Len Deighton was born in 1929. He worked as a railway clerk before doing his National Service in the Royal Air Force as a photographer attached to the Special Investigation Branch.

After his discharge in 1949, he went to art school – first to the St Martin's School of Art, and then to the Royal College of Art on a scholarship. It was while working as a waiter in the evenings that he developed an interest in cookery – a subject he was later to make his own in an animated strip for the *Observer* and in two cookery books. He worked for a while as an illustrator in New York and as art director of an advertising agency in London.

Deciding it was time to settle down, Deighton moved to the Dordogne where he started work on his first book, *The IPCRESS File*. Published in 1962, the book was an immediate success.

Since then his work has gone from strength to strength, varying from espionage novels to war, general fiction and non-fiction. The BBC made *Bomber* into a day-long radio drama in 'real time'. Deighton's history of World War Two, *Blood, Tears and Folly*, was published to wide acclaim – Jack Higgins called it 'an absolute landmark'.

As Max Hastings observed, Deighton captured a time and a mood – 'To those of us who were in our twenties in the 1960s, his books seemed the coolest, funkiest, most sophisticated things we'd ever read' – and his books have now deservedly become classics.

By Len Deighton

FICTION
The IPCRESS File
Horse Under Water
Funeral in Berlin
Billion-Dollar Brain
An Expensive Place to Die
Only When I Larf
Bomber
Declarations of War
Close-Up
Spy Story
Yesterday's Spy
Twinkle, Twinkle, Little Spy
SS-GB
XPD
Goodbye Mickey Mouse
MAMista
City of Gold
Violent Ward

THE SAMSON SERIES
Berlin Game
Mexico Set
London Match
Winter: A Berlin Family 1899–1945
Spy Hook
Spy Line
Spy Sinker
Faith
Hope
Charity

NON-FICTION
Action Cook Book
Fighter: The True Story of the Battle of Britain
Airshipwreck
Basic French Cooking
Blitzkrieg: From the Rise of Hitler to the Fall of Dunkirk
ABC of French Food
Blood, Tears and Folly

LEN DEIGHTON

Bomber

Events relating to the last flight of an
RAF Bomber over Germany on the night
of June 31st, 1943

HARPER

Harper
An imprint of HarperCollins*Publishers*
77–85 Fulham Palace Road,
Hammersmith, London W6 8JB

www.harpercollins.co.uk

This paperback edition 2009
1

Previously published in paperback by Grafton 1978

First published in Great Britain by
Jonathan Cape Ltd 1970

A catalogue record for this book is
available from the British Library

ISBN: 978 0 586 04544 2

Typeset by Palimpsest Book Production Limited,
Grangemouth, Stirlingshire
Printed and bound in Great Britain by
Clays Ltd, St Ives plc

Introduction

Bomber was the first fiction book written using what is now called a 'word processor'. In 1969 that name did not exist. It was an IBM engineer visiting my home at the Elephant and Castle in London to check my golfball typewriter, who asked me: *'Do you know how many times your secretary has retyped this chapter?'* He waved pages in the air.

'Half a dozen times?' I said defensively. I knew my wonderful Australian secretary Ellenor only retyped chapters when her typewritten words were almost obscured by my handwritten changes.

'Twenty-five times,' said the IBM man. *'Your poor secretary!'*

I tried to look repentant.

Along the street at the mighty Shell Centre, IBM had installed banks of computer-driven machines that produced printed in-house essentials such as instruction manuals.

'Come along and see them,' urged the IBM man. Being somewhat obsessed by machinery (while not really understanding it) I went along. Soon I became the only private individual permitted ownership of an IBM MT 72 computer. It was the size and shape of a small upright piano. I was very proud of that machine, I showed it to everyone who visited me, but it was Ellenor who mastered it.

My friend Julian Symons said I was the only person he knew who actually liked machines. *'Perhaps you should write a book about them*', he said, only half seriously. That was the start of *Bomber*. Does everyone hate machines? Perhaps they do; so suppose I wrote a story in which the machines of one nation battled against the machines of another? It had already happened. I had been bombed quite a lot in London. The night bombing campaigns were fought in complete darkness, with both the enemy aircraft and the terrain below depicted only as tiny blips and blobs on glass screens. The combatants never saw their enemies. It had a spooky fascination for me but would such a grim mechanical theme overshadow a story's human element?

The human element was already a difficult aspect of writing such a story. Most of the characters – both British and German – would be able-bodied young men chosen for their physical, emotional and psychological similarity. To make it more difficult, my preliminary notes showed that I would need a cast of well over a hundred of these similar young people. This meant a style that would bring a character to life in only a sentence or two of dialogue. And do it well enough for the reader to pick up on that character two or three chapters later. And I was determined to do it without resorting to crude regional pronunciations.

It was daunting. I began to talk to experts and discovered how deep I was going to have to dig for my research. German radar was very advanced by 1943; it was only after that that Anglo American technology took the lead. But Germany lost their technical lead and lost the war too. That meant that very few people had taken any interest in the history of German air defences. I went to Germany and sought out the technicians and radar operators as well as the night-fighter pilots and Flak crews. Then I had to put their explanations together well enough to understand the basis of the German air defence system. The more I studied it, the more the subject fascinated me. Long after *Bomber* was finished, I wrote *Goodbye Mickey Mouse*, a totally different sort of book, about the American strategic bombing campaign. The contrast between the social environments astounded me and I needed to wipe this *Bomber* research from my memory in order to get to grips with the Eighth Air Force.

If 1943 German radar controllers and night-fighter veterans were a complex challenge, then wait until I started to delve into the social life, scandals and Nazi-led politics of a small Westphalian town. Everyone seemed to have a war story. One lady found for me some striped overalls that she had made from her nurse's uniform. A man I met in a restaurant had kept all his wartime documents and when I showed interest in them insisted that I kept them. My wife Ysabele's fluent German was the key to this conversational research and greatly expanded the number of people and stories available to me.

It was almost overwhelming but it was too late to stop, and anyway I enjoy research. One large room of my London home was devoted entirely to *Bomber*. I collected everything available: films, air photos, logbooks, letters, recordings, tele-printer orders and target maps. Pasting aeronautical maps together I covered one whole wall with northern Europe. Tapes of the bomber routes, turning-points, dog-legs and feints showed each aircraft in the story. Tabs for times meant I could see where each fighter or bomber would be at any chosen moment.

The anchor of the story was to be found in England's Bomber Command airfields. I knew many of them from my time in the RAF and I returned to see them again. My RAF veterans were great companions with anecdotes galore, and I had flown in Mosquitos and Lancaster bombers. In Germany Adolf Galland found for me some of the best of his night fighter crews. The Dutch air force allowed me to spend some time on a military airfield that was very little changed from 1943. By amazing luck I was able to find, enter and climb around one of the very few Luftwaffe 'Opera House' command centres just days before its demolition began. It was a vast echoing place and by chance the demolition crews had left all the electric lights burning, probably for safety reasons. My good friends at London's Imperial War Museum gave me a room filled with Luftwaffe instructional films about the night-fighter version of the Junkers Ju 88 and by bending the rules a little I also got to climb inside one.

Right from the first notes I had decided upon the twenty-four hour time format. It meant that I would describe only one RAF bombing raid but I could depict it in detail. By describing mechanical elements (such as the number of fragments into which the average anti-aircraft shell breaks) I wanted to emphasize the dehumanizing effect of mechanical warfare. I like machines but in wars all humans are their victims.

Len Deighton, 2009

Although I have attempted to make its background as real as possible this is entirely a work of fiction. As far as I know there were no Lancaster bombers named 'Creaking Door', 'The Volkswagen' or 'Joe for King'. There was no RAF airfield named Warley Fen and no Luftwaffe base called Kroonsdijk. There was no Altgarten and there were no real people like those I have described. There was never a thirty-first day of June in 1943 or any other year.

L.D.

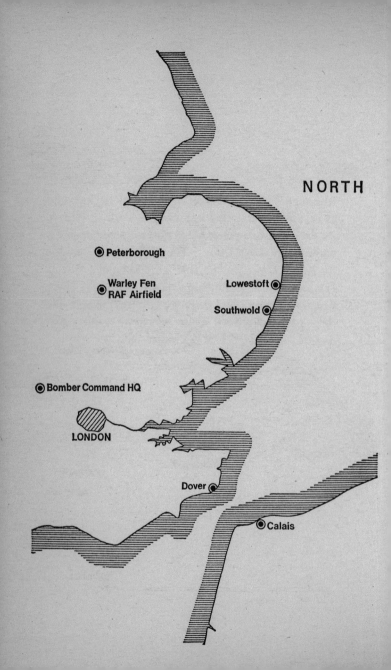

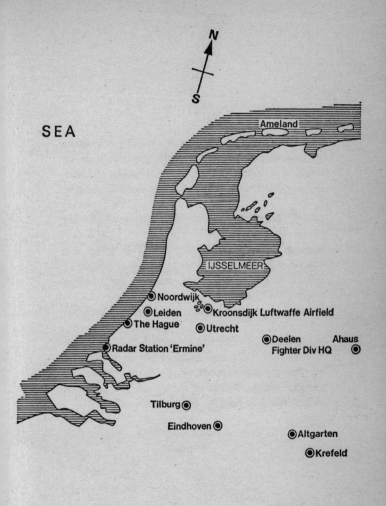

N

S

SEA

Ameland

IJSSELMEER

Noordwijk

Leiden   Kroonsdijk Luftwaffe Airfield

The Hague   Utrecht

Radar Station 'Ermine'   Deelen   Ahaus
Fighter Div HQ

Tilburg

Eindhoven

Altgarten

Krefeld

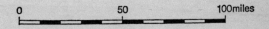

0   50   100miles

Ritual: A system of religious or magical ceremonies or procedures frequently with special forms of words or a special (and secret) vocabulary, and usually associated with important occasions or actions.

Dr J. Dever,
Dictionary of Psychology (Penguin Books)

Between February 1965 and July 31st, 1968, the American bombing missions in Vietnam numbered 107,700. The tonnage of bombs and rockets totalled 2,581,876.

Keisinger's Continuous Archives

The attitude of the gallant Six Hundred which so aroused Lord Tennyson's admiration arose from the fact that the least disposition to ask the reason why was discouraged by tricing the would-be inquirer to the triangle and flogging him into insensibility.

F. J. Veale,
Advance to Barbarism (Mitre Press, 1968)

CHAPTER ONE

It was a bomber's sky: dry air, wind enough to clear the smoke, cloud broken enough to recognize a few stars. The bedroom was so dark that it took Ruth Lambert a moment or so to see her husband standing at the window. 'Are you all right, Sam?'

'Praying to Mother Moon.'

She laughed sleepily. 'What are you talking about?'

'Do you think I don't need all the witchcraft I can get?'

'Oh, Sam. How can you say that when you . . .' She stopped.

He supplied the words: 'Have come back safe from forty-five raids?'

She nodded. He was right. She'd been afraid to say it because she did believe in witchcraft or something very like it. In an isolated house in the small hours of morning with the wind chasing the clouds across the bright moon it was difficult not to fall prey to primitive fears.

She switched on the bedside light and he shielded his eyes with his hand. Sam Lambert was a tall man of twenty-six. The necessity of wearing his tight-collared uniform had resulted in his suntan ending in a sharp line around his neck. His muscular body was pale by comparison. He ran his fingers across his untidy black hair and scratched the corner of his nose where a small scar disappeared into the wrinkles of his smile. Ruth liked him to smile but lately he seldom did.

1

He buttoned the yellow silk pyjamas that had cost Ruth a small fortune in Bond Street. She'd given them to him on the first night of their honeymoon; three months ago, he'd smiled then. This was the first time he'd worn them.

As the only married couple among Cohen's guests, Ruth and Sam Lambert had been given the King Charles bedroom with tapestry and panelling so magnificent that Sam found himself speaking in whispers. 'What a boring weekend for you, darling: bombs, bombing, and bombers.'

'I like to listen. I'm in the RAF too, remember. Anyway we had to come. He's one of your crew, sort of family.'

'Yes, you've got half a dozen brand-new relatives.'

'I like your crew.' She said it tentatively, for just a few trips ago her husband had flown back with his navigator dead. They had never mentioned his name since. 'Has the rain stopped?' she asked.

Lambert nodded. Somewhere overhead an aeroplane crawled across the cloud trying to glimpse the ground through a gap. On a cross-country exercise, thought Lambert, they'd probably predicted a little light cirrus. It was their favourite prediction.

Ruth said, 'Cohen is the one that was sick the first time?'

'Not really sick, he was . . .' He waved his hand.

'I didn't mean sick,' said Ruth. 'Shall I leave the light on?'

'I'm coming back to bed. What time is it?'

'No,' said Ruth. 'Only if you want to. Five-thirty, Monday morning.'

'Next weekend we'll go up to London and see *Gone with the Wind* or something.'

'Promise?'

'Promise. The thunderstorm has passed right over. It will be good flying weather tomorrow.' Ruth shivered.

'I had a letter from my dad,' he said.

'I recognized the writing.'

'Can I spare another five pounds.'

'He'll drink it.'

'Of course.'

'But you'll send it?'

'I can't just abandon the poor old bugger.'

There were cows too, standing very still, asleep standing up, he supposed, he knew nothing about the country. He'd hardly ever seen it until he started flying seven years ago. There was so much open country. Acres and acres young Cohen's family had here, and a trout stream, and this old house like something from a ghost story with its creaking stairs, cold bedrooms and ancient door latches that never closed properly. He reached out and ran his fingers across the tapestry; they'd never allow you to do that in the V and A Museum.

Some of the windowpanes were discoloured and bubbly and the trees seen through them were crippled and grotesque. At night the countryside was strange and monochromatic like an old photograph. To the east, over the sea beyond Holland and Germany, the sky was lightening enough to silhouette the trees and skyline. Eight-tenths cloud, just an edge of moonlight on a rim of cumulus. You could sail a whole damned Group in over that lot, and from the ground it would be impossible to catch a glimpse of them. He turned away from the window. On the other hand they'd have you on their bloody radar.

He walked across the cold stone floor and looked down at his wife in the massive bed. Her black hair made marble of the white pillow and with her eyes tightly closed she was like some fairy princess waiting to be awoken with a magic kiss. He pulled the curtains of the ancient four-poster bed aside and it creaked as he eased his body down between the sheets. She made a sleepy mumbling sound and pulled his chilly body close.

'He was just tense,' said Lambert. 'Cohen's a bloody nice kid, a wizard damned navigator too.'

'I love you,' Ruth mumbled.

'Everyone gets tense,' explained Lambert.

3

His wife pulled the pillow under his head and moved to give him more room. His eyes were closed but she knew he was not sleepy. Many times at night they'd been awake together like this.

When they married in March it had rained when they arrived at the church, but as they came on to the steps the sun came out. She'd worn a pale-blue silk dress. Two other girls had married in it since then.

Her face pressed close to him and she could hear his heart beating. It was a calming, confident sound and soon she dropped off to sleep.

The one-time grandeur of the Cohens' country house was defaced by wartime shortages of labour and material. In the breakfast room there was a damp patch on the wall and the carpet had been turned so that the worn part was under the sideboard. The small, leaded windows and the clumsy blackout fittings made the room gloomy even on a bright summer's morning like this one.

Each of the airmen guests was already coming to terms with the return to duty and each in their different ways sensed that the day would end in combat. Lambert had smelled the change in the weather, and he chose a chair that gave him a glimpse of the sky.

The Lamberts were not the first down to breakfast. Flight Lieutenant Sweet had been up for hours. He told them that he had taken one of the horses out. 'Mind you, all I did was sit upon the poor creature while it walked around the meadow.' He had in fact done exactly that, but such was his self-deprecating tone that he was able to suggest that he was a horseman of great skill.

Sweet chose to sit in the Windsor hoopback armchair that was at the head of the table. He was a short, fair-haired man of twenty-two, four years younger than Lambert. Like many of the aircrew he was short and stocky. Ruddy-complexioned, his pink skin went even pinker in the sun, and when he smiled he looked like a happy bouncing baby. Some women found this irresistible. It was easy to see why he had been regarded as 'officer material' from the day he joined up. He had a clear, high voice, energy, enthusiasm, and an unquestioning readiness to flatter and defer to the voice of authority.

'And an ambition to get to grips with the Hun, sir.'

'Good show, Sweet.'

'Goodness, sir, I can't be any other way. That sort of thing is bred into a chap at any decent public school.'

'Good show, Sweet.'

Temporarily Sweet had been appointed commander of B Flight's aircraft, one of which Lambert piloted. He was anxious to be popular: he knew everyone's nickname and remembered their birthplace. It was his great pleasure to greet people in their hometown accent. In spite of all his efforts some people hated him. Sweet couldn't understand why.

This month the Squadron had been transferred to path-finder duties. It meant that every crew must do a double tour of ops. Double thirty was sixty, and sixty trips over Germany, with the average five-per-cent casualty rate, was mathematically three times impossible to survive. Lambert and Sweet had already completed one tour and this was their second. Actuarily they were long since dead.

Sweet was telling a story when Flight Sergeant Digby came into the room. Digby was a thirty-two-year-old Australian bomb aimer. He was elderly by combat aircrew standards and his balding head and weathered face singled him out from the others. As did his readiness to puncture the dignity of any officer. He listened to Flight Lieutenant Sweet. Sweet was the only officer among the guests.

'A fellow drives into a service station,' said Sweet. His eyes crinkled into a smile and the others paid attention, for he was good at telling funny stories. Sweet knocked an edge of ash into the remains of his breakfast. 'The driver had only got coupons for half a gallon. He says, "A good show Monty's boys are putting on, eh?" "Who?" says the bloke in the service station, very puzzled. "General Montgomery and the Eighth Army." "What army?" "The Eighth Army. It's given old Rommel's Panzers a nasty shock." "Rommel? Who's Rommel?" "OK," says the bloke in the car, putting away his coupons. "Never mind all that crap. Fill her up with petrol and give me two hundred Player's cigarettes and two bottles of whisky."'

It was unfortunate that Sweet had cast the driver as an Australian for Digby was rather sensitive about his accent. Appreciative of the smiles, Sweet repeated the punch line in his normal voice, 'Fill her up with petrol and give me two hundred cigarettes.' He laughed and blew a perfect smoke ring.

'That's a funny accent you're using now,' said Digby.

'The King's English,' acknowledged Sweet.

'I hope he is,' said Digby. 'With a ripe pommy accent like his he'd have a terrible time back where I come from.'

Sweet smiled. Under the special circumstances of being fellow guests in Cohen's father's house he had to put up with a familiarity that he would never tolerate on the Squadron.

'It's just a matter of education,' said Sweet, referring as much to Digby's behaviour as to his accent.

'That's right,' agreed Digby, sitting down opposite him. Digby's tie had trapped one point of his collar so that it stood up under his jawline. 'Seriously, though, I really admire the way you fellows speak. You can all make Daily Routine Orders sound like Shakespeare. Now, you must have been to a good school, Flight Lieutenant Sweet. Is that an Eton tie you're wearing?'

Sweet smiled and fingered his black Air Force tie. 'Harrods actually.'

'Jesus,' said Digby in mock amazement. 'I didn't know you'd studied at Harrods, sport. What did you take, modern lingerie?'

6

Sweet saw Digby's attitude as a challenge to his charm. He gave him a very warm smile, he was confident that he could make the man like him. Everyone knew that Digby's record as bomb aimer was second to none.

Young Sergeant Cohen played the anxious host, constantly going to the sideboard for more coffee and pressing all his guests to second helpings of pancakes and honey.

Sergeant Battersby was the last down to breakfast. He was a tall boy of eighteen with frizzy yellow hair, thin arms and legs and a very pale complexion. His eyes scanned the room apologetically and his soft full mouth quivered as he decided not to say how sorry he was to be late. He had less reason than anyone to be delayed. His chin seldom needed shaving and most mornings he merely surveyed it to be sure that the pimples of adolescence had finally gone. They had. His frizzy hair paid little heed to combing and his boots and buttons were always done the night before.

Batters was the only member of Lambert's crew who was younger and less experienced than Cohen. And Batters was the only member of Lambert's crew who would have contemplated flying under another captain. Not that he believed that there was any other captain anywhere in the RAF who could compare with Lambert, but Battersby was his flight engineer. An engineer was a pilot's technical adviser and assistant. He helped operate the controls on take-offs and landings; he had to keep a constant watch on the fuel, oil, and coolant systems, especially the fuel changeovers. As well as this he was expected to know every nut and bolt of the aeroplane and be prepared 'to carry out practicable emergency repairs during flight' of anything from a hydraulic gun turret to a camera and from the bombsight to the oxygen system. It was a terrifying responsibility for a shy eighteen-year-old.

Until recently Lambert had flown fifteen bombing raids with an engineer named Micky Murphy, who now flew as part of Flight Lieutenant Sweet's crew. Some people said that Sweet should never have taken the ox-like Irishman away from Lambert after so many trips together. One of the ground-crew sergeants said it was unlucky, some of Sweet's fellow officers said it was bad manners, and Digby said it was part of Sweet's plan to arse-crawl his way to become Marshal of the Royal Air Force.

Each day Batters hung round the ground crew of his aeroplane watching and asking endless questions in his thin high voice. While this added to his knowledge, it did nothing for his popularity. He watched Lambert all the time and hoped for nothing more than the curt word of praise that came after each flight. Batters was an untypical flight engineer. Most of them were more like Micky Murphy, practical men with calloused hands and an instinct for mechanical malfunction. They came from factories and garages, they were apprentices or lathe operators or young clerks with their own motorcycle that they could reassemble blindfold. Battersby would never have their instinct. He'd been a secondary-school boy with one afternoon a week in the metal-work class. Of course Batters could run rings round most of the Squadron's engineers at written exams and luckily the RAF set high store by paperwork. His father taught physics and chemistry at a school in Lancashire.

I marked your last physics paper while on fire-watching. The headmaster was on duty with me. He'd given the sixth form the same sample paper but he told me that yours was undoubtedly the best. This, I need hardly say, made your father rather proud of you. I am confident however that this will not tempt you to slacken your efforts. Always remember that after the war you will be competing for your place at university with fellows who have been wise enough to contribute to the war in a manner that furthers their academic qualifications.

This week's sample entrance paper should prove a simple matter. Perhaps I should warn you that the second

8

part of question four does not refer solely to sodium. It requires an answer in depth and its apparent simplicity is intended solely to trap the unwary.

Mrs Cohen came into the breakfast room from the kitchen just as Battersby was helping himself to one pancake and a drip of honey. She was a thin white-haired woman who smiled easily. She pushed half a dozen more upon his plate. Battersby had that sort of effect upon mothers. She asked in quiet careful English if anyone else would like more pancakes. In her hand there was a tall pile of fresh ones.

'They're delicious, Mrs Cohen,' said Ruth Lambert. 'Did you make them?'

'It's a Viennese recipe, Ruth. I shall write it for you.' They all looked towards Mrs Cohen and she cast her eyes down nervously. They reminded her of the clear-eyed young storm-troopers she had seen smashing the shopfronts in Munich. She had always thought of the British as a pale, pimply, stunted race, with bad teeth and ugly faces, but these airmen too were British. Her Simon was indistinguishable from them. They laughed nervously at the same jokes no matter how often repeated. They spoke too quickly for her, and had their own vocabulary. Emmy Cohen was a little afraid of these handsome boys who set fire to the towns she'd known when a girl. She wondered what went on in their cold hearts, and wondered if her son belonged to them now, more than he did to her.

Mrs Cohen looked at Lambert's wife. Her WAAF corporal's uniform was too severe to suit her but she looked trim and businesslike. At Warley Fen she was in charge of the inflatable rafts that bombers carried in case they were forced down into the sea. Nineteen, twenty at the most. Her wrists and ankles still with a trace of schoolgirl plumpness. She was clever, thought Mrs Cohen, for without saying much she was a part of their banter and games. They all envied Lambert his beautiful, childlike wife, and yet to conceal their envy they teased her and criticized her and corrected the few mistakes she made about their planes and their squadron and their war. Mrs Cohen coveted her skill. Lambert seldom joined in the chatter and yet his wife would constantly glance towards him, as though seeking approval or praise. Cheerful little Digby and pale-faced Battersby sometimes gave Lambert the same sort of quizzical look. So, noticed Mrs Cohen, did her son Simon.

It was eight-fifteen when a tall girl in WAAF officer's uniform stepped through the terrace doors like a character in a drawing-room play. She must have known that the sunlight behind her made a halo round her blonde hair, for she stood there for a few moments looking round at the blue-uniformed men.

'Good God,' she said in mock amazement. 'Someone has opened a tin of airmen.'

'Hello, Nora,' said young Cohen. She was the daughter of their next-door neighbour if that's what you call people who own a mansion almost a mile along the lane.

'I can only stay a millisecond but I must thank you for sending that divine basket of fruit.' The elder Cohens had sent the fruit but Nora Ashton's eyes were on their son. She hadn't seen him since he'd gained his shiny new navigator's wing.

'It's good to see you, Nora,' he said.

'Nora visits her mother almost every weekend,' said Mrs Cohen.

'Once a month,' said Nora. 'I'm at High Wycombe now, Bomber Command HQ.'

'You must fiddle the petrol for that old banger of yours.'

'Of course I do, my pet.'

He smiled. He was no longer a shy thin student but a strong handsome man. She touched the stripes on his arm. 'Sergeant Cohen, navigator,' she said and exchanged a glance with Ruth. It was all right: this WAAF corporal clearly had her own man.

Nora pecked a kiss and Simon Cohen briefly took her hand. Then she was gone almost as quickly as she arrived. Mrs Cohen saw her to the door and looked closely at her face when she waved goodbye. 'Simon is looking fine, Mrs Cohen.'

'I suppose you are surrounded with sergeants like him at your headquarters place.'

'No, I'm not,' said Nora. They seldom saw a sergeant at Bomber Command HQ, they only wiped them off the black-board by the hundred after each attack.

After they had finished eating Cohen passed cigars around. Digby, Sweet, and Lambert took one but Batters said his father believed that smoking caused serious harm to the health. Sweet produced a fine ivory-handled penknife and insisted upon using its special attachment to cut the cigars.

Ruth Lambert got up from the table first. She wanted to make sure their bedroom was left neat and tidy, no hairpins on the floor or face powder spilled on the dressing-table.

She looked back at her husband. He was a heavy man and yet he could move lightly and with speed enough to grab a fly in mid-air. His was a battered face and wrinkled too, especially round the mouth and eyes. His eyes were brown and deep-set with dark patches under them. Once she had written that his eyes were 'smouldering'.

'Then mind you don't get burned, my girl.'

'Oh Mother, you'll both love him.'

'Pity he can't get a commission. Do him more good than that medal.'

'A commission isn't important, Father.'

'Wait until you're living in a post-war NCO's Married Quarters. You'll soon change your tune.'

He felt her looking at him. He looked up suddenly and winked. His eyes revealed more than he would ever speak. This morning for instance she had watched him while Flight Lieutenant Sweet was theorizing about engines, and had

11

known that it was all nonsense by the amused shine in Sam's eyes. Sam, I love you so much: calm, thoughtful and brave. She glanced at the other airmen around the table. It's strange but the others seem to envy me.

Mrs Cohen also hastened away to pack her son's case. Left to themselves the boys stretched their feet out. They were puffing stylishly at the large cigars, and clichés were exchanged across the table. They could talk more freely when a chap's mother wasn't there.

'We'll be on tonight,' predicted Sweet. 'I feel it in my corns.' He laughed. 'We'll put a little salt on Hitler's tail again, eh?'

'Is that what we are doing?' asked Lambert.

'Certainly it is,' said Sweet. 'Bombing the factories, destroying his means of production.' Sweet's voice rose a little higher as he became exasperated by Lambert's patronizing smile.

Cohen spoke for the first time. 'If we are going to talk about bombing, let's be as scientific as possible. The target map of Berlin is just a map of Berlin with the aiming-point right in the city centre. We are fooling only ourselves if we pretend we are bombing anything other than city centres.'

'What's wrong with that?' said Flight Lieutenant Sweet.

'Simply that there are no factories in city centres,' said Lambert. 'The centre of most German towns contains old buildings: lots of timber construction, narrow streets and alleys inaccessible to fire engines. Around that is the dormitory ring: middle-class brick apartments mostly. Only the third portion, the outer ring, is factories and workers' housing.'

'You seem very well informed, Flight Sergeant Lambert,' said Sweet.

'I'm interested in what happens to people,' said Lambert. 'I come from a long line of humans myself.'

'I'm glad you pointed that out,' said Sweet.

Cohen said, 'One has only to look at our air photos to know what we do to a town.'

'That's war,' said Battersby tentatively. 'My brother said there's no difference between bankrupting a foreign factory in peacetime and bombing it in wartime. Capitalism is competition and the ultimate form of that is war.'

Cohen gave a little gasp of laughter, but corrected it to a cough when Battersby did not smile.

Lambert smiled and rephrased the notion. 'War is a continuation of capitalism by other means, eh, Batters?'

'Yes, sir, exactly,' said Battersby in his thin childish voice. 'Capitalism depends upon consumption of manufactured goods and war is the most efficient manner of consumption yet devised. Furthermore, it's a test of each country's industrial system. I mean, look at the way we are developing our aeroplanes, radios, engines, and all sorts of secret inventions.'

'What about man for man?' said Digby.

'Surely after the great victories of the Red Army you don't still subscribe to the superhuman ethic, Mr Digby,' said Battersby. 'Evils may exist within our social systems but the working man who fights the war is pretty much the same the world over.'

They were all surprised to hear Battersby converse at length, let alone argue.

'Are you a Red, Battersby?' said Flight Lieutenant Sweet.

'No, sir,' said Battersby, biting his lip nervously. 'I'm just stating what my brother told me.'

'He should be shot,' said Sweet.

'He was, sir,' said Battersby. 'At Dunkirk.'

Sweet's rubicund face went bright red with embarrassment. He stubbed his cigar into a half-eaten pancake and, getting to his feet, said, 'Perhaps we'd best get cracking. Just in case there's something on tonight.'

Digby and Battersby also went upstairs to pack. Lambert was silent, sipping at his coffee and watching the cigar smoke drifting towards the oak ceiling.

Cohen poured coffee for himself and Lambert. The two

of them sat at the table in silence until Cohen said, 'You don't believe in this war?'

'Believe in it?' said Lambert. 'You make it sound like a rumour.'

'I think about the bombing a lot,' admitted Cohen.

'I hope you do,' said Lambert. 'I hope you worry yourself sick about it.'

On the Squadron Lambert usually spoke only of technical matters and like most of the old-timers he would smile without committing himself when politics or religion was discussed. Today was different.

'What do you believe then?'

'I believe that everyone is corruptible and I'm always afraid that I might become corrupt. I believe that all societies are a plot to corrupt the individual.'

'That's anarchy,' said young Cohen, 'and you are never an anarchist by any measure. After all, Skipper, society has a right to demand a citizen's loyalty.'

'Loyalty? You mean using another man's morality instead of your own. That's just a convenient way of putting your conscience into cold storage.'

'Yes,' reflected Cohen doubtfully. 'The SS motto is "my honour is my loyalty".'

'Well, there you are.'

'But what about family loyalty?'

'That's almost as bad: it's giving your nephew the prize for playing the piano when the little boy down the street plays better.'

'Is that so terrible?' asked Cohen.

'I'm the little boy down the street. I wouldn't have even got as far as grammar school unless a few people had let a prize or two go out of the family.'

'What you are really saying,' said young Cohen trying to make it a question rather than a verdict, 'is that you don't like bombing cities.'

'That is what I'm saying,' said Lambert and the young

navigator was too shocked to think of a reply. Lambert drained his cup. 'That's good coffee.'

Hastily Cohen reached for the pot to pour more for him. He wanted to demonstrate his continuing admiration and regard for his pilot. 'Coffee isn't rationed,' said young Cohen.

'Then fill her up, and give me two hundred Player's.'

The roses on the table were now fully open. Lambert reached out to them but as he touched one it disintegrated and the pale-pink petals fell and covered the back of his hand like huge blisters.

'Men are disturbed by any lack of order.' The voice by his shoulder made Lambert start for old Mr Cohen had entered the room without either of them hearing him. He was a tall man with a handsome face, marred only by a lopsided mouth and yellow teeth. He spoke the careful style of English that only a foreigner could perfect. However a nasal drone accompanied his flat voice which gave no emphasis to any word nor acknowledged the end of a sentence.

'You and I might be able to see the virtue of chaos,' he continued, 'but dictators gain power by offering pattern, ranks, common purpose, and men in formations. Men want order, they strive for it. Even the world's artists are asked only to impose meaning and symmetry upon the chaos of nature. You and I, Sergeant Lambert, may know that muddle and inefficiency are man's only hope of freedom but we will not easily convert our fellow men.'

'You are mocking me, Mr Cohen.'

'Not me, Sergeant. I have seen men line up to dig their own graves and turn to face the firing squad with a proud precision. I am not mocking you.'

'The British are not easy to regiment, Father.'

'So they keep telling me, my son, but I wonder. In this war they have gained the same sense of national identity and purpose that the Nazis gave the Germans. The British are so

15

proud of their conversion that they will almost forgo their class system. I see the clear eyes and firm footfalls of the self-righteous and that is a good start on the road to totalitarian power. History is being quoted and patriotic songs revived. Believe me, the British are proud of themselves.'

There was a commotion outside as Digby stumbled down the stairs with his suitcase but Mr Cohen did not pause.

'Some day, in the not-so-far-distant future, when the trade unions are being particularly tedious, students are being unusually destructive, and the pound is buying less and less, then a Führer will appear and tell the British that they are a powerful nation. "Britain Awake" will be his slogan and some carefully chosen racial minority will be his scapegoats. Then you will see if the British are easy to regiment.'

Sergeant Cohen smiled at Lambert. 'For goodness' sake don't argue with him or we'll be here all day.' He got to his feet.

'I wouldn't mind that at all,' said Lambert. The old man bowed courteously. As the two airmen went into the hall old Mr Cohen followed Lambert closely, as if to separate him from his son. Lambert turned to the old man and waited for him to speak but he didn't do so until his son had left.

'All fathers become old fools, Lambert,' he said and then stopped. Lambert looked at him, trying to draw the words from him as one does with a man who stutters. The words again came in a rush: 'You'll look after the boy, won't you?'

For a moment Lambert said nothing. Sweet came down the stairs. He took the old man's arm and said airily, 'Don't worry about that, sir,' but Cohen had selected only Lambert for his plea.

Lambert said, 'It's not my job to look after your son, sir.'

Young Cohen was still within earshot on the balcony above them. Digby saw him and felt like tugging the back of Lambert's tunic in warning.

Lambert knew they were all listening but he didn't lower his voice. He said, 'It simply doesn't work like that. A crew all need each other. Any one of them can endanger the aircraft. Your son is the most skilful navigator I've flown with, probably the best in the Squadron. He's the brains of the aeroplane; he looks after us.'

There was silence for a moment, then Mr Cohen said, 'He certainly should be good, he's cost me a fortune to educate.' The old man nodded to himself. 'Look after my boy, Mr Lambert.'

'I promise.' Lambert nodded to the old man and hurried upstairs cursing himself for saying it. How the hell could he protect anyone? He was always amazed to get back safely himself. He passed young Cohen who was coming downstairs with a large case.

When he was alone with his son the old man said, 'You hear that? Your Captain Lambert says you're the best.'

Mrs Cohen appeared from nowhere and brushed her son's coarse blue uniform distastefully.

'His captain says he's the best. Best on the Squadron, he said.'

Mrs Cohen ignored her husband. She pulled a piece of cotton from her son's sleeve. 'I see that Mr Sweet, the officer, is wearing gold cufflinks. Why don't you take yours with you? They look so nice.'

'Not in the Sergeants' Mess, Mother.'

'How old is Captain Lambert?' she said.

'He's not a captain, Mother, he's a flight sergeant. That's one rank above mine. We call him captain because he's the senior man on our aircraft.'

His mother nodded, trying to understand and remember.

'Twenty-six or twenty-seven.'

'He looks much older,' said Mrs Cohen, looking at her son. 'He looks forty, an old man.'

'Do you want him to fly with a child?' said Mr Cohen.

'This Mr Sweet can help to make you an officer, Simon.'

'Oh, Mother, you've been talking about me.'

'Would it be so bad, Simon?' said Mr Cohen.

'It would mean changing to another crew.'

'Why?'

'They don't like officers flying under NCO captains. Anyway, it would make Lambert's job more difficult, having me sitting behind him with shiny little officer's badges. And we wouldn't be together in the Sergeants' Mess. And perhaps I'd have to go away to a training school.'

'Quite a speech,' said Mr Cohen. 'The most I've heard you say all weekend.'

'I'm sorry, Father.'

'It doesn't matter. But if Mr Lambert is such a fine fellow, why is he not an officer? You tell me he has more experience, medals, and does the same job as your friend Mr Sweet.'

'Surely you know the English by now, Father. Lambert has a London accent. He's never been to an expensive school. The English believe that only gentlemen can be leaders.'

'And this is the way they fight a war?'

'Yes. Lambert is the best, most experienced pilot on the Squadron.'

Mrs Cohen said, 'If you became an officer perhaps you could fly with Mr Sweet.'

'I'd rather fly with Lambert,' he replied, trying to keep his voice amiable.

She said, 'You mustn't be angry, Simon. We're not trying to make you stop flying.'

'That's right. Just thinking of you earning more cash,' his father joked.

'I keep telling both of you I'm just not ambitious. I'm never going to be an officer and I'm never going to be a philosophy professor like Uncle Carol. Nor a scientist like dad. I'm not sure I could even run the farm. This job I'm doing in the Air Force . . .'

Cohen raised a finger to interrupt. 'There is a common mistake made by historians: to review the past as a series of errors leading to the perfect condition that is the present time. It's a common mistake in life too, especially in one of our closed societies like a school or a prison camp. It's easy then to forget that the outside world or future time exist. Now in the middle of 1943 your Messrs Sweets and Lamberts seem to have attained the highest pinnacle of prestige and achievement. But it's all glamour and tinsel. When the war is over, being the finest bomber crew that ever flew across Germany won't get any of you so much as a free dog licence.'

'You've got the wrong idea, Dad. I don't like being in the Air Force. It's dangerous and uncomfortable, and a lot of the people I work with are pretty nasty fellows.' The old man looked up quizzically. 'But if nasty fellows can destroy the Fascists I'll put up with it. I know how to do my job theoretically at any rate so don't worry about me. You've both got to understand that this is my life now. The whole of my life and I've got to live it in my own way. Without gold cufflinks or your talking to anyone about commissions or pocket money even. And most of all, no more parcels.'

Mrs Cohen nodded. 'I understand, Simon, I always over-do things. I've embarrassed you with your captain, have I?'

'No, no, no, it's fine. It's been a wonderful weekend and wizard food.'

'Wizard,' repeated Mrs Cohen, making a mental note of the superlative. She reached for her handbag but after a warning glance from her husband did not open it.

'Have a good journey, Cosy,' said his father.

'My nickname is Kosher. Kosher Cohen they call me.'

'So what's wrong with that?' asked his father. Kosher smiled but did not answer. The old man nodded and patted his son on the arm. They were closer than ever before.

'Nora Ashton always asks about you,' said Mrs Cohen. 'She's a fine girl.'

The hall clock struck nine. 'I must go. They are waiting. There's probably too much moon but we might fly tonight.'

'Over Germany?'

'There's not time to go far on these short summer nights.

19

Probably we'll be dropping mines into the North Sea. All the boys like that, it's a milk run but it counts as a full operation.'

Digby heard the last bit of that. 'That's right, Mrs Cohen, these gardening trips go off as quiet as a Sunday in Adelaide.'

'Phone me in the morning, Simon.'

CHAPTER TWO

'One thing about these short summer nights,' an elderly Wing Commander said, 'we can usually shortlist the target files and have them in the old man's hands the moment he makes the decision.'

Nora Ashton, the young WAAF officer, smiled at him briefly and then went back to checking the target files. Each one had been started on orders from the Targets Selection Committee at Air Ministry. She identified each file by its code name: Whitebait was Berlin and Trout was Cologne. The code names were the idea of the Senior Staff Officer, who was a keen angler. Recently he had taken up collecting butterflies and moths but the C-in-C said that code names like Broad-bordered Bee Hawk would be inconvenient. Inside each target file there were population figures, industrial descriptions, photos and intelligence about searchlights and guns. The files varied a great deal: some files were as fat as phone directories and packed with reports from resistance workers and secret agents, while many contained little that didn't appear in a pre-war city guide. Others were contradictory or out of date, and some were so thin that they scarcely existed at all. In each file there was a record of Bomber Command's previous attacks.

'The Ruhr tonight,' said the elderly Wing Commander. 'I'll bet you my morning tea-break: Essen or Cologne.'

'What, on my wages?' said the WAAF officer. 'When you buy three or four sticky buns.'

He shrugged. 'You would have lost.'

Quickly she picked up a newspaper and turned to the astrology section. Under Aries it said, 'Someone dear to you will make a journey. Financial affairs promising.' She folded it and pushed it into the drawer.

She said, 'Some day I'll take you up on one of your bets. Anyway, look at the moon chart. After the casualties we've had on recent light nights they might decide a full moon is too dangerous.'

'Too dangerous for some ops,' said the Wing Commander, 'but the Ruhr looks messy on radar screens. Moonlight gives a visual identification of the target. If the Met man predicts some cloud cover they'll go, and the Ruhr's the only logical target.'

The girl looked up and nodded agreement. It was 09.05 hours; another hour and a half before morning tea-break.

She said, 'What was the weather like when you came in, sir?'

'Quite delightful, a perfect summer's day – not a cloud in the sky.'

'I do hope so,' said the WAAF officer. 'Last night I had to get out of bed and close the window. The rain came down in torrents.' She had planned to have her hair done that afternoon: rain would ruin it.

'My garden needed the rain.'

'So did the Met people: they'd been forecasting it every day for a week.'

Neither of them raised their eyes to the Met map on the wall where was written the finest weather prediction that money and daring could provide. Each hour it was amended according to reports from weather stations, aeroplanes, and ships at sea.

* * *

There was certainly no indication of prevailing weather conditions from inside this underground Operations Room, known to its inmates as 'the hole'. The air was clean and at constant temperature and the bright lights shone unchanging night and day. Here arrived the strategic requirements from Churchill's Cabinet War Room and from Air Ministry. From here went the orders that sent four or five thousand airmen into a three-dimensional night battle over Germany.

Every square foot of wall space was crammed with information. At desks around it sat the top brass of Bomber Command, an awe-inspiring array of rank. An Army officer sat near a hot line to the C-in-C Home Forces and a naval captain clutched an armful of Enemy Shipping reports. Two American officers had small change spread across a desk top while a WAAF officer explained for the third time that thirty of these big coins made half a crown. 'Then what makes a whole crown?'

'Nothing makes a whole crown,' said his colleague, 'it's like saying what makes a bit. Two bits may be a quarter but you can't have a bit.'

'I think I've got it,' said the first American doubtfully.

At this moment the SASO (Senior Air Staff Officer) and the Group Captain i/c Operations began to give the C-in-C a summary of the previous night's bombing of Germany. All eyes were on the thirty-foot-wide blackboard upon which the previous night's objectives and orders were chalked in yellow and results added in red.

Even as they spoke a sergeant climbed the ladder and altered the Failed to Return tally from 26 to 25. 'What's that make it?' asked the C-in-C.

'Four point five per cent.'

'Not bad, I was expecting worse.'

'What are we going to get tonight?' the Met man was asked.

'Here are the predicted positions of the fronts for midnight. Well-broken cloud all along the north-west coast but clear from Hamburg northwards. Residual thundercloud with thunderstorms near the cold front.'

'The Ruhr?' The elderly Wing Commander heard the C-in-C's question to the Met man and nodded significantly.

The Met man shuffled his notes. 'At present thunderstorms are moving across the Rhine with this cold front but they will clear by this afternoon. Midnight: thin layer of medium cloud somewhere between 1,000 and 20,000 feet but it will probably have gone by 01.00 hours. There's a chance of a little stratocumulus at 2,000 to 3,000 feet. Expected visibility moderate.'

'What about Northern France?'

'Fine; moderate visibility. Well-broken layer cloud in north-west.'

'And the weather over UK for the aircraft's return?'

'Fine. A little stratocumulus at 2,000 or 3,000 feet. Excellent visibility.'

The C-in-C walked slowly across the highly polished floor to look at the quarter-inch map of Northern Europe that almost covered one wall. Each of the target towns was marked by a colour-coded reference on a flat pin. He looked back towards the moon chart, then moved nearer to peer at the Ruhr. The short routes were marked with coloured tapes and his eyes scanned them, calculating the flying times and fuel-loads that each target would demand.

As the C-in-C followed the routes a knot of staff officers moved with him, murmuring discreetly like Harley Street specialists about to collaborate on an expensive job of surgery. Always their glances went back to the Met wall. As the moment of decision arrived the officers ceased to talk. The only sounds were the air-conditioning and the clock. Suddenly the voices began again; the decision had been taken.

'Target files, Harry,' a young Group Captain called to the elderly Wing Commander, for, although it was a high rank on the squadrons, in this place a Wingco was a dogsbody.

Nora Ashton pushed it towards him. Once again they had guessed the target to within a few files.

'Krefeld as primary, Bremen as weather alternative,' said the C-in-C. 'H-Hour will be 01.30 hours. No gardening tonight.'

In the centre of the room were large drafting-tables. On one was a map showing enemy radar and night-fighter units. Another displayed overlapping photographs mounted together to make a mosaic of the whole Ruhr. The C-in-C walked across to one and tipped it flat. The Krefeld target file was open and large-scale maps, target maps, plans, diagrams and vertical photos were arranged around it.

'What's our availability?'

'We've much better deliveries from the factories this month. We are showing 783 heavy bombers, 148 mediums. The strength of the training units is unchanged.'

'Well, I'll use 650 heavies and 100 mediums. This target will give them all a chance.'

'Very good, sir.' The Staff Officer put a form headed 'C-in-C's Daily Allotment of Targets' on the table, and arranged the most recent reconnaissance photos of the target.

'Krefeld then, with 750 aircraft. I'm going to increase the proportion of high explosive to incendiary bombs slightly. I know that the HE raises dust at the beginning but we need the blast damage in order to expose the interiors and have something to set alight. Let's have twenty-five minutes' pause before the second wave goes in. That increases the risk from night fighters but gives us a chance of killing his firemen and policemen and air-raid people. I'll give that second wave mostly HE; one-third of the aircraft will carry one bomb fused for long delay to keep them worried.'

While he was talking, the C-in-C filled in the Daily Allotment of Targets form.

'Put some Mosquitoes over Berlin to make the sirens go and some leaflets on to Ostend. I want the Berlin route and the Ostend route near enough to our main stream route to confuse them.' The C-in-C passed the written order to the Controller. He got up slowly and left the Operations Room.

As he stepped out into the daylight the sentry gave a smart salute. Bomber Command HQ was hidden in thickly wooded countryside but the sky seen through the beech trees was clear and blue.

The centre of the depression had moved across Northern England and out into sea-area Dogger. It was a young, vigorous depression and pulled the cold front eastwards after it, leaving England to enjoy a period of anticyclonic weather. There would be no rain.

Even before the C-in-C was through the door the SASO was on the phone to the first of the Group commanders.

'It's Krefeld tonight, old boy. Weather alternative Bremen. Our Met chaps seem sure the weather will clear but we'll have the usual Met conference call. I want to leave it as late as possible today. Naturally you'll plan for sky marking just in case . . .'

He glanced at the clock marked Double British Summer Time. It showed 09.55 hours. Alongside it another clock set to Central European Time showed that German clocks were set to the same time.

CHAPTER THREE

'Aren't you glad we no longer live in Krefeld?' Anna-Luisa asked.

'You said there would be lions and tigers, and wild animals,' the little boy said accusingly.

'There are lions and tigers, and yesterday I saw an elephant in the woods near Frau Richter's farm.'

'You're always saying that,' the little boy said with a chuckle. 'You just make those stories up.'

'If you've finished your egg you ought to get along to school. It's nearly nine o'clock.'

She took a handkerchief and wiped a trace of egg from his lips. Hansl hurried to get his schoolbooks. 'Take your raincoat, Hansl,' she called. 'I'm sure it will rain.'

Anna-Luisa made sure his coat was buttoned and his collar straight. She checked the schoolbooks in his case and ran a comb through his short hair. When all was approved she gave him a little salute. 'All is in order, Herr Leutnant, say goodbye to Pappi.'

The little boy saluted gravely. Anna-Luisa reached for a second egg and placed it carefully in the simmering water.

'Breakfast, Herr Bach,' she called.

Neither the little boy nor his father, for whom she was preparing breakfast, belonged to Anna-Luisa. She was a member of the RADwJ, a uniformed labour force of mothers' helps and social workers. A little over a year ago she had gone to work for Frau Bach in Krefeld, twelve kilometres away in the Ruhr district. She had liked the job, adored the child, and Frau Bach had been a not unreasonable employer. Within a month of her starting work Frau Bach had been killed in an air raid. Herr Bach and his elder son Peter, an infantry private just eighteen years old, had been flown back from the Russian Front. The authorities had a simple solution. They wanted to evacuate little Hansl to a Hitler Youth camp in the Protectorate of Czechoslovakia, but Herr Bach preferred that Anna-Luisa should stay with the boy. He wanted some place that he could think of as home, although the cost of renting an apartment just for one ten-year-old made terrible demands upon his Oberleutnant's pay.

Herr Bach's cousin suggested that they should move into this apartment in the town of Altgarten not far from the Netherlands border. It had been the home of Gerd's father but had been unoccupied since the old man's death almost two years before. Gerd had loaded Bach's salvaged furniture into his grocer's van and brought it here from Krefeld. That was a year ago, and since then August Bach, Luftwaffe Oberleutnant and Commanding Officer of radar station 'Ermine', had learned to call it home. Now that he was stationed on the Netherlands coast he was able to see his small son every two or three weeks. Last Christmas his grown-up son Peter had also come home on leave. It was a happy time.

'Breakfast is ready, Herr Bach,' called Anna-Luisa.

'Did you hear the thunder?' asked Bach.

'I made Hansl take his raincoat.'

'It's just a summer storm,' said Bach. 'If it does rain it will soon be over.'

'I hope so,' said Anna-Luisa. 'You've such a long journey.'

When August Bach sat down to breakfast she noticed that he was wearing his best uniform. She approved of his uniform, for although he was forty-six years old he was tall and slim and his greying hair served only to emphasize the tan on his face. At his throat the Pour le Mérite medal glittered.

'The milk is sour. The thunder must have caused it,' said the girl.

'It doesn't matter.'

'This is the last of the real coffee you brought. Do you know, Herr Bach, I am so used to ersatz coffee that the real beans you bring from Holland keep me awake at night.'

'Where is an egg for you, Anna-Luisa?'

'There were only two, Herr Bach, the hens are not laying, and they cost six Reichsmarks each. There is a terrible shortage this month.'

'Have this one. The Luftwaffe live well in Holland. Only last week Willi, my Stabsfeldwebel, laid his hands on some cream.' He passed the egg to her.

'You'll never believe me, Herr Bach, but I don't remember the taste of cream.'

'I believe you,' said August Bach. 'I'll speak to him when I get back and see if he can't find some for me next month when I come.'

'Did you notice, Herr Bach, little Hansl has picked up this terrible local accent?'

'Like my cousin Gerd's,' said August smiling.

August Bach watched the girl eating his boiled egg. She looked up and smiled. What did an accent matter? She was very beautiful, especially when she smiled. Without her he would have no home and, unless you counted the occasional printed postcard from a Hitler Youth camp in the Protectorate, no young son either. Nowadays the children were being evacuated farther and farther away. Bombed-out children from Cologne had gone to Bulgaria and Hungary.

'Herr Bach,' said Anna-Luisa. 'Is it true that many RADwJ girls are going to work on flak sites? There is a rumour that they will even be manning the guns.'

Bach had always feared that some day Anna-Luisa would decide that looking after little Hansl was not a great enough contribution to the war effort. Worse still, he feared that the RAD bureau would decide that for her, but here in the country the pace of things was slower. There was no RAD bureau in Altgarten, no SA, and even the Party HQ was closed on market day.

'Are you unhappy, Anna-Luisa?' he asked. 'Are you thinking of leaving us?'

'I would never leave you, Herr Bach,' she said. 'Never. I will look after Hansl all the rest of my life.'

'Now, now, Anna-Luisa, you mustn't make promises like that.'

'I will, Herr Bach. I will. I love Hansl as though he was my own child.'

'Then why do you ask me about the RAD girls going to the gun sites?' asked August.

She got to her feet and began to clear the breakfast table. 'Have you finished your coffee?'

'Yes.'

'I'm sorry, but there is now only the ersatz.'

'Answer me, Anna-Luisa.'

'Herr Bach,' she said. She was standing at the sink now with her face turned away from him. He waited for her to continue. She was attractive in her neat white blouse and brown skirt with her blonde hair drawn back into a severe knot. Why had he not noticed before her long slim legs and strong young arms? Undressed, she would look . . . he killed the thought immediately. She was only a child, perhaps a year or so older than his infantryman son. Her service in the RAD was a patriotic duty. It was his job to look after her, not lust after her.

'Are there' – she paused – 'any RAD girls working at your radar site?'

August Bach didn't laugh, although the thought of girls in that desolate spot on the Dutch coast made him realize how little she understood the rigours of his life there.

'There are no girls, Anna-Luisa. I only wish there were,'

he joked. And he looked up at her, still smiling, to discover her face racked with tears. He took his handkerchief to dry her eyes. 'Anna-Luisa, whatever is the matter?'

'Be careful of the washing-up water on your fine uniform,' she said, raising her face to him, and the next moment he found that he was kissing her. She was sobbing as though she would never stop. It was difficult to understand what she was saying, but August Bach suddenly found that everything made sense to him. 'I love you, Herr Bach,' she said. He smoothed her blonde hair and made little clicking noises with his lips in the hope that it would stop her crying.

'I love you,' she said again. 'Whatever shall we do?'

'You can stop calling me Herr Bach for one thing,' he said.

'What will people say?' she said.

'Does it matter?'

'This is a little country town, Herr August . . .'

'Just August.'

'August . . . people gossip here. There is no telling what stories will go round.' He had his arms round her and felt her sobbing gently. He patted her shoulder awkwardly and paternally.

It was a damnable situation. Almost the whole town knew August's cousin – Gerd Böll the grocer – and through him half the town knew August. Often strangers would talk to him in the street as though they were lifelong friends. 'We must take things slowly,' said August. Anna-Luisa nodded.

'Oh, for God's sake,' he said, 'do you think they're not gossiping about us already?'

'They are,' said Anna-Luisa, 'but it does not matter. I love you.' He held her more tightly and less paternally.

'And I love you,' said August and he realized that he did. All these months of spending his leaves in the same house with this young girl. No wonder neighbours talked. To her he must have seemed unnatural or inhuman. He looked at her; she was a simple girl and for her perhaps he was a frightening figure. He asked himself to what extent he had been hurrying back here to see the child and to what extent because it was his home, a home that Anna-Luisa had created, a place where his favourite foods were placed before him and his favourite records near the gramophone. August realized that all these months he had been hurrying back to Anna-Luisa. 'I love you, Anna-Luisa,' he said. 'I want you to marry me.' She raised her reddened eyes to him. Her hair had fallen forward. She was remarkably beautiful even in this disarray. Even more beautiful, perhaps.

'There are my parents, Herr Bach. You will have to visit them or at least write.'

'I will do that today,' he said. He stroked her head again and took her hand. It was a slim hand reddened by hard work, scrubbing floors and washing Hansl's clothes and August's shirts.

'Damn, damn, damn,' said August Bach under his breath, and then began to undress her, still declaiming loudly about how foolish they were. He unpinned the RAD swastika brooch from her blouse and set it aside carefully.

'How old are you?' he asked suddenly.

'Twenty-two,' said Anna-Luisa.

'Well, there you are,' said August. 'It's stupid, absolutely stupid,' but he did not undress her more slowly. The nearby church clock struck nine and a horse and cart clattered past the house. It made their intimacy more conspiratorial to hear the town going about its business just a few yards away.

'I love you, Herr Bach,' said Anna-Luisa.

'August,' insisted August.

'You'll write?'

'Every day,' swore August.

'And to my father?'

'This afternoon.'

'I love you, Herr August,' said Anna-Luisa. 'I love both of you. We shall make a perfect family. You just see. I will

32

buy new fabric for the front-room curtains, and Hansl needs new shoes.'

He pulled the pins from her hair and it tumbled down over her face. He had never seen her with her hair loose. It had always been rolled tight at the nape of her neck in a style suitable for her uniformed appearance. She laughed and kissed him again. By now they were in the bedroom and the big brass bed creaked loudly as she climbed onto it. August leaned across the bed to her, but she moved aside and giggled at outwitting him. For a moment, a terrible moment, August thought that she was just teasing him. It was the sort of thing that a young girl might do to an ardent lover of forty-six. But no sooner had the thought entered his mind than she undressed herself. Still standing on the bed, she threw her starched white uniform blouse across the room and stepped out of her brown skirt. Her underwear vanished as if by magic and there she was, naked, spinning round before his startled gaze. She pulled back the bedclothes and slid under them. Only her tousled flaxen hair and bright blue eyes were visible as she pulled the eiderdown up to her nose. It was the yellow silk eiderdown, that his wife had been so proud of, Bach remembered. They had saved so long to buy it.

He unbuttoned his uniform jacket and put it across the back of a chair.

'Don't come to bed with your medal on, Herr August. It hurts,' she called.

He pulled the black-and-white ribbon of the Pour le Mérite over his head.

'Show me.' He threw the beribboned medal to her. He continued to undress while she looked at it.

She put the ribbon over her head and admired herself in the mirror, stiffening her naked body like a soldier on parade. The blue and gold of the medal matched her eyes and hair.

'It's the Pour le Mérite, isn't it?' she asked.

'That's very clever of you.'

'I asked someone about the cross you wore at your throat. What did you do?'

'I shot down eleven English aeroplanes in the first war.'

'You must have been only a boy.'

'I was seventeen when I shot down the first one.'

She opened her arms to him and he climbed on to the bed with her.

'You know,' she told him in a whisper. 'I have seen this room a thousand times from every place. I have even crawled under the bed to sweep and clean but I never thought I would see the room from this viewpoint.' Her skin was soft and warm and contrasted with the cold stiffly starched sheets under his touch.

'In future you will see it from this viewpoint as often as you wish,' he said with a smile.

'I shall always wish it so,' said Anna-Luisa seriously. She touched his face with her fingertips and he caught the harsh smell of kitchen soap as it mingled with her cologne.

'It's a gloomy room,' said August. The wallpaper was dark and the oak wardrobe huge and ancient. They were both reflected in its mirror. Their eyes met. A streak of lightning came through the lowered blind and lit them momentarily like a flashbulb. There was a growl of thunder. Anna-Luisa blushed and looked away. Hung here and there were old family photographs; unwanted in the sitting-room, but difficult to throw away. On the washstand a basin and jug glinted in the rosy light coming through the pink blind. A potted plant silhouetted against it shivered in the draught from the window. Anna-Luisa touched the Pour le Mérite medal. She grinned. 'It looks better on me,' she said.

'It does,' he agreed, and reached out for her.

'And the red ribbon?'

'For the East Front,' he said. 'The Eisbeinorden.' The cold-feet medal.

'That must have been terrible.'

34

'It was.' His voice was muffled as he kissed her ear.

'Herr August,' she whispered as they began to make love. 'Shall I always sleep in this bed now?'

'Yes,' said August. Close to, he noticed that her hair was almost white and under its fringe her eyes were reddened by sobbing, and the tip of her nose was too. She smiled at him again. The light faded and there was the chilly gust of air that precedes a storm. Without hurry August made love to her as the thunderclouds darkened the gloomy room.

Afterwards she clutched him very tightly and made his arm wet with her silent tears. He reached for his cheroots and lit one. He wanted to tell her everything he had ever done and show her everything he had ever seen. There was so little time before he must go.

'Will you be kind to me, Herr August?'

He kissed the side of her nose. 'Kindness in a man is a quality few women admire,' he said. 'Especially very young, very beautiful women.'

'I shall always admire you, Herr August. Tell me about the medal.'

We were all victims of these symbols and trinkets, totems and taboos, thought August Bach. Why should the girl be attracted by the blue enamelled cross? What could it mean to her?

'The aeroplanes were different then. Biplanes: fragile little affairs of sticks and fabric.' Why was he using those old clichés? They were tough little planes and agile too. Not like today's sophisticated metal machines so full of fuelpipes, radio gear and delicate equipment that even a heavy bump on take-off made something malfunction.

'They were painted with strange patterns of mauve and pink and grey. I can remember them.' It wasn't true. He could no longer remember the difference between a Halberstadt and an Albatros. It was the smell that he remembered, the fuel and the dope, shrill smells that caught the back of the throat. He remembered too the sound of the Mercedes motor firing and the roar of it echoing against the side of the hangar.

'I remember the day I shot down my first Englishman. It was a beautiful day, not a cloud in the sky.' Or was he telling it correctly? Surely that was the day he got the telegram about his mother dying. It was pouring with rain the day he shot down his first Englishman.

'Were you afraid?' asked Anna-Luisa.

'I was afraid that someone would think I might be afraid,' he said. It was a conventional answer. The true answer was that at eighteen he didn't have enough intelligence to be afraid with.

'Did you see the Englishman?'

He tried to remember. 'It was a two-seater. I saw the pilot's white silk scarf floating out of the cockpit. I came out of the sun.'

'Were you proud?'

'I'd killed two men, Anna-Luisa. It's a terrible thing.' He wondered what sort of men they were or might have become. The British should never have sent men out in those BE-2s, not over the lines anyway. After he landed and claimed his first victory his Staffel commander said, 'A BE-2, I suppose.' This one had already been shot up but he fought like the devil. On the third pass the gunner ran out of ammunition. He waved and pointed to his gun. A white-faced fellow with a moustache, no youngster. The pilot seemed unable to open the throttle. He looked over his shoulder to see how close the attack was coming. They stood no chance. He went out to the crash, to salvage the roundel markings as a trophy, but there was blood all over the canvas upon which they were painted. Both British flyers were dead. The sentry told him that one of the medical orderlies had kept an Englishman's scarf. He'll sell it for five marks, said the sentry. Bach had declined.

'I want to walk with you, Herr August. Can we go shopping together?'

'And we will lunch together at the Stube,' he answered.

'It will be wonderful, August.' She stroked his head.

'We will walk everywhere, Anna-Luisa. Everyone shall see us arm in arm.'

'I love you, August. I shall always love you.'

The room lit up bright pink.

'One thousand,' said Anna-Luisa. 'Two thousand . . .' When he puffed at his cheroot he found it had gone out. He reached for his matches and relit it carefully, then he held up the match and Anna-Luisa blew it out but still counted on. When the thunder came she pronounced the storm to be four kilometres away. There was still no sound of rain.

'Did you know how to tell how far away a storm is?' she asked.

'You can never be sure,' said August.

CHAPTER FOUR

The huge layer of cold air that was approaching Altgarten moved eastwards across Europe at twenty miles per hour. As it moved, the cold front's sharp edge chiselled under the unstable humid summer air and levered it skywards to form thunderclouds. There was thunder too and lightning and in places rain. Eighty miles north-west of Altgarten the rain fell upon the IJsselmeer, the great inland sea that opened the heart of Holland to the northern storms. At first the rain was light and constant, dropping from the low nimbostratus cloud like black columns that propped up the sky. Then came the rain from the cumulonimbus, falling ten miles, right through the nimbostratus, and crashing in great sheets upon the rough waters of the IJsselmeer. The wind had veered to the north and sudden gusts of it pushed the rain horizontal. It deluged the little lakes near Utrecht. Hundreds of ducks, herons and hundreds of other water-birds sheltered miserably along the water's edge and under wooden piers from which even the anglers had departed. At Kroonsdijk the rain beat upon the farm-style buildings and the duck pond and hammered the flat cobbled and asphalt causeways, so that fine spray rebounded like tall white grass.

In building number thirty-one the rain awoke Oberleutnant Baron Victor von Löwenherz when even the thunder had failed. He looked at the clock; it was ten o'clock Central European Summer Time and the barometer had fallen dra-

38

matically. He reset the barometer, for when the pressure started to rise and the wind steadied and backed he would know that the cold front and its line squalls had nearly passed. Löwenherz took a close interest in the weather, for he was a pilot and Kroonsdijk was a Luftwaffe night-fighter airfield.

The military installations had been designed to look like Dutch farm buildings. The big roofs that sloped almost to the ground and the timber exteriors disguised concrete block-houses. The shutters painted with gay peasant designs were made of six-millimetre steel. Instead of a rectangular fire hydrant tank, here was an oval pond, and upon it the Luftwaffe had installed ducks to complete the illusion. Grazing near the runways were herds of pantomime cows made from lath and plaster. The subject of jokes and derision, they were enough to deceive the air cameras.

Outside the window, motor vehicles and beyond them twin-engined fighter aeroplanes were parked under the trees. Nothing had been left to chance. This site had been selected, surveyed and decided upon, the architect's plans had been completed and all was ready, three years before Holland was invaded. Now Kroonsdijk had become a key factor in the air defence of Germany. It lay upon the direct route from the bomber airfields in Eastern England to the heart of industrial Germany, as a toll-gate on a dark busy road.

It was not surprising that Oberleutnant Baron Victor von Löwenherz had many times been photographed for the Nazi magazines *Der Adler* and *Signal*, for he was the personification of National Socialist propaganda – although they often chose to omit his title, for the new Nazi state had created its own aristocracy. Tall, slim and elegant, his hair was blond and by this time of year the sun had turned it almost white. His face had the sharp-edged, bony look that sculptors invent and his teeth were white and even.

He jumped out of bed and did his physical exercises: twenty press-ups, eight hundred paces on the spot, knees high, stretching, knees bending and arms flinging, watched with deadpan interest by the young bulldog that was lying in its usual spot under the writing-table. Löwenherz's room was small and rather dark, for windows were kept as small as possible to reduce the danger from blast and shrapnel. In one corner was an iron bedstead with grey blankets which he now carefully remade, folding each corner neatly and expertly as he had done every morning since he joined the Army as an officer cadet in 1937.

For well over three hundred years the Löwenherz family had supplied soldiers to Prussia. A Heinrich Löwenherz had served under the mighty Wallenstein and shared his grim defeat by Gustavus Adolphus at Lützen in 1632. But Heinrich's son had become a senior officer in the Kriegskommissariat of the Great Elector and had lived to see the Swedes driven from the battlefield of Fehrbellin some forty-three years later.

There was a painting of Heinrich on the staircase of the house in Grawiec. A pale-faced man with the Löwenherz nose and dark, broody eyes. His beard and moustache are trimmed in the Spanish style and he is wearing the broad lace collar and red sash even upon his breastplate and leather fighting clothes. As a child, Victor had been frightened to go past it down the stairs, especially after dark when there were only flickering candles to light the hall and the howl of wolves came from the hills above the village.

In the First World War Baron Hans-Georg von Löwenherz – Victor's father – had lost an arm at Langemarck, Ypres, serving with the Prussian Guards, and had gone on to become a staff operations officer. After the war he had taken command of one of the secret instruction schools that the Reichswehr formed to replace the Military Academy forbidden by the peace treaty.

It was natural that Victor should go into the Army and although he had never been truly happy as a cadet he could look back upon it with pride and pleasure. Tucked into the corner of a silver-framed portrait of his mother there was a fading snapshot taken in Austria – at the time of the Anschluss. Five smiling cavalry officers, their caps bearing the commemorative Brandenburg dragoon eagle of which they had been so proud. The following day, in Linz, they had caught a glimpse of the Führer himself. A month later Löwenherz had been transferred from the Army to the Luftwaffe and was a part of the intensive aircrew training programme that followed the Munich Agreement.

He looked again at those boys who had been his close comrades through the agonies of cadet school. They'd teased him mercilessly when they heard of his application to become a flyer, but they'd come to the railway station at four-thirty in the morning to bid him goodbye. He looked at their childish faces; the amateur photo was creased and faded. One was buried in Narvik, another had been crippled in an amphitheatre near Sparta, the third was an Oberst on Manstein's staff at Army Group Don. The fourth was commanding a Bewährungs-kompagnie (a suicide unit for enemies of the régime) near Kharkov.

The group in the small ivory frame was his class at the Neu Bieburg A/B Flying School, with an old Bücker biplane in the background. Only half of those recruits finally got their wings.

Twenty-five men sepia-toned and defaced by youthful signatures: pupils and instructors at Schleissheim Fighter Pilot School. He was blinking in the strong sunlight. He'd just completed two hundred flying hours when that photo was taken. It had seemed a lot at the time. Scowling in the front row was his present commanding officer who, like most of the instructors there, had just returned from fighting in the Spanish Civil War. To Löwenherz he had seemed a remote and glamorous figure with his four victories over Loyalist Spanish planes. Now, he supposed, the new replacements on his Staffel saw himself as a similarly forbidding figure: distant and coid and expert. Löwenherz hoped so.

41

He stopped looking at the photos and pulled on his silk dressing-gown before going to the end of the officers' billets for a shower. He scrubbed himself energetically under the cold water and dried himself thoroughly. He had a catlike grace of movement that fitted his fastidiousness with food and his concern for clean personal linen. When he returned to his room he spent forty minutes ironing the shirts and underclothes that he had washed and left to dry the previous night.

When Löwenherz finished he put away the electric iron and dressed carefully. He inspected his gleaming high boots and fixed the Iron Cross and the German Cross Order to the pocket of his newly laundered tunic. He briefly checked his appearance in the mirror: the white tunic was immaculate and he slanted the white-topped cap rakishly. The bulldog came out from under the table and prepared for the walk through the woodland to the Officers' Mess.

'It's wet outside, Bubi,' he warned, but, like his master, the dog enjoyed walking through the fragrant grass. The rain had ceased and sunlight shone upon the wet grass. The dog sniffed each patch of it and ran across the road and cocked its leg at the slit-trench bomb shelters. Löwenherz used to scold Bubi for doing that, but since the shelters had never been used from the day they were dug he had ceased to care if the dog fouled them.

As Löwenherz stepped out from his quarters four Dutch civilians arrived carrying mops and brooms. Behind them cycled Feldwebel Blessing, the civilian staff overseer. The Feldwebel dismounted from his bicycle when he saw Löwenherz and saluted him with precision. Blessing was a young, over-weight Bavarian with heavy features and small piercing eyes.

'Good morning, Feldwebel Blessing,' said Löwenherz. 'There's rust in the water supply again. The same trouble as last March, I suspect.'

'It will be investigated, Herr Oberleutnant.'

'Excellent, Blessing, I am confident that it will.' Although he was unpopular, Blessing's efficiency was a byword and his civilians kept the billets clean and shining. A few generals like Blessing in the OKW and perhaps we shouldn't be on the defensive in the East, nor preparing Italy for an Allied invasion, thought Löwenherz. Blessing cycled energetically away towards the main barracks with Bubi barking at his rear wheel. Löwenherz walked towards the Officers' Mess and soon the dog returned, racing after him, splashing through the puddles.

Along the perimeter fence sat hundreds of sea-birds driven inland by the summer storm. Bubi chased them along the fence, barking and jumping high into the air. Lazily the wet white blobs stretched their wings and circuited briefly before settling back into place.

As he neared the Officers' Mess, Löwenherz recognized one of his pilots walking towards him through the sun-spotted woodland. The boy would probably have avoided a meeting with his Staffelkapitän if he had been looking where he was going.

Christian Himmel was a twenty-two-year-old Unter-offizier. His basic pay was one hundred marks per month plus another forty marks in Wehrsold (war pay) and seventy-five marks Fliegerzulage (flying pay). This, even allowing for income tax and contributions to Nazi funds and winter relief, still left him with more comforts than he had known in civil life and just double what his father earned as a gardener. He was a muscular boy with short untidy hair that he inexpertly trimmed himself. His face was round and his serious mouth full-lipped. 'Angel-face' he had been called at the camp where he had done his labour service, and the lack of wrinkles in his clear skin did make him look like one of those carved cherubs that crowd together around the altars and pulpits of the baroque churches near his Bavarian hometown.

Himmel was shy, although no one at Kroonsdijk had less

43

reason to be daunted by Oberleutnant von Löwenherz than he had. In July 1940 during the Kanalkampf (as the Luftwaffe named the early period of the Battle of Britain) the circumstances had been very different. Löwenherz was a young ensign newly posted to a Messerschmitt 109 squadron where Himmel was a very experienced pilot, with a Polish Lós bomber and two Spitfires to his credit and a novel reputation. It was said that Himmel had shot down more enemy aircraft than he claimed, and on at least three occasions he had been more than generous in allowing kills to be credited to others.

Löwenherz's first two kills – a Hurricane and a Defiant – had a considerable number of Himmel's bullets in them, as Löwenherz was the first to admit. But Löwenherz had been Himmel's wingman, and, as Himmel said, a good wingman should share credit for every victory. A wingman flew two hundred yards on the beam of his leader and covered him from stern or quarter attack. The leader navigated, led the attack and made the decisions. Himmel had done that well. Himmel was also a skilled mechanic. His concern for the aircraft on the Staffel amounted almost to hypochondria, an obsession that was his excuse for being shy, silent and alone. When he spoke with his ground-crew men he tried to confine the conversation solely to technical matters. Sometimes Löwenherz could almost believe that Himmel ticked and whined and roared, and made better contact with his machines than with his fellow men.

'Good morning, Himmel.'

'Good morning, Herr Oberleutnant,' said the boy. There was a gust of wind and Himmel, clad in black mechanic's overalls, shivered.

'Plugs still oiling up, Christian?'

'They fitted new rings but that was just a waste of labour, Herr Oberleutnant. There's only a very slight improvement.'

The dog made playful rushes at the Unteroffizier's boots. Himmel pretended to punch Bubi's head and the dog

44

growled and made fearsome open-fanged passes at his fast-moving hands.

'Kugel won't be able to do it today. The Major has had trouble with his supercharger capsule. He's given strict instructions that his plane must be ready this evening.'

'Then Kugel will be busy,' said Himmel.

'Very, very busy,' smiled Löwenherz, picturing the pot-bellied old mechanic facing the Gruppenkommandeur's wrath.

Löwenherz said, 'I'll tell him to do a run up when you land tonight. If you're still getting a drop in revolutions I'll tell him he must fit a new engine. How's that, Christian?'

'Thank you, Herr Oberleutnant.'

'Are you going to breakfast?'

'I'm not hungry. I will have coffee when it's sent out to the dispersal. Shall I take Bubi with me?'

Löwenherz passed Bubi's collar and lead to Himmel. Bubi barked happily. Löwenherz watched the young NCO and the dog move out of sight through the trees. Himmel was running and the dog chased him until Himmel's black overalls merged into the patches of shade.

The temperature had dropped slightly in spite of the sunshine and Löwenherz noticed that the gusts of wind were coming from the direction of the HQ buildings to the north-west. The cold front had moved well past Kroonsdijk now, and the great cold air mass was steadying. When he reached the Officers' Mess he looked at the barometer; it had risen. Everything pointed to a few days of fine summer weather.

Löwenherz was a methodical man. He deposited his peaked cap on the cloakroom counter and picked up a copy of the *Berliner Börsen-Zeitung* that was set aside for him. He looked up the prices of his Daimler-Benz, Zeiss Ikon and Siemens shares. He believed in good solid companies. He'd bought a few shares of Sachs Engineering because it was owned by the father of his radar operator and, although they had done wonders until a year ago, they had now begun to

45

stick a little. He thought he might sell. He looked at the back page for the annual reports but there was nothing of interest. Neither was the war news of any great importance. The war was at a time of hiatus. He didn't want to fold the paper and stuff it into his pocket for it would make bulges in his newly pressed uniform jacket. So he rolled it carefully and took it with him. There were no new notices on the board. Glancing at his reflection as he passed, he smoothed his hair and opened the door of the dining-hall.

The Mess Hall was a large sunlit room with long refectory tables and a high ceiling. At the far end there was a patriotic mural covering the entire wall. Firm-jawed soldiers and radiant girls in peasant costume and flaxen plaits marched with flags under a canopy of bomber formations. There were posters that reminded crews of the dangers of careless conversation in public places. Another depicted a gull in flight: 'Pilots, he too is your enemy!' A photo of a birdstrike-damaged plane was also shown. A cartoon pilot said, 'If you are lost, climb to safety height. Don't descend through cloud, it's dangerous.'

Over the serving-hatch there were listed the civilian rations side by side with the more generous Wehrmacht issue of the same items. 'Remember . . .' it was headed.

There were two officers of his Staffel sitting over a pot of coffee. Löwenherz joined them. Some of the tables were set for the 'brunch'-style meal that the night-fighter crews had at midday after sleeping late. It was still only ten AM and as yet these three flyers were the only ones up and about.

'Can I join the *Kaffeeklatsch*?' said Löwenherz.

'The whole points system should be revised,' said Leutnant Kokke, a young Berliner. He was a swarthy man with long black hair, full moustache and a beard trimmed just close enough to fit under his oxygen mask. Löwenherz noted his grubby grey shirt and unpolished boots. Kokke was noted for his devastating sarcasm and polished flying skill, but he was invariably the untidiest officer on the unit. Löwenherz decided that he must speak to Kokke about this on a more suitable occasion.

Kokke went on, 'On the Eastern Front any fool can shoot down a dozen a day. One hundred victories, two hundred victories, what's it matter? Any day now they'll have a fellow there with three hundred victories.'

'While we struggle and sweat to see who will be the first man to get thirty,' complained Beer, a sad little Leutnant from Regensburg who before the war had been a racing-car driver. His face was lined with worry and his wavy hair surmounted a very tall forehead. He too was trying to grow a moustache but after nearly three weeks its growth was less than luxuriant. He fingered it for a moment before laying aside his copy of the *Völkische Beobachter* and sipped at the bitter coffee.

A Mess waiter put a plate of chopped raw swede on the table along with a fresh pot of coffee. The Luftwaffe medical authorities said it would improve night vision. Few aircrew ate it, fewer still believed in it, but Löwenherz bit into a piece now to set a good example. Then he reached for a tin of vitamin tablets and took two.

'Do you think the tablets improve night vision, Herr Oberleutnant?' asked Beer.

'Night adaption,' corrected Löwenherz.

'Yes,' said Beer.

'There's a whole world of difference,' said Löwenherz.

'And you think the vitamin A tablets improve night adaption?' asked Beer.

'It's on orders,' said Löwenherz. 'Two each morning before breakfast and two immediately before flying.'

'They should revise the points system,' said Kokke. 'At present a pilot has to destroy, say, thirteen four-engined bombers at three points each and a twin-motor escort at two points in order to get a Knight's Cross. At night! My God, we should get a Knight's Cross just for finding one. And now with this wet weather our radar aerials will be all to hell.'

Beer nodded agreement. It was all Kokke needed to expound further. 'Why, on the Eastern Front you can knock down a couple of antique American Airacobras and a couple of LaG3s every morning before breakfast and get yourself a sheet-metal tie in a week or two. Isn't that right, Herr Oberleutnant?'

'Are you two still talking about Knight's Crosses?' said Löwenherz. It was no surprise, though, that's what everyone in the Gruppe spent their spare time talking about; perhaps the whole damn Luftwaffe did. 'Knocking down Ivans is not so easy,' said Löwenherz. 'I've never seen a LaG3, but its newest variant is the La5FN. It's got fuel injection, a 1,650-hp motor, and the exhaust gases – carbon dioxide and nitrogen – are passed into the fuel tanks as a precaution against incendiary bullet hits. It's got two cannons with supplementary rockets. A Red pilot defected with a new one last month; I flew it at Rechlin Testing Centre. It's a good plane.'

'How fast?' asked Kokke.

'I got nearly 400 mph out of it at 15,000 feet.'

'That's fast,' said Beer.

'But what can it do at higher altitudes?' asked Kokke.

'It doesn't matter what it can do higher,' explained Löwenherz. 'It's a low-altitude air war in the east. If the Ivans are ground strafing, or bombing at low level, then we've got to come down low and fight them.'

'I suppose so,' agreed Kokke.

'What's more,' said Löwenherz, 'our technical people say its air-cooled motor will be simpler to service in bad winter conditions than the liquid-cooled ones are. The report also said that the airframe will take more punishment.'

'We could do with a few of those La5s to replace these crappy old wrecks that we have to nurse through the air,' said Kokke.

'There's nothing wrong with the Richards,' said Beer. 'Last year I was flying 110s. That really is an obsolete design.'

'Nothing wrong with the Richards?' scoffed Kokke. 'Where did you read that, the *Völkische Beobachter* in 1937?' He tapped off criticisms on the fingertips of his stubby pianist's hands. 'Designed as a dive bomber, we're using it as a night fighter. Four years out of date. Poor pilot visibility. Very high landing-speed. So, land a dive bomber with poor visibility at night with a high landing-speed and you've got a handful of aeroplane.'

'I like having a handful of aeroplane,' said Löwenherz. 'Anyway, next year we'll have the Heinkel 219.'

He was inclined to agree with Kokke about the Ju88R, especially in respect to the landing-speed, but the last thing he was prepared to do was to destroy the confidence his aircrews had in their equipment.

'With all respect, Herr Oberleutnant,' said Kokke, 'next year might be too late.'

'By next year we shall all be on the East Front,' said Beer. He helped himself to bread and cherry jam. A wasp was buzzing round the table and Beer shooed it away nervously.

'You're a miserable bastard,' said Kokke. 'When shall I ever hear you say a cheerful word?'

'Well, I don't say defeatist things like you do,' said Beer. He smiled thinly as he said it, but there was more than a trace of accusation in his voice.

'What did I say?' Kokke reached for Löwenherz's *Börsen-Zeitung* and swatted the wasp with a loud crack.

'The war in the east was like a travelling circus and a travelling zoo battling in a wilderness to decide which should put on a show.'

'Are you sure you didn't just make that up?' asked Kokke.

'Oh, shut up,' said Beer angrily.

'More coffee, Herr Oberleutnant?'

'Thank you, Kokke,' said Löwenherz. He watched the bearded man handling the coffee cups. Those were a musician's hands. Kokke had wanted to be a professional pianist until the war had interrupted his studies. By now a

49

career of the sort he'd once hoped for was impossible. He had only to touch the Mess piano to know how much skill had slipped away from him. Kokke poured coffee for Löwenherz and grinned at him provocatively. Some people said the young Berliner was an agent provocateur in the pay of the Gestapo. Löwenherz suspected that to be a story Kokke himself had circulated to provide an excuse for constant criticism of the régime and its methods and equipment.

'Here's to our Knight's Crosses,' toasted Löwenherz with coffee.

'I'll not drink to yours,' said Kokke smiling. 'If the bloody thing isn't on its way by now, it must be because they've decided to stop awarding them.'

Löwenherz bowed gratefully at the compliment. He had gained more than enough victories for the coveted Knight's Cross to be at his neck. His seniority and experience deserved a promotion but the Führer's birthday, a traditional date for promotions to be announced, had come and gone.

The pilots drank their coffee in silence, and Löwenherz held his napkin carefully in his free hand lest a drip of coffee fall upon his gleaming white summer jacket. Somehow Löwenherz always had the answer and the technical data to back it up. It was amazing how he found time to handle the office routine and paperwork that fell to him as Staffel Leader, as well as reading and remembering all the intelligence reports, doing the same blind-flying minimum that he had ordered for his Staffel, consistently winning the clay-pigeon stakes as well as maintaining a string of girlfriends from Brussels to Wilhelmshafen.

Finally it was little Beer who spoke. 'The Knight's Cross is always conferred by Hermann Göring in person?'

'A visit to Karinhall' – Löwenherz nodded. 'And the cauliflower for the Knight's Cross means an audience with the Führer.'

'With the knives and forks they give you a two-bedroom apartment at Berchtesgaden,' said Kokke mischievously.

'It's all right for you two to talk of Oak-leaves and swords,' said Beer. 'You, Herr Oberleutnant, have twenty-eight confirmed victories, and Kokke has twelve, but as yet I have none and might never get one.'

'Cheer up,' said Kokke. 'We all have the Iron Cross on our pocket.'

'That makes it even worse,' said Beer. 'How do I explain that mine was awarded for doing twenty flights without ever catching sight of a *Tommi*?'

'Perhaps you'll get a chance tonight if the weather clears,' said Löwenherz.

Beer pinched his face and refused to be cheered up. 'Each night the controller sends up his most successful crews first. They get the first crack at the Englishmen while the rest of us spend all day practising instrument-flying and all night playing chess.'

'It's necessary for the defence of the homeland that the best crews are put into battle as soon as the first radar contact is made,' said Löwenherz.

'Beer thinks the war has been arranged solely for his sport,' said Kokke.

'You must remember that these bombers are tearing the hearts out of our cities,' said Löwenherz. 'Ask Kokke if he prefers the best crews to go up first when it's his town of Berlin that's being bombed, or ask poor old Oberfeldwebel Krugelheim, my chief mechanic, whose wife was killed in Stuttgart last April.'

Kokke added, 'Or Leutnant Klimke, my radar man, whose wife and three children were killed in a bombing raid on Duisburg last Christmas, one day before he went on leave.'

'All I want to do,' protested Beer, 'is help shoot the murdering bastards out of the sky.'

'Don't be downhearted,' said Löwenherz. 'You will soon have your opportunity.' He finished his coffee and wiped his mouth carefully with his napkin. He stood up and after nodding a good day to them he eyed Beer's black leather zipper-jacket, breeches and high boots.

'You're not thinking of flying in those boots, Leutnant Beer?'

'No, sir,' said Beer.

'Good. There is a regulation about it. The Luftwaffe medical service has informed High Command that foot injuries are very difficult to attend to if the injured crewman is wearing close-fitting high boots.'

'I read your memo, sir.'

'Excellent, then that's clear. Good morning, gentlemen.' He looked at his newspaper with the remains of the wasp spattered across the headline in ugly brown stains. He didn't pick it up.

They both nodded goodbye to him.

'*Kaffeeklatsch*,' said Beer; 'patronizing bastard.'

'May I quote you?' said Kokke.

'It's all right for a *Krautjunker* like him,' said Beer. 'Son of a baron, enormous estates in East Prussia well out of the reach of the RAF . . .'

'That's why he's worried about those Russian aeroplanes,' said Kokke. 'You know, the mechanics across on Staffel number three have got a nice fiddle going. When the long-range Aunty Jus fly in with spares, the crews bring tins of caviar from Odessa to swap for bottles of Dutch schnapps. They say that that tall Oberfeldwebel with the motorcycle is making a fortune out of it. The other day the mechanics opened a tin of caviar out there on the dispersal apron. They were sitting around in the sun eating it, when Löwenherz walks up. The Oberfeldwebel gives him a big salute and spreads a great heap of caviar on a biscuit and offers it to him. "Beluga caviar, sir," he says. Löwenherz looks down his nose at it and says, "Never mind what kind of caviar it is, Oberfeldwebel. Have you washed your hands?"'

Kokke laughed heartily at his own story but Beer didn't.

'Prussian bastard,' said Beer. 'And that damned white jacket he wears as though this was a peacetime training school. Did you notice him looking at your dirty shirt? I bet there'll be another reminder about officers' appearance circulated next week.'

'Screw him,' said Kokke.

'He's always wiping his mouth and fingers,' said Beer. 'He makes me feel like I'm suffering from some sort of contagious disease.'

'You are,' said Kokke. 'It's called poverty.'

'Well, you know what I mean. And I hate men who wear cologne. He's obsessed with cleanliness, he's always in that shower whenever I want to use it.'

'Which isn't often,' said Kokke. 'Well, that's probably because he's terrified of getting a dose of clap from all those girls he runs around with.'

'One of these days, Kokke, you're going to get yourself arrested saying things like that.'

'Yes, well I can always count on you to help. Fancy telling Löwenherz that stuff about the East Front.'

'A man should be prepared to live with the statements he makes,' said Beer.

'You know, Beer, sometimes I think you would have made a bloody wonderful Pope.'

As Löwenherz reached the foyer of the Mess half a dozen aircrew officers were arriving for their noon meal. He nodded curtly to each of them and collected his peaked cap from the orderly in the cloakroom. In the foyer there were soft leather chairs and low tables with copies of *Luftwelt*, *Signal* and *Der Adler* scattered on it. Sitting nervously on the edge of his armchair was Blessing, the man in charge of civilian labour. Sitting next to him, leaning well back and reading the *Deutsche Zeitung*, there was an elderly man in civilian clothes. Blessing tapped the other man on the knee. He lowered his paper and looked up. Blessing nodded towards Löwenherz. The man was too old to be local civilian labour, and his clothes were a little too good and of German cut. My God, thought Löwenherz, it must be a relative of some recent aircrew casualty. The man reached for a soft hat and leather briefcase, got to his feet and approached Löwenherz with a sad smile.

'Oberleutnant Victor von Löwenherz?' said the man. The suit he was wearing was of pre-war quality but had been darned carefully at the corner of the pocket. There were three pens in his waistcoat and under it he was wearing a grey home-knitted sweater. The man's eyes stared calmly at him through gold-rimmed spectacles. His eyes were moist, as old men's eyes become, but they were as active and alert as they had ever been. His face was heavily lined and had the mauve tints that afflict the skin of heavy drinkers. His stiff white collar was of an ancient style and the knot of his tie was secured by a gold pin. A doctor or lawyer most people would have guessed him to be, and rightly. Blessing saluted carefully while the man extended a hand to Löwenherz. It was while they were shaking hands that the man said 'Heil Hitler' in a disinterested voice that he also used for commenting on the weather. He smiled bleakly and introduced himself. 'Feldwebel Dr Hans Starkhof of AST Nederlands, Group IIIL.'

The man's eyes flickered short-sightedly behind his spectacles and yet Löwenherz wondered whether this myopia – like his hesitations and eyebrows raised in surprise – was a ruse feigned for his own purposes. The man watched for Löwenherz's reactions to his low rank and the manner of its coupling to his doctorate, and to the Nazi greeting with his soft civilian handshake. He watched too for the reaction to the word AST – the Abwehr, or Military Intelligence, office: the technique of surprise was one that Starkhof had perfected many years ago as a criminal lawyer in Hamburg. There was always work for a criminal lawyer in Hamburg and a surprise immediately upon meeting could often help a case to a quick conclusion. From Löwenherz came no reaction, but Starkhof still had a card to play.

'Perhaps I should introduce . . .' he half turned towards Blessing.

'Feldwebel Blessing I already know,' said Löwenherz coldly.

'Ah, yes, precisely, which is why I should tell you that Blessing is employed by RSHA and has a SIPO rank of Untersturmführer.'

'May I see your identity papers?' asked Löwenherz.

'Alas, we carry none except a Wehrpass, but you may phone my office if you are worried.'

'I am not worried,' said Löwenherz.

'Excellent.' He gestured towards the entrance. 'We'll talk as we walk,' he suggested. 'You'll perhaps feel more comfortable in the open air.' He put on his trilby hat and stepped out into the sunshine. The three men walked down the long gravel drive, their shadows sharply drawn on the path by the warm sun. When he realized that Löwenherz had no intention of speaking first, the man said, 'There has been a theft of some documents, Herr Oberleutnant.' He paused but still nothing came from Löwenherz. 'Some secret documents,' he added. 'We are in no doubt about the identity of the thief.'

'I am sure,' said Löwenherz, 'that you have not come here to boast to me of your success.'

'Precisely,' said the man in civilian clothes. 'We should value your frankness and aid.'

'You will in any case be treated to the former,' said Löwenherz. 'As to the latter, until you are more forthcoming who knows what it might entail?'

'Dear comrade Löwenherz,' said Starkhof. 'You must be patient with an old man. Secret documents have been stolen and they must be recovered.'

'This is the Medical Centre, Herr Doktor,' interrupted Blessing.

'They were stolen from this building,' Starkhof explained to Löwenherz. 'We know the thief but lack the . . .'

'*Corpus delicti*,' supplied Löwenherz.

'Precisely,' said Starkhof. He turned to his colleague, 'The *corpus delicti*, Blessing, that's what you must find.'

They stood on the road between the farm-like headquarters buildings. Everywhere was quiet, for the true working day of this night-fighter station had not yet begun. A lorry rattled noisily through the main gate loaded with oil drums. Outside the Pay Section a line of men had formed and assumed the relaxed attitudes with which Servicemen accept inevitable delay. From the Medical Centre two orderlies were bringing chairs and piling them together in the sunshine, while from inside came the sound of buckets and mops and tuneless singing.

Starkhof said, 'The thief first misappropriated the documents. It was later that he stole them.'

'If that means that someone hid them behind a cupboard and went back for them later, why not say so more clearly?'

Eagerly Blessing said, 'The papers were secreted behind a cupboard and the thief did return later. How did you know that?'

'Deduction,' said Löwenherz. 'And I'll tell you another deduction too.'

'If you . . .'

'Comrade Untersturmführer Blessing' – the old man interrupted them. He raised a finger at Blessing. 'My witness, I believe.' He smiled; Blessing nodded.

The old man said, 'My dear Löwenherz. We should both be most interested in your deduction.'

Löwenherz said, 'You knew where the documents were, and yet did not retrieve them. Then you hoped to catch the thief taking them to some other place . . .'

'Or other party,' nodded Starkhof. 'Excellent, Oberleutnant.'

'You do not have the documents therefore you did not catch the thief in . . .' Löwenherz paused.

'You were about to say *flagrante delicto*, my good friend. Do say it.' In a quick aside to Blessing the old man added, 'Red-handed, my dear Blessing.' Blessing smiled.

It was difficult to be sure whether the man was trying to make a fool of Löwenherz or of Blessing. When Löwenherz walked forward again the others kept by his side.

Löwenherz said, 'Since Blessing pointed out the Medical Centre to you, I deduce that you have not seen it before. So it was' – Löwenherz feigned difficulty with the SS rank and pronounced it in a precise and ponderous manner – 'Untersturmführer Blessing who set a trap for the thief but was outwitted.'

'*Sunt lacrimae rerum*,' said the man to Blessing. 'Tears are a part of life, as I said to Blessing at the time.' Blessing scowled.

'Is it someone on my Staffel?' said Löwenherz.

'There you go again,' said Starkhof. 'Straight to the heart of the problem. Yes, it's someone on your Staffel.'

'Unteroffizier Himmel,' supplied Blessing.

'Young Himmel,' said Löwenherz. 'Why, that's impossible. I'd stake my life on Himmel.'

'Is that your considered opinion, Herr Oberleutnant?' asked Blessing weightily. They walked in silence for a moment, then Starkhof said, 'Of course not, the Herr Oberleutnant was speaking merely as a comrade in arms. Such sentiments nobly become front-line soldiers.'

'Would you stake your life on this thief Himmel?' persisted Blessing.

'My dear Blessing,' said Starkhof. 'The Oberleutnant often does exactly that. For isn't Himmel one of his most experienced pilots and thus essential to the safety of the whole Staffel?'

'Young Himmel is a fine pilot, hard-working and loyal,' said Löwenherz.

Blessing said, 'You went to breakfast at a few minutes to ten?'

Löwenherz said, 'I spoke with you.' He said it quickly and defensively, and was angry at himself.

'And you gave Himmel your dog?'

'Himmel took my dog to the dispersal.'

'Did Himmel often walk your dog?' asked Blessing. He smiled at Löwenherz and filled the simple question with complex innuendo.

'The dog chooses carefully the people with whom it will walk,' said Löwenherz.

'Himmel was one of the chosen people?' said Blessing.

'You seem better provided with malice than with evidence,' said Löwenherz. 'Perhaps it's merely that Himmel is easier to apprehend than the real thief who seems to have eluded you so effortlessly when the crime was committed.'

'Dear comrade Löwenherz,' said Starkhof wearily. 'You are not the judge in this case and, even if you were, it is not Blessing who would be on trial. We have asked your assistance merely to recover the documents which we believe – with excellent reason – Himmel stole from the Medical Centre.'

'How can I help?'

'Thank you, Herr Oberleutnant. That is what I was hoping that you would say.'

'Earlier,' added Blessing.

'Blessing,' sighed the older man, 'there are times when I believe that making witnesses hostile is your sole creative endeavour.' He turned again to Löwenherz. 'Last night Unteroffizier Himmel had this document in his bedside locker. This morning when Blessing arrived at his billet to arrest him he was not there. Neither was the document. The only person he met this morning was you . . .'

'What do you suspect Himmel did?'

'There are many possibilities: he might have learned it by heart and then destroyed it; he might have buried it so that he could return to retrieve it; or he might have handed it to an accomplice.'

'You don't seriously think Himmel is a spy?'

Starkhof shrugged.

Löwenherz said, 'How did he gain access to this document?'

'By accident, we think. He was due for a routine medical check on the fourteenth of the month. Eighteen NCOs attended the Medical Section that morning. Himmel was tenth; when he saw the Medical Officer to have his card signed the document was on the desk.'

'Sounds circumstantial,' said Löwenherz.

'I don't think so,' said Blessing.

'I rather agree with Löwenherz,' said Starkhof. 'The way the evidence is at present it would be difficult to put a very good case.'

'Impossible to put a case at all unless you mean against Blessing for incompetence.'

'That's rather severe, Herr Oberleutnant,' said Starkhof. 'But I must say, Blessing, you will come out of this looking rather foolish, and your chiefs are probably expecting you to prove that a young SIPO officer can run circles around an antique Abwehr Feldwebel like me.'

Blessing said, 'I will take that chance.'

'There's the Medical Officer too,' said Starkhof reflectively. 'He was undoubtedly negligent. Secret papers should go into the safe.' He noted Löwenherz's face. 'Never mind, as long as the culprit is caught and the papers recovered there will perhaps be no need to bring any of Himmel's colleagues or superior officers into this. You hear me, Herr Oberleutnant?'

'I do.'

'Splendid. Young Blessing and I searched along the perimeter this morning. In the hedge, in the ditch, and then retraced our steps on the far side of the fence. Nothing there, I'm afraid. I'm glad to see you're concerned about the fate of the doctor. A charming man, I thought, something of an aristocrat one might almost think.' He smiled. 'If it wasn't for that unfortunate Austrian accent.'

'Where are you taking me?'

'Taking you? My goodness we're not taking you anywhere, Oberleutnant. You have your duties for the Third Reich just as we do, but if you can spare us a moment, the Kommandeur was kind enough to take an interest in our problem.'

Löwenherz looked carefully into the man's wrinkled face. Starkhof stared back coolly with an amused contempt for all the world. On the estates in Prussia Löwenherz had seen the same easy-going manner among the senior farm hands and foresters. It was the quality one looked for when employing or promoting such men. Some policemen had it and so did high-court judges, It came from dealing with many people and being able to predict their reactions well in advance. It came from the certainty that no one would ever disobey the suggestions that made orders unnecessary.

They walked into the Operations Building, Blessing in the lead. The Kommandeur must have seen them through the window for he stepped out to greet them. He was dressed in boots, breeches and grey uniform shirt. At his throat dangled the coveted Knight's Cross. 'My good Untersturmführer Blessing,' he said, 'and Herr Doktor Starkhof.'

'Heil Hitler,' said Blessing.

'Heil Hitler,' said the Kommandeur.

'Heil Hitler,' said Starkhof, doffing his hat cheerfully to the Kommandeur.

Major Peter Redenbacher put on his jacket and buttoned it. He was thirty-three years old: elderly by fighter-pilot standards. He commanded Löwenherz's Staffel of ten aircraft plus two other Staffeln that shared Kroonsdijk. He was an impressive man in spite of his battle-scarred appearance. His shortness of stature and some false teeth were common among those who had grown up in the blockaded Germany of the First World War. His powerful arms were an inheritance from his furnace-worker father in Essen, and his clear blue eyes and full-lipped mouth from his hardworking *Mutti*. The thick muscular legs were developed in his teens by sixty-eight-kilometre weekend cycle rides to a DLV gliding club. Most weekends he had come no nearer to a flight than hauling the winch, positioning the club's sole glider or helping to build a second one. The small scar visible under his closely cropped blond hair dated from a heavy landing at Wasserkuppe, on the bare high plateau of the Rhön. That year he had won a minor prize in the National Gliding Championships. The permanently arched little finger on his left hand had come under a Communist boot after holding a Nazi standard aloft in Essen in 1927. The sustained hatred that made him a killer was born in March 1923 when he saw a French officer of the occupying army strike his father and uncle for not removing their hats as a military funeral passed. The cold confident gaze dated from 1934 when he was one of twenty chosen from four thousand applicants to go to the Deutsche Verkehrsfliegerschule at Brunswick. This airline pilots' school was a secret training centre for the Nazi Air Force. When the Luftwaffe was officially born in 1935 Peter Redenbacher was stunting a Bücker Jungmann biplane above the heads of Hitler, Göring, the foreign Press and a deliriously happy German crowd. His forearm scarred badly because there was no doctor in the Spanish village of San Antonio when a Republican Rata shot his He51 down in flames there in November 1936. He landed by parachute in the village. The Russian pilot did a low pass over the rooftops and waved to Redenbacher from the open cockpit: a big smile and an ancient leather flying helmet, and low enough to see that the pilot was a woman. No one would believe him, until in January 1937 a high-ranking Russian woman was shot down near Madrid.

It was at the Schleissheim fighter school near Munich that a pupil turned without power on take-off, thus writing off an old He50 biplane that would have floated unharmed to the ground hands off. It was the worst crash of all. The pupil died and Redenbacher spent six weeks in hospital. Although he would never admit it, even to his wife, still to this day in cold weather the base of his spine ached like the very devil.

His four victories in Spain, fourteen on the East Front and thirty-two French, RAF and US aeroplanes downed had brought him a Knight's Cross with Oak-leaves and made him something of a celebrity. He had been shot down over the sea by an American P-47 the previous May, and had spent four miserable hours bobbing from wave-top to wave-top perched on a one-man dinghy. He was too old to take that sort of punishment without suffering after-effects. A medical board had detected his symptoms in spite of Redenbacher's denials. Now he had been advised that a staff job was to be his. Meanwhile he flew every sortie possible.

When he went to spend the rest of his life flying a desk he'd asked that Löwenherz should take over as Gruppen-kommandeur. He had been one of his pupils at the fighter school, and one of his best. Redenbacher was glad to have a young aristocrat like him in his Gruppe because, for Redenbacher, National Socialism meant the end of classes and social groupings. During all the wars of the last century only a hundred or so German NCOs had been made officers. In this war, under National Socialism, thousands and thousands of rankers had so far been commissioned. There were, at that moment, twelve Nazi generals who had come from the ranks. It made Redenbacher very proud to be a member of the Wehrmacht. It had become a simple matter of being a good Nazi.

Redenbacher looked at the men across the room. The young SIPO officer was a good Nazi. There was no other explanation. Only a dedicated young officer would be happy to do his duty as a lowly Feldwebel engaged on menial tasks. The old Abwehr man was a more doubtful case. Why had he never been promoted to officer rank? That shrewd old swine, like too many men in today's Germany, guessed Redenbacher, survived by evading conflict. Major Redenbacher walked round his desk, but he did not sit down behind it, neither did he invite the others to sit. There were in any case only two chairs. The white-painted office was bare and austere: only a framed portrait of the Führer, one of Reichsmarschall Göring, and a small photo of Redenbacher and his wife framed by Nazi banners on their wedding day.

The major's table-top was clear and efficient. A gleaming piston-top from the wrecked Heinkel biplane stood near the blotter. It would have made a fine ashtray for anyone who dared to smoke here. Instead it was a paperweight but there were no papers awaiting attention; the trays were empty, ink-wells full and sharpened pencils placed to hand. The major picked one up and tapped the table-top reflectively. He raised his eyes to Löwenherz. 'What do you make of Himmel, Victor?'

Löwenherz came correctly to attention, his white-topped cap clutched tight under his arm. 'He has six years' service, sir. Service record excellent.' Löwenherz related Himmel's Service record. It was easy to remember, for so much of it was the same as his own.

'But is he loyal, Victor? Is he a true National Socialist?'

'Yes, Herr Major.'

Blessing came to a noisy attention. 'With respect, Herr Major, loyalty is something best left to my department.'

'I'm sure my Oberleutnant had a reason for testifying to Unteroffizier Himmel's loyalty,' said Redenbacher. He nodded to Löwenherz.

'Himmel was one of the pilots assigned to the Führer's Kurier flight in March 1941 for three months. All personnel were cleared for security by Kommandostab RF-SS.'

For a moment there was a complete silence.

'Why the devil didn't you say so, man?' said Starkhof

angrily. Redenbacher admired the way in which Löwenherz had caused the old man to lose his careful temper.

'No one asked me, Herr Doktor.'

'That was over two years ago,' said Blessing.

'If his clearance had been changed recently, I would have been informed,' said Redenbacher.

'Even our Kommandostab security people are not infallible,' said Blessing, taking folded papers from his pocket. 'Let me read you a part of a letter written by Himmel . . .' There was a knock at the door. 'Come in,' said Redenbacher.

Leutnant Kokke entered. He was the Gruppe Technical Officer in addition to his other duties. In his hand he was carrying neatly drawn training schedules for the coming twelve-week period.

'I'm sorry, sir,' said Kokke. 'I will come back.' He ran a hand through his black untidy hair.

'Come in, Kokke,' said Redenbacher. Kokke was an excellent example of the new order. From the melting-pot into which National Socialism had poured the old Germany had come men like himself and Kokke. In the old days they would have had no chance to become professional officers. Kokke pretended that he would sooner be a musician, but this cut no ice with Redenbacher who recognized him as a man born to be a pilot as few men were. He still had much to learn, there was no short cut to experience, but Kokke might be a great flyer of tomorrow's Reich. Even now – Staffelkapitäns excepted – he was one of the best pilots on the Gruppe. He had top grades in navigation, instrument-flying and engine: theory and practical. He reminded Redenbacher of the oil-stained old pilots home fresh from the first war, with their medals, tall stories, hard drinking and acid *Galgenhumor*.

Many people thought that Redenbacher was too soft on Kokke, but this was because he knew that Löwenherz kept a tight rein on him. He looked at them now. Young Löwenherz in his white jacket, standing primly with his cap under his arm like a fashion-plate, and Kokke, relaxed and smiling, with his shirt bulging under his short Air Force jacket and bread-crumbs on his tie.

'Do you know what brings these officers here today, Kokke?' asked Redenbacher.

'No, Herr Major. Is it something in connection with the ablutions?'

'No,' said Redenbacher. 'The man you have in the past known as Feldwebel Blessing, overseer of the local foreign labour, is an officer of the Sicherheitspolizei.'

'*Ach so!*' said the satanic Kokke with a smile. 'Congratulations, Blessing.' He said it as though Blessing too should be surprised at his new status.

Blessing clicked his heels.

'Unteroffizier Himmel has stolen some documents,' said Major Redenbacher. 'At least it is alleged so. He spoke with the Herr Oberleutnant here shortly before breakfast. You were seated by the window, Kokke. Perhaps you saw Himmel this morning.'

'He spoke with Herr Oberleutnant Löwenherz.'

'I have just said so, but did he meet anyone else?'

'Didn't he meet Blessing?'

'No. I was waiting to arrest him at his barracks,' said Blessing.

'But didn't I see you tiptoeing through the woods, Blessing? I would have sworn it was you. Your ears, if you don't mind my saying so, and a huge fat arse very reminiscent of yours came past the Mess window just about ten o'clock. I turned to my friend Beer and said, "Tell me if my eyes deceive me, Beer, but doesn't that look very like the big protruding ears and great arse of our friend Feldwebel Blessing who cleans the ablutions?" At the time of course I had no way of knowing that Blessing was an officer.'

When Kokke stopped speaking Major Redenbacher said nothing; he flicked open the training schedules that Kokke had drawn neatly in coloured inks. This inquiry was distasteful to him. They all waited for him to comment. The gossip on the Staffel said that Redenbacher had not been truly well since his ditching last May. Some said that he would soon be posted to a less active unit. In which case, thought Kokke, that humourless stuffed-shirt Löwenherz would probably take over the Gruppe. Ah well, he was a fine pilot, bloody efficient and fair-minded, so it could be worse. He'd never replace Redenbacher in Kokke's eyes though. The Major was a tough, barnstorming veteran who would break every rule in the book for his men. What was more, unlike Löwenherz, Redenbacher had a sense of humour. Redenbacher still said nothing.

The old Abwehr man said, 'If you did speak to Himmel, you may as well tell me, Blessing.'

Blessing was indignant. 'You are not taking this clown's words seriously?'

Kokke said, 'Don't you remember, Blessing, the dog tried to bite you?'

'If you saw Himmel with the dog, say so,' said the old man severely to Blessing.

'Of course he saw them,' said Kokke. 'Look at his boots, look for yourself.' Even Major Redenbacher looked away from the schedules and stared down at Blessing's grass-wet boots.

'That's where the Oberleutnant's dog peed on his boots. You know how that dog pees everywhere, and Blessing was mistaken for a tree by the careless beast.'

Blessing knew that he was being provoked by Kokke but he kept his temper and even managed a ghost of a smile. It was important that Redenbacher should not think him vindictive or precipitate.

Starkhof took off his spectacles in a gesture which had once been a part of his courtroom technique. 'Did Himmel have a parcel? It was foolscap size with a brown cover.'

'It's difficult to remember,' admitted Kokke. 'As I said, there was so much activity.'

'Thank you, Leutnant Kokke,' said Starkhof.

'Blessing,' said Redenbacher, 'what evidence do you have against Unteroffizier Himmel?'

Blessing was still holding Himmel's letter. He said, 'This is a letter from Himmel to his father dated May 27th, 1943.' He skimmed through it mumbling, '"Weekend . . . well and happy . . . thanks for the home-made bread . . ." Ah, here we are!' Having found the place, Blessing's voice changed to one of stern officialdom. '"Do not be alarmed when the English terror bombers get through because that too is part of the Führer's plan. Grandmama and Cousin Paul had to die and our cities must be laid waste as part of a great strategic scheme that my poor brain cannot guess at. It's the very measure of the genius of our highest commanders that they can allow the *Amis* and *Tommis* to drop bombs on us while they lose the war. What fools the Russians must be to think that they are winning the war merely because they are advancing on all fronts. What simpletons the British were to fall into the trap of destroying the Afrika Korps and capturing the whole of North Africa when all the time our beloved Führer had planned it thus. Trust the Führer, he is full of surprises."'

Blessing looked up triumphantly.

'Well?' he said. The words had brought a terrible silence upon the group.

'Well what, Blessing?' said Kokke. 'Wasn't it a noble letter?'

'The traitorous swine,' said Blessing. 'The sarcasm stands out a mile.'

'What sarcasm?' said Kokke. 'Did you detect sarcasm?' he asked Starkhof.

'Styles of writing can be deceptive,' fielded the old man.

'Perhaps you'd better point out which passages seem preposterous and quite beyond your belief, Blessing,' said Kokke.

Blessing looked again at the letter. No one spoke. Aircraft

were doing circuits and bumps. One approached down the funnel, slid on to Runway 25 and, at the very moment of landing, gunned the throttle and climbed away into the circuit again. The sudden noise of the motors being opened up to full power shook the windowpanes. Three more did it before Major Redenbacher said, 'I think you'd better tell me what other evidence you have against Himmel.'

Blessing came to attention again. 'The stolen document was in his bedside locker last night and the previous night.'

'How do you know that?'

'My staff reported it.'

'I see,' said Redenbacher. 'How many of your civilian staff work for the Sicherheitspolizei?'

'Respectfully, Herr Major, I could not say.'

'But they have keys to bedside lockers?'

'Yes, Herr Major.'

'My quarters are cleaned by your local civilians, Blessing. Do they have a key for my bedside table?' Blessing did not answer. Redenbacher said, 'What about this Operational HQ. Do your staff examine my files and desk here in this office?'

'Not regularly, Herr Major.'

'Only when you instruct them to do so, eh, Blessing?'

'With respect, Herr Major, we must confine the conversation to the arrest of the spy Himmel. I request permission to take him to the Wehrmacht Prison in The Hague where a case against him will be prepared.'

' "Be prepared"?' echoed Redenbacher indignantly. 'This is Nazi Germany 1943, Blessing, not some damned little South American republic. We work by the rule of law, not by the odds and ends of guesswork that you assemble when you've slept too late on the morning you should have made your arrest. My soldiers are entitled to freedom and bread and the rule of law. If you want to deprive my combat station at front-line readiness of one of its most skilled pilots, you must provide the proper work from your side.'

'With respect, Herr Major, fighting Communist spies and traitors is also front-line work. It is your duty to let me take Himmel to prison where he belongs.'

'I don't need you to remind me of my duty, Blessing,' said Redenbacher. 'As for fighting Communists, I was doing that in the streets of Essen when you were still wetting your bed.'

'You are refusing to let the prisoner be taken away?' said Blessing.

'No, no, no,' interrupted Starkhof. 'The Herr Major has made his position very clear, Blessing. And a very reasonable position it is too, if I may say so.' He nodded at Major Redenbacher and smiled. 'He feels that you are going off at half-cock and wants to prevent you making a fool of yourself. He's advising you to procure more evidence, prepare your case more thoroughly, and I agree with him. At this moment I really couldn't support you, Blessing. I think you'd better release this fellow Himmel, on the Kommandeur's assurance that he's kept confined to the base.'

Starkhof had judged his timing nicely. His previous silence enabled him to sound like an arbitrator (although he would have said 'like a judge').

It took Blessing a few seconds' silence to realize that he had been outmanoeuvred by the wily old Abwehr man.

'Heil Hitler,' Blessing called loudly, stamping into the salute.

'Heil Hitler,' replied everyone in the room, but Kokke's voice was shriller and louder than the others. Blessing left before the the old man, who took his time shaking the hand of each of the airmen. As he got to the door he turned and smiled to them. 'You young gentlemen have had your fun with Blessing, and it might well result in Himmel's dossier becoming my sole responsibility. If it does, gentlemen, then when I return we must talk more seriously than we have today. We will start afresh. And you must be careful of what you tell me, for as we lawyers say, "*Decipi quam fallere est tutius*".' He smiled again. 'Herr Oberleutnant Löwenherz will translate.' He closed the door.

'It's safer to be deceived than to deceive,' translated Löwenherz.

'What a character!' said Kokke.

'He's an Abwehr man,' said Löwenherz. 'There's no love lost between them and the SIPO.'

Redenbacher said, 'Victor, do you think that he precipitated the arrest of young Himmel just to take over control of this case by those very means?'

'Yes, sir, I do,' said Löwenherz. 'I realize now that my conversation with him on the way way here was largely dedicated to making me antagonistic to Blessing.'

'The old fox,' said Redenbacher. 'If I thought he was deliberately sabotaging the work of the Sicherheitspolizei I'd report him.'

'I wouldn't help those bastards get their hands on my worst enemy,' muttered Kokke.

CHAPTER FIVE

There were many inhabitants of Altgarten who could remember it a half-century ago. By that time the cramped little houses built for the men who made the railway had become slums and although each doorstep had gleamed white and the curtains in each window were clean and pressed, few people then would have wished to walk through the town after dark. There was not enough work at the gasworks to help Altgarten's poor and the unemployed stood on street corners and waited for their wives to return from scrubbing and washing and cooking in other person's homes. Nor did the land provide for the desperate. In those days a wet spring would inevitably mean a hungry winter.

Now in 1943 the Burgomaster could look across a thriving town where never a hand was idle, although many of its menfolk were in far parts of the world. He saw them in the corridors of the Rathaus, for the Servicemen came here to have their leave documents endorsed and signed. Young Tornow had just come home on leave. He was now a Kapitänleutnant. He looked elegant in his dark-blue naval uniform with gold braid rings on his cuff and the snappy white-topped summer cap that U-boat captains favoured. Tornow's father owned the Altgarten printing works and had servants, a fine house and a fast Mercedes car.

'Hello, Tornow,' said the Burgomaster, passing him on his way to lunch at Frenzel's. 'This is fine weather for you sailors, eh?'

Hans Tornow had grown used to such remarks. He had long since given up explaining that he was an accountant in the Paymaster's department at Hamburg, a grim old building with tiny windows and inadequate lights. As for the ocean, he hated those occasions when he had to take cash to ships anchored in the Elbe, for even the slightest swell made him a little queasy. 'Yes, Herr Bürgermeister, it's sailors' weather,' said Tornow.

All Altgarten envied those citizens who had chosen that weekend to begin their holiday, for the weather promised to be superb. In spite of the thunder the black clouds had passed and it was sunny. No rain had fallen upon the town for over three weeks. The air was crisp and dry. For the last week the humidity readings had not risen above forty-five per cent and had gone as low as thirty. The old centre of Altgarten was principally of wooden construction and its timber was dry and contracted.

Winds up to fifteen miles an hour fan the flames of a large fire but a faster-moving wind can make even a small fire into a disaster. This day the wind came in gusts from the potato fields and orchards and the strongest gusts measured eighteen miles an hour. As a fire hazard the town of Altgarten had few equals.

The buildings in Dorfstrasse were parched and dusty and the once-red swastika flags that rippled in the wind had faded to a light pink in the sunlight. Many of the vehicles moving along the busy roads were horse-drawn and the horses hurried as they neared the end of the journey. From Frenzel's a considerate drayman brought water for the two grey cart-horses that had delivered the beer and watched them as they drank greedily.

Fire fascinates men and fire services never run short of recruits. Johannes Ilfa had always wanted to be a fireman.

72

It was an ambition interrupted at the age of twelve by a short-lived desire to enter the priesthood. In 1935, aged eighteen, Johannes had entered the Altgarten fire service as a trainee. A hard-working and intelligent son of a Bierkeller owner, he had risen in rank until in 1942 he had been selected for attachment to the Cologne brigade and had been on duty there during the night of May 30th, 1942, when the town was attacked by almost one thousand RAF bombers. In this and other attacks Johannes had seen terrible sights. In fact he had offered comfort and last rites to more people than had any priest in Altgarten. In one raid the previous winter a shell splinter had punctured his lung. For one month he was in hospital and then he was posted back to Altgarten. In smoke it pained him to breathe even now but he never mentioned this.

For Ilfa, membership of any Nazi organization was out of the question. He could still only see the Nazis as the coarse Bavarian toughs who frequented his father's bar and staged fights in order to get away without paying their bill. If he must be a part of their war, then the fire service provided him with a way of fighting only the evils of it.

He was a battle-scarred veteran of twenty-six, a dark-eyed man with short hair which he kept carefully brushed and a large moustache of which he was quite proud. His teeth were even and white and so much water had kept his hands white too and lately his rank had enabled them to become soft like those of a girl. But his body was hard and his physical condition was excellent except for his lung. Over short distances his energy was exceptional and he had won many a bet to race younger firemen to the top of the practice tower with the hook-ladders.

He was a Gruppenführer, the senior man on the finest and newest engine in Altgarten. He sat beside the driver and directed his seven-man crew as they extricated pedestrians from under buses, pulled the electrocuted off live cables, sawed free young children trapped in railings and dealt with chimney fires and hayrick blazes.

Today the fire station was cool and quiet and the sun glinted on the polished brass hose fittings and on the engines. Respirators, gloves and steel helmets were lined up neatly. Under each hung the metal discs with the letters that enable messengers, hosemen, attack troopers and water troopers to be recognized in the smoke and heat of a fire.

So far there had been no alarm. Johannes Ilfa was lecturing the full eighteen-man complement of the Altgarten fire brigade upon the various types of RAF bombs. On the classroom table there were dummy examples of the small phosphorus canister, the 30-lb phosphorus bomb, the 250-lb liquid fire bomb (benzol and rubber) and the hexagonal 4-lb incendiary stick bombs.

'The 30-lb phosphorus bomb is 810 millimetres long. You'll recognize it by its dark-red colour and a broad light-red band around the body,' read Johannes Ilfa aloud from an instruction book. He smiled. 'Unless of course it goes off.'

Some of the firemen laughed a short quiet nervous laugh. 'Pieces of flaming phosphorus will fly thirty metres or more and will keep floating down for fifteen seconds, so don't run towards it too quickly. If you get the smallest piece of flaming phosphorus anywhere upon your clothing you must immediately remove that clothing and douse it thoroughly in water. Then scrape it all off, otherwise it will ignite again as soon as it comes out of the water.'

A fireman asked a question. 'How do you do that in the middle of an air raid?'

'I don't write these handbooks, I just read them.' He paused. 'Just don't get any of the damned stuff on you.' He rubbed his moustache nervously. He'd seen phosphorus bombs and they horrified him.

Some of the students wrote in their notebooks. Any one of them was liable to be assigned to one of the fire services in the Ruhr, in which case he would need to know what the war was like.

'That's the end of the lecture,' said Johannes Ilfa looking at his wristwatch. The senior fireman called the class to attention and when Ilfa had gone he dismissed them for lunch. Seven of the men lived sufficiently near to eat at home and they hurried to the cycle shed to collect their bikes.

The fire station was at the unfashionable end of Mönchenstrasse. Two young Waffen SS soldiers cycled past it on their way to the shops of Dorfstrasse. The Scheske twins were just eighteen and until last month they had never been more than five miles from their native town of Insterburg on the Pregel in a distant part of East Prussia. Here in the extreme west of the homeland, so near to Paris and Brussels and Amsterdam, about which they had read in their schoolbooks not long ago, there was so much to see. Even this cycle ride into Altgarten to fetch some razor blades for the guard commander held promise enough for both boys to be carrying their new Exacta cameras.

They were shy lads and did not respond to the teasing their Slavic name drew from the race-conscious SS men stationed at the Wald Hotel camp. Everything about the new Nazi Germany was an adventure. Together they had been the mainstay of the Hitler Jugend choir back home and at party celebrations they were invariably chosen to augment the SA men's choir. Alas, at their camp in Altgarten there was no choir. Mausi had suggested that they find out if there was a choir at the Liebefrau church, but luckily Hannes was in time to prevent him making a complete fool of himself by suggesting such a thing in front of the other SS men.

So now they sang lustily as they cycled through the town. It was the chorus that often ended the Party meetings back home.

> '*When the SS and the SA*
>   *March up in formation. Taratata!*
> *Firm is the stride.*
> *Firm is the pace,*
> *Left two three four, everyone wants to join*
> *And so one marches today through every little town*
> *And every German girl dreams of this today*
> *Because the black SS and the brown SA*
> *Have what pleases everyone today*
>   *And it's the most beautiful thing in the world.*'

They finished it in polished harmony. 'We'd better hurry,' said Hannes, 'or we'll miss lunch.'

'What must we buy?'

'The commandant's medicine from the druggist, razor blades for the guard commander, a smoking cure for the fat fellow in the cookhouse and I want some colour film.'

'If we missed lunch we could take some photos of the old market place where the vegetable stalls are.'

'Good idea, let's miss lunch.'

An elderly Saxon TENO engineer named Ueberall – Fuchs to his friends because of his red hair, now turning grey – had also decided to miss lunch. He waited as the two cyclists passed him before crossing the road. 'Nazis,' he muttered under his breath as he heard the song they sang. He'd heard it as the prelude to many a brawl in which he invariably found his friends ranged against the singers. That was when Fuchs had worked as a diesel fitter for a boat company on the Elbe. As a young man he'd been a keen trade unionist and even now he worried that old documents would be found and bring him under police scrutiny.

Fuchs was a huge man with giant's hands and a square jaw, but his shrill Saxon voice did not belong to such a man. He, more than anyone else in the pioneer battalion, disliked military life. The previous year some skilled engine fitters had been released to factory work but Ueberall's application had been turned down. Now he looked forward only to his card-playing evenings, for it was the nearest thing to being a civilian that he'd managed to find in the Army. He liked his two friends very much: Gerd Böll had been a college professor and Oberzugführer Bodo Reuter never had occasion to remind him that he was also his senior officer.

Fuchs Ueberall often missed lunch, and almost always it was in order to play skat. All three men wondered sometimes what they had in common besides a similarity of age and outlook, a lack of family responsibility and an easily renewed faith that they would win the next game. But, as Gerd said one day, wasn't that enough to have in common?

CHAPTER SIX

When choosing a site for an airfield it doesn't matter that the ground is not flat, for it can easily be levelled. The deciding factor is drainage. The inhabitants of Little Warley had always known that the potato fields to the east of the village drained into Witch Fen. The land between there and the line of ash trees at The Warrens is hard, fertile and as black as coal. Its subsoil is firm enough to take the weight of a bombing plane. So it was no surprise when, as war began, Air Ministry teams surveyed the place and pronounced it suitable for a Bomber Command airfield. After that came earth-moving machinery, concrete mixers and asphalt pourers. A tarmac cross was drawn across Warley's countryside and around it went a road complete with a circular pan for each aeroplane. Men dug sewers and drains, laid water pipes and strung power lines. Telex and phone cables crossed the fields. Corrugated-iron Nissen huts appeared as if by magic, huddled together like wrinkled grey elephants sheltering from the cold East Anglian winds. There were hangars too: black cathedrals higher than the church steeple and wider than the graveyard. Finally out of the clouds came the sound of an aeroplane and ten minutes later Warley Fen was truly an airfield.

The box-like Control Tower stood alone, commanding a view as far as Witch Fen. Behind it dozens of buildings provided the complex necessities of Service life from A to

Z. Armoury, Butchery, Cinema, Dental Surgery, Equipment Store, Flying Control, Gunnery Range, Hairdresser, Instrument Section, Jail, Kitchens, Link Trainer Room, Meteorological Section, Navigators' Briefing Room, Operations Block, Photographic Section, Quarters for Married Officers, Radar Building, Sick Quarters, Teleprinter Section, Uniform Store, Vehicle Repair Yard, Water Tower, X-ray Department, YMCA Hut, and a zebra-striped Aerodrome Control Post. Later there were also added a large vegetable garden and extensive pig pens.

A sign was painted – RAF Station Warley Fen – and erected at the entrance. The wooden shed there was painted red and white and adorned with a notice: ALL VISITORS MUST REPORT HERE. In no time at all it seemed as though the village had always known the bustle of one thousand and eighty-three noisy airmen: bicycles were stacked outside the Bell every evening and Mrs Jenkins had had to write NO CIGARETTES on her window in whitewash in order to save a few smokes for her regulars. There were girl airmen too, to the villagers' dismay. They flaunted painted lips and waved hair and worked as hard as the men. Sometimes they were heard to swear as hard as the men, too. They set an awesome example to the village girls. Some said the whole aerodrome was a 'black Satan's nest' and hurried past it after dark, especially if the roar of aircraft was rattling the village windowpanes like a thousand furies.

Dispersed all round the aerodrome were the Squadron's bombers sitting on their tarmac circles. The six-foot-high fence that surrounded the airfield was little more than a boundary mark, for human logic had torn great holes in it where it had blocked the paths that led from the dispersals to the Bell. Even the armed sentries who stood all night at the main gate would, their duty finished, wander off through gaps in the fence to save themselves a hundred extra yards walk along the perimeter track. It was through one of these gaps that the Bedford lorry bumped and caused them all to lose their balance. Digby and Battersby hit their heads against the metal uprights. 'Hold on!' shouted Flight Lieutenant Sweet from his seat in the cab.

'Now he tells us,' said Digby as the lorry pulled up in front of B Flight offices. The tailflap crashed open and Sweet took Mrs Lambert by the waist and floated her down in a movement that would have done credit to the Sadlers Wells ballet company. Still holding her by the waist, Sweet gave her a decorous kiss. '*Droit du Seigneur*, Lambert,' he called. 'The driver will take you to the Ops Block, Mrs Lambert; it looks like there's something on for us. It's a good thing that I decided to look in here first.'

The Lancaster bombers were alive with airmen. Engine mechanics, riggers, electricians, instrument fitters and radio mechanics swarmed all over the great four-motor aircraft. The newcomers automatically looked across to the north corner of the airfield. There a group of hillocks looked like prehistoric burial mounds with a concrete entrance to each. It was all surrounded with blast walls and laced with pulleys and tackle. Inside that was the bomb store. Around it were queues of bomb-trains. Armourers bent low over fuses and fins, and patted the bombs into place on the trolleys. There were general purpose bombs and high-capacity bombs and target indicators and canisters packed with ninety shiny 4-lb incendiaries. No one was painting 'Hello Hitler' on them; that was something the Press photographers did. For armourers there was nothing humorous about a bomb.

'Looks like we're on the battle order, chaps,' said Sweet. 'There's a bit of luck. I'll enjoy putting some HE amongst the squareheads.'

'Bombs or mines?' said Digby.

'Can't see,' said Cohen.

The Flight offices were a complex of tin huts which rattled as one by one the engines were tested up to full revs. The Sergeant clerk saluted as Sweet entered the shabby little room marked B Flight Office. Eric, the airman clerk, stopped typing and stood up at attention. It was a dismal place. There were two filing boxes, two tables and two chairs. In the corner there was a sink with chipped railway cups and a brown metal teapot upside down to drain. A notice board on the wall was crammed with ancient announcements and memos. The blackboard was marked to show the serviceability of B Flight's Lancasters. Above it Sweet had had the lettering bod write 'B Flight Bombs Best' in Saxon lettering. There was a dirty smudge under it where another opinion on the subject had been clumsily erased.

'Good morning Percy, good morning Eric,' said Sweet. 'Are we on?'

'Yes, sir; maximum effort,' said the Sergeant.

'I hear you're making a book on the Squadron cricket match on Saturday, Eric. Put me down for five bob.'

'On us, sir?' said Eric.

'You cheeky sod,' said Sweet. 'Aren't I the best batsman in the Group?'

'That's it, sir.' Sweet smiled appreciatively and patted Eric's shoulder.

Sweet picked up a tin of pennies and shook it. A hand-lettered label said 'Village Children's Xmas Party'. Last year and the one before that, the clerk Eric Sedge and LAC Gilbert, the Squadron artist, had arranged it, but this year Sweet had put the full force of his persuasive personality behind it. Smilingly he demanded contributions from all ranks and insisted that any raffles or sweepstakes held among the lads of B Flight must pay ten per cent 'tax' to the Christmas party.

'How much more since Friday, Eric?' Sweet rattled the tin again.

'A few pennies, sir.'

'Get the names in the book?'

'I don't put down less than sixpence.'

'Get them all in the book, Eric. It's only fair. Then at Christmas we'll see which section has contributed most.'

'Yes, sir.'

'And put the teapot on, Eric.' Sweet walked through the door marked 'B Flight Commander'. It was very hot inside and a wasp was buzzing hysterically. Sweet hit the wasp with a rolled-up copy of *Picture Post* and then opened the window. He scooped up the wasp and put it outside. He leaned out far enough to see Lambert talking to his wife. Sweet inhaled the perfume of freshly cut grass and looked long enough at two airmen on fatigues for them to go back to work. Sweet sat down at his desk. Over it a poster with the slogan 'Bread is a munition of war, don't waste it' had a Johnny Walker label obscuring the first word. The office was equipped from many sources. There were pub ashtrays, a cinema seat, a Victorian wardrobe containing Sweet's working uniform and some spare flying kit. There were also a small stove with a home-made chimney, a threadbare piece of antique carpet and a suitcase full of gramophone records (including a course in spoken German). Through the window were the Lancasters he commanded, standing on the skyline like a frieze.

Sweet's own plane was S for Sugar, although by now he had persuaded almost everyone on the Squadron to call it S Sweet. It was the newest aeroplane on B Flight. Its Perspex was bright and clear and its interior shiny bright. It had one bomb painted on its nose.

Lambert's aeroplane – O Orange – on the other hand, was an ancient machine, with line after line of yellow bombs totalling sixty-two. From outside it looked the same as the other bombers, covered for the most part in black matt paint with dull green and brown on the upper surfaces. But if you went inside and looked at the bright alloy formers in its nose and wondered why the port side of the interior had dulled and tarnished while the starboard interior was gleaming fresh silver metal, you might guess that it had not escaped unharmed from its sixty-two trips. She had been back to Servicing Flight for major surgery. She'd had a new tail section, the port flaps were new, and the nose and port wing had several riveted plates where flak had holed her. Bomb-doors were the most vulnerable part and this plane had used up eight of those.

When Lambert's crew had first got her fifteen trips ago they had looked with silent awe upon the battle-scarred machine until Micky Murphy the Flight Engineer said, 'A creaking door hangs the longest.' Digby christened her 'Creaking Door'. The machine seemed to revel in the name and although she flew like a bird, the tail section did creak a little, especially over the target. Or so swore Flight Sergeant Digby.

If one hadn't known what a cynical unimaginative type Digby was, it would be easy to accuse him of sentimentality about Creaking Door. It had cost him many pints of beer to hear its life story from Flight Sergeant Worthington. For bombers belonged to the ground crew; aircrew only borrowed them.

Creaking Door was one of the very first Lancasters ever built. The factory was producing a disastrous two-motor aeroplane and as an emergency measure the designers asked if they could try putting two extra motors on it. The Air Ministry experts said no, the factory ignored them and begged, borrowed and stole bits and pieces in order to try it anyway.

'That's how the best bombing plane of the war was designed. What a typical pommy fiasco.'

'I told my father that it was a fine example of British engineering genius,' said Battersby.

'An accident, sport. But she's a beaut, a real vintage beaut.'

'What remarkable luck,' said Binty Jones, the mid-upper gunner, looking up from his comic book. 'We'll sell her to one of those museum places when we have finished with the clapped-out old wreck.'

'Money, that's all you dills think about,' said Digby. 'I'm

talking about art. I'm talking about history. Yes, planes like this will be in museums when the war is over, preserved as a masterpiece of twentieth-century taste and culture and beauty.'

'We all will,' said Lambert.

'I should have known better than trying to talk seriously to you mob,' said Digby.

Next in line along the dispersal was L Love, which was having a new name and symbol painted to surmount the fifteen yellow bombs on its nose: 'Joe for King' was now its name. Sergeant Tommy Carter flew 'Joe for King'. He was a handsome red-haired orphan from Newcastle. After the orphanage he'd become a messenger boy and then a New-castle policeman until his inspector found him reading *Das Kapital*.

'What the devil are you doing with that damned rubbish, Constable Carter?'

'It's for my evening classes, sir. I've got *Mein Kampf* here in my other pocket.'

'Don't bring that poison into my police station, Con-stable. Do you understand?'

'I do, Inspector.'

Two months later he joined the RAF. He had a huge ginger moustache that had originated as a disguise for a scarred lip. He'd encouraged it into the slightly clownish handlebar shape that was fashionable among many aircrew. Tommy Carter thought the RAF was the most marvellous thing that had happened to him, and Joe for King, he said, was the finest Lancaster ever manufactured. The machine was fifteen trips old; Tommy's crew had done eight of those with the exception of Collins. He was their bomb aimer. Only survivor of a crash landing in February, he'd completed twenty-nine trips. Tonight would be his last before going for a rest.

The next Lancaster bomber was Z Zebra. It was almost out of sight behind the ash trees of The Warrens, where even in daylight wild rabbits ran across the tarmac pans. Under the shade of Zebra's wingtips, in the damp-smelling black soil, there were now puff-ball mushrooms for frying and in the autumn delicious blewits in fairy rings and red fly agaric that men said could kill.

'The Volkswagen', they called Z Zebra. Its skipper was Pilot Officer Cornelius Fleming; newly commissioned, with three hundred and fifty flying hours at training schools, he was a soft-spoken introvert from York, an ex-student of medicine. He had done his elementary flying training in Alberta. Canada's bright lights and informality were a startling change after blacked-out wartime Britain, and the ease with which he'd got lost flying over the prairie had been a fearful lesson in its dimensions. Three times a week he wrote to Tracy Rybakowski, a girl in Edmonton. After the war he was going back there to marry her and make his fortune, but so far he'd not told his parents. His brief time in medical school had now faded so far into his memories that he couldn't believe that less than two years ago his ambition was to be only a doctor.

It came as no surprise to Fleming and his crew to find that as newcomers they'd been assigned to one of the shabbiest aircraft on the Flight. When they'd first climbed into it the interior was littered with old newspapers and oily rags and the Elsan lavatory had not been properly emptied. There was a faint but pervasive smell of sweat, excrement and rotting meat. Fleming had conscripted his whole crew for the cleaning job. Now the plane smelled of fresh oil, metal polish and disinfectant. As Fleming had remarked, now it smelled 'as clean as a hospital', but he'd regretted the comparison as soon as he'd made it. Naming the plane 'The Volkswagen' had been part of Fleming's desire to give the dirty old Z Zebra a new image.

Fleming's bomb aimer and rear gunner were also officers. All three of them were standing around Fleming's Austin Seven watching one of the electricians fix into it a length of

Air Ministry wiring. The car was undergoing a major over-haul at the expense of His Majesty. The three officers had come to B Flight, with the rest of Zebra's crew, six weeks ago, but so far they had not flown on an operation. They spent most of their time together and felt estranged from everyone else, for, as Fleming had remarked to Sweet, most of the other flyers of B Flight – including four of Fleming's own crew – shared the Sergeants' Mess with their ground-crew counterparts. It sounded like a provincial working man's club. 'Think yourself lucky not to be a member of it,' Sweet had said smiling; 'the only conversation is speculation, intoxication and fornication. Wait until you go to a Ser-geants' Mess dance, then you'll get an insight into the great unwashed.'

Sweet, however, had no time for anything more than passing affability and they seldom saw him. They drifted around B Flight aimlessly. Faith, Hope, and Charity, the sergeants called them. They were creedless bishops, lost in a chapter of rough-tongued Jesuits. They knew that the first three operations by a new crew risked five times the normal casualty rate. They exchanged the litany of technical gen and letters from home and awaited their baptism. It would come tonight.

A mile or more away across the airfield Sweet could see the nearest of the other Flight's aircraft, and to the right of it, beyond the bump, the Control Tower. On its roof a Meteorology WAAF officer was reading the instruments in the louvred box. At the south end of the runway there was the Aerodrome Control Post, and behind that the steeple of the thirteenth-century church in Little Warley village. He had a good view from here. He looked back to where the lorry that had brought them back from their weekend was turning round before going back along the main road past the village and entering the main gate empty, with Form 658 correctly signed just as Sweet had fiddled it with the Transport Officer. Near the gap in the fence Flight Sergeant

Lambert was saying goodbye to his wife, who was getting a lift to the Safety Equipment Section where she worked.

'Be a good chap, Eric,' said Sweet. 'Tell Lambert that I want a word with him. And on second thoughts I think the Bedford had better go back to the MT section straightaway. Can't be too careful.'

'I'll tell the driver,' said Eric.

'And apologize to Mrs Lambert. She'll have to walk. I really am sorry, tell her.' When the airman left, Sweet closely examined his face in a wall mirror. He wondered why his skin went red and mottled in the sun instead of bronzed and handsome.

'Take my bike, Ruth,' said Lambert.

'I can't ride a bicycle, Sam. Not in this uniform skirt. I'll walk.'

'You'll be all right?'

'It's only a mile. It will do me good.'

'Mr Sweet would like a word with you, Chiefie,' said the clerk.

Lambert kissed his wife goodbye. 'You'll know where we are going tonight before I shall.'

'Look after yourself, Sam.'

'I love you, Ruth. I'll pop in and see you before we go.' As he walked back to the Flight office, airmen were forming a line to await the arrival of the NAAFI van with morning tea and cakes. Lambert looked at his watch; it was ten to eleven.

Inside the Flight office, Flight Lieutenant Sweet was finishing a story as Lambert entered. '". . . stop doing that, Sergeant," she says, "I hold the King's commission."' The two clerks and Sweet laughed.

He was still smiling as he turned to Lambert. 'Well, the flap's on, Sambo. Looks like everyone else around here has stolen a march on us. You'd better get your crew together and get your NFT done as early as possible. Captains and navigators at 3.30 this afternoon, main briefing at 5.0 PM.'

'Can I change out of best blue into working uniform?'

'That would mean you all going back to the Sergeants' Mess, and by the time you shower, shave, shampoo and scrounge some coffee it'll be lunchtime.' Sweet smiled knowingly. 'No, get cracking right away. Borrow parachutes and helmets from Tommy Carter's bods or Mr Fleming's crew.'

'Any buzz on the target?'

'Even if I did have, I'd not be able to tell the chaps.' He moved some papers on his desk. 'Oh, and by the by there's a bit of a crew reshuffle. From tomorrow, young Cohen will be navigator S Sweet. Digby will be with me too. My chaps – Teddy and Speke – will be coming to you. You're damned lucky to get them, Sambo, they're damned good blokes.'

'Transfer?' said Lambert in amazement.

'I know it's damned rotten for you, Sambo. It's just the sort of thing we all hate happening when chaps are crewed-up and happy, but Cohen is a raw kid, I'm going to have to nurse him a little.' Sweet found a packet of cigarettes locked in a desk drawer. He rarely smoked but now was an exception. He offered them; Lambert declined. Sweet exhaled the smoke urgently. 'Look, I know what you are thinking, Sambo, but this is the last thing I wanted, I can tell you.' He found a packet of peppermints in the drawer and offered one of those to Lambert but he shook his head.

'Your navigator stinks, and that bomb aimer Speke is what's keeping you at the bottom of the photo ladder,' said Lambert. 'I don't want to fly with them. You took Micky Murphy, my engineer, last month, after we'd had fifteen trips together. Isn't that enough for you?'

'Ah! So that's it,' said Sweet. 'It's just because you think it's a bad swop. Had it been Grimm, that duff wireless operator of yours, you wouldn't have minded. Well, I don't run my fights like that, my friend.'

'Of course I would have minded. Jimmy Grimm is one of my crew. I don't want any of them shuffled around like nuts and bolts. They rely on me to look after them. All of them.'

Sweet put his cigarette down and came round his desk. He put a consolatory arm around Lambert's shoulder. 'Now, now, Sambo, you're upset. Don't say something you might regret. I hate unpleasantness, any sort of unpleasantness. You know that.'

Yes, thought Lambert, providing you can get your own way without it.

'Look, old chap,' said Sweet. 'The new arrangement won't take effect until tomorrow. It's not my idea, you have my word on that. Some bloody chairborne wonder in the Ops Block. Take it easy. We may all have gone for a Burton by tomorrow, eh?' Sweet smiled in an effort to cheer Lambert up, but failed to do so.

'If that's all, sir, I'll get started.'

'Good show, Sambo.' He squeezed Lambert's arm affectionately. 'Look, about this damned business, tomorrow I'll get the CO in a corner of the Officers' Mess and threaten that you and me will do a low-level attack on Air Ministry if he doesn't let you keep your crew intact.'

'I want to speak to him myself,' said Lambert.

'You've no idea what a blimp he is. Old buffers like him are a menace to all of us. It's no good you even asking for an interview, you'll just have to trust me. If I can't squeeze it out of the old man when he's got a couple of nips inside him after dinner, there's no chance of you doing it in the cold light of dawn in the Squadron office.' Sweet laughed reflectively, then he asked, 'You've not reconsidered the cricket team? We're playing Besteridge at the weekend. They've got a strong side.'

'I'm committed next weekend, sir,' said Lambert.

'Pity. It might have made all the difference to the old man's attitude.'

Lambert said nothing. Sweet said, 'Think it over, Sambo; a couple of cricket victories – especially inter-Command victories – could put you well in with the old man. And with me.' He smiled to show he was joking. 'Not that I won't do all I can for you anyway, you know that.'

There was a knock at the door. It was Flight Sergeant Micky Murphy, the engineer who had recently been transferred from Lambert's to Sweet's crew. He was a huge Irishman with a white complexion, a square protruding jaw and a gap-toothed smile that he used between sentences as regularly as he breathed. He glanced at Lambert and smiled.

'Well,' said Sweet. 'Did you find the trouble with the under-carriage?'

'That we didn't find,' said Murphy. 'We've bled her out and she's as nice as ninepence, but we found no fault unless it was the microswitch playing false.'

'It wasn't the switch,' said Sweet.

'Did you try the lever a few times?' asked Murphy.

But Sweet threw the questioning back at his engineer. 'Are you sure you switched the indicators over to their reserve, Paddy?'

'First thing I did, sir.'

'Call me Skipper, for God's sake, Paddy,' Sweet insisted. 'It's that hydraulic fluid; I told you I wanted only Intava 675.'

'At this time of year it can make no difference,' said Murphy. 'I still think there was nothing wrong. All the undercarts stick sometimes. Lowering the lever a couple of times will often do the trick. No need for the emergency compressed air. It's a big job once the compressed air is in the system.'

'I'll decide when there's a need to use the compressed air, thank you, Chiefie. How soon will she be ready?'

'She's still on the jacks and the boys will be wanting to work the undercarriage a few more times to be on the safe side; it's a fine test for the whole system. After that we reinflate the emergency air bottle, top up the reservoir, sign the 700 and off we go.' Flight Sergeant Murphy smiled nervously.

'For God's sake stop grinning, Paddy,' said Sweet. 'S Sweet has got a date over Hunland tonight and I don't intend to miss it, so get mobile. And this time don't mix the hydraulic fluids when you top up.'

Murphy was about to explain what the handbook said about hydraulic fluids but finally nodded.

'These engineers just want to blind us with science,' said Sweet to Lambert after the man had left.

'Yes, sir,' said Lambert unenthusiastically.

'That's the spirit, Sambo, all any of us want is to make B Flight the best damned bomb-delivery service in East Anglia, eh?'

Lambert didn't answer. Sweet gave Lambert an encouraging smile, for he didn't want him to feel annoyed about losing men of his crew. It was Sweet's especial pride that he was one of the most democratic officers on the camp. He might almost say *the* most democratic. It had become a standard joke now that at the Sergeants' Mess dances Sweet would turn up wearing a sergeant's uniform. Sometimes he could be persuaded to sing *Tea for Two* close to the microphone. The sergeants appreciated an officer who knew how to be one of the boys. It would need only one miserable bastard like Lambert to spoil the whole atmosphere.

Eric the clerk looked round the door. 'Will you be wanting transport to the Officers' Mess for lunch, sir?'

'Affirmative,' said Sweet. It was only a quarter of a mile by the short cut, but the path was always muddy. Last week he'd felt a perfect fool when some ass in the Mess had pointed to his shoes and said, 'Been running B Flight through the assault course, Sweetie? Nothing like it for working up an appetite.'

Even Munro, the Squadron commander, had joined in the laughter. Good thing the Group Captain hadn't been there at the time. The Groupie was a real old Sandhurst blimp: fussy as hell about officers' appearance; no flying gear in the Mess, not even roll-neck sweaters, and him leading the officers in to meals like some old dowager duchess saying, 'I'm employed to kill Huns,' as though he'd actually seen one through a gunsight. Still, the buzz was that Munro was getting a station of his own. They might decide to give a flight lieutenant his scraper-ring and a chance at the job.

'Righto, Sambo my lad, off you go on a night-flying test.' And then, 'Oh, by the by, Lambert.'

Lambert turned.

'The armourers have removed a panel from your rear turret. You authorize that?'

'I did.'

Lambert's attitude made Sweet think that perhaps a higher authority had ordered it. He trod warily. 'What's the idea?'

'To see better.'

'Than through clear polished Perspex?'

'You opened this window just now to see what I was doing.'

Sweet smiled.

Lambert said, 'Anyway, the Perspex was badly marked, the Sergeant armourer was about to change it. I decided it was worth a go.'

Again Sweet smiled. 'It's just a matter of good manners, Flight. As your Flight commander it would be nice to be informed.'

'Written memo. On your desk last Thursday. It came back signed, so we went ahead.'

'Yes, quite. I meant keep me informed how it works out. A good idea of yours, Lambert.'

'Sergeant Gordon's idea, sir. If it works he deserves the credit.'

'OK, Lambert. Off you go, and don't forget the Christmas Party tin on your way out, laddie.'

Lambert, who was four years older and six inches taller than Sweet, saluted and left.

* * *

When Corporal Ruth Lambert had walked a little way along the road she overtook the Bedford lorry that Sweet had sent away. It was waiting for her.

'Jump in, Mrs Lambert,' said the driver.

'Thanks,' said Ruth.

'Bloody officers,' said the driver.

As the lorry passed near to where Creaking Door was parked, one of its engines started. Four birds, frightened by the noise, flew out of the hedge in front of the lorry. The driver braked in time for the birds to climb steeply into the sky.

'Crows,' said the driver. "Where I come from they say, "One for sorrow, two for mirth, three for a wedding, four for a birth".' He glanced at Ruth and grinned. 'Four for a birth,' he repeated.

'Three of those were rooks,' said Ruth.

'Oh well,' said the driver, 'I don't believe any of that stuff anyway.'

Other motors started, until the noise was shattering. Flight Sergeant Worthington waited for Lambert. They walked without speaking to the aeroplane. Flight Sergeant Worthington had been in the RAF twenty-eight years. His overalls were pressed and starched, and his tie was knotted tight against his collar. His face was red and highly polished and he could climb inside a greasy engine and emerge without a hair out of place. He regarded all airmen who had joined the RAF after war began as nothing better than amateurs. 'Which war, laddie?' The way in which aircrews were automatically given sergeant's rank and membership of the Mess he saw as a terrible heresy. Some evenings when the weather was bad he'd sit at the bar, with pints of beer arriving automatically at his elbow, while he told his fellow men of his peacetime Odyssey to this Ithaca. He'd tell of Bloody April 1917, the rigours of the Khyber Pass, the boredom of Habbaniyah and the cruelties of Uxbridge depot. Whether or not he noticed that the young aircrew were the most dedicated part of his audience and kept the beer pots coming was not certain, but lately his tirades were more jocular than venomous.

Lambert had joined the Regular RAF in 1938. In Worthington's eyes he was one of the few 'real airmen' on the camp.

It was January 1936 when Lambert became a part-time airman. He'd had great difficulty in getting six whole weeks off from his job in the garage, but the new manager thought it would be rather smart to boast of a qualified pilot on the staff and let him go, without pay, of course. Lambert went to an airfield in Scotland and was the first of the Volunteer Reserve sergeants to be trained under the new scheme. At the end of his course he had soloed and from then on every weekend, wet or fine, was devoted to training. He flew Hawker Harts and sometimes, as a special treat, a Fury. To be nearer the aeroplanes he got a job as an aero-engine fitter at the flying club that shared the field with the RAF reservists. Now and again the club would let him air test a light plane, or even instruct.

'Take him up for a spot of dual, a few flick rolls and a loop. No spins and for the Lord's sake don't let the silly little bastard try a landing.'

'Thanks, I'd like to do that.'

'There's no one else here, Lambert, and I can't leave the office.'

In 1938 the RAF offered any VR pilot with more than two hundred and fifty flying hours a chance of six weeks with a Regular RAF squadron. Lambert volunteered immediately and after six weeks flying Hurricanes he joined the Regular Air Force. He was disappointed to be assigned to twins, especially when war broke out and his old VR squadron was given Hurricanes. However, twin-motor aircraft proved to be a new sort of complication and he liked the challenge. When after a tour on Wellingtons and a DFM he first got his hands on a Stirling his envy of fighter pilots disappeared never to return. The four-motor planes made him happy and if he had to be in the RAF in order to get hold of one of them then he would put up with it.

Worthington put his spectacles on and studied the snag book before looking at Creaking Door to compare it with the initials of the men who cared for it. For Worthington also felt possessive about these aeroplanes. As he saw it, the Air Ministry had wisely put this aeroplane into his good keeping. Without regarding the bomber as his own personal property he was a little disquieted when Lambert – and Lambert's amateur crew – took it away overnight and subjected it to indignities and aerobatics and corkscrewing. Sometimes they brought it back damaged by chunks of enemy metal.

Worthington ushered Lambert through its entrance. Like a lecherous medico with a young girl, Worthington stroked and caressed each grip and bulkhead as they passed through the aeroplane. Her walkways and handholds gleamed like fine silver where so many other men had done the same. It was dark and confined in the slim belly, no wider anywhere than the smallest of today's motor-cars. They had to crouch as they moved forward, but Worthington continued to speak. His voice was resonant and to punctuate his words he tapped with his knuckles and the metal sang a note of anxiety and affection like a nervous patient under the scrutiny of a specialist.

'She's a game old bitch, Sam,' said Worthington, 'but she's not getting any younger.' He allowed Lambert to fit himself into the narrow pilot's seat and took a quick glance out of the window to be sure that his fitters were hard at work on the starboard inner engine.

'That starboard generator was giving us half a volt this morning on the run-up. We found a wiring fault but I'm still suspicious of the genny. It's reading high. Your engineer is going to watch the readings on the air test.' Worthington allowed himself a smile. 'I've given the poor kid a good drilling about it because the accumulators will explode if he lets a big overcharge build up: oxygen and hydrogen, see?'

'Yes, I had heard, Worthy.' Lambert touched the control column and rested his feet upon the rudder bar.

'Yes, well, one of these days you'll be glad I'm a bit of an old woman.' He discovered a mark on the Perspex and cleaned it with his newly laundered white handkerchief.

'Is that the only thing, the genny?'

'Apart from that, she's bang-on. The Squadron average oil consumption is 13.2 pints an hour. All of Creaking Door's motors are better than that: 11.5, 12.8, 10.5, 12.4. A good bus. In fact, a bloody good bus.'

Worthington gave Lambert the snag book.

'NFT right away, Chief. Could you ask the Sergeants' Mess to save seven lunches?'

'Meat pie,' said Worthington, 'or what they call a meat pie. Horrible stuff. Does Mr Sweet know what the target is?'

'If he does, he's not saying. With a full moon perhaps we'll be gardening.'

Worthington shook his head. 'Bombs, lots of high capacity, incendiaries galore; it's a town. Target indicators too. We are on number two tanks: six hundred and fifty gallons of juice, at a gallon a mile. Plus ten per cent for stooging around . . . three hundred miles away?'

'We can't go far on these short summer nights,' said Lambert, still avoiding the unavoidable.

'The Ruhr,' said Worthington.

'Happy Valley,' said Lambert dolefully. 'That will cheer the boys up.'

'If that bloody genny plays up bring her back. Don't try to press on, OK?'

'OK,' said Lambert. He wondered if Worthington said things like that to give him an alibi for survival, for he wasn't the sort of man to libel Door's machinery gratuitously.

'Spam,' pronounced Worthington dolefully. 'That's what gives that meat pie a funny taste.'

They both looked across to Joe for King.

Lambert said, 'It's funny, Chief, the way they paint the number of raids the *machine* does. None of the bomb-scores on our aeroplanes coincides with the number of raids the crew has done, it's just the number of raids the machine has done. It's as though the plane goes to bomb Germany of its own predatory volition, as though it takes us along just for the ride.'

Worthington decided that it was a little flutter of nervousness. 'Old planes are lucky planes, Sam.'

'Sometimes I think it's just the machines of Germany fighting the machines of Britain.'

Worthington looked at Lambert's dark-rimmed eyes. 'You're not on the booze are you, son?' he asked quietly. Lambert shook his head.

'Sleeping all right?'

'I wake up a lot,' Lambert admitted. 'I have a funny dream about a kid's birthday party. He's there with this cake and on it there's half a dozen candles. When he goes to blow them out his head melts like wax. Funny dream, eh? I mean, considering I've got no kids.'

'Seen the quack?'

'He thinks the Air Force is divided into officers and malingerers. Can you imagine me reporting sick with a dream?'

'Yes, he's no help with my bunions either. Still, perhaps you won't dream it again now you've told someone.'

'It's that bloody Mess food,' said Lambert laughing, and wondered how Worthington knew that he'd never spoken of his dream before.

'You don't want to think about it all too much.' Worthington changed the subject. 'Not playing in the cricket match, Sam? I'd like to see some of those slow bowls again.'

'I'm taking the missus up to London.'

Worthington self-consciously dabbed a finger of spittle at

a corner of Perspex that the cleaning rag had missed. 'They'll keep on at you, Sam. I've seen it happen before. Why don't you play a couple of games, get the bastards off your back?'

'I ask myself that every day, Chiefie.'

Worthington finished his tiny cleaning task and looked at Lambert. 'It's the sensible thing, son. You can't fight the Luftwaffe and the RAF too. It's the sensible way, the comfortable way, the logical way.'

'That must be the reason, then,' said Lambert. Worthington looked at his friend. He'd had too much: too much combat, lost too many pals, took too much responsibility for his crew. Lambert had had it, Worthington decided. He'd seen them go like this before. He shook his head sadly and changed the subject. 'Great God, look at all this stuff.'

All round Warley Fen airfield the Squadron's Lancasters were being bombed up. Girl tractor drivers backed the bombtrains under the open bomb-doors. The dark-green bombs came in all shapes and sizes although most were 500-lb general-purpose or 500-lb medium-capacity bombs: heavy steel cases with relatively small explosive charges inside them. They were the most widely used, and most notoriously ineffective, bombs the RAF dropped. For every ten successfully delivered by Bomber Command six failed to explode.

When the war began Bomber Command's missiles were small and its instruction books advised using a 40-lb GP against a house (only if occupied by troops, of course). For a fuel plant a 250-lb GP was recommended. The ineffectiveness of the old bombs and the new style of war demanded simpler weapons. Huge 8,000-lb canisters – little more than steel dustbins – without nose or tail fin were crammed full of explosive and named high-capacity bombs. They were designed for use against housing and just one of them could destroy a street.

Curiously shaped containers were packed with ninety 4-lb sticks of magnesium, each of which would burn with spluttering white flame and ignite almost anything it touched.

Because they were acting as a pathfinder squadron there were marker bombs too. They exploded with pretty colours: red, yellow and green, each colour denoting the authority and experience of the crew that dropped it. Few markers were prettier to see than the 'Pink Pansies': 4,000-lb medium-capacity bombcases stuffed full of benzol, rubber and phosphorus that ignited on impact with a great pink flash of fire easily spotted for miles.

Pretty and not so pretty bombs were winched slowly up into the bombers' black bellies. Calculations had determined their positions in the bay and the fuse-setting control link had been adjusted so that a touch of the bomb aimer's button could release the great weight without upsetting the aeroplane's centre of gravity. The bombs' fins had been straightened and their casings washed so that no patch of mud would spoil their balance as they dropped through the air.

The armourers worked carefully, remembering perhaps the accident at Scampton the previous March, when a 4,000-lb bomb – a cookie – fell out of a bomber during bombing up. It had exploded. The blast of it had completely destroyed six Lancasters and badly damaged five.

The first victim of the Krefeld raid died at 12.49 hours Double British Summer Time at B Flight, but it wasn't due to carelessness. Tommy Carter's aeroplane was the one involved. The carriers had been lowered from its bomb-bay and the bombs winched up into it. Its bombing up had been completed and Aircraftwoman Jenkins had driven the bombtrain clear of the aircraft's belly. Aircraftman Grigson, an electrician, was sitting just inside the rear gun turret, from where he could see B Flight office and was far enough away from the aircraft's door to be able to spring into life checking the wiring if an NCO should enter the aeroplane. It was a well-chosen place to hide while smoking a forbidden cigarette.

Aircraftman McDonald, armourer, had been fitting fuses

all the morning and now he was crouched under the bomb-bay checking each bomb container. He noticed that one jaw had two shiny cuts in it and guessed that they had been made by shapnel during a previous operation. He grasped the metal jaw and tugged it. A part of it broke off in his hand. 'Christ,' said McDonald as the 1,000-lb medium-capacity bomb wrenched itself free and fell upon him. The bomb did not explode but as it hit the tarmac the ground shook. Inside the bomber Aircraftman Grigson, halfway through his cigarette, knew immediately what had happened. He scrambled out and ran to the tractor and moved the remaining bombs away from the aircraft. He then disconnected the loaded bomb-trolley and returned on the tractor to report to the Sergeant armourer who was the only person at Warley who ran towards the mishap. Grigson quite forgot the cigarette in his mouth and when the Sergeant saw him smoking he screamed with a terrible rage and put him on a charge. He was sentenced to extra fire picket for seven days.

No one felt the vibration more than LAC Henry Gilbert, a forty-three-year-old rigger from Lewes. A Sunday painter before the war, he had made a reputation as an artist at Warley Fen airfield. His ladder was on the hard-standing at the nose when the bomb tumbled on to McDonald less than four yards away. The ladder shook and LAC Gilbert paused in mid brush-stroke. He had completed his fine portrait of Joseph Stalin wearing a crown and was halfway through writing 'Joe for King' under it. Later, much later, he continued work, but the last part of the lettering was very shaky.

Everyone on B Flight was now looking fearfully at Joe for King.

'Holy Mother of God,' said Micky Murphy, who had been retracting the undercarriage of Sweet's Lancaster for the fourth time when he felt the ground tremble. Together with two fitters and Battersby he was full-length in a pool of oil waiting for the bang. '. . . And in my bloody best bloody blue.'

'L Love,' said Worthington to Lambert when they stopped running and looked back.

'You dropped your false teeth, Bert?' shouted Door's electrician to his pal who was helping him to set up snares along the rabbit warrens behind B Flight. They had dropped into a ditch.

'My oath. Someone will be put on the pegs for that,' predicted Digby, looking across the airfield to where Joe for King was parked.

'Mind your toes,' muttered Corporal Hancock, armourer, who was winching an identical bomb into The Volkswagen. He stopped work and crouched low on the tarmac. Fleming and the other two officers of his crew, who had been watching Corporal Hancock's work, didn't flinch. They looked at each other but said nothing.

It took forty-five minutes to fit a new jaw in Joe for King. By that time the bomb, the inside of the starboard bomb-door and the tarmac had been hosed down by the duty crew. The ambulance had come and gone and so had Groupie, the Adjutant and the Squadron medical officer. Two firemen in new white asbestos suits had spent thirty minutes wearing looks of bleak disappointment. McDonald's mangled remains had been put into the storage shed at the back of the Medical Section – sometimes called the mortuary – and a Sergeant clerk in the Orderly Room had sent a priority telegram informing McDonald's father in Dundee.

Two Sergeant armourers winched another bomb into the bomb-bay. The one that had fallen was taken to the far side of the airfield to await the Bomb Disposal Team. Within an hour of the accident the aeroplane was pronounced bombed up and fully operational, but Tommy Carter, ex-police constable from Newcastle, who was flying her that night complained that it was a bad omen.

CHAPTER SEVEN

Altgarten was a small country town with nearly five thousand inhabitants. Five hundred of them had moved there since the regular bombing of the nearby Ruhr district – the so-called Battle of the Ruhr – had begun in March.

In the Middle Ages a great monastery had marked this crossroads where the trade in Flemish cloth met German iron. A fine stone bridge had once been needed to cross the stream that trickled along Mauerstrasse, the eastern boundary of the town. Altgarten never grew large, for a bigger trade route passed south of here, connecting Cologne to the important seaport of Bruges and its Venetian ships. Altgarten remained a spot on the map where travellers changed horses and gulped beer hurriedly in order to reach the Dutch border or Cologne before dark. The monastery fell into ruins, and its orchards – the fame of which had spread as far as Amsterdam – became a wilderness and were gobbled up by the town. Eventually, of the medieval buildings only the Liebefrau church remained, and fruit and vegetable farms covered the flat surrounding country and row upon row of greenhouses trapped the sunshine. There were silk factories too, and now that they were making harness in the sheds behind Frau Kersten's farm, parachute manufacture provided work for nearly two hundred townspeople, mostly women.

The town centre, around Liebefrau church, was a cobbled triangle of seventeenth-century houses. When the military convoys passed through, the policemen had to divert them to Bismarckstrasse and past the railway station, for the heavy lorries would never have been able to negotiate the narrow cobbled streets of the old town. The war had brought great change to Altgarten, or at least it seemed like great change to the people who lived there, for few of them had witnessed the rest of Europe turning from butterfly into earthworm.

Of course the flowers and fruit on the farms had given place to vegetables, but that had happened long before the war. The disused factory near the brewery had become a cage for Russian prisoners of war while they worked on widening the main road, but at the rate the Russians worked they would be there for years. They were a dirty lot, always hungry, and they seemed to spend most of their time hanging around the town watching the gutters anxiously for cigarette butts. Lately they'd brought from door to door madonnas carved from old crates. Catholic residents exchanged potatoes, cigarettes and bread for them.

The hospital had expanded enormously since the air raids upon the Ruhr had increased. There was an annex and a training centre for Red Cross 'Samariter' (as they called the young trainees who did the three-week emergency nursing course). Adjacent to these buildings there was a big hutted camp where amputee casualties from the Eastern Front came for convalescence and learned how to use their new false limbs. These establishments dominated the town. Some afternoons Dorfstrasse was so crowded with medical staff and convalescent soldiers that local people felt out of place there.

Where Winkel's was once a sea of blossom there was now a Technische Nothilfe camp, full of specialist troops ready to send heavy rescue and repair convoys to bombed towns in the Ruhr. Lately the TENOs had been building a railway siding there for their heavy equipment. It was heavy work and each night they drank a lot of Frenzel's thin wartime beer.

The housing estate on the north side of town, intended as rehousing for the slums around the gasworks, was now occupied by doctors and TENO engineer officers, which did nothing to endear the visitors to the locals. Not that everyone complained about the influx of personnel. Herr Frenzel, who owned the best restaurant in Altgarten, never complained. The downstairs bar was always full of TENO engineers and was sometimes a little rowdy, but the restaurant upstairs was chic. It commanded a view across Liebefrauplatz of the church itself and the seventeenth-century houses beyond it. This was the very heart of Altgarten and these buildings, from this viewpoint, were its proudest asset.

The Liebefrau was one of the hall-style churches that you get only in the north. The tracery windows were extra large to let in the sparse northern light, and the roof was extra steep to shed the winter snow. Its slim buttresses ran down like anchor chains stretched tight by a stiff tide and behind it the white houses were like chalk cliffs against which it was moored.

By lunchtime the cold front and its dense dark low cloud had passed eastwards over Altgarten without causing rain. Now the whiter clouds moved gently, shrinking in the subsiding air to reveal blue sky beyond and permit golden pools of sunlight to hurry through Liebefrauplatz, finger the ancient church walls and transform the gloomy interior with its glowing stained-glass pictures. In front of the church a crowd was gathered at a highly publicized fund-raising drive. Anyone contributing two marks to Winter Help was invited to hammer a nail into a wooden map of Britain. Since the Burgomaster had driven home the first nail that morning many of the town's most influential people had joined in the witchcraft. The map was studded with a pox of nail-heads that concentrated around London, for only the tallest could reach Scotland. A Hitler Jugend fanfare band was playing, helping with the Winter Help collection. The boys played loudly and expertly and the music was audible inside Frenzel's in spite of the rattle of dishes and the chatter.

'Frenzel's Stube' was spelled out in carved wooden letters across the doorway. The upper storeys were ochre-coloured plaster and carved black beams built upon a brick first floor. The ancient house was bent and bowed like an illustration from a book of fairy stories and the interior was dark even on a sunny day like this. There were other, more luxurious restaurants in the old town, but none had Frenzel's chef or was able to get meat as good as Frenzel's served. Whether he obtained the meat on the black market was a matter of constant speculation. Meanwhile Frenzel's Stube was patronized by Altgarten's most important citizens and none of them asked questions. There was good wine in Frenzel's cellar and champagne and old brandy too. For those with money to pay there were Bayonne ham and paté Strasbourg studded with truffles. For without Britain and the USA, and with the mark pegged artificially high, Germany had become the best customer for Europe's home-grown luxuries.

Müller, who owned the parachute factory, came to Frenzel's almost every night. Nazi Party officials held banquets here. The commanding officer of the TENO engineers was a regular and so was the electricity station chief. So also was Frau Kersten who ran the vegetable farm. Tonight, however, was to be special. The Burgomaster was sitting near the window with Herr Frenzel himself, planning every detail for the Burgomaster's fifty-third birthday dinner.

Walter Ryessman, the Burgomaster, was six feet two inches tall, a white-haired ex-cavalry officer with a duelling scar on his forehead. He had joined the Nazi Party in 1928 when dignified upper-class members were in short supply. The Burgomaster was still an ardent Nazi but also a German of the old school. He was a calm dignified man to whom honour meant telling the truth, fighting to the death and ruthlessly rejecting all non-Aryan influence. Over half of Altgarten's population had grown up in Catholic homes but the Burgomaster's political creed did not extend to anti-Catholic persecution. The crucifixes in the Volkschule had, of course, been removed and destroyed and there was no longer any religious instruction but no policemen had ever been posted at the church to record the names of worshippers. As Herr Ryessman had boasted at a Party gathering in Dortmund, 'No non-Jewish citizen who is prepared to march forward with National Socialism to victory and honour need fear injustice from me.'

But the Burgomaster's greatest and most popular triumph was a bureaucratic one. Just five months previously he had, by string-pulling, form-filling and judicious bargaining, saved the bells of the Liebefrau church from being melted down for armaments. The response from all sides had surprised him. In one month he had managed to find favour with Catholics, traditionalists, historians and colleagues. Oddly enough, Herr Berger – senior full-time SS officer in Altgarten – had been one of the first people to congratulate him.

'Not a large affair,' the Burgomaster explained. 'Eighteen persons, most of them of my family.'

'I understand,' said Frenzel. 'I will personally supervise the Herr Bürgermeister's food and wine and service.'

'A Burgundy. The same one as last year.'

'I have it written down,' said Herr Frenzel.

'Who's that with Herr Bach?'

The Burgomaster had respect for August Bach. Not only had Bach had a distinguished career in the First World War but he was a man of good family and a serving officer of the Luftwaffe, a true German, honourable and silent. Furthermore, his cousin, Gerd Böll – although a frivolous and unconventional fellow – was one of the town's most prosperous tradesmen. Mind you, if Bach had paid a little more attention to practical politics he could have done far better for himself than Oberleutnant's rank. A man with the 'Blue Max' – the highest decoration of the first war – at his throat should be a general. What couldn't the Burgomaster have done if he'd had that medal.

'His housekeeper,' said Frenzel without looking up, for he had already surveyed his restaurant and amended his knowledge of his fellow citizens.

'He's lunching with her?' asked the Burgomaster.

'Yes,' said Frenzel.

'How long since his wife was killed?'

'Thirteen months,' said Frenzel, who had already calculated it.

'She's a very beautiful girl,' said the Burgomaster.

'A beautiful girl,' agreed Frenzel. 'Her father is from Breslau: a high-ranking official of the Propaganda Ministry.'

'Indeed,' said the Burgomaster. He fingered the Party badge in his lapel.

August Bach was seeing an Anna-Luisa that he had only suspected might exist. She laughed readily and was delighted with everything he said and did.

'I'm glad to see that Herr Frenzel's sausages also burst out of their skins,' she said and giggled. She wasn't used to drinking two large glasses of wine at midday. 'They are full of bread,' she explained, solemnly stabbing the *Mettwurst*.

'No,' said August. 'It's a secret ray the British have. A man in London flicks a switch and every sausage skin in the Ruhr splits from end to end. The great *Wurstwerfer*, is the British secret weapon.'

She searched his face, for she had not yet got used to the idea that this man was capable of teasing her, then she laughed at his silliness and her own happiness. It was a nice laugh.

'*Kirschtorte*,' said August; 'Frau Frenzel makes it herself.'

'Yes,' said Anna-Luisa, gazing into his eyes without hearing him.

She was still laughing as they came out of Frenzel's through the bar room. At the bar there were several people they knew. A group of TENO engineers waved to Anna-Luisa and she blew them a kiss.

'They are friends of little Hansl's,' she explained. 'Last week they took him for a ride on the heavy crane. He loved it. Everyone likes your little son, August.'

They had walked only a few paces along the street when they heard a voice calling August's name. Across the road there was a grey van with the name 'Gerhard Böll' painted on its side. Gerd himself was driving. He got out and came across the road.

Gerd Böll had been a widower for four years. He was a cheerful little man, with long arms and large powerful hands which combined to make him look like a laughing bald gorilla. This resemblance Gerd did nothing to disguise, and after a few glasses of the schnapps which he distilled in the garage behind his grocer's shop he would swing around lamp posts and frighten people picking their way carefully through the blackout. At least, he used to frighten passers-by in this way but by now too many local inhabitants had grown used to it. Gerd Böll's practical jokes were often of a more complex nature that befitted a man who had once been a doctor of engineering at Leipzig University. Gerd Böil had two grocer's shops in Altgarten and a relative managed another one in Krefeld. Each evening he reported with his van to the air-raid defence office at the Rathaus. For putting his van at the disposal of the Luftschütz he was eligible for sixty litres of petrol per month. After particularly heavy air raids upon the Ruhr cities Gerd took his van to the bombed areas to help. Sometimes at the bar he would tell hair-raising stories of the death and damage he had seen and the TENO engineers would add tales of their own.

'August,' he called. 'I've been looking for you. I stopped by at the house hoping for some of that real coffee.'

'What is it? We were shopping this morning.'

'It can wait,' said Gerd. 'I didn't know you were with Anna-Luisa.'

'We are going to be married, Herr Böll,' she said.

August's cousin looked so surprised that both Anna-Luisa and August laughed. 'Is it so awful?' Anna-Luisa asked him.

'It's wonderful news,' said Gerd Böll.

'It looks like it,' August said.

'I'm sorry,' said Gerd.

'Herr Oberleutnant,' called a rough voice from the roadway. Parked against the kerb there was a Kübelwagen, the military version of the Volkswagen. Its camouflage was hidden under ancient mud and its equally dirty windscreen was folded flat upon the bonnet. There were dents in its side and four rusting bullet holes ran in a line above the rear wheel. The car bore SS registration plates and the rear seat was piled high with kit. In the front sat an unmistakably Russian driver and alongside him a Waffen SS officer in a very battered leather coat and dust goggles. The officer threw Bach a perfunctory military salute. 'There is an SS unit here?' He looked at Anna-Luisa appreciatively.

'The Wald Hotel,' said August.

'Which way?'

Gerd said, 'Go to the end of this road and then turn right following the old walls. The Wald Hotel is where the trees begin. You'll see the black-and-white sentry boxes.'

'Thank you,' said the officer.

'It's no trouble,' said Gerd.

'Heil Hitler,' said the officer. He glanced at Anna-Luisa again and without waiting for Gerd to return his salute he gave the driver his instruction in a language unknown to the others. They watched the car pull away with a roar. It steered round the horses and carts that moved slowly past the Liebefrau church, their metal wheels rattling on the cobblestones like drum-rolls. They stared after it for a few minutes.

'What was it you wanted?' August asked Gerd.

'It can wait until your next leave.'

'I'll be back here in two weeks,' said August.

'That's fine,' said Gerd. All three looked at each other in silence, wishing to break away and yet not knowing how.

'I go back to my unit in an hour,' said August. 'But first we must buy a ring, and then I will write to Anna-Luisa's parents.'

'I mustn't delay you,' said Gerd, but he didn't take his leave.

'There's something wrong, Gerd.'

Gerd took August's hand and gripped it warmly. 'Enjoy yourself, August, and you too, Anna-Luisa. There is little happiness in the war for anyone.'

They walked slowly across Liebefrauplatz. 'He's usually such a cheerful man,' said August. Gerd drove past them and waved again.

'He's a funny man,' agreed Anna-Luisa. 'Everyone says that he's the jolliest man in Altgarten.'

'He's not jolly today,' said August Bach. 'He's in a very strange mood.'

'Anyway it didn't rain,' said Anna-Luisa, anxious to make him smile again.

'That's true,' said August, smiling down upon her and hugging her arm secretly. 'Although they say the farms need some rain. The countryside is very dry.'

CHAPTER EIGHT

The River Ouse bisects pathfinder country. To the north of the river, acres of the ancient forestlands darken the road with shadow, but suddenly through a gap in the trees the far horizon is glimpsed across the dead-flat peaty land that slopes down towards the south-west. Rain draining off the airfields could make the sleepy, almost motionless, Ouse into a torrent that overflooded its banks and filled the shady lanes with deep mud even in high summer. For there were many airfields, or, put another way, just one airfield, and over it the winged monsters slid, as once went the pterodactyls that are still found fossilized in the nearby chalk quarries.

The day was half gone. The machines were ready and the Daily Inspection Forms initialled. The drone of circuiting bombers had not ceased since early morning. Creaking Door got the green light from control and Lambert's right hand pushed the throttles gently forward as he had a thousand times. He kept the port ones slightly ahead to correct the swing. Behind his shoulder he felt young Battersby leaning against him to let him know he was there. He brought the tail up quickly. There was that exhilarating feeling of the back of the seat pushing hard against the spine as five thousand horsepower gripped the air and fifty thousand pounds of aeroplane teetered on tiptoe before relinquishing the last touch of spinning tyres on runway. Battersby took the throttles, sliding his hand under the pilot's as before him

Micky Murphy had done for fifteen NFTs and the fifteen operations that followed them. Now Lambert needed both hands to haul back upon the control column and force the dark nose up through the horizon. Lambert gave the rudder bar an extra touch, for Battersby hadn't kept the port throttles quite far enough ahead.

Cohen was calling out the air-speeds from his indicator beside the navigation desk: 95, 100, 105, and then suddenly Creaking Door was airborne. Battersby had seen the rudderbar movement and corrected the throttles precisely.

'Climbing power,' chanted Lambert.

'Climbing power,' Battersby answered.

'Wheels up.'

'Wheels up.'

There was only sky. The horizon had dropped out of sight like a spent hoop.

'Flaps up.'

'Flaps up.' Battersby closed the flaps and there was a grinding sound as they slid back into the wings.

'Cruising power.' Battersby didn't move the throttles with the considerate slowness that an airline check captain would approve. He altered their position with an abrupt indifference that slowed the forward speed with a jerk and changed the roar to a lower tone.

The nose dropped a trifle. The Lancaster assumed its flying stance.

'Just one round the garden,' said Lambert. It was a way of telling Cohen that he wouldn't need fixes or navigation for the short trip.

There was a click as a microphone was switched on. 'It's meat pie,' said Digby from the front turret. He should have been behind Lambert on take-off but he preferred to be in front and Lambert didn't mind. 'But late lunches will probably have potato cheese.'

'Skipper,' said Binty Jones from the top turret, 'is that glycol on the port inner?'

Lambert looked out. He was fond of this aeroplane. Seen through this aged Perspex, the world was not bright and new but ancient and yellowed like parchment. Polished a thousand times, the windows had become a delicate optical system that edged the landscape with haloes and made of the sun a bundle of gold wire. He looked at the engine-covers. Battered by riggers' feet and chunks of ice, there was around each panel screw a white calligraphic crosshatching of screwdriver scratches. From the exhaust dampers came a blue feather-like jet of flame. Its heat had baked the oil spill upon the cowlings. Like antique enamelware the dark-brown stains shone with a patina of deep reds and rich greens. Above the exhaust pipes upon the matt paint of the engine-cover there was one shiny patch. It was catching the bright afternoon sunlight and gleaming like a newly minted penny. Battersby also glanced at it briefly, then turned back to his panel. He was determined to do his job by the book, better than Murphy even.

'Fuel pumps of all tanks off,' reported Battersby. 'No warning lights.'

'A coolant leak can be real big trouble,' said Binty, always a Jeremiah.

'What do you think, engineer?' asked Lambert.

'It's just an oily footmark,' said Battersby. 'I saw the rigger do it. I should have had it wiped, I'm sorry.' He didn't turn away from his panel.

Lambert looked at the mark again: it was the shape of a rubber toe. He tapped Battersby on the arm so that he looked round. Lambert grinned at him. The white-faced engineer was relieved not to be reprimanded.

'That generator behaving, Batters?

'Perfectly, Skipper.'

Digby was full-length in the nose watching the sunny landscape slide under him. He switched on his intercom. 'Skipper, did they tell you what it's going to be tonight?' As always when Digby was trying to wheedle something his accent had become more nasal, drawing each word to its fullest possible extent like soft chewing-gum.

'Yes, thanks,' said Lambert. He leaned to his right and bent his head low to watch Digby's reaction.

'Come on, Skipper,' said Digby looking back to him. 'Give us the gen.'

'It's Hamburg,' volunteered Jimmy Grimm the wireless operator. 'The Orderly Room WAAF told me. The blonde job'.

'Big deal,' said Binty scornfully from the upper turret. 'Who told her, the Groupie last night in bed?'

'Skip,' coaxed Digby. 'I've got the calculations to do. I should be told.'

'It's a five-tank job: 2,154 gallons,' said Lambert.

Squinting into the hot sun coming through the nose panel Digby nodded. Lambert continued, 'The whole Squadron is bombing the shit out of Adelaide.'

They all heard Binty's catcall of joy even without his intercom. 'That's the one, Skipper,' said Flash Gordon from the rear gun turret.

'You pom bastards,' said Digby cheerfully.

'Sticky beak,' said Lambert. It was one of Digby's favourite insults.

Jimmy Grimm hunched lower at his table under the racks of radio equipment and grinned. He was sending the favourite operator's test signal: 'Best bent wire best bent wire best bent wire'. Who knows who first invented this strange phrase with its jazz-like rhythms, known to RAF operators and Luftwaffe monitoring services alike?

Lambert began a gentle turn. Under the banked wing the green countryside tipped slowly forward like a child's soup plate waiting for a spoon. The Great North Road was black with traffic: long military convoys and civilian lorries lumbered slowly down England's ancient spine.

Lambert looked at the dazzling blurs made by the air-screws and superimposed them as he juggled the throttles.

Watching the stroboscopic effect enabled him to synchronize the engines. Lambert noticed that Battersby was looking at him. He grinned. Then he ruined the harmony and pointed to the throttles for Battersby to try.

Binty heard the motors go out of synch suddenly and said, 'What's the matter with the motors?'

'Nothing,' said Lambert. 'Battersby is handling the controls.'

'Then let me off,' said Binty.

'Don't be a fool,' said Lambert. 'It's better that he should know as much as possible.' There was a fearful silence.

North-west of Huntingdon the countryside changed suddenly. No more weatherboard houses and thatched cottages, now yellow-brick dwellings and rusty sheds. Windswept allotments full of caterpillar-nibbled cabbages, shallots, wire fences and old cars propped on wooden blocks until petrol supplies returned. Here the fields were brightly coloured: light yellow, gold, green potato fields and bright blue ones full of cabbages.

Round came the flat angular fens and the Ouse through which had waded Angles, Saxons and Jutes. Danish Vikings too had plundered this land and left their names upon the map. The circle of Bourn airfield came into sight and around it the hovering flies that would be with them tonight.

Godmanchester: unmistakable, two Roman roads like spokes in its central hub.

'Another Lanc ahead,' said Digby. It crabbed along, the wind pushing it askew. It was not of their squadron. Nor was it a training flight from Upwood OTU or Woolfox Lodge. Lambert looked at the strange Lancaster. He tried to see it anew as though he had never seen a Lancaster bomber before. It was a brooding machine; thirty tons of it. Even counting motors and turrets as one and excluding nuts, bolts and rivets there were fifty-five thousand separate parts. Over three miles of electrical wiring, generators enough to light a hotel, hydraulics enough to lift a bridge, radio powerful enough to talk to a town on the far side of Europe, fuel capacity enough to take it to such a town, and bomb-load enough to destroy it.

Lambert held his speed. It was just enough to close distance inch by inch. Is this the view a fighter pilot will have just before pressing the button that will blow them all into eternity? Tonight? The prim red, white and blue roundels on the plane ahead were symbols of Britain. Its brown-and-green upper surface was a formalized version of the land, ploughed and verdant, over which it flew. Like primitive voodoo objects the brightly painted aircraft defied the enemy, and upon them were painted the little formalized yellow bombs, or symbols of aeroplanes destroyed, that showed how powerful was the magic they could work.

Lambert had seen enough of the other Lanc. He had got too close for comfort. Lambert moved the control column and adjusted the throttles and pitch control. Creaking Door lifted like a showjumper, leaving the other plane far below. That was better. Even a sneeze from a nervous gunner was enough to send a bomber into violent evasive aerobatics and like most pilots he feared mid-air collision more than flak and night fighters put together.

Stop climbing. Straight and level while he saw where he was. Six or seven miles away to starboard the countryside lapped around Cambridge, a ramshackle rash of workers' dwellings and speculators' suburbia. In its centre, lush with green courts and beflowered backs, the great university, its spires grinning like dragons' teeth daring the untutored to seek admittance. Beyond this citadel the countryside turned green again and there were more airfields. Below him passed RAF Oakington, Lancasters dotted along its perimeter. Gentle turn. Warley somewhere off to port lost to sight amongst the fenland. He saw the other Lanc turn that way. This was the flying Lambert liked, in the clear light of a fine summer's day. This was how he'd fancied it would be on the day he'd volunteered.

Lambert was flying straight and level now. No compass needed, for below him, glinting in the sun like a twenty-mile-long steel needle, was the man-made Bedford River.

'Lambert's compass, I call it.' The voice startled Lambert. Kosh Cohen was at his elbow, sitting on Battersby's folding seat and staring out of the window like a day tripper.

Lambert smiled.

'You always come over here, Skip,' said Cohen. 'Is this where you're going to live after the war?'

'Perhaps,' said Lambert. 'Your toys OK?'

Cohen nodded.

'Let's go and get some lunch,' said Lambert and he let the nose dip. Cohen folded back the seat and returned to his dark curtained booth. Since Lambert was flying by visual landmarks there was little for Cohen to do. He had sorted his maps and given the Gee and H2S the routine test. Although it was notoriously prone to technical failures, he was proud of the top-secret radar set that showed him the ground through fog, mist, cloud or darkness like some god bringing wrath to a sinful Babylon. Only 'selected crews' had the new equipment.

Lambert's voice came over the intercom asking each crew-man if their equipment was in order. Cohen pushed the mask to his mouth to answer yes into the microphone. On his first two operations he had vomited before the aircraft had even crossed the English coast. Apart from the humiliation, it meant that Creaking Door had to lose precious height so that he could clean himself up before clamping the oxygen mask back to his face for the rest of the trip. Now he knew the smell of fear, for it lingered in his face mask and was a constant reminder of the dangers of being too imaginative. He sharpened pencils and prepared the elastic strap that held pencils, rulers and protractors from flying loose during violent evasive action. He looked at the topmost map and read to himself the names of Channel ports. He had passed through them on holiday before the war. He switched his

117

microphone on. 'Batters,' said Cohen on impulse. There was no answer for a moment, then the engineer answered, 'Engineer here, who is it?'

'Kosh, Batters. What mob was your brother in at Dunkirk?'

There was no reply for some time. Cohen was debating whether to call again when Battersby answered.

'I made that up, I'm afraid,' he said. 'My brother is in a reserved occupation, an electricity sub-station.' There was a stunned silence over the crew intercom. Then Battersby said anxiously, 'You weren't thinking of telling Mr Sweet?'

'No,' said Cohen. 'I wasn't.'

Lambert could see Warley Fen straight ahead. The mile-long runways were distinct on the landscape like a black Chinagraph cross scrawled upon a coloured map. Lambert took a quick look round to be sure there were no other aircraft in the circuit. High above them he saw a thin streak of a condensation trail in the upper atmosphere. The aeroplane making it was just a speck.

'Look at him go,' said Cohen. Lambert guessed he was standing under the astrodome. He was like a kid on an outing whenever they were in the air.

'It's the Met flight, on his way to look at the weather over our target,' said Digby.

They looked up at the dot. 'With that sort of altitude,' said Lambert, 'a man could live for ever.'

At 32,000 feet the Spitfire had begun to spin a white feathery trail in the thin moist air. The pilot watched the trail in his mirror and put the stick forward. The highly polished Spitfire Mk XI responded with a shallow dive. The altimeter needle moved slowly backwards until, as suddenly as it began, the white trail ended. Immediately the pilot corrected his plane into straight and level flight. This was his optimum safety height for today. No enemy could bounce him from above without leaving a telltale trail. Now he need only watch the air below. He checked the notepad and pencils strapped to his knee for the tenth time. He settled back comfortably and ran a finger round his collar; the cockpit was very warm. Few men had seen the world from this height. Few men knew that it was only a layer cake: a rich-green England base with a layer of light-green ocean on it, then Holland, brownish and flecked with clouds along the coastline. Then the distant horizon, perhaps as far as two hundred miles away, disappearing into white mist like whipped cream. Upon it blue sky was heaped until it could hold no more. To the Ruhr and back would take the Spitfire only ninety-two minutes. He'd have time for a game of tennis before tea.

In the thirteenth century East Anglian wool merchants had brought back from the Low Countries wealth, brickmakers, architects and a taste for fine Dutch houses. There were many houses as well preserved as Warley Manor, with its distinctive curved gables and fine pantiles. Before the war it had been the home of a Conservative Member of Parliament. Art students had regularly come to sketch it. They had sat on the lawn shaded by the ancient elm trees, and had tea and cucumber sandwiches in the Terrace Room. Now it was the Officers' Mess of RAF Station Warley Fen. The Terrace Room was furnished with long polished tables. Between the tables white-jacketed airmen moved carefully, setting the lunch plates with white linen napkins and gleaming glass-ware. Through the folding doors from the anteroom came the cheerful shouts of young commissioned aircrew, and a gramophone record of Al Bowlly was playing gently in the background. The sunlight made patterns on the carpet and the glass doors had been opened to let the tobacco-smoke escape.

There were sixteen Lancaster bombers at Warley Fen. Each one had a crew of seven. Of these one hundred and twelve operational crewmen, eighty-eight were sergeants.

(The Sergeants' Mess was a series of corrugated iron huts interjoined.)

The remaining twenty-four flyers were officers; they shared this mess with another forty-eight officers ranging from the Padre to the Dental Officer, plus some WAAF officers like Section Officer Maisie Holroyd. She was a plump thirty-eight-year-old woman who had spent eight years running a cheap 'meat and two veg' dining-rooms in Exeter. At Warley Fen she was the Catering Officer and even the people who found the present food unappetizing agreed that she did a better job than any of her male predecessors.

The non-operational officers were mostly middle-aged. They wore medals from the First World War and inter-war campaign ribbons from Arabia and India and a very high percentage had pilot's wings on their tunics. Of the twenty-four operational flyers, thirteen were born in Britain. The others were three Canadians, four Australians, two Rhodesians, and two Americans who still had not transferred to the USAAF. Seven officers wore the striped ribbon of the DFC, including Flight Lieutenant Sweet of B Flight.

Had he been asked what his talents were, Flight Lieutenant Sweet would not have put flying a bomber anywhere near the top of his list. Nor, which would have surprised his fellow airmen even more, would he have claimed to be a popular leader of men. Sweet felt himself particularly well fitted to be a planner of air strategy. Some of his boyhood ambitions had come to nought, for instance his desire to be six foot tall and his ambition to be head boy. In addition, there was his dream of winning the hundred yards' sprint and being Captain of the Southern Counties Public School Cricket Eleven, but these were lesser hopes.

His desire to be a strategist had not diminished with time as had the desire to be a professional cricketer, nor had it become unreal like his hopes of being six foot tall. The war would continue for at least ten more years, Sweet had decided. There was time enough for this ambition. When we had conquered the Germans the Japs would be next on the list, and look how long the Chinks had spent trying to hold them off: since 1931. After that we'd probably have to put the Russians in their place. It was going to be a long war and Sweet had decided to spend the greater part of it on the staff side: making decisions, formulating plans, forging strategy. These were the things of which wars were made. Naturally a young ambitious staff officer would have had a dangerous war behind him and a couple of gongs. These would be his credentials, his way of making the old-timers listen to reason. Two tours of bombers, DFC and bar and a job at High Wycombe: this was Sweet's ambition.

He could handle a bit of schoolboy German and French. Next he'd learn some Russkie or Jap, or perhaps even Mandarin. He bought two whiskies and walked across to the solemn-faced Education Officer, an elderly schoolteacher who had joined the station only that week. Education officers were often called 'schoolmasters', and never more aptly, for this bespectacled pilot officer had, until ten weeks before, been teaching History and Languages at a secondary school in Harwich.

'How are you finding things, sir?' said Sweet deferentially.

'Splendid,' said the Education Officer, wondering why he should have been sought out by this gay young hero.

'Wizard,' nodded Sweet. 'That's wizard. My name's Sweet, Flight commander B Flight. Look, sir, I would appreciate your advice. Considering the way the world is going – the war and everything, you know – I'd like to hear a broader view than we' – quick look round – 'get in the Mess.'

The Education Officer looked at Sweet with interest. It was quite amazing that these boys – in spite of their rank badges and medals – were only a year or two older than his sixth form back in Harwich. Younger in a way, for the war had prevented their minds expanding in the normal manner. They thought of nothing but the technical skills of their job. Most of them failed to realize how narrow and uncommercial those skills were. After the war the poor devils would suffer when they started looking for a job, just as he had, as a young infantry officer, after the previous war. A brilliant first year at Oxford with its crowning achievement a commission in a yeomanry regiment. My God, what a fool!

It goes without saying we are all proud of the sacrifices you have made, Captain, and the decoration you won, but when there are so many men after so few jobs, it would be irresponsible and unfair to our shareholders to take anyone without experience or even a degree.

He had gone out and joined the Peace Pledge Union. 'I remember war, and I will never support or sanction another.' And yet here he was supporting another, with these curious young men. How different they were from the chaps he soldiered with in 1914. Half these kids hadn't even got their matriculation exam. He was amazed at the superficial nature of their conversation: flying, booze-ups and bints. Even their cynicism was ingenuous. He said, 'I'd be glad to help if I can.'

'It's not really for me,' said Sweet. 'It's for my cousin. He's a pretty clever chap. No degree, but he could get one at any time, just like that.' Sweet clicked his fingers. 'He was asking me a few questions the other day. He thinks my advice is worth taking. Can't think why.' Sweet laughed. 'He's in the Army, he stands a good chance of a job on staff. They are putting together the real brains now to start planning the invasion.'

'Really,' said the Education Officer.

'Yes. This chap will be a brigadier in no time at all. Anyway this fellow . . .'

'Your cousin.'

'What?' said Sweet. 'Oh yes, my cousin. He's got German and French pretty well buttoned up and he's thinking of having a crack at the old Russian or the old Jap. What do you think would be best? Perhaps Mandarin? I mean, you can't tell the way it might go. What would you have advised the chap to study?'

'He'd do best to concentrate still on his French and German. Conversational practice. Vocabulary building, perhaps working solely with military books.' Sweet was looking rather blank. The EO felt that he was expected to continue. 'He should try translating some of the *Manuscrit de mil huit cent treize* by Baron Fain, who was Secretary of Napoleon's Cabinet. Or there's Danilewski's *Denkwürdigkeiten aus dem Kriege 1813*; I translated a piece of that once to pass the time away in France. Then for the Battle of Waterloo there's the famous *Documents inedits* by the Duc d'Elchingen . . .'

'If I want to read about our victory at the Battle of Waterloo,' said Sweet, 'I don't need any French blighter to tell me about it.' He laughed ironically.

'But for your cousin . . .'

'Oh, my cousin doesn't need that sort of thing,' said Sweet. 'He thinks internationally: Russkie or Jap. Perhaps you don't think internationally.'

'I'm afraid I never do,' said the Education Officer.

'My cousin always does,' said Sweet. 'So do I. Look here, sir, I know that in the first war the trenches in France were full of poets and all that, but because chaps beat the Mess up once a week, de-bag some poor blighter and have a little horse-play you mustn't think that they are a lot of shallow-minded musclemen. I mean, these chaps do their bit; some win a gong or two by luck or judgement.' Sweet smiled. 'But that doesn't mean that when the shouting's over they can't enjoy some good poetry and music and sit down and try and think what the world really means to the common man.'

'I don't jump to conclusions,' said the Education Officer. 'As it is I'm rather proud to be sharing a Mess with so many interesting young men.'

'Nice of you to say so, sir.'

The Station commander was standing alone near the

cupboardful of Squadron silver. Sweet thought he was counting it. The Mess Sergeant thought he was trying to see if the rearmost cups were polished. Actually he was trying to decide if the Command swimming trophy was solid silver or only plated. Sweet turned back to the Education Officer. 'There's an operational matter I must speak about with the Stationmaster.'

The Education Officer followed Sweet's gaze. 'Oh certainly,' he said. 'Don't let me hold up the war.' He sniffed burned fat and watery cabbage and decided that he wasn't hungry. He missed his wife's home cooking more than he'd thought he would. What good was he doing here?

'And thanks awfully,' said Sweet as he moved among the earnest young drinkers around the bar. The light through the glass doors gave them haloes of sunshine. Sweet addressed the Groupie directly. 'All alone, sir? Have I pestered you about my collection for the village children's party?'

'Hello, young Sweet, yes, you had a quid from me last week.'

'Of course, sir.'

'Your team going to knock spots off those Besteridge chaps on Saturday?'

'I think so, sir. Mind you, Flight Sergeant Lambert is going up to London on a pass. I was rather counting on his slow bowling. Two of their team played for their county before the war to say nothing of this professional they've got. But Lambert's set on taking his wife up to London. He says he doesn't like playing for the Air Force.'

'Bad show that, but I'm sure you'll win, Sweet. I'm going to stonewall for you. Anyway, I've got ten bob on us.' They both laughed and the Groupie bought Sweet a small beer.

Sweet said, 'There's a story, sir, that you scored a century for 3 Group before the war.'

'That's true enough. I also played for Fighter Command one year. Before I got this touch of arthritis, or whatever the quack says it is, I was quite a sought-after bat.'

124

'That's what I heard.'

'Oh come along, Sweet, I'm sure I've bored you with the story of my batting at Sandhurst . . . when the umpire tried to catch the ball . . .' and the Groupie was launched into his reminiscences.

Several officers moved aside, for the Group Captain's stories about his cricket prowess were familiar to most of the Mess. His narrative was laced with monosyllabic four-letter Anglo-Saxon words which helped the Group Captain to establish a democratic camaraderie with his virile young officers. This, at any rate, was his theory. For this reason the Mess still had male waiters and barmen when most others had airwomen doing these jobs. The Groupie finished his anecdote flushed and happy. He said, 'If your team win on Saturday the chances are the AOC will invite you for dinner.'

'Yes, I'd heard he does that.'

'Give you a chance to tell him your theories about staff planning and strategy,' the Groupie said chuckling.

Sweet bowed his head modestly. Groupie said, 'But you're a Flight commander now, Sweet. You're finding out a thing or two about running a unit, eh?'

'In a small way of business,' admitted Sweet modestly. 'But I must say I had no idea of the amount of paperwork necessary just to get an aeroplane into the air.'

The Groupie gave a short ironic laugh. 'Now you are finding out where the real war is being fought, laddie. Saturation bombing of airfields with Air Ministry bumf, memos, requests and bloody nonsense, each prepared in triplicate and filed under waste paper, what?'

Sweet smiled at the Group Captain to indicate how much he shared his contempt for chairborne warriors. 'Especially when all a chap wants to do is get to grips with the damned Huns, sir.'

'That's it,' exclaimed the Groupie enthusiastically. 'I'm employed to kill Huns, and by God, my squadron will kill more Huns of all shapes, colours, sizes and sexes than any other in this man's air force or I'll know the reason why.' The Groupie smiled and self-deprecatingly added, 'At least, that's what I've told Air Ministry a few times, eh?'

'Yes, sir,' said Sweet. 'In fact, on this matter of killing Huns there's something you could help with . . . I say, I'm sorry to talk shop and all that . . .'

'Now then,' said the Groupie. 'You know my views about those bloody squadrons where they taboo shoptalk in the Mess.'

'Well, on this business of killing Huns, sir. There's a pilot – a damn good chap, experienced, decorated and all that, a good NCO – but he told me that he thinks our bombing attacks are "just old-fashioned murder of working-class families".'

'Confounded fifth columnist!'

'Yes, sir, I knew you'd be annoyed, but that's not all. This war, he says, is just the continuation of capitalism by other means.'

'That's Karl Marx he's quoting.'

'Yes. It's a misquote of Clausewitz actually, sir.'

'It's a bloody disgrace. A chap on my station you say?'

'Flight Sergeant Lambert, sir. It might be just a touch of the jitters, mind you.'

The Groupie's face changed. 'Lambert again, eh. Still, he's got a good, hasn't he? And we've got to remember that Karl Marx is on our side now. Got to hand it to the Russkies, Sweet, they've put up a jolly good show lately. This Stalingrad business could be the turning-point of the war.'

'I only thought, sir . . . knowing your views on killing Huns.'

'You did right, laddie. I'm a Hun-killer, as you well know, only way to get the war won. I'll be looking into it. If he's going to lose his nerve for killing Huns it will be better to put the chap on to something he can manage.' The Mess waiter caught the Groupie's eye. He nodded. 'Cleaning our latrines, for instance.'

126

'I thought you'd better know, sir.'

'Quite right,' said the Groupie. 'But then you usually are, young Sweet, but don't say I said so, what?' They both smiled.

'Oh, by the by, sir. Perhaps you've heard about this little experiment I'm doing on one of the rear turrets.'

'I heard something about it. What are the details?'

'Well, it came to me one morning when I opened the window in order to see more clearly . . .'

In the hall a corporal struck the gong; its soft sound echoed through the old house. 'Come along, gentlemen, let the prisoners eat a hearty lunch.' The Groupie always said that at lunchtime. In the evenings he said 'hearty dinner'.

He turned back to Sweet. 'I saw you talking to our new schoolmaster. Nice chap, isn't he?'

'Indeed he is, sir. A very good type indeed, sir.'

'And gives the Mess a bit of style having a VC here, what?'

'VC, sir?'

'The schoolmaster my boy, Pilot Officer Pearson, VC. Don't tell me you didn't make a beeline for that purple ribbon. Everyone does. Nineteen-seventeen; killed twelve Huns with a sword and dozens more with hand grenades, held a section of Boche trench for two hours until reinforcements arrived. Fascinating, what? Seeing an officially accredited hero in the flesh.'

'Yes, sir,' said Sweet, trying to remember what he had said, 'but let me tell you about this silly little idea I've had about the Perspex in rear turrets . . .'

The Lanc that Lambert had followed came in to land on Warley Fen's main runway. There were no squadron letters or call signs, no bombs painted on its side, no pet names. There were no guns in the turrets nor gunners to man them. There was not even an engineer to help with the fuel change-overs or assist with the controls. It made a perfect landing and obeyed the tower's instructions with a care that was unusual. A Hillman car sped out to the bomber and waited while the pilot checked through the procedures with the ground crew and the Engineer Leader. The engineer officer was Sandy Sanderson, a slim-hipped Lothario who had bet ten shillings that he'd have lunch with the ferry pilot. He lost. The pilot, a twenty-year-old brunette in the uniform of the Air Transport Auxiliary, declined with a knowing smile. Is it dangerous, her mother had once asked her? Only after you land, Mother. As well as flying the four-motor aircraft entirely alone she had eaten three cheese sandwiches while doing so. By missing lunch she would have time to get back to the storage unit and deliver another aircraft before finishing work for the day.

There were always new modifications on the planes coming from factories, and this group, like most of the others, had special requirements that had to be incorporated. Wing Commander Munro and Sandy didn't finish their ground inspection until ten minutes to three.

It was a quarter past three when they hurried up the steps of the Mess. Munro had missed lunch and would make do with spam sandwiches and a glass of lemonade. Not that there was any harm in having a glass of beer at lunchtime even when they were on Battle Order but he felt that he should be marginally more abstemious than his men. Sandy drank lemonade too.

Munro was a wealthy, desiccated landowner with a fragile manner and little or no sense of humour. In 1941 he had been injured in the leg by flak. There were three or four splinters still hiding somewhere in his ankle. For a time he had needed a walking-stick and even though he had stopped limping ages ago he had never relinquished the walking-stick. He marched around the aerodrome brandishing it like a laird striding through the heather. He was a tall slender man with a lined face and a stubby moustache. His closely trimmed hair was grey at the temples and although most of the men flying that night would be wearing white roll-neck sweaters and stained battledress, Munro was never seen on duty in anything other than his well-tailored barathea with his hand-made shoes polished like patent leather. Like his civilian worsteds and tweeds, Munro's uniforms had a patina that only years of valeting can bestow. The elbows and cuffs were reinforced with patches of soft brown leather and there was a special pocket where he kept a box of Swan Vesta matches. He reached into it and carefully lit his pipe, even though it seemed to be burning well. Often at meetings and briefings this gave him a moment's pause in the conversation. It was, like many of his mannerisms, an old man's habit. He was thirty-five years old and yet few people would have guessed him to be younger than forty-five. This would not have surprised Wing Commander Munro. He preferred to look forty-five. Munro had been an officer since 1932, although he had spent a year of peacetime as a civilian. His wife Sarah was running the whole estate now. It was a beastly war for her: extra acres under cultivation but many of the staff in the Army. She was looking so much older.

There was a letter waiting for him in the rack. It was written in bold good-humoured handwriting, on a sheet torn from an accounts book.

Darling,

How can I thank you for the magnificent handbag? It arrived on my birthday which represented a brilliant piece of Munro organization. I don't think I'd like to see London at the present time. From your description it sounds like an international madhouse. I like the way you are always telling me to never trust strangers and yet you are really absurdly generous with those unregenerate ruffians from the old squadron whenever you meet them (which usually means whenever you enter a public-house). Perhaps you should grow a large moustache again at that!

The beans are going to be magnificent; aren't you clever? You must be here to taste the first of them. Those dashed aphis are all over the roses as usual and they just drink up the spray, belch, and call for more. The strawberries are doing very well and tomorrow I'm jam-making with cook. I'll send you a pot of it.

Now you mustn't worry about us. We both know that it will take a few years for Peter to build his strength up to that of other children but he has fresh air and there is plenty of milk here still. If he went to Canada who would give him the love that we give him, and what is more important?

You remember how short of breath he was when you were on leave at Christmas? Now he is just as bad again. It's pitiful to hear him at night and I want to breathe for him, the darling. He's so good about it all and Dr Crawford says that it must be painful for him sometimes.

We miss you darling but you must worry only about bringing yourself home to us safe and well. Save your concerns for yourself and your men. Here all is well apart from Peter and for him it's simply time and rest and fresh air. I would not have told you anything of this but you made me promise. I will see you some time soon. Take care my darling, do take care. From your untidy slut of a farmhouse wife and dung-spreader-in-chief at 2 AM and the accounts not complete.

Love,

SARAH

'That girl and her cheese sandwiches,' said Munro.

'Yes, sir?' said Sandy, looking up and suddenly alert.

'Not a bad idea that.'

'Indeed, sir?'

'Eating in the air.'

Munro carefully folded the letter and replaced it in the envelope. He took a gold propelling pencil from his pocket and listed upon its back the things he must do before briefing time.

CHAPTER NINE

In the cryptic style of teleprinter Meldekopf 1 – I/Ln Funkhorch-Regiment West – the radio monitoring and interception department of 12th Fliegerkorps HQ received from Palais Luxembourg, Paris (HQ of the 3rd Air Fleet) the so-called WIM report. This was the collated result of hostile radio traffic, navigational bomb and radar aids, IFF and jamming devices. Largely, however, it was based upon the brief radio tests made by RAF wireless operators. Radio tests before lunch usually indicated a bomber being readied for a raid that evening. Jimmy Grimm's 'best bent wire' signal was just one of the hundreds heard in Paris. The Luftwaffe's No 1 Fighter Division HQ at Deelen was told unusually early to expect a heavy RAF attack that night.

Fernschreiben
+KR   31.6.1943   GEHEIM

MELDEKOPF 1
FUNKBEFEHLSSTAND WEST
LUFTFLOTTE 3, HOH.NAFU

GLTD
HVO 1. JAGD-DIVISION
FUNKBEFEHLSSTAND MITTE
WIM – MELDUNG

RAF WITH APPROX 600–700 (AMONG THEM PERHAPS
90 TWO-MOTOR) EXPECTED TARGET WEST GERMANY

MELDEKOPF 1
BR.B.NR.3567/43 GEH
GEZ.BOFINGER,LT.

CHAPTER TEN

There were vehicles that every sentry at the Wald Hotel could recognize. For instance, the commanding officer's Mercedes, the daily mail and ration lorries and the afternoon transport that went to the railway station. For these the ornate hotel gates were folded back well before their arrival. At the approach of an unrecognized vehicle, however, it was customary to challenge it and scrutinize the driver's papers before the gates were opened. The muddy Kübelwagen did not decrease speed when the two SS sentries walked to the middle of the road. Mausi Scheske held up his hand but finally stood back behind the sentry box. It was to the credit of the other sentry that he did not jump aside until the last moment when the front offside mudguard caught him a glancing blow on the leg. Damage to his knee-cap resulted, some weeks later, in the removal of a cartilage. The motor stopped after striking and bending a spray of wrought-iron oak-leaves. Its mudguard suffered another dent.

'Officer of the guard!' bawled the man in the front seat of the car, making no attempt to get out nor sparing a glance for the sentry who had been knocked full-length upon the gravel. Guard dogs barked and six armed and equipped soldiers stumbled to be first out of the gatekeeper's lodge that was now used as a guardroom. They were clamping their helmets to head and fixing bayonets and all the time were treated to loud complaints from the officer.

'Open the gates, pick that fool up. Officer of the guard! Why aren't you saluting? Where's that man's pack? Officer of the guard! Move these clowns off the path. You know how long you lot will survive on the East Front? Twenty-four hours. Why is that helmet dirty? Where in the name of bloody blue blazes is the officer of this pitiful shambles of a stumbling band of crippled incompetents? Officer of the guard!' He screamed as loud as possible and the starlings in the nearby trees rose into the blue sky in alarm. No less alarmed were the Scheske boys, Mausi and Hannes, who for the first time were seeing a Knight's Cross winner, grimy with the dust of battle, here before their very wide eyes.

'Yes, sir?' said a young officer, still breathless. He'd heard the noise while lying on a bed in the guardroom with his boots off.

Fischer yelled his own particulars like a recruit: 'Sturm-bannführer Fischer from Panzergrenadier-Division "Leibstandarte Adolf Hitler" on attachment to SS Division "Hitler Jugend", Beverlo, Belgium.' Give these kids and armchair soldiers the whole lot in the teeth, that was the only way to treat them.

'Yes, sir,' said the young officer. He took Fischer's travel papers. He'd heard that a new élite SS division was being formed. 'That's the sort of unit I'd like to be assigned to.' Quietly he added, 'A man forgets he is a soldier in these backwaters.'

'So I notice,' said Fischer. He opened his leather overcoat to replace his papers, which the young officer of the guard had not examined. The Knight's Cross tinkled against his top button and he saw the young man's eyes drawn to it. More than anything else the young officer wanted that. A Knight's Cross holder could do no wrong. Headwaiters provided the best tables and hotels their best rooms, queues vanished, girls submitted and even senior officers showed respect. How, he wondered, had this dirty fellow gained his.

He looked at both of the men in the car. Each of them

had a P38 pistol in a leather holster strapped to his waist with a lanyard from its butt. On the VW's dashboard there was a machine pistol in metal clips. There was an oily rag around its bolt and deep into the clumsy wooden stock of the gun the name Fischer had been carefully carved. So had a line of twenty-eight notches.

Fischer removed his peaked cap and wiped its sweaty leather band with a dirty handkerchief. His skull showed pink through the closely cropped hair. On it were the white worm-like scars of childhood bumps and falls and a long furrow that could only have been made by a bullet. He tucked the handkerchief into his sleeve as the English were reputed to do. The young guard commander noted this fine touch of sophistication.

'I want petrol and a new set of plugs.' Fischer rubbed his oil-blackened hands together briefly. 'We've had trouble with the motor.'

'And food, bathroom and bed?'

'The motor first.'

'Immediately, Herr Sturmbannführer,' said the young officer.

Now the sentries were alert and stiff with anxiety. That's all they needed, thought Fischer, a real soldier here to light a fire under them. The young officer's accent was that of a country boy. Racially pure, outstandingly fit and as ideologically sound as a dull-witted yokel could be. It all fitted Waffen SS selection policy but sometimes Fischer wondered if the policy was sound.

'Your kit to your room?' said the boy slowly.

'And put a guard on it. I'm carrying valuables.'

'Yes, sir.'

'And feed my driver and give him a place to sleep. He hasn't closed his eyes for fifty-six hours.'

The young officer looked at the high-cheeked driver.

'Are we taking Asiatics into the SS now?'

'We have a whole division of them in training – 14th

SS Freiwilligen-Division Galizien. Two hundred and fifty of them have gone to the Junkerschule. By the time you get to the east they'll have Ritterkreuze dangling on their collars and you'll be saluting them.'

'Ostvolk?'

'The Reichsführer says they are comrades. You don't object?'

'No, sir,' called the young man loudly. Fischer gave a sour smile.

The gates were wide open. Fischer signalled with his finger that the driver should start up.

The young officer said, 'Follow the gravel drive. You'll see the old hotel building. I'll phone ahead so that they'll have orderlies to attend to your baggage. And I will phone the kitchen too.'

'You're getting the idea, boy,' said Fischer as the car rolled forward. He turned to his driver and in careful German said, 'Petrol, sparking plugs, bath, food, sleep. It's now 15.00; the Kübelwagen ready by 22.00.' He held up his fingers.

'*Frauen?*' said the driver.

'No *Frauen*, you big ape,' said Fischer. 'This is Germany. Wait until we are across the border.'

Half understanding, the Ukranian smiled so that his narrow eyes almost closed. He nodded his head.

The inhabitants of Altgarten wore the tired faces that years of war, blackout, rationing, overtime and loneliness bring to the people that endure them. The uniforms were coarse and the civilian suits threadbare. The girls' dresses were homemade, although here and there in the crowd one saw fine furs or pearls that had made a journey in a soldier's kitbag.

'What time do you leave?' asked Anna-Luisa. She was giving his shoes an extra polish as she always did just before he returned to duty.

'Three o'clock,' answered Bach. 'A staff car will take me.'

'I'm impressed.'

'An old friend, on the staff of General Christiansen. He has to go from Dortmund to The Hague several times a month. He often gives me a lift.'

'You shouldn't have told me.'

'I want to tell you everything,' he said. She packed clean laundry into his case, folding and smoothing it with a new-found dedication.

Sometimes Oberst Max Sepp travelled in General Christiansen's Mercedes, complete with imperious horn and flying pennant. Today Bach was disappointed to find him in a Citroen. It was a factory-fresh car specially made for the Wehrmacht and newly painted Luftwaffe blue, but it hardly compared with the Mercedes and its throaty roar and silver supercharger pipes. Even Max was less impressive than usual, hunched in a badly creased cape and battered peaked cap. As they stood on the pavement August glanced into the sky. It was a habit he would never lose. Six miles in the sky above him the Met observation Spitfire pilot had seen the whole sweep of the cold front and its attendant hammerhead clouds and black twig-like base. He scribbled upon the note-pad attached to his thigh and while his attention was distracted from the controls the aeroplane lost 500 feet of altitude. This brought it low enough for condensation trails to form, although only for a minute. At 420 mph that minute meant a thin white scar seven miles long across Krefeld's blue sky.

'One of our fighters,' said Max. August didn't reply; he threw his leather overcoat on to the driver's seat and got in.

Max Sepp was a plump white-haired man in his middle fifties. He was on the staff of the Military Governor of the Netherlands. He was Controller of Civilian Fuel Supplies, about which, as he freely admitted, he knew little or nothing. Before the war he had been a forestry official.

'This is the life,' said August, settling into the back of the car with Max as the driver closed the door and saluted. Anna-Luisa waved and August waved back.

The car moved off. 'The best job in the war,' said Max. 'When I go on leave I feel ashamed at the arduous life they lead on the home front.'

The driver had done this same journey a thousand times. From Mönchenstrasse where Bach lived he drove across Dorfstrasse, the big main street, and into Richterend, the short cut round the back of St Antonius Hospital. The old building was dwarfed by the new training centre behind it, while on their left lines of unpainted huts on the waste ground stretched as far as Sackgasse and the slums behind the gas-works.

'What's that bloody great place?' asked Max. 'A concentration camp?'

August Bach looked at his friend a moment and glanced at the back of the driver's head before replying. 'No,' he said finally, 'it's a medical centre for amputees. Men from the East Front and civilians from the bombed cities. They learn how to use false limbs there. They take a walk into Dorfstrasse . . .'

'And frighten the kids and look at the empty shops. Lovely.'

'Is that what a concentration camp looks like, Max?'

'If either of us knew that, my dear August, we would probably not say.'

'Probably wouldn't be sitting here,' said August.

'How right you are.' Max Sepp smiled grimly. He looked out of the window as the car turned the corner at Frau Kersten's fruit farm and jolted heavily over a badly repaired place in the road.

'An air raid?' asked Max.

'Altgarten's one and only. Last March. An RAF plane jettisoned incendiary bombs across the potato fields and two high explosive bombs. One on the road, one on Frau Kersten's outhouse. She has French prisoners of war working on the farm now. She made them fix up the barn and mend the road.'

'They did a better job on the barn than on the road.'

'She didn't give them the road to live in.'

'Smart woman, Frau Kersten,' said Max with a laugh. The car turned north-west on to the road that they would follow to Nieukerk and all the way to Arnhem. On the left, Frau Kersten's potato fields stretched away to the flat horizon. Long lines of bent figures were lifting the waxy yellow potatoes that August liked so much. There were children among them, for the schools had given older boys the traditional holiday to help with the crop. As lines moved forward their forks raised the dry soil so that the breeze carried it in dust clouds across the fields behind them.

'They are fine potatoes,' said August.

'Ah, potatoes! How could the Wehrmacht fight without them. Frau Kersten must be doing very nicely out of the war, August. A smart woman. Now that's a direction you might be looking.'

'What do you mean, Max?' August couldn't help laughing at the face Max pulled in answer to him.

'What do you *think* I mean, you old rogue,' said Max. 'You think I believe you spend all your time embracing your binoculars and flirting with those seagulls around that radar station of yours.'

'Just lately the RAF have been keeping me busy.'

'Not too busy for that, August.'

'I'm in love, Max, I'm going to get married.'

'To the RAD girl?'

'Yes.'

'We have a lot of RAD girls working in the Military Government. It never works out.'

'Whatever do you mean?' said August.

'Marriages with the RAD girls clerks. We have a couple of requests every month. I usually post the girl away. Unless she's pregnant. In that case I post the man.'

'You're a cold-hearted swine, Max.'

'Your girl . . . is she? . . .'

140

'Damn you, Max, no. At least . . .'

'There you are, August. Face the truth, old friend. A moment's fun, a convenient relationship.' He paused. 'For a *time*. Not for a marriage, August.'

'I love her, Max.'

'See how it goes for a month or two.'

'There's a war on, Max. And God knows how old I'll be when it ends! No, this is right for me. And right for her too.'

'Cigar?'

'Thank you.' August sniffed at it appreciatively.

'The Controller of Civilian Fuel Supplies, Netherlands, is a post that brings a privilege or two.'

'All right, she's just a naïve young girl, but I've had enough of complex sophisticated people. If she'll put up with my devious complications, I'll be happy to have her simple soul.'

Max smiled and lit the cigar for him. For quite a long time they both looked out of the car windows without speaking. It was odd, thought August, one can know a man for many years, and then suddenly half a dozen sentences reveal how little communication there truly is between the two of you. Perhaps all human relationships are like that. Perhaps the best that he could hope for in a marriage to Anna-Luisa was that disenchantment would come slowly, and the bitter aftermath of disenchantment – the black despairing hatred – never even begin. He looked at Max; how indolent and comfortable he was. He leaned back, his eyes closed as they sped along the clear main road.

'Our roads,' remarked Max. 'Could we have imagined such wonderful roads when we were children?'

'Could we have imagined war on two fronts and the need to move armoured divisions on interior lines?'

'You're a miserable fellow today. Admit the Führer's roads are wonderful.'

'The roads are wonderful, but are roads the thing we most urgently need? I can't help thinking that the great

Autobahnen were built across the land in order to convince us that Germany is not a conglomeration of disparate and unfriendly principalities.'

'Well, today I bless the fine roads, for we have a detour: Deelen.'

'Will it make us late?'

'You won't miss your appointment with the *Tommis*.'

'How late?'

'Sixty kilometres to Deelen, Deelen to your radar site can't be more than one hundred and fifty kilometres, even after dropping me off in The Hague.'

'How long at Deelen?'

'Stop being so nervous, August. We'll have no local traffic in the border zone, a few convoys between Utrecht and The Hague and then nothing at all in the prohibited coastal zone. When we get to Deelen you'll be fascinated. I'll have to drag you away, you'll see.'

The first traffic holdup was on the far side of Geldern. Teenage officer cadets, stripped to the waist and gleaming with sweat, were working like a chain-gang to replace a damaged bridge section in record time.

They were only a couple of kilometres past that when an oncoming convoy halted them again. August watched the twelve-ton half-tracks, and the 8.8 cm flak guns they trailed, creep past. It was a large battery complete with fire-control equipment and personnel in full battle order. Three of the guns were crewed by Flakhelfer. These Hitler Jugend, some only fifteen years old, were dwarfed by the seats of the giant tractor. Their steel helmets came low over their unsmiling faces. They wore brightly coloured badges and shoulder-patches and red and white swastika armbands. At their waists each one had a dagger.

'Hitler Jugend volunteers,' said Max.

'Conscripts,' said August.

'Kids?'

'That's it.' How soon would Hansl be accoutred thus and

fed into the endless war? Max counted the guns as they rolled past. 'Twenty-eight guns,' exclaimed Max. 'Fantastic.'

'Grossbatterie; under centralized fire control. At first it was two or three sites combining, now they have up to forty guns under one control.'

'Is that good?'

'At least the flak keeps the RAF up high. Without flak the *Tommis* would come down on the deck and put their bombs into our factory chimneys.'

'You know, August, my friend, there are quite a few homeless civilians living in the Ruhr who would prefer that.' He laughed.

A flak officer noticed the dark-blue Citroen with its Luft-waffe number plates and came across to apologize for the delay. He was a stern-faced young man, steel helmet, fair moustache and a non-regulation pair of soft kid gloves that came into view as he saluted.

'There are road repairs in Geldern,' said Max Sepp. 'You won't get these contraptions through the town.'

'I know, sir,' said the officer, 'but we turn off to Wesel before the roadworks.'

'The road into the Ruhr from Wesel is even worse,' said Max. 'I know this district well.'

'Our destination is Ahaus,' said the flak officer.

'Why Ahaus?' said Max. 'If it was left to me I'd pull all the flak back into the Ruhr. There you can be sure of a crack at the terror flyers. You'll be lucky to see any *Tommis* at Ahaus.'

'The policy is still an air defence corridor along the Netherlands border,' said August.

'My lads are keen,' said the officer. 'They'll be dis-appointed unless they see action soon.'

August replied, ' "No great dependence is to be placed in the eagerness of young soldiers for action. For fighting has something agreeable in the idea to those who are strangers to it." '

The flak officer was puzzled. He pulled at the fastening of his glove.

'Vegetius,' supplied August.

'A Roman military writer of the fourth century,' explained Max Sepp.

'As the Herr Oberst wishes,' said the officer respectfully. Three huge searchlights trundled past them. He saluted again and swung aboard one of the slow-moving tractors to join his young enthusiasts. The Citroen moved forward.

'You shocked the fellow,' said Max.

'I didn't mean to,' said August.

'Why worry?' said Max. 'With that medal at your throat you can afford to be blasé about heroism. But in case you should think me an untutored serf, Vegetius was also the man who said, "Let him who desires peace prepare for war!"'

'We all say something we don't mean once in a while,' said August.

Max laughed, and August wondered if he had not been too quick to judge his old friend.

There was another quarter of a mile of the traffic jam before the cause of it was revealed. There a Bedford Army lorry and an Opel car were locked in embrace. A young NSKK man was directing the traffic on to the grassy verge around the debris while three other NSKK men were extricating the unconscious driver from under the lorry's bent steering column. The rear part of the Bedford had broken through a hedge and from it boxes of fruit had fallen and split open. Pigs from the orchard were making the most of their good luck.

'Those bloody British lorries,' said Max. 'They shouldn't allow them on the road.'

'But after Dunkirk there were so many.'

'With right-hand steering. Half of these lorry drivers are Motor Corps kids. They are taught to drive in three weeks and then they come on the road and kill anyone who gets in their way.'

The NSKK boy waved them forward and they bumped on to the grass. It was well ploughed up now and the Citroen's wheels were spinning for a moment before getting a grip. Max leaned out of the car as they passed the traffic man. 'Those right-hand drives are death traps,' he said.

'I don't speak German,' said the traffic man. 'I am French.' He had the same green-and-black uniform that the Germans had but he wore a tricolour badge on his sleeve and now he tapped it. Max was furious. 'What bloody use are they?' he shouted loud enough for the boy to hear.

August said, 'We're short of manpower, Max. Russia is drinking our population as fast as we can get them there.'

'A Frenchman,' said Max angrily.

'They are a logical race. They should make good traffic police.'

'Huh,' said Max. 'Logical. They put a knife between your ribs and spend an hour explaining the rational necessity for doing it.'

'That sounds like a lot of Germans I know.'

'No, a German puts a knife into your rib and weeps a sea of regretful tears.'

August smiled. 'And after the Englishman has wielded the knife?'

'He says, "Knife, what knife?"'

August laughed.

From there on, apart from a traffic jam in Kleve and a long line of traffic crawling through a military police check at the Waal bridge, they moved fast. August dozed off until Max nudged him.

'We'll be at Deelen in five minutes or so,' said Max.

'Deelen air base or the Divisional Operations Room?'

'Number One Fighter Division. They control the whole damned air battle there: the whole of the Netherlands, Westphalia, Rhineland-Palatinate, and even parts of Hesse and Belgium. Been there before?'

'Last year.'

'Ah yes, the old sanatorium buildings. Wait till you see the new bunker. When I first saw it, August, I realized for the first time that, no matter what the *Amis* and *Tommis* do, they can never win against organization like ours. On the control map there is every night fighter, bomber, flak unit, civil-defence unit. It's like magic.'

'We need every bit of magic we can get, Max. Last year the RAF kept flying right through the bad winter weather. There was no chance for a breathing-space. We must stop these people within the next few weeks or we can be sure they'll keep bombing us right through next winter. What's the good of winning a war if our families, our homes, our cities, museums, and culture are bombed to destruction. We can move our Tiger tank factories deep underground, but we can't put Speyer Cathedral or Cologne underground.'

'The experts at OKL say that if we can crack the morale of the bombers this year, they'll give up bombing the cities.'

'The only way I know of cracking their morale is shooting them down.'

'Well, of course. They say if we could bring their casualty averages up by just two and a half per cent, the RAF would have to change their tactics.'

'Now you understand why I mustn't be late back,' said August. 'A short summer night like tonight, the moon almost full. If they come tonight and we don't knock down a record number of them we don't deserve to win.'

The Luftwaffe Citroen stopped at the first of the HQ's road blocks. The Luftwaffe sentries with their sub-machine-guns looked strangely out of place in the candy-striped sentry boxes. An elderly sentry checked their papers and waved the car on. It had rained heavily here and the striped box made dazzling reflections on the shiny road. The bunker itself was in beautiful forestland south of the airfield. The tall beech trees were dripping on to the sunlit paths and beyond the woodland patches of heather were near to flowering.

They got out of the car. There was a smell of resin from

the sun-baked pine trees and also the damp dark smell of mould. Deelen airfield was only a stone's throw beyond the trees and from there August caught the sound of a light aircraft. He waited until it came into view above the trees. It was a white two-seater biplane climbing steadily and earnestly without showmanship.

'That's what I call an aeroplane,' said August. 'If only flying had stayed like that, instead of giving way to scientists, horse-power, calculating machines and control systems.'

'You mustn't complain about that, my good August,' said Max. 'You are a controller, remember.'

The white biplane banked and turned neatly. Its fabric was still wet with rain and its wings flashed in the sunlight. The little plane kept climbing in spirals, like the diagrams in training manuals. Then, just as deliberately, it set course on a reciprocal of its take-off path and passed over them again. Before they could turn away the puttering of the white trainer was drowned by the roar of a twin-engine Junkers. The great black machine appeared over the leafy oak trees like some new sort of flying beetle. Its sting-like aerial array seemed to quiver as it searched for the other plane. In a moment it had gone.

'What a beauty,' said Max. 'For the time being, I'll take the calculating machines and horsepower every time.'

The bunker was truly gigantic. Its entrance road sloped down to a levelled site several metres below ground level. In spite of this the bunker towered above the surrounding woodland. It was as high as an apartment building and as long as a city block. Its roof was three metres of concrete laced with steel rods and heavy steel girders. Every lesson learned in the first years of war had been embodied in its design.

'It's indestructible,' said Max. 'It will stand there for hundreds of years after the war is over. Even if you wanted to remove it, it would be impossible.'

Max was enjoying August's surprise. 'Take no notice of all those windows in the wall,' said Max. 'That's just to give some light to the office workers. Behind that layer of offices, the concrete internal structure is many metres thick.'

The doors were one-centimetre steel, hung on hinges as big as fists. The concrete corridors were noisy with Luftwaffe personnel, many of them young girls. Max Sepp knocked briefly upon an office door and marched into an office crowded with Luftwaffenhelferinnen, uniformed girl com-munication auxiliaries. Max was on first-name terms with them. He collected a metal document-case and gave it to his driver to carry. Max settled down to gossip with one of the girl auxiliaries. From among the young officers who received Max's cigars one elected to show August the 'Opera House' itself. He was a dark-eyed young man. He put the cigar away in his desk and reached for his cap. He had grown a blunt black moustache to imitate the one Dolfo Galland, the popu-lar young general of fighters, wore. August guessed he'd smoke his cigar in similar mimicry. With a seeming disregard for convention or discipline he kept his left hand thrust deep into his jacket pocket in a rakish manner that well suited the night-fighter clasp on his chest and German Cross on his top pocket.

The young Leutnant took August upstairs. The outer shell of corridors gave on to the inner chamber at three levels. At the top of the staircase they passed through another identity check by an armed sentry. The Leutnant said to August, 'There is a drill on at present – Pheasant Alert – so we must keep very quiet.'

As they entered the cool dark Battle Room August shook his head in disbelief. The Leutnant smiled; every visitor was amazed. It had become a show place for top Nazi VIPs and this was the place to stand for a first glimpse. As August's eyes became accustomed to the gloom he saw that it was indeed like an opera house. Seated rank upon rank in front of them were Helferinnen, each one crisp and neat in her white uniform blouse. He saw only the backs of their heads, as would a person standing at the rear of a steep theatre balcony. Far below him, in the orchestra stalls, were rows of high-ranking control officers. Everyone's attention was upon the stage. For hanging where a theatre's curtain would hang there was a glass map of Northern Europe. The green glass map was fifteen metres wide and its glow provided enough light for August to see the rows of white faces peering at it and the papers on their desks. On the walls beside the map there were weather charts and a complex board that showed the availability of reserve night fighters. The cool air, silent movement and green light conspired to make the atmosphere curiously like that of an aquarium.

Each of the girls in the balcony with them had a spotlight. From the fresnelled lens of each one was beamed a small white T to represent a constantly moving RAF bomber or a green T to represent the fighter hunting it. As the map-references came over the girls' headsets they moved the white bombers across Holland and Northern Germany in a neat line. Down in the stalls the phones were in constant use and there was a shuffle of papers and movement. The air-conditioning made a loud humming sound and it was cool enough inside this vast concrete bunker to make August shiver even on this warm summer's day. From here phone and teleprinter cables stretched across the land to airfields, watchtowers, radar stations, radio monitors and civil-defence headquarters. Even U-boats, and flak ships off the Dutch coast, reported aircraft movements to this bunker which the Luftwaffe had christened the Battle Opera House.

Overlapping circles of light had appeared on the map. Each one was a radar station like August's own. Each one had two night fighters circling above it waiting to pounce upon a bomber coming into range of its magic eye. Now and again one of the T lights was switched off as a bomber was destroyed.

The young Leutnant had noticed August's Pour le Mérite

149

and decided that he was worth a fuller explanation than most of the rubberneck visitors that he showed around. He pointed to the six rows of stalls far below them.

'It's in the two front rows that the battle decisions are made. The Major-General third from the left is the Divisional Controller. On each side of him he keeps an Ia – Operations Officer. On the far left is the NAFU or Chief Signals Officer. Second to the right of the Div Controller, the officer with the yellow tabs is the Ic or Intelligence Officer. The old man on his right is the senior Meteorology man. The second row of officers, the ones speaking into phones all the time, are Fighter Controllers carrying out the orders. On that same desk there's a Flak Officer, Radar Controller and Civil Defence Liaison.'

'Who is the man in the tinted-glass office on the left?' asked August.

'Radio Intelligence Liaison Officer. He only comes out to talk with the Divisional Controller. Even then it's in a whisper.' He smiled, he had the cynical attitude to boffins that operational pilots always have.

The T-shaped lights moved slowly in a straight line towards Berlin.

'What do you think?' asked the Leutnant.

'It's damned impressive,' said August.

'It's not always as calm as this, I'm afraid. On a real raid things get more hectic. I've seen them shouting at each other down there.'

'And those little white lights don't disappear so quickly,' said August.

'Ah,' said the Leutnant. 'That's the real difference, I'm afraid.' He spoke like a man who knew how big the sky was on a dark night.

They watched the 'air raid' proceed for a few more minutes. Still the white T lights that represented the bombers kept on their narrow line. The controllers practised dealing with the 'stream tactics' that the RAF had developed as a way of overwhelming the radar defences of just one zone instead of presenting single targets piecemeal to several radar sets and accompanying night fighters.

'What about the Mosquito they send in to mark the target? If our planes could get up high enough to knock that down, the stream wouldn't know where to drop their bombs.'

'Exactly,' said the Leutnant. He swung lightly round on his toes with his arm stiffly akimbo, giving him a curious effeminate stance. He eyed Bach speculatively and then decided to confide a secret.

'Tonight we have a surprise awaiting them.'

'The Ju88s supercharged with nitrous oxide?'

' "Ha-ha" they call them – laughing gas, you see – you've heard about them, eh?'

'What idiot thought of that code name?'

'And 12.8 guns on railway mountings, we are going to try everything we know tonight. I don't know, some fool in Air Ministry, I suppose.'

'If they cooperate by flying over the railway guns,' said August doubtfully.

'They always come in from north to south, and always towards the Ruhr because – we think – that's the limit of the electronic range. So we can make a guess at it. We'll be more or less in position.'

'Radio intercept predict a big one tonight,' said August. He looked at his own radar station on the glass map, its range indicated by a dull lit circle. It was exactly placed between the RAF bomber airfields of East Anglia and the Ruhr. 'I'm at Ermine,' said August.

'I know, sir,' said the Leutnant. 'I don't think you'll have much sleep before morning.' Now August could see that the young Leutnant's stiff left arm was artificial.

CHAPTER ELEVEN

Like all such depressions, this one had been born when moist air from the Azores met the cold dry air of the Arctic. The resulting muddled air mass moved eastwards over Britain until it reached the sea area to the west of Denmark which was called Heligoland. Here the centre of the depression paused. Hinged upon this depression, the cloud-marked cold front, like a thousand-mile-wide door, swung across Europe at twenty miles an hour. The front curved because its southern edge couldn't keep up the pace. That southern end had only reached Bilbao in Spain when the centre was darkening the skies of Lyon and the northern sector was deluging the streets of Esbjerg with torrential rain.

In the high-pressure region that followed the front the heavy air subsided, warming by compression as it dropped. There was no more than the lightest of breezes, the clouds shrank even as you watched them, and the sun shone.

England had had its thunderstorms during the night and a morning of sunshine, but already a little cumulus had appeared over Wales and parts of the West Country. At Kroonsdijk, however, where the cold front had only recently passed, the skies were blue and the sun warmed the wet grass.

Unteroffizier Himmel eased himself into the pilot's seat of his Ju88 parked at the end of the dispersal. The sun had been upon the metal fuselage for several hours and now the seat and controls were hot to touch and the smell of warmed fuel was as powerful as *Glühwein*. It was a luxury to be alone for a moment and apart from the sounds of the ground crewmen doing their pre-flight inspection it was as peaceful as a country graveyard. Himmel looked at the wet grass where an oil-patch made a rainbow pattern of red, yellow and mauve. A sandpiper landed and bobbed around the brightly coloured grass looking for worms until a mechanic closed the dinghy stowage hatch forcibly enough to frighten it back into the air.

The old piece of fuselage that the fire section had set alight sent a quill of white smoke into the still air. At its nib, Leutnant Beer in overalls was wielding a fire extinguisher under the command of Horst Knoll, the senior NCO of the fire section. Horst was a bad-tempered fellow who hated officers and did his best to make their lives as uncomfortable as his legitimate duties permitted.

'On to the base of the flame,' he was shouting to Beer, who was reluctantly closing in upon the foul-smelling wreckage and cursing. Horst Knoll, knowing exactly what the moving lips were saying, smiled and urged him forward all the more. 'Don't be afraid of the smoke, Herr Leutnant, get much closer and put the jet on to the base of the flame. Much closer, Herr Leutnant, much, much closer.'

At the far end of the line of matt-black aircraft Major Redenbacher's aeroplane poked its snout from the dark hangar. Most of the spare mechanics were working on it. Suddenly the peace was shattered by the sound of engines. A Junkers with Leutnant Kokke at the controls was also preparing for an air test. Its chocks were pulled aside. Kokke gave a blip of throttle to start it moving around the perimeter. It moved away beyond the Alert Hut where the aircrew spent so much time. Outside it a dozen aircrew – air tests completed – sat sunning themselves. Most of them were younger than Himmel and few had been in the Luftwaffe as long as he had, but they'd come from all manner of units as their clothing showed. They'd seen service on war fronts from Finland to Egypt: British Army bush shirts, Czech flying boots, old Hitler Jugend shorts and Swedish leather jackets. Some sat shirtless, eyes closed in the deck-chairs, two played chess and some sprawled full-length on the wet grass arguing about engines and firepower and girls and promotion and medals.

No matter how much Löwenherz disapproved of their unsoldierly appearance it was a standing order of Major Redenbacher that at their Alert Huts the aircrews could 'dress informally, always providing that the regulations concerning the wearing of identity tags around the neck are not disobeyed'.

Three flyers were standing in the hut doorway. Himmel looked at his watch and guessed that they were listening to the BBC, for this was the time that they broadcast the flyers' programme. The carefully written technical talks always ended with a list of Luftwaffe personnel newly captured and newly dead.

Suddenly there was a loud thunder of cannon-fire and they all swung round to the firing butts. Above it a thin veil of blue smoke showed where Löwenherz's plane was having its guns harmonized by the armourers. Someone made a joke, and then Himmel saw them all laugh and relax. It was the long wait for nightfall that built up the tension. That's why Himmel always left his air test as late as possible.

One of Himmel's ground crew removed the rudder lock and then walked round the aeroplane to check the ailerons and control surfaces. Himmel slipped his toes under the rudder-bar loops and fastened his seat straps. He ran his hand down his oxygen-lead connection to check it and then moved the control column forward and back and twisted the antlers to be sure that the controls were free of obstruction. Old Krugelheim, the chief mechanic, was getting a little impatient. Under his black overalls he was shirtless and without trousers, but still he sweated as he paced about under the nose of Himmel's machine. He kept looking across to the hangar and Major Redenbacher's aircraft. The cowling had been removed from its port motor and its most intimate parts bared to the oily inquiring hands of the fitters. The black-garbed men stood on a platform, arrayed around the disembowelled motor like witch-doctors at a Black Mass. One of them, chanting a line from a textbook, bent low into its entrails and flashed a torch deep inside. His open hand appeared and worldlessly a spanner was put into it.

Krugelheim looked up to where Himmel sat in the cockpit high above him. 'The fuel pump,' explained Krugelheim.

Himmel hoped sincerely that the black men would work their healing magic soon, for it was 15.20 hours already and if his own plane was not in service by nightfall, when the killing began, the Major had a habit of taking the nearest one. Himmel's plane – Katze Four – was the nearest.

He slid the cockpit fully open and called down to the chief mechanic, 'Have you seen Unteroffizier Pohl?'

'No,' said old Krugelheim. 'He's probably still talking to the Signals Officer.'

'These aerials are a trial to us,' said Christian Himmel. The old man walked under the nose to look closely at the 'toasting fork'.

'It's the rain,' he said. 'If they stay dry for a few days they work perfectly. Here comes Pohl now.'

Someone in flying overalls, yellow lifejacket and para-chute harness emerged from the hut, but it wasn't Himmel's radar operator. For a few paces he was obscured by the tail of another Junkers 88, but as he came round it they recog-nized Löwenherz. On this warm day none of the other flyers were wearing flying overalls. Like Himmel most wore light-weight helmets, shirts, shorts and lifejackets. It was just like Löwenherz to be in full flying gear.

'What does the bloody Staffelkapitän want?' said old Krugelheim. As if having a faulty fuel-line on Major Reden-bacher's machine wasn't enough trouble for one day.

'Cheer up, Kugel,' said Himmel. 'We'll soon find out.' To call the grumpy old Oberfeldwebel 'Kugel' was a privilege earned by only the most seasoned of Kroonsdijk's NCOs. Although it meant 'bullet', the pot-bellied old chief mechanic was short enough in stature to realize that it also meant 'globe'. Kugel came close under the cockpit.

'You were in his Staffel during the Kanalkampf, weren't you, young Himmel?'

'He was in mine. I took him on his first operational sortie as my wingman. He was a lively fellow in those days.'

'Then the war has sobered him,' said the old man.

'It's sobered a lot of us,' agreed Himmel.

'Huh,' exclaimed the mechanic bitterly.

Himmel smiled at the old Oberfeldwebel. His misanthropy was what kept these aeroplanes in such good order. The old man too had been a lively youngster once, but there are more casualties of war than the doctor ever sees. Kugel clicked his heels as Löwenherz walked past him without a word and proceeded to inspect and waggle each control surface to be sure they were unlocked and free of obstruction.

Himmel looked down to the hatch as Löwenherz climbed up the metal ladder. The soft inner hatch opened and his head appeared level with the floor of the cockpit behind Himmel's feet. 'I'm flying with you instead of Pohl,' he said. One of the ground staff passed Löwenherz's briefcase up through the hatch.

Himmel nodded and turned to exchange a pained glance with the chief mechanic below while Löwenherz strapped himself into the radar operator's seat behind him. The backs of their heads almost touched, but between their seats there was a slab of steel armour. The Staffelkapitän carefully made sure that his intercom cable went down his back and was clipped to his overall. It was an inconvenience, but Löwenherz had read of several cases of aircrew being strangled by their own radio leads and it was a pet subject for his memos. Himmel hoped that he wouldn't notice that his leads were not correctly positioned.

'All set, Christian?' fussed Kugel. 'It's warm today, radiator gills full out while you're taxiing, then fully closed for take-off. Watch the cooling indicator.' Himmel nodded. '*Frei!*' yelled Kugel.

'*Frei!*' replied Himmel and pushed the button. The starter motor whined, jerking the blades. A bright blue flame escaped from the exhaust, in spite of the dampers. Then there was an ear-splitting roar. The panel vibrated and the instruments blurred. Himmel throttled back. He started the other motor and waited while the fuel- and oil-pressure needles came alive. The whole plane was rocking on its tyres now. He slid the side window closed in spite of the heat, for it was one of Löwenherz's well-known instructions. The instrument panel and the windscreen chattered with the pulse of the motors. He pushed the throttles wide open and saw the rev counters flick around to 2,800. Even through his flying helmet the sound was piercing. The ground crew had hands clamped against their ears and their black overalls rippled in the wind. Two of them tugged the chocks away from the wheels.

Himmel took an extra look round the cockpit: flaps up, mags off, undercarriage locked, fuel full, straps fastened, oxygen ready, brakes on. The instruments were colour-coded: yellow for fuel, brown for oil and blue for air. Each of them read correctly and yet still Himmel worried. All pilots did, this was the moment of worry, once they were airborne the tenseness would ease a little.

Himmel hooked his oxygen mask into the forehead of his helmet and pushed closed the studs of his throat mike. Löwenherz, taller than little Pohl, struggled to notch the seat back. Himmel was about to help but decided that Löwenherz was not the sort of man who liked being helped.

'Pilot to radar operator,' said Himmel self-consciously. 'All correct?'

'All correct,' said Löwenherz.

In his rear-view mirror Himmel saw Löwenherz fingering the radar controls.

'Katze Four to Control, request permission to take off.' The Controller told them to move off. Himmel released the brakes and the aeroplane rolled forward. Old Kugel waved him away like a swarm of flies.

Control told him to taxi to the far side of the airfield, wait until Katze Two was airborne and then move on to the end of the runway. He moved slowly along the perimeter track and past a wrecked Junkers 34. It had been there ever since Himmel could remember and had become a landmark for the aerodrome. Three months before, a salvage gang had removed the motor, only to find that it was an ancient Bristol Jupiter instead of the German power unit they had expected. A typical Luftwaffe balls-up, thought Himmel. So now the disembowelled plane had its rusting motor displayed alongside like a museum exhibit.

Parallel with the fence was the water-filled ditch, bright green now that summer sun had covered the surface with tiny cress plants. The dijk itself was two and a half metres higher than the aerodrome and upon it was the road to Utrecht. Its edges were neatly marked in white paint and its surface cobbled with the large stones that the Dutch call 'children's heads'. Military convoys buzzed upon it like angry bees and the wooden wheels of local cyclists crawled along with a bone-shaking clatter. Along the dijk road came a company of metalshod infantry. Himmel noticed the tired sweaty soldiers look his way with envy as they trudged past under the weight of full packs, blankets and rifles. They were singing, '*In der Heimat, in der Heimat, da gibt's ein Wiedersehen*'. In the homeland we'll meet again.

Himmel and Löwenherz watched Kokke's plane as he ran its engines to maximum revs and then roared along the runway climbing steadily towards the east. Then Himmel followed.

It wasn't one of his best take-offs, but to have Löwenherz sitting calmly behind you waiting to do the routine radar-interception test that was really the duty of meek little Unter-offizier Pohl was downright disconcerting.

The land flashed past beneath them. The sun shone down upon Kroonsdijk so that half of each street went black with shadow. Children pointed at them, a dog fled, a horse needed comforting. Gulls went into the air like a handful of white confetti, caught the breeze and in unison swooped back towards earth. The undercarriage thumped into the nacelle. A line of laundry wriggled, cyclists stopped. A silk patch of blue lake was tacked to green countryside by the taut fishing-lines of a hundred anglers, hoping to supplement their meagre rations. The flat heathland was like purplish-brown sandpaper scratched with irregular pale footpaths. The fields and lakes grew smaller as they fell away. An empty road grew busy, reached a fishing village and ended. Boats crammed tight to crowded quays, then there was just the empty blue water of the IJsselmeer. Over it there was a haze of summer heat like smoking fat on a frying-pan.

Control called him. 'Katze Four steer 090 for practice air interceptions. Rendezvous at two thousand metres, grid reference: Heinz Marie nine.'

Himmel pulled a map from his flying boot. 'Deelen,' supplied Löwenherz before he could unfold it. Himmel spread the map and glanced down at the ninth square of the H and M reference. Of course Löwenherz was right. Himmel smiled; the big plane was flying perfectly. In the mirror he saw Löwenherz look over his shoulder.

'Is this gun loaded?' asked Löwenherz.

'Yes, sir.'

'I'll test it while we are over water,' announced Löwenherz.

Behind him he heard a burst of firing as he tested the gun. What a good thing the ground crew had loaded it. They often didn't bother, for in the night fighter's war these little machine guns, swivelled round by the radar man, weren't much use. Himmel could smell the sour cordite fumes and tightened the oxygen mask against his face. They were circling Deelen when their airfield control called them to say that Kokke's Junkers had returned to Kroonsdijk with a technical fault. Leeuwarden airfield would supply an aircraft for them to test the airborne radar. They must go to Ameland, an island off the northern coast of the Netherlands.

It was Löwenherz who first saw the plane below them. It was only when you saw another aircraft in the sky that you realized how fast you were moving. It was a white biplane, an Arado 66 with a red warning streamer flying from its wingtip. It seemed a long time since Löwenherz had flown his first solo.

'See that, Himmel?' said Löwenherz. 'Below to port?' The little trainer crawled across fields of ripening rye and dark fir woods.

'He's going well, sir, steadier than I was.'

'And steadier than I was too,' agreed Löwenherz. 'Come round behind him; perhaps I can pick him up on the radar.'

'He's very low. I think we'll get ground echoes,' said Himmel, but he put the plane's nose down and came round to creep up behind the pretty machine that was popping along merrily like a toy.

'I'll put the Kurier dead ahead,' said Himmel, using the code word for enemy aircraft. The little white biplane had become an enemy bomber, for in what magical rites and rituals do we not manufacture an enemy from clay or wax. Or even from wood and fabric. The doll that looks like your enemy is called by his name. Stick pins into it and set it alight and believe that those same misfortunes will befall the ones you hate. Pretending it was dark, the two men acted out their game, stalking after the white quarry with all the skill that their years of war had taught them.

Himmel's head twisted and turned like an anxious sparrow's. Veteran fighter pilots survived by scrutinizing every sector of the sky regularly and Himmel never rested his eyes on one thing for more than a moment. Victor Löwenherz, on the other hand, with some effort of willpower concentrated solely upon working the radar. As far as he was concerned the plane was under Himmel's control. His father had always boasted that he could ride better, shoot better and even groom the horses and polish the equipment better than any man under his command. Similarly Oberleutnant Löwenherz was proud of his skill on the radar sets. Of course it was all very simple when your pilot was steering at the machine ahead for a test. In the black of night when the pilot relied solely upon his radar man's guidance it was very different. He adjusted the controls again but the elevation tube was a mess and the range tube was almost as bad. It was closing far too fast. Himmel throttled back and even used some flap, but the old biplane was so slow that Himmel had to break away to port and come round behind him again.

In his mirror Himmel saw Löwenherz crouching close to the three radar screens. He said, 'You're right, Himmel, the ground echo at this height just wipes out the elevation blip. We're probably scaring the fellow half to death.'

And scaring me too, thought Himmel. Here we are, perhaps the two most responsible and experienced pilots on the Staffel, compiling a blueprint for an air disaster: low altitude, speed close to stalling and formating on a strange aircraft. An accident investigation board would pillory both of us should anything happen.

Himmel rolled the little control wheel to close the flaps. He pushed the yellow throttle-knobs and the engine note modulated from baritone to tenor. It was a relief to open up the motors. The Richards were powerful machines but the heavy radar equipment and clumsy aerial array on the nose made them only too easy to stall. He made a wide arc round the little white biplane so that it wouldn't be thrown around by the propwash. Himmel smiled as they passed, for the pilot had been so closely concerned with holding his horizon steady that he noticed the Junkers now for the first time. He stared in amazement at the huge black machine and its secret radar aerials. Then the white biplane dipped as the pupil began looking for his airfield.

The Junkers climbed steeply and continued north, skirting Leeuwarden to the west and continuing out to sea. To starboard lay Terschelling, one of the largest islands in the Frisian chain. The weather was excellent except on the far northeastern horizon where ice crystals of cunimbus clouds reached miles into the air and wore the dark skirt of falling rain. They continued over the Frisian Islands and out into the North Sea. Flecks of cloud made shadows on the water below them and sometimes there were shreds of white stratocumulus large enough to swallow the plane for a moment.

A few miles out they saw a coastal convoy. Keeping well clear of the wrecks that litter this coast, but inside the minefields that protected it, the convoy was making good progress through the calm sea. The Junkers was low enough to see the seamen moving on the decks and some of the old coal burners were making columns of smoke tall enough to reach them. They were a battered collection: half-painted funnels, rusty winches, dribbling scuppers and misplaced hatch-covers. Some of the deck cargoes were only half covered and a deck party was working feverishly on the tarpaulins. Himmel wondered why they bothered. The grimy condition of the coasters was belied by the fresh rain that had glossed their decks and given their hulls the polish of old jackboots. Two freighters had deck cargoes of honey-coloured fresh timber looking good enough to eat. There were Danes and Dutchmen; ancient coastal tankers low in the water, and at the front two French cargo liners making down the coast with machinery and chemicals. They were sailing the routes they had always sailed, some since before the first war. Strange that now they should have German naval destroyers, frigates and UJ boats fussing around their formations and

162

German aircraft protecting them from the determined attacks of RAF planes. Stranger still when some of those RAF planes were manned by Frenchmen, Dutchmen and Danes. Two UJ boats – converted trawlers of about four hundred tons – detached themselves from the convoy and hurried to the rear. Now the convoy began changing course, but kept convoy discipline and good formation. Each wake was scratched crisp and white upon the azure ocean. It was a beautiful sight, enhanced by the red-and-yellow lights that climbed higher than the masts. The light cruiser was covered in winking lights as though every seaman aboard was sending a message to the plane, as indeed he was. Suddenly there was an explosion.

'They're firing at us,' yelled Löwenherz, but his voice was drowned by the fierce bangs of the shells bursting around them. Now Himmel knew what was under the tarpaulins: guns. A near-miss rocked the aeroplane and wrenched the port wing upwards. He didn't correct. He let the aeroplane skid down in a violent sideslip. Each exploding shell hung a new black smudge in the sky but the old smoke did not disappear, it slowly turned brown and the air around them was blotched with smelly smoke like a three-dimensional disease. The plane dropped through the bursting shells until the extra lift of the down-pointing wing, and the Junkers' lateral stability, flattened it into straight and level flight just a hundred feet over the wave-tops.

Now they were within range of the flak ship's 3.7 cm guns and even the multiple 2-cms. The pom-poms added a new descant to the bass rhythms of the heavies. Himmel let down even lower until they were only ten feet above the water. The sea was a different colour close to: a cold steely grey flecked with dirty spumé. Broken timber and refuse pockmarked its heaving surface, and so did the splashes of flak shells.

Himmel moved the throttles forward and, with touches of rudder, danced across the wave-tops low enough for spray to mottle the windscreen. The ship's gunners were aiming off skilfully. Their yellow lights spanned the water to make a fairy bridge between aeroplane and convoy. Soon they were far enough away for the bridge to fall into the water behind them. Himmel reset the trim wheel and pulled the nose up into a gentle climb.

Ahead was Holland. Marking its coastline high in the air there was another 'land' of cumulus conjured up by the sea breeze from a cloudless sky. Himmel kept the Junkers' nose up. By the time they reached the coast they would be above those clouds. How beautiful they were: dark grey undersides, golden rims and fluffy white tops with occasional gaps revealing intense blue sky above.

'Are you all right, sir?' asked Himmel.

'I'm fine. Is the aircraft functioning?'

'It took a couple of knocks but the controls are working.'

'That was damned remarkable flak, Himmel.'

'They get a lot of practice.'

'They get trigger-happy too,' said Löwenherz.

They both laughed too much and the tension was relieved.

'Do you remember that fellow they called Porky?' asked Löwenherz.

'Ostend in May 1941. When Karl Reinhold phoned him at the Alert Hut and told him he'd been awarded the Knight's Cross . . .'

'. . . for low-level attacks against friendly shipping,' hooted Löwenherz. 'Then he phoned me, but luckily you'd warned me that they would play pranks upon the new boys.'

'They always did.'

'You saved me being made a fool of, Christian.'

'You were a good wingman.'

'And now I'm your Staffelkapitän. It's funny how things work out.'

'You should be the Kommodore,' said Christian Himmel.

'For God's sake, Christian, why did you take those documents?'

'Is that why the Herr Oberleutnant came along?' Himmel had moved into the respectful third person.

'Of course it is, Christian.'

'It was a matter of honour, Herr Oberleutnant.'

'Honour?'

'Those documents shame us all.'

'What are you saying? What sort of documents were they?'

'They didn't tell you, eh? Well, perhaps they were ashamed. Even shame is progress.' Himmel reached into his flying overalls and pulled out a bulky document with brown-paper covers. He passed it over his shoulder to Löwenherz. 'Read it first, Herr Oberleutnant. Then you'll see why I have to go through with this.'

It was not an impressive-looking dossier. There was a metal clip holding it together and a Luftwaffe eagle rubber-stamped on to the cover. Along the top it said 'Luftwaffe High Command: Medical Corps: Secret'. It wasn't a printed document. It was a duplicated typescript and in places the words were scarcely legible.

'Go through with what?'

'Please read it, sir.'

At first Löwenherz was inclined to return it to Himmel unopened. He feared he was being drawn into a tacit con-spiracy. For some time he stared out from the cramped little pulpit and watched the green sea creep past. By the time they crossed the coastline the cumulus fractus was below them, but only by an arm's reach. It stretched before them like a blinding white wasteland of ice and snow. The motors held a bass note like an organ pipe and the plane trembled with its power. Oberleutnant Löwenherz made his decision: he undid the metal clip and began reading the stolen medical report.

The convoy resumed the proper course after its evasive zig-zagging. The destroyers and other armed ships hurried up and down, chivvying the merchantmen into line with loud-hailers and signal lamps. At the rear the light cruiser *Held* maintained a dignified straight course like a mother hen. The *Held* had been the 3,500-ton light cruiser *Jan Koppelstok* of the Royal Netherlands Navy until 1940 when she was seized by the Germans and refitted as an anti-aircraft ship. In the forecastle battery, hidden by the steel door, a gunner named Franz Pawlak was smoking a cheroot. His loader cleaned the breech of the 10.5-cm Model 37 with care and affection. They were both wearing the hooded fur-lined winter clothing that had been designed for the Russian Front. It gave them some protection against the piercing North Sea winds that even in the middle of summer chilled professional sailors to the bone.

The gun crews suffered even more, for many of them were ex-Luftwaffe personnel, most of whom found it hard to adapt to the rigours of a seaman's life. Obergefreite Franz Pawlak did. He had joined the Luftwaffe during the Battle of Britain, when cinema newsreels showed pilots relaxing in deckchairs between jousting amid puffy white clouds, yelling 'Spitfire' and smiling in the sunlight as high-ranking leaders shook their hands firmly and garlanded them with medals. Franz had been washed out of pilot school after a very bumpy solo landing. His marks in navigation theory had precluded his transfer to observer school and by the time he arrived as an officer candidate for the flak service he was confused and demoralized. He flunked, and was now an Obergefreite on a flak ship with precious little chance of becoming anything better. Franz loathed all aeroplanes with a terrible and sustained hatred. The previous month he and his gun crew had been credited with an RAF Blenheim bomber shot down. The gun barrel wore a white ring to celebrate it. Franz wanted to add another ring only a little less than he wanted to become a civilian again. His K3, a plump butcher's delivery boy from Königsberg, was flushed with the exertion of loading 15-kg shells on to the awkward, steeply inclined loading-tray. He was arguing with Franz. 'You can't paint a white ring on the barrel until the destruction of the plane is confirmed. That's the captain's orders.'

'You saw it come down,' said Franz. 'Now am I the best gunner in the whole damn convoy?'

'It may have dived to sea level to avoid the gunfire, Admiral.' Both his friends and his enemies called Franz Pawlak 'Admiral'.

'Get the white paint. We shot it down, I tell you.'

'I still say it might have been one of ours.'

'What are you talking about, Klaus, every gun in the convoy was firing,' said Franz.

'They didn't start until you did,' said Klaus.

'Exactly. When I started, old glass-nose gave the order.'

'I'm still frightened it might have been one of ours. It looked very like a Junkers 88 and it flew south to escape.'

'Beaufighter. A Bristol Beaufighter. Anyway, it was an aeroplane,' said Franz. 'Aeroplanes drop bombs and any aeroplane that comes within range of this contraption gets shot at. Now will you get the white paint?'

'Whatever you say, Admiral. We'll be the only gun on the *Held* with two victory rings, providing the old man doesn't make us paint it out again.'

'I tell you something, Dikke,' said Franz, prodding his friend in the belly. 'We're averaging eight and a half knots and if that damned Danish bucket doesn't have any more steering-gear trouble we'll be sailing past the Hook of Holland by midnight. That's the place for aeroplanes; the RAF are over there nearly every night lately.' He stroked the barrel of the big gun. 'By tomorrow morning, Heini, we might have three rings on our *Würstchen*. Now wouldn't that be something to write to your cousin Sylvia about?'

Klaus Munte looked at his friend and smiled, but if there was anything he hated more than to be called 'fatty' it was to be called Heini. 'By tonight the war might be over,' said Munte.

'It won't be over for me,' said Pawlak.

In this, as in so much of his plausible patter, he was wrong.

What Löwenherz had before him was one of the most bizarre, macabre and horrifying documents produced by a civilized society.

'Freezing Experiments with Human Beings' was a thirty-two-page report drawn up by Dr Sigmund Rascher of the Luftwaffe Medical Corps, helped by a professor of medicine at the University of Kiel. The experiments took place at Dachau concentration camp and consisted of putting naked prisoners into ice-water or leaving them out in the snow until they froze to death. Their temperatures were taken from time to time and recorded by the doctors. After death there was an autopsy.

Dr Sigmund Rascher had moved the Luftwaffe's decompression chamber from Munich to Dachau concentration camp a few kilometres down the road. Two hundred prisoners were put into this chamber and each was depressurized until his body exploded. The report on this series of experiments was sent to the Medical Inspector of the Luftwaffe in the summer of 1942.

The third and final part of the stolen file was a report of Dr Rascher's 'warming experiments'. These were even more perverted. Male prisoners were frozen almost to death in ice-water and then placed in a bed between two naked women. (The women were prisoners from Ravensbrück concentration camp.) Dr Rascher noted in great detail the sexual reactions of the half-dead men and to what extent these improved their chance of survival. He reported in a paper dated February 1943 and marked Secret.

It stabbed Löwenherz to the heart of his belief. Of course he had misgivings; few men didn't. Baron Löwenherz, his father, had not disbelieved the rumours; he called them symptoms of unrest. The Nazi Party was a bridge to sanity, a stage between the 1918 breakdown on the home front and

168

the return to a natural state of things where a strong German officer corps held Germany's honour in trust. For the time being the nation was in the hands of these Bavarians and among them there were some villainous rascals, but better this sort of revolutionary than the Bolshevik variety, who was prepared to butcher families because their hands were clean or their names patrician. Inventive, creative men are inclined to be ruthless, the baron had told him. We must work with these Nazi *condottieri*, just as Leonardo had to work with Machiavelli, with Cesare Borgia and with his Count Sforza; just as three centuries later the Industrial Revolution pushed aside philosophers and humanitarians so that single-minded despots ruled Europe. They put children up chimneys and women down mines, they bullied, cheated, bribed and literally worked their employees to death. They caused misery and strife but, as we now know, the Industrial Revolution put Europe a century ahead of the rest of the world.

Now the Nazis are transforming Germany with a similar single-minded ruthlessness. Of course we can't approve of the sort of things that occur, these camps that people speak of in whispers, the witch-hunts for Jews and Communists, the 'gunboat diplomacy' that Hitler used to annex Austria and then Czechoslovakia. These things are bad things, but they are all things that Britain did, or would have done if necessary, to achieve its position as a world power. If Hitler cheats he cheats for Germany, if he steals he steals for Germany, if he kills then this he does for Germany too. If he needs our help then the officer corps must give it, generously and unstintingly.

All these things that his father had told him Löwenherz explained to Christian Himmel, but Christian remained unconvinced.

'But what would you achieve if you gave these unpleasant documents to the British? Would you like their propaganda people to reveal such things to the world?'

'I? Give them to the British?' said Himmel. 'Is that what they told you?'

'Then what do you want with the papers?'

'It's very simple,' said Himmel. 'These things are being done in our name, Herr Oberleutnant. Oh, it sounds very grand when you say it's for Germany, but these things are being done on behalf of us aviators. The research will be used to help us survive should we force-land in the ocean or the Arctic. But, Herr Oberleutnant, do you know a flyer who wouldn't sooner die than have these disgusting experiments done to prisoners?'

'None,' agreed Löwenherz. 'But that's because we should ask them the question while they are warm and dry and on the ground, perhaps sitting back in the Mess with a cognac in their hand. Ask a flyer that question a few moments after he has crashed in the cold sea and perhaps he'll decide differently.'

'I won't.'

'No. Because you are an idealist, Christian. I remember the time when you spoke of the Nazis as though they were saviours of our land.' Exactly, in fact, as the old baron had spoken of them. 'Now you're disillusioned,' continued Löwenherz. 'You're bitter and resentful of your own ingenuous feelings. You're angry because the Nazis have never delivered something they didn't promise.'

'Of course I am,' said Himmel, 'but that doesn't mean I was right then, nor that I am wrong now.'

'It means that you should consider matters at greater length and not rush headlong into danger.'

'No, with respect, Herr Oberleutnant, no. We have all delayed too long. While the victories arrived on schedule we all put our conscience in pawn to success. It's only now, when the future looks less rosy, that we are beginning to wonder if the "new order" has been built upon sand.'

'But the documents, Himmel. What do you want with them?'

'I made twenty-three photographic copies of the documents. Each copy was sent by normal mail to a Luftwaffe officer. I considered the list for a long time, Herr Oberleutnant. You are number twenty-three; that is your copy. The original has been posted to the Medical Inspectorate of the Luftwaffe in Berlin.'

There was silence. A tuft of cloud was decapitated by the black wing. Other larger tufts raced after it. Then Löwenherz said, 'It doesn't make it legal because you sent it only to Luftwaffe officers. It was a highly secret document.'

'It's hardly less secret now that twenty-three Luftwaffe officers have a copy. But from now on they can't pretend they don't know of these things. They must protest. They must raise their voices. From now on they can never say they have not heard of concentration camps . . .'

'What do you know of concentration camps, Christian?'

'I know, sir, that at least three airmen at Kroonsdijk have spent time in such places for small political offences. Even if we have three times the average, that still leaves one man on every Luftwaffe airfield who has been in such a place. How much longer can the whole nation pretend that they don't know what we are doing in Europe, from Bordeaux to Leningrad: prisoners tortured, civilians killed, hostages executed? Now this is something that puts the honour of the Luftwaffe in jeopardy. Reichsmarschall Göring will have received one of these copies. He will understand what must be done.' A large cloud-fragment swallowed the aeroplane and disgorged it.

'They will arrest you, Christian,' said Löwenherz. 'Perhaps as soon as tomorrow.'

'Yes,' said Himmel. 'Tomorrow I shall be arrested. But tomorrow I shall not be agonizing with my conscience, nor shall I be making excuses for the Nazis, nor shall I be fighting so that even more foreign prisoners can be experimented upon in concentration camps by insane doctors wearing the same uniform that I am wearing.'

'Stop talking, Himmel. I must have time to think.' The cloud-top was higher inland and suddenly the Junkers was totally enveloped in it. Now that it was pressing against the window it was no longer soft, dry, white, sun-tipped and inviting. It was grey, wet, cold and threatening. They could see nothing. The cloud gave a curious unnatural constant light to the cabin, and the two men sat very still, brightly lit and shadowless, like specimens on a microscope slide.

CHAPTER TWELVE

When August Bach emerged from the gloomy chill of the air-conditioned Divisional Fighter Control bunker it was 17.15 hrs CET. The day had ripened into one of those mellow summer afternoons when the air is warm and sweet like soft toffee and anyone with an ounce of sense is reclining in the grass smelling the honeysuckle and wild strawberries, half listening to the insects, and watching blues and brimstones fluttering fast enough to avoid the swallows above them that glide and wheel and wait and wait.

Both Max and August dozed contentedly, hypnotized by the sunlit countryside that moved past like a swinging watch. The dark-blue Luftwaffe Citroen made good speed down the main road from Arnhem past Utrecht all the way to the small town of Tempel, where it turned off north through Leiden, heading towards The Hague where General Christiansen, First World War ace fighter pilot, was now Military Governor of the Netherlands.

They were beyond Leiden before Max awoke from his reverie. He stirred and lit cigars for both of them.

'You were on the East Front last year, August. Perhaps now that the sun shines on the great grasslands of the Ukraine you wish you were back there: birch forests, long summer evenings, buxom country girls, balalaikas, caviar, medals arriving with the mail.'

'That's what it says in the recruiting pamphlets. All I

remember is endless snow, my eyelashes iced over and on Christmas morning one of the sentries frozen alive so that we had to hack his rifle out of his hand with an axe.'

'So that's how you all got *Eisbeinorden*?' said Max.

'That's how we all got *aufs Eis geführt*,' said August. It meant 'led up the garden'. Max looked anxiously at his driver but he seemed not to have heard.

'Were you ever stationed with your son?'

'For a month. Near Lake Ilmen in March of last year. His battalion was pulled out of the line after their casualties had reached sixty per cent during the winter offensive. For a month they were on communication assignment not two miles from the airfield where I had my radar installation.'

'That was good.'

'He is not commissioned yet, so I couldn't take him to our Mess. It was in any case only a grain store with a stove and some old chairs.'

'You must have had plenty to talk about.'

'Staying warm. That's all anyone talks about in a Russian winter. My Luftwaffe unit was still wearing its summer uniforms. Peter's infantry regiment had some overcoats they had taken off Russian backs and some odds and ends of furs and lined boots that Goebbels had persuaded German civilians to part with. Peter bribed his quartermaster to let me have some coats and hats. In return I showed him how three skilled men, under cover of darkness, could steal two dozen loaves from a mobile bakery unit. It makes a man very proud to exchange such knowledge with his son.'

'For a month you were together?'

'It was the first day of the spring thaw when they left: March 15th. There was a watery sun that noon and for an hour there was the slightest of breaks in the intense cold. I went down to the railhead to say goodbye. His unit had found a piano factory almost intact. When they fired bullets into the lines of pianos there were strange resonant trills and jangling overtones. Hand grenades made a demented musical scream. Peter said it was the best fun he'd had since the attack on Vyasma the previous October.'

'Are you frightened for the boy, August?'

'My God, Max, I am.'

'Could you not arrange a posting? After all, he has served on the Russian Front for . . . what, eighteen months?'

'Twenty-one months. He'd never forgive me, Max. How would he feel? How would any of us feel?'

'Not doing our duty, you mean? I'd feel damn good, August. What would you do if you were posted back there? Would you do your utmost to avoid it?'

'Who knows, Max?'

'Seriously, August.'

'For God's sake, Max! Do you think I've never thought about it? Do you know what it's like to find yourself wishing your own son would have his leg shot off, just so he will survive?'

'I'm sorry, August.'

'Forget it, Max. It's not good to think of these things in advance. In war all things are possible and nothing inevitable.'

'Who said that?'

'I said it,' said August. 'There is but a second of time, a stroke of a pen, a misinterpreted look, a fingered trigger . . . between us and a Knight's Cross, a court-martial, sainthood or eternal damnation.'

'Do you hear from your son?'

'Every few weeks.'

'And he hates the war as you hate it?'

'Max, my friend, I have to tell you he likes it. We have given our world to our children. Can we be surprised that these children are destructive? Every fit, aggressive youngster who tries hard can get himself a bomber or a U-boat or an artillery battery and wreak havoc upon the world that it's taken us old men so long to put together. Nineteen-year-old children creep up on a 20,000-ton merchant ship, press a button, and watch it die, writhing like a wingless fly. They set fire to great cities and turn our society upside down in return for bits of coloured ribbon. Where have we failed, Max? What manner of children will they breed, and what manner of world will they shape? We ask them to count their victims like head-hunters, marking each death with a notch, a painted tally or a new promotion. What will they unleash upon us, Max?'

'Dare I say you are a hypocrite, August, my friend? You pronounce judgement upon the men who fight, you call our heroes murderers, but you do not disdain the respect and admiration due to a fighter-pilot expert. And at your throat you wear your trinket, your tally is well known and gains for you respect from soldier and civilian alike. Oh no, August, you want to eat your cake and throw it into the faces of lesser men like me.'

'You don't understand.'

'Then explain.'

'You are confusing heroism with morality. A man can be brave and yet do dishonourable things. His individual act might be honourable and yet the result dishonourable.'

'Give me an example, August.'

'The RAF bomber crews. They are brave men, the risks they run are high and yet they kill women and children.'

'You go too far, August. They are cowardly monsters. They drop their bombs and take to their heels in the darkness leaving people to burn.'

'So do our U-boat crews who torpedo a merchant ship and steal away in the night leaving people to drown. Yet both are brave.'

'Talk, talk, talk, August. You know as well as I do that we are all victims of circumstance. When the order comes we shall press the trigger, merely because the individual cannot challenge a system. Why try? As you said earlier, whether a man is commanding a U-boat, allocating civilian fuel supplies or even flying an RAF bomber is largely a matter of chance.'

'Perhaps you are right, Max. Perhaps I have too much time to think.'

He watched the people on the crowded pavements of The Hague. For every happy bemedalled young officer there were a hundred men and women who looked tired and dejected.

'Ah, August, my friend. Why so sad? This was but a friendly fight, such as two old friends might have over a cigar.' The car turned into the Plein and the Luftwaffe sentry saluted the car without caring if it was empty or full.

'Go carefully with me, Max. A man in love is fragile.'

Max smiled. 'But it's a good cigar, eh, August?'

'Magnificent.'

'Then take the box. A man in love never knows when he might need a box of cigars.' August tried to refuse them but Max closed his hands around August's and pressed the big box of cigars on to him. 'Major Georg Tuchel will be doing this run for the time being. Phone him here any weekday morning if you want a ride. I have already spoken with him, there'll be no difficulty.' Max turned to the driver. 'Take the Oberleutnant to radar station Ermine. I'll log you for another two hours and see you in the morning at the usual time.'

The driver closed the car door and saluted Oberst Max Sepp. Max stayed on the steps and waved to August as the car departed.

For nearly an hour the driver drove silently, but as they entered the prohibited zone August sensed that he had something to say. He offered him a cigar but he preferred a cigarette. Here near the coast he was driving more slowly. It was a strange, deserted place. Occasionally they passed a farm cart with its heavy-footed Zeeland horses, or a bicycle with homemade wooden tyres slapping the cobbles.

When the last village had vanished behind them the narrow concrete road became a sandy track and suddenly the North Sea appeared through the mist. The scrubby grass-topped dunes are twenty or thirty feet high and beyond them is only a table-flat beach of fine sand and then the sea. From it had come the dense white mist that clings like icy steam and reduces visibility to fifty feet. The sentries were wearing their overcoats and they walked stiffly around the radar station which, like this whole coastline, was a forest of barbed wire and steel stakes.

The bushes and wire-like grass had been bent double by the wind from the sea. In the lee of the dunes the air was still and the white mist scarcely moved, but the bushes were still deformed and bowed. The only creatures happy to be there were the birds which skimmed low over the bunkers and could breed protected by barbed wire. Even the bird-watchers couldn't get near them now and five hundred square miles of Northern Europe's coast had become a vast nature reserve guarded by the Wehrmacht.

The Citroen's tyres slid in the soft sand, but the driver insisted upon driving Oberleutnant Bach right to the very door of his quarters. He always did. He opened the door for August and saluted him formally.

'Thank you,' said August. 'See my Feldwebel and he will fix you up with some eggs.' The boy nodded. It was all exactly as it always was, except for one thing. 'It's about the Herr Oberst,' said the driver nervously.

'What about him?' said August.

'I think the Oberleutnant would like to know that the Herr Oberst has been ordered to join an infantry regiment on the Russian Front: Orel. Many officers have. They go on Thursday. We shall miss the Herr Oberst.'

'So shall I,' said August. 'Thank you.'

The driver saluted again and walked across to get his eggs.

CHAPTER THIRTEEN

'It upset me, Victor, I can tell you that. Couldn't eat a bite of lunch.' The Medical Officer shook his head in brief silent anguish. 'I've seen it before, Victor. Exhibitionism.'

'What do you mean?' asked Löwenherz.

'That surprises you, does it?' Hans Furth, Kroondijk's Medical Officer, pointed to a cupboard which contained his bottle of brandy and glasses but Löwenherz declined. 'With all you fit young men a doctor doesn't have much of a chance to show his mettle. My job has become that of a psychiatrist.'

'Psychiatry? I thought you disdained that Jewish science, Hans.'

Hans smiled. 'Go back as far as Henry the Navigator and you'll find that navigation is a Jewish science, but that doesn't mean we can ignore it.'

'If you go back far enough, you'll probably discover that gravity is a Jewish science,' said Löwenherz.

'That's in order. It's the Luftwaffe's job to ignore gravity.' Hans chuckled.

'Himmel, you said, was an exhibitionist,' said Löwenherz.

'Life is a game for me, Victor. If you sat behind this desk you'd watch the whole panorama of human life pass: tragedy, humour, honour, disgrace, death and injury.'

'And you reported your suspicions to the SIPO?' persisted Löwenherz.

'Mustn't get on the wrong side of the law, Victor.'

'But only last week you said you'd never voted for the Nazis and wished Austria had never come under Nazi control.'

Hans Furth leaned well back in his swivel chair. A plump man in his middle thirties, he was Austrian by birth, doctor by training and airman by conscription. He affected the smart leather zip-front jacket that the flyers liked and many of their youthful mannerisms. His clothes were clean and well pressed and his thick black hair was freshly washed and combed straight back. His face was ruddy, his eyes blue, and his small, unnaturally red, girlish mouth was always ready to talk and smile. He smoked his cigar carefully without spilling the ash anywhere except into the ashtray and he frequently touched his face, running a fingertip along his lips or round his eyes to be sure that everything was in its rightful place. 'You're trying to catch me out, Löwenherz Victor,' he smiled. It was a Viennese affectation to invert the names like that and today Löwenherz found it an irritating one.

Furth levelled his cigar like a javelin between finger and thumb. 'I'm a working-class lad, you're an aristocrat. Our sort gave the Nazis little or no support in the old days, Victor. Their strength came from the middle-class clerks and unemployed ex-officers: fertile ground, Victor.'

'I'm interested in this business with Himmel,' said Löwenherz, making one more effort to get the conversation back on his intended lines.

'Damned interesting case,' agreed Hans Furth. 'I've been through his medical dossier again this morning and I think I've solved the question to some extent.' He leaned back like a woman with uncomfortable stays and gave a matronly tug to the bottom of his short jacket.

'How?' asked Löwenherz.

Furth leaned forward and lowered his voice. 'I can't prove it, but it's my guess that he's not racially pure. I was reading in the paper the other day that more Jews commit thefts than Aryans do, by a considerable margin.'

'That sounds very unscientific,' sighed Löwenherz.

The doctor smiled at the window as if he shared a secret with the furnishings. 'My dear Baron, you are hardly in a position to deny the effects of breeding. It took a thousand years of breeding to make you what you are. The Jews . . .'

'Everyone in the world has a thousand years of breeding behind them,' said Löwenherz irritably. 'Perhaps these days Jews have more motive for theft than do Aryans.'

'This is my theory,' continued Hans Furth. 'We Germans have been bred as a systematic nation and this fellow Hitler understands us . . .'

We Germans, thought Löwenherz, as he listened to the doctor's sing-song Viennese accent, nibbling the German language like *Sachertorte* and showing his teeth at every bite.

'. . . Revolutionize a systematic nation by means of political theory and you have an instrument. Harness the military caste to that instrument and you have a weapon. Allow the politicals to have their own armed forces – the Waffen SS – and create a climate in which they and the military are in constant and dynamic struggle and then your weapon will conquer the world.'

'There's still a large piece of the world unconquered,' said Löwenherz.

'I know,' said Furth, smiling and nodding. 'It's fascinating to see what will happen.'

'Like a game of bridge,' said Löwenherz.

'Better,' said Furth. 'Bridge was never half as exciting. My training as a doctor and as an officer has given me a unique chance to become an expert on the German psychology. Do you know, I can tell what sort of symptoms a man will have according to the rank he holds. For instance, no German NCO would dare to come in here complaining of indigestion, just as few officers come to me with foot ailments. Funny folk, we Germans, eh?'

Yes, thought Löwenherz, and if the Russians get here then this plausible joker will be occupying some comfortable seat in their military administration amusing the occupying power's officers with these same cynical observations on German character and weakness. And they will be laughing and throwing him an extra box of cigarettes and saying, gay fellows these Austrians.

'I don't like any sort of unpleasantness, Victor. All I want is to be left alone.'

'And people like Himmel try to involve you?'

'Don't misunderstand me, I like this fellow Himmel. But this isn't an important enough matter for you or me to get involved with. He's an exhibitionist, Victor. Most of the people who get into trouble are exhibitionists.'

Löwenherz could think of no response. He looked at Furth, who ran his little finger nervously along his eyebrow.

'I didn't invent the world or any social system in it,' said the doctor. His smile endorsed this disclaimer. 'Man is a crafty animal and a vicious one. You'll never alter that, Victor. Don't tell me that your ancestors didn't fight, cheat and kill to win and hold your family estates.'

'I must get along, Hans.'

'I've offended you.'

'No,' said Löwenherz. 'I'm sure you never offend anyone.'

Löwenherz didn't bring up the matter of Himmel again. He knew that he would merely be treated to glib and elementary generalizations.

'Speaking as your medical adviser,' said Furth, 'you could do with a couple of days' rest. I can arrange for guns and accommodation and we'll shoot wild pig. This business has upset me too, I can tell you. I was fond of young Himmel. The Mess will buy the meat for sausages. Take you out of yourself, Victor. What do you say?'

Löwenherz laughed, and this puzzled the doctor. 'I've arranged all the shooting I can handle at present, Herr Doktor,' he said. 'Thanks all the same.' He got to his feet. Perhaps there was a more direct way to handle this business.

* * *

The Alert Hut was littered: chairs empty, newspapers abandoned, amendments to operational orders unread, fur-lined jackets unneeded in the warm afternoon sun. By now Löwenherz had had a chance to think about the dossier. How many influential Luftwaffe officers would be needed to make a protest legal, or at least difficult to punish? The Medical Officer was obviously scared stiff by Blessing and Starkhof, but how many protests had already been made about the experiments? To what extent was opinion already being rallied? Perhaps the document was in the doctor's office because the Luftwaffe Medical Inspectorate were circulating it for comment.

Starkhof could answer all these questions but Löwenherz was determined to give no information in return. The phone was best; after all one could always hang up if the fellow became objectionable.

Even from the first moment that he lifted the telephone he was nervous. His father would have known how to handle this situation but Victor didn't. On the other hand, his father would not have handled it; he would have left it very much alone.

'Herr Doktor Starkhof, please,' he told the operator. There was a short pause. 'Hello, von Löwenherz,' said the old man. He always used the 'von'. He knew that Löwenherz would think it uncouth but that amused him. 'I thought you might give me a call.'

It was startling that Starkhof had guessed who was calling, and Löwenherz needed a moment or two to collect his wits.

'It's about the stolen dossier, of course,' said Löwenherz.

'Sent you one through the post, has he? Dear me, can't think why our people failed to intercept that. Well, you make fifteen. Any idea how many others he sent?'

'No.'

'Pity. Any letter?' said the old man.

'No.'

'No matter.'

'Are you going to come here and collect it?'

'Nervous, eh? Well, that's all right, Baron. Hold on to it until tomorrow. There's no hurry. I have fourteen copies here on my desk.'

'There's nowhere really secure that I can lock it, unless I give it to the Kommandeur to lock in the safe.'

'No, no, my boy, don't worry about it. There were nearly three hundred copies of that report circulated throughout the medical services. In Nuremberg there was a conference of ninety-five scientists discussing the report. Each of them had a copy and at least four were mislaid, so there's no need for you to get too excited about that one copy.'

'So it's been circulated? Did anyone else . . . I mean was there? . . .'

An aeroplane flew low overhead rattling the windows; Löwenherz was glad of a chance to stop speaking.

Starkhof said, 'Ah, the baron has been speaking with young Himmel, I can tell. No, of course there was no reaction, except that Doktor Rascher was sent Göring's thanks on behalf of the Luftwaffe. He also received a letter of thanks from the Medical Inspector of the Luftwaffe and many congratulations from his medical colleagues.'

Löwenherz felt lonely, degraded and sick as his hopes drained away. Was this the way Himmel had felt when talking with him, in the cool crisp clean air? If so, Himmel's resolution had not faltered. 'Did you read the dossier, Herr Doktor?'

'I did, von Löwenherz. I did.'

'And? . . .'

'What do you want me to say, von Löwenherz? If you use your brains for one moment, you will realize that I can provoke you with any treasonable or scurrilous statement that I care to invent. Afterwards I should merely plead that I did it in my line of duty. Now stop being so foolish. Go back to your aeroplanes and leave this business to me.'

184

'You are not interested in my opinions?'

'Not in the slightest, my boy. If you know nothing important, then I shall be wasting my time. If you know something important, I prefer to hear it tomorrow, when the dossier has been officially passed to my department. A dramatic break-through today would simply mean promotion for our friend Blessing. While wishing him all the good luck in the world, I am not going to work to secure a promotion for him. Tell me tomorrow.'

'You are returning tomorrow? To arrest Himmel?'

'Correct. It will be very quiet and discreet. My paperwork will be in order and by tomorrow morning you and your friend Kokke will have had time to reconsider your attitude. You'll see the wisdom of cooperating with the law.'

'What will Himmel get?'

'Punishment? Well, that depends. If he recants, pleads guilty, cooperates with us in respect of helpers, instigators and fellow plotters or leads us on to a whole network of conspirators, then he will get ten or fifteen years.'

'You don't believe it was a conspiracy?'

'No, I don't. But if he wants to persuade me, I'll listen. He has some Dutch civilian friends in Kroonsdijk that I'm not entirely happy about. They have more than enough butter and schnapps down there in Kroonsdijk village. Some of it is filtering back to your air base. Himmel could provide me with the chance I need to open up a big black-market racket.'

Löwenherz found the Abwehr man's frankness disconcerting.

'What if these documents bring Himmel support from influential Luftwaffe officers?'

'We live in a society where influence can be a trump card,' said old Starkhof cagily. 'But I'd wager that they'd face execution along with Himmel.' Drily he added, 'Although I've heard of cases where suicide cheated the law of a high-ranking victim.'

185

By now Löwenherz's carefully prepared arguments had gone dry in his mouth. He felt a strong distaste for this cynical old man who had confidence enough to say things that other men only whispered.

'You seem very sure of that?'

'My boy, this is what I do for a living. I am not as ambitious as you; I don't want to reform the law or judge its transgressors. I merely bring law-breakers to justice. If tomorrow your friend Himmel is making the laws and my colleague Blessing breaking them, then I will deliver him to justice with the same calm objectivity.' There was a trace of self-mockery in old Starkhof's voice.

'Smug complacency, you mean,' said Löwenherz.

'My very sentiments,' said Starkhof. 'I so wish I had the Herr Oberleutnant's fine vocabulary.'

'Good day to you, Feldwebel Herr Doktor.'

'Good day, my dear Baron.'

CHAPTER FOURTEEN

The teleprinters in the Operations Block had been clattering since lunchtime. The message from HQ Bomber Command had gone to the Group HQs and from there the messages reached the airfields including Warley Fen.

CONFIRMING TELEPHONED ORDERS FOLLOWING ARE
EXECUTIVE ORDERS FOR THE NIGHT OF JUNE 31ST, 1943

There followed a gibberish of abbreviations and code words that defined the nature of the attack. Flare colours, air and ground marking, cascade heights and times, turning-points, assembly areas, bombing heights and times, bomb-loads and Met forecasts giving the predicted winds at the bombing heights and conditions at base airfields at the time of return.

Hurriedly the technical officers began to build the plan into lectures and diagrams that would constitute the after-noon briefing. Flight Lieutenant Giles, the Bombing Leader; Flight Lieutenant Ludlow, the Navigation Leader; and John Munro, the Squadron commander, conferred. The Meteoro-logical expert expressed the doubts that forecasters always have about other men's predictions.

The executive orders were as yet communicated only to those who had to know. As an added security precaution, the guardroom had been told to close the main gate and forbid personnel to leave the airfield except with the written permission of the Station Adjutant. In spite of the gaping holes in the perimeter fence the embargo was observed by everyone – partly because there was so much work to do that no one could find an opportunity to get away for a lunchtime beer in the Bell.

Deprived of the noise and movement of the airmen, the village became as quiet as the airfield was busy. When an attack was being prepared even the public bar of the Bell maintained a decorous sobriety.

Cynthia Radlett, the barmaid, had wiped the tables, rinsed and polished the glasses, fetched more bottled stout from the cellar and swept the floor. She looked enviously at the four farmers who had been drinking and gossiping ever since lunchtime. Now it was almost opening time again. Those who complained of women chattering could never have listened to farmers' talk. It was a good thing that the village policeman was busy out on the green facing Mr Wate's spin bowling, or he'd be complaining about them drinking after closing time. At last one of the men came to the bottom of his glass. He put it down with a sigh and wiped his lips.

'Beans I told him, put in beans. Anything else and the wire-worm will eat them.' The three men nodded and stole a glance at Ben Thorpe.

Old Ben's voice was rasping and slow. 'Ten Acre was always full of wireworm.'

'Are you sure you don't want to walk up to Parson's Meadow, Ben?'

'Nah,' said the old man and blew his nose loudly. They could not tell how upset he was, for an old man's eyes are always wet.

'After the war you'll never know the difference.'

'Nah,' snorted Ben. 'It's the finest piece of grazing for a hundred mile. My dad weeded it and dunged it himself for nigh on fifty years and his dad afore.' The old man was

188

crying now, there could be no doubt of it. 'I shan't watch them plough her up and sow their damned 'taters there. I'll not live to see her back to grazing again.'

'Weorf' is the old English word for draught animal. Warley meant a place where such animals could graze. Now the War Agricultural Committees had given grazing to the plough and one of the few patches of grassland left was the lower end of Trimmer's Meadow that the village used as its cricket field. Today it was only a knockabout match, but towards opening time a small crowd of airmen and villagers gathered outside the Bell. They applauded the batsmen, advised the bowlers and dozed in the afternoon sun.

No previous cricket season could equal this one: Royal Engineers Norwich Depot versus RAF Warley, A Flight versus the village; teams from all over East Anglia came to play cricket on the green, shove-ha'penny and darts in the public bar and drink the Bell's warm bitter. The cricket pitch was smooth and flat, although since it was slightly below sea level it was muddy in wet weather. The RAF had sent carpenters to rebuild the old scoreboard and the Station artist – LAC Gilbert – had supervised its repainting. Sammy Thatcher's shed had been moved and rebuilt. Although it could only hold one team at a time, there were no smiles when it was referred to as the pavilion.

Today Bill Beacham, village policeman and domino champion, was the last man batting for the scratch team the village had put up. He hadn't scored for nearly a quarter of an hour but none of Mr Wate's spinners daunted him and he stonewalled with grim determination. The war had brought Police Constable Beacham promotion to sergeant and when the RAF moved in he had been officially told to 'cooperate with the RAF police in matters affecting Service discipline and national security'. There was even talk of him having a police constable to help him. 'Help him home from here on a Saturday night,' said Cynthia, and everyone laughed because like most good jokes it wasn't a joke at all.

The Group Captain proudly boasted of an unbroken record of friendship between his airmen and the people of the village. Like most official thinking, the Group Captain's was purely negative. He meant that there were no instances on paper of physical, social or legal hostilities. On the other hand there was no great affection either. When a villager announced the arrival of a lorryful of airmen outside the Bell with the remark, 'Here come the Wehrmacht,' this too was a joke that wasn't a joke.

There was still another half-hour before the Bell was officially open, but Cynthia took a pint of bitter outside to where Sam Thatcher was working at the base of the ancient oak tree that marked the boundary line.

'How is it going?' asked Cynthia.

Sam took the head off his pint before answering. 'Same as that tree behind Percy's house. It's rotten inside.'

'What a shame.' She wiped her wet hands on her apron.

'It's getting old, Cynthia. It's probably stood here for a hundred and fifty years or more.' Sam had been drilling deep into the tree and pushing bonemeal mixtures into it to feed the wood. He put down his glass and finished plugging up a hole.

'Will that save it?'

'It will give her another fifty years, Cynthia.'

'You'd better do my guv'nor after you've finished this tree.'

'Now, now,' said Sam Thatcher, 'don't start.' He had no wish to be drawn into the feud between Cynthia and her employer. He looked across the pitch to where Police Sergeant Beacham was still blocking the frantic bowling, and beyond him to the airfield. 'They're off again tonight.'

'Looks like.'

'And that old wind's going to change,' said Sam.

'Rain?'

'No, not yet awhile, or my feet would tell me. But during the night that wind will swing round and they'll be coming in right over our heads just about the time I'm turning over.'

'Don't say that, Mr Thatcher. I can't get back to sleep when they wake me.'

There was a flutter of applause as Bill Beacham was clean bowled.

'What I don't understand', said Cynthia Radlett, 'is what they do all day. I mean, they don't go raiding until after we close at night. I know they have to test their aeroplanes in the morning but what do they do there all day?'

'They have to work out their navigation and decide where to drop their bombs. They do a lot of talking up there at the aerodrome.'

'Well, I don't know,' said Cynthia Radlett, 'but it's terrible for our business when they go off raiding.' It was five-thirty. She walked back to the Bell and started serving drinks.

The most literary and sophisticated officer at Warley Fen was, by common consent, Flying Officer Longfellow. He was, appropriately enough, the Intelligence Officer. A tall blue-eyed man of thirty-eight, in his youth he had been an amateur boxer of some repute at Cambridge where he studied classics. After Cambridge he had worked on a small newspaper in the Midlands and graduated from that to a national daily. He had never excelled at news-gathering but had always been able to provide, at short notice, a couple of thousand words on the College of Cardinals (at the death of a Pope), helium (airship disaster), or surrealism (record price at Sotheby's). Nor was Longfellow too proud to cover a wedding or review a film. In 1936 he left the newspaper's full-time staff and went to live in Cornwall. He became the science correspondent. A few thousand words a month earned enough money to keep himself, his young wife and two kids in a small cottage with a view of the sea while he laboured on a book. It was a murder mystery, set in a

Cornish tin mine, and although he modestly referred to it as a whodunit he had inserted the description 'a psychological study in depth of the mind of the criminally insane' into the publisher's blurb. The *Scotsman* found it promising, *The Observer* thought it had grip, but a left-wing weekly said that 'hand-made, and thus readily identified, cigarette ends have become a careless vice among the sort of villains who people this year's mediocre detective fiction'. He was stuck halfway through a sequel about a carefully organized bank robbery when the war began. Longfellow volunteered.

An Intelligence Officer's special responsibility was the Briefing Room. At Warley Fen it was a large wooden hut that could seat one hundred and fifty aircrew on benches. There was a stage at one end and behind it a map of Europe that stretched the width of the hut. Covering the map there was a red curtain that swept aside at the pull of a string. It had become usual for the Station commander to pull the string.

Along each side of the hut there were windows. They should have been shuttered at briefing time but lately the weather had been so fine and warm that they'd been left open. There were the usual 'Careless talk costs lives' posters and a notice board with Intelligence memos fastened to it with bright red pins. Specially arranged by Flying Officer Longfellow were the 'This is your enemy' displays: photos and three-view drawings of Bf110 and Junkers 88 night fighters as well as some speculative Air Ministry diagrams of what the newer German fighter planes might look like.

From the ceiling hung models of both enemy and Allied aircraft, each one clearly marked with its designation and wing span. Then there was the Accident Board with photos of aeroplanes drunkenly askew after sliding off the runway or with a prop blade eating up a tailplane after a taxiing collision. At one side of the stage there was the easel standing ready for the Met Department's Cloud Board (icing cloud in red, non-icing cloud in blue, all stacked to show altitudes).

On the other side of the stage, reaching to the ceiling, there was the Photo Ladder. This didn't denote a proficiency in photography but showed the accuracy of the bombing, bomb explosions being plotted from the flashlight photo that each bomber took as its bomb-load landed. Lambert's crew were in the top quarter of the ladder but Flight Lieutenant Sweet's crew were well down.

Longfellow was proud of this Briefing Room upon which he and his clerks had spent so much time and energy. It embodied all the freshness and appeal of a commercial display or a newspaper layout. It was kept up to date every day and on the notice board there were a world map and a bulletin with a first-class summary of the war on all fronts, as well as a note on yellow paper in which Longfellow attempted to predict the strategic aspirations of the fighting powers. This supposition was clearly headed 'Intelligence Guesswork'. Often during the day aircrew would wander into the Briefing Room, looking at the new displays or leafing through newspapers or copies of *Flight, Aeroplane Spotter, Tee Em* or one of the other technical magazines. Longfellow often claimed, 'There's not another Briefing Room in the whole of Bomber Command where the crews pop in and look round when there's no briefing. Even if most of them only want to see Jane in the *Daily Mirror*, doze for half an hour and scrounge a coffee, by the time they wander out again they could have seen something that will save their lives.'

Cosily full of bacon, beans and fried eggs – a rare luxury – none of them now dozed. The room was full with the crews of all sixteen bombers. The men, sitting stiffly upright and white-faced with tension, were waiting for permission to smoke. As the time of danger approached men grew lonely and the flyers were dividing into their assigned crews. They exchanged comments and smiles with men they didn't like and had only briefly seen since the previous operational flight four days earlier. For now men were drawing close, not to their friends but to six men who for the next few hours would share their good or fatal fortune.

Lambert's two gunners for instance, Binty Jones and Flash Gordon, had a deadly feud dating from over two months before, but now they were exchanging jokes just as they'd done in the old days. They had met at the gunnery school and promised each other that they would insist on being in the same crew. They were thickset young men chosen, like most air gunners, for the short stature that enabled them to fit into the power-operated turrets. Flash was a dark-complexioned, gap-toothed Nottingham miner, a real pit-man who'd worked at the coalface on the trickiest seam. His hair was very long and with the aid of generous amounts of hair cream he arranged it in long shiny arabesques. For fear of disturbing its patterns he would avoid wearing a uniform cap. His liking for gold-plated identity chains, skull-and-crossbone rings and white silk scarves and his unmilitary bearing had given him his nickname. He shared it with a strip-cartoon hero of the same patronymic. His wide mouth smiled easily. Digby had said, 'He hasn't got a mouth but a small hinge on the back of his neck.' He was, in fact, proud of his white teeth. In spite of being exempt from military service he'd volunteered on his twenty-first birthday. He hated the pit; his only ambition was to survive the war and get an office job with a local tobacco factory. He was a cheerful boy with lots of energy and endless questions. He always wanted to know what his fellow airmen did in civvy street and he was not too shy to ask how much they earned doing it. Flash Gordon manned the rear gun turret.

Binty, a Welsh milkman – Jones the Milk – was also twenty-one. He usually manned the mid-upper turret, although a few times when Flash had a head-cold they swapped. Flash often got head-colds because, he said, the rear turret heater didn't work properly.

Binty had joined the RAF when he was seventeen, which made him a peacetime airman by a few weeks. He believed

194

that the superiority of the peacetime recruit was manifested by his very short hair, shiny boots and buttons, and razor pleats that he made by treating the inside of each crease with a layer of soap. His smartness was thus virtually unique among the aircrew NCOs. He was not beyond reprimanding airmen and even corporals for minor faults like having a pocket unbuttoned. This made him very unpopular.

He affected the old soldier's vocabulary, sprinkled with mispronounced Arabic and adapted Hindi. Bint was his word for young girl and he used it frequently, for in spite of an unappealing face he was a womanizer of renown. He had quick eyes and a brain which he described as shrewd but which the rest of his crew knew was cunning. However, none of them would allow an outsider to describe Binty Jones as cunning and they all appreciated that his cleanliness and efficiency extended not only to his sex-life and motorbike but also to his Browning machine guns. Artfully he had laid a claim to the upper turret for which there were only two guns.

Binty and Flash had flown fifteen operations, all with Lambert. They had been close pals for nearly a year; drinking, whoring, fighting, and sharing girlfriends, gunnery exam answers, cigarettes and a 350-cc BSA motorcyle, until they had met a woman named Rose in a pub in Peterborough. Her husband was a corporal in the Eighth Army fighting in the desert. Flash Gordon said they shouldn't see her any more but Binty said she was a sure thing and now spent more nights at her apartment than he did on the base. 'No one can have their wives within forty miles of their base,' said Binty, 'but Station Standing Orders don't say you can't have someone else's wife.' The two gunners hated each other but now you would never have guessed it. Binty sat reading a tightly wadded *Beano* comic and nodding while Flash told him about a motorcycle that an electrician on A Flight wanted to sell for fifteen pounds. Flash admired Binty's knowledge of motorcycles.

A fat fly buzzed and settled on Digby's hand. Even a finger prodded at it failed to move it. 'Lazy old bugger,' said Digby.

'Put him out the window,' said Lambert. 'He's probably just finishing his second tour.' But Digby tipped it on to the floor and Jimmy Grimm put his boot on it.

The briefing was running late. It was already 17.05 hours by the big clock but half of the chairs on the platform were still empty. The Assistant Adjutant, Jammy Giles, was there, of course, tipping back in his chair until it nearly fell over, laughing noisily and joking with a group of flyers in the front row. The Intelligence Officer, Longfellow, was also there. He always arrived early to be sure that his precious charts and diagrams were set up and to check that the route was correctly taped on the big map and the curtains closed upon it. He stood behind Jammy and steadied the chair each time it teetered too far back. But Jammy never toppled over. 'Jammy' was another word for easy or lucky and Flight Lieutenant Giles was lucky.

Outside in the corridors of the Operations Block there was the clatter of a relex machine as more orders arrived from Group. There was a pungent smell of floor polish and sweet tea and the clerks were hurrying with last-minute orders and modifications for the briefing officers. Standing in the corner of an empty office in the same block was Wing Commander John Munro, the commanding officer of the Squadron. While the Group Captain had control of the entire airfield from Dental Surgery to Smithy, John Munro commanded the bombers and their crews. Not that either of them would be likely to get into an argument about how things should be done. Air Ministry had carefully delineated their respective areas of responsibility.

If there was one man who had stamped this Squadron with his personality it was John Munro. Its faults were his and its virtues were his and its skills were his too. Now Munro was tired. There was no need for him to fly on so many raids, but he felt that he must. He flew and he kept his desk-top clear and tidy. He was not among the most popular officers on the Station. He knew that but he was unconcerned. Airmen brought before him knew that they could expect just punishment but little sympathy. He knew that the men called him Himmler but he was perceptive enough to know that there was a paradoxical element of respect and affection in the nickname. Munro's most celebrated virtue was that he spoke to the men coming before him for judgement with exactly the same tone of voice and listened to them with the same degree of attention that he gave the AOC. As one of his gunners had said after they had been badly shot up over Duisburg, 'He's not as cool as a cucumber, he's as cold as a bloody iceberg.' One night in the Mess Jammy Giles, full of thin beer and hoarse from singing, had pronounced loudly, 'Munro is a gentleman and gentlemen are now obsolete. This is the age of the technician.'

'The age of violence,' PO Cornelius Fleming had argued.

'Then we should be all right, old cock,' said Jammy. 'Seeing as we are the technicians of violence.'

'But Munro's a good type, isn't he?' asked Fleming.

Jammy suddenly sobered up. 'He's all right, Fleming my boy. Men don't come straighter than that tall, thin, humourless, toffee-nosed old sod.'

Now Munro was in the vacated office leaning on his walking-stick and puffing at his pipe. Around him there were the Engineering Officer and three senior ground staff NCOs including Flight Sergeant Worthington.

There was a problem. Carter's aeroplane – Joe for King – which had dropped the bomb that afternoon had developed an electrical fault and would not be serviceable in time for the raid.

'Our only reserve is the one that came in this afternoon,' said Worthington.

'Could do, Mr Sanderson?' the CO asked the Engineer

Officer, who in turn raised a quizzical eyebrow at the three NCOs.

'She'll have to go without an air test,' said Worthington.

'Get your best chaps on it and keep me in the picture, would you?' Sandy nodded assent.

'We'll be putting the new flame traps on the exhausts. Permission to bomb her up in the hangar while we work?'

Munro looked at his watch. 'No choice, Mr Worthington. And rip as much of that armour plate out of her as you can manage.'

'It's a long job, sir,' said Worthington.

'Group's boffins say we get an extra foot of altitude for every pound of weight we lose.'

'We'll leave the armour behind the pilot, sir?'

'I don't think any one of the crew will want you to take that out, Mr Worthington,' said Munro with a smile.

Worthington saluted and hurried away to round up his bods and break the bad news that they would be working frantically through their mealtime and on through the evening.

'Carter to take the new kite, John?'

Munro raked a match into his pipe and spoke with it still in his mouth. 'Seven trips, or is it eight? Average pilot; what's his flight engineer like, Sandy?'

'Ten trips actually, sir. His engineer is Gallacher. Apprentice toolmaker, argumentative, thin on theory but practical enough. They'll be all right.'

'That's settled, then.'

'Shall I tell him?'

'I'll tell him,' said Munro. 'He'll probably be a bit needled.'

Munro's own ground-crew chiefie was still standing nearby. 'What is it, Chief?'

The old NCO saluted gravely. 'What time will you be doing your air test, sir?'

Oh Lord, he had quite forgotten that he still had his own

NFT to do. His poor crew, they had been hanging around all day, and now they would probably have to fly while the rest of the Squadron were enjoying the evening meal. 'Immediately after briefing, say 18.15 hours.'

'Very good, sir.'

Munro reached into his pocket and looked at the list he had written on the envelope of the letter from his wife. He'd forgotten to put the NFT on it. If he'd seen another officer behaving as he had done over the past two months he would have grounded him without argument. But a commanding officer can't ground himself, in spite of those little talks the quack had given him. There were the lads in the crew, of course, but then they might have been flying with some chap straight from an Operational Training Unit, which would have endangered them even more. It was a problem that would solve itself; tonight would be his last operation. Next week he was to hand over to a new CO.

By the time Munro reached the Briefing Room everyone was there and the Groupie was hovering at the door waiting for the crews to come to attention. Munro walked to the platform and waited until the room was silent. 'Gentlemen, Station commander,' he called.

The crews got to their feet as the Groupie's footsteps clicked smartly down the centre aisle. He sprang agilely up on to the stage and tossed his gold-encrusted cap into a chair. He smiled, smoothed his white hair and looked at the great crowd of men as though wondering why they should be standing at attention.

'OK, chaps,' he called breezily. 'Sit down and light up.'

Near the front he saw Tommy Carter's bomb aimer who had completed twenty-nine trips. Tonight would be his last, for if he returned safely he would be screened to some safe job for a few months. He was nineteen.

'Collins, have one of mine,' said the Groupie and flung him a packet of cigarettes.

Collins caught the packet, took a cigarette and passed

them along the line to Carter and the rest of the crew of Joe for King.

'Thank you, sir. I'm passing them down the line.'

'You saucy bastard,' said the Groupie. 'No wonder they call you Tapper.' The Sergeant gave a shy smile.

There was a roar of delight from the crews, for Collins had earned his nickname from his constant pleas to borrow a few shillings until payday. The Groupie smiled. Napoleon, he knew, had used the same simple device to endear himself to his soldiers. And this brilliant fellow in Africa gave away cigarettes by the cartload, so it was said. Not that the Group Captain was a cynical man. On the contrary, he was imbued with a simple desire to have his aircrews like and respect him with the same intense feeling that he had for them. He would have given almost anything to fly with them to bomb Germany. Twice he had flown unofficially as an extra crew member, but the AOC had heard of it and warned him against doing it again. The Groupie described himself as a Hun-killer. The crews mostly thought of him as a harmless eccentric. In fact he was a lonely man desperately trying to believe that the company of youth would offset the approach of old age. He swept the laughter away with a movement of his hand. The crews sat silent, waiting to hear the name of the target.

In the few moments before the curtain rises at the opera there is a sound, a presence, an indefinable and unique mood. The audience are hushed and expectant, their throats are tight and even the nervous coughs are shrill and have an overtone of hysteria. Imagine then the mood that would prevail if – like these crews – it was the audience that were about to mount the stage: mouthing their dialogue lest they forget it, noting their cues, worrying about lights and timings and fussed over by a dozen stage managers who will take the blame should the performance become a disaster. It was a complex theatrical drama that this audience were about to stage and one mistake would bring them, not a boo or a jeer or a poor review but a sudden, nasty, fiery death.

The Group Captain tugged the cord and the curtains parted with a squeak of metal rollers.

'The target for tonight,' said the Group Captain, 'is Krefeld in the Ruhr.'

The captains and navigators had already been briefed, so it was no surprise to them. Many of the engineers had guessed from the fuel-loads and some of the remainder had heard by now, but there were still enough wireless operators and gunners to greet the news with a soft sincere groan. There had been rumours and bets that it would be a pushover target. Krefeld was no pushover. Happy Valley was Happy Valley: the best-defended target zone in Europe.

Lambert, Cohen and Micky Murphy had arrived together from the previous briefings upstairs. Seated behind them were Flash and Binty, the two gunners, and Digby, who was smoking a small cigar. Cohen had his notebook open in front of him. The raid was detailed there in neat handwriting with times in large numbers down one side. Lambert had some notes on the back of an envelope but he knew he would never refer to it. The routes and details that seemed so baffling to the newcomers were second nature to him; he had seen the techniques grow from the days when they had little more briefing than the name of the target and time of take-off.

On the stage the technical officers were seated in a line, with the Groupie standing like a vicar opening a church fête. Beside him, on a table covered with a grey blanket, there was a carafe of water and a glass. He moved it aside as he always did and turned to the map. Beribboned gaily with red-and-white tapes, the route to and from the target made a squat diamond shape centred upon the North Sea. The enemy coastline was defaced with ugly red blotches of flak around the cities of Amsterdam, Rotterdam and The Hague, while the right-hand tip of the diamond poked into the biggest red patch of all, the heavily defended heart of Germany's heavy industry – the Ruhr.

'Krefeld, heavy industry, textiles, light industry, communications,' reeled off the Groupie. 'It's a big show tonight: over seven hundred Bomber Command aircraft operating, with leaflet-dropping by Operational Training Units. Zero 01.30 hours. Take-off 24.20.' The Group Captain eyed the five journalists and Flight Lieutenant from Air Ministry Press Office who had seated themselves quietly at the rear of the room. He spoke to them rather than to the aircrews, who had heard it all before. He spoke slowly and deliberately and avoided jargon, as much as one can avoid it when dealing with a series of new techniques that have been named as they were invented.

'Any target in the Ruhr is difficult to identify. Even though the Met man tells me there will be little or no cloud and a full moon, there will be industrial haze lying over the target area; there always is. Take no chances, chaps. No guesswork. Tonight we are flying as part of the pathfinder element and it's important that we put up a good show. Don't bomb or mark out of sequence. One plane can spoil the entire raid and that means they'll send us back to do the job properly next week. So let's get there and mark it accurately so that the Main Force can hit it once and hit it bloody hard.' The Groupie sat down while a ripple of agreement ran round the room. No one wanted to go back next week.

Flight Lieutenant Ludlow, the Navigation Leader, stood up. The shy ex-bank clerk from Guildford had become an actuarial curiosity. He was now on his third tour. Only two per cent of airmen survived three tours. Some called him 'the immortal Lud'. He had briefed the navigators upstairs an hour before but now he outlined the route for the sake of the others. As usual he mumbled so quietly that the crews at the very back couldn't hear properly, but the ones who chose to sit at the very back usually didn't care. 'Assemble over Southwold on the coast. You'll need little or no change of course until the turning-point at Noordwijk on the Dutch coast. There will be yellow markers at the turning-point but

202

don't come back and complain that you didn't see them. They are for the Main Force boys and as pathfinders you're now expected to pinpoint places like that without the markers. Met says there will be no cloud, but if he's wrong there will be sky markers above, the cloud.

'From there it's straight run down to the target. I'll be placing a yellow fifteen miles from the target and you must go in to bomb over that yellow datum-line marker. If you don't you'll be crossing the bomber stream. By the time you reach the datum marker navigators must have their ground-speed calculated so that captains and bomb aimers have an exact time to the aiming-point. That's all. Anyone with queries can see me afterwards.'

Some of the new boys were scribbling away furiously. Cohen could see PO Fleming and his officer navigator checking and rechecking every word of the briefing. The rest of Fleming's crew sat close and watched approvingly as he prepared the spell that would bring them safe through the night. Not all of the crews were together. Sweet always sat at the front with a group of officers. His engineer – Micky Murphy – sat next to Lambert just as he had always done. On the other side of Lambert sat Battersby, studying the oil and grease on his hands. He noted with pride that they were fast becoming real engineer's hands like Murphy's.

Digby leaned forward to Murphy and Lambert. 'Faith, Hope and Charity are writing their memoirs,' he whispered.

'Yes, I remember what it was like on my first trip,' said Lambert. 'I was more frightened of making a mistake on my log than of tangling with a night fighter.'

All of the new crews had arrived in the Briefing Room at least five minutes early. For fear of taking some veteran's allotted seat they had all stayed close together near the back of the room. Like new boys at school they were anxious not to attract attention, but when Jammy Giles stood up it was to this part of the Briefing Room audience that he addressed himself.

Flight Lieutenant Giles was the Squadron's Assistant

Adjutant and also its Bombing Leader. Thirty-three years old, he had joined the RAF during the Munich Crisis. He had first flown as a gunner, when any erk standing around at take-off could become an air gunner without training or brevet or sergeant's rank. At that time he had been an LAC, almost the lowest form of Air Force life. Later, when his job had been made official and he'd got three stripes, he had delighted in swapping jobs with other aircrew. He had flown as gunner, as wireless operator, and even as second pilot. He had proved particularly skilled at bomb-aiming; so much so that at the end of his first tour he had got the DFM and a job as instructor. The discipline at the training school had been so irksome that he had applied for a commission and to his surprise got one. Now that the importance of his job had been recognized by the creation of the air-bomber category, Jammy had become an important man at Warley.

The eleven men in the room who had already completed a tour of operations were quieter and more introspective than the newer crews. Jammy was a notable exception. He was noisy, balding and inclined to plumpness; all due, he boasted, to the vast amounts of alcohol he consumed. Amid a less stringently selected group of men Jammy's physique would have gone unremarked. Amongst these aircrews, however, his slight paunch was Falstaffian, his pate Pickwickian and his cheerful nose Cyrano-like.

This was emphasized by the build of his pilot, Roddy Peterson, a tall thin doleful Canadian. He had a dry, savage brand of humour that Jammy had taken to immediately and now excelled in. Laurel and Hardy they were often called. Before joining up Jammy Giles had lived with his mother in a three-room basement in the London suburb of Morden and worked as a clerk for a building contractor. Now he was a bemedalled officer; a Flight Lieutenant. It was a transformation beyond his wildest dreams and he refused to think of what he would do when the war was over. In any case he didn't expect to survive it.

'All right. Belt up there and listen,' said Jammy. 'I don't care how many times you've heard it before.' Several times in the past Jammy had brought some inattentive crew member up on to the stage and asked him to repeat the briefing. Jammy knew how to make such a man feel like an infant; the crews became quiet and attentive.

'First the PFF Mosquito aircraft will mark the target with red markers. Their gear is much more accurate than anything we have, so their reds are what the Finders must look for. The Finders will put long sticks of flares over the reds. Mixed in with the Finder aircraft there are Supporters – and these are mostly crews on their first couple of trips – who are carrying only high-explosive bombs. That's because incendiaries could be mistaken for red markers. Remember, all you Supporter crews, it's your job to shake up the defences with your HE. Aim at the reds; if you don't see them I'd rather you brought your loads back here than made a mistake. And don't go round again, save that for the experienced crews. All right. Next over the target are the Illuminators – they will be dropping short sticks of flares right on the aiming-point which they will identify from the light of the Finders' flares. Lastly, the Primary Markers will arrive and put yellow markers down upon the aiming-point which will be lit by the Illuminators' flares, Aircraft with Y equipment will check by radar and visual means because the whole main bombing force will be looking for those yellows. It's been carefully planned, lads, so it's up to you to check and double-check before you mark. We don't want any more Pilsens and there won't be if you all pull a finger out.'

On April 16th, 1943, a mistake by the pathfinders resulted in an attack being centred on a huge Czechoslovak lunatic asylum at Dobrany instead of the Skoda arms factory at Pilsen. The horror was compounded by the loss of thirty-six RAF aeroplanes and Pathfinder Force was still smarting from the shame of it.

There was a flurry of coughs and affirmative grunts.

Lambert passed his cigarettes amongst his crew. Micky Murphy took a cigarette. 'What do you think, Sam?' he asked.

'It sounds carefully planned,' said Lambert guardedly.

'That's what they say about contraception,' said Micky, and smiled to reveal his gap-teeth. He smiled at Battersby too. The boy grinned back, pleased to be included in the joke.

Upon the stage Jammy continued, 'All right. The last wave are Backers Up. You are carrying green TIs. First look for any remaining reds because they are from the Mosquitoes. If there are no red TIs look for yellow ones from the Primary Markers. I'll be there watching you with my beady little eyes and if any of you mess up my pretty pattern of coloured lights I'll have your guts for garters. All right?' The crews laughed and Jammy gave a brief guffaw. He always said that at the end of his briefing. A new joke would have worried them; at this time they preferred things that were old and familiar.

'All right, one more thing,' said Jammy. 'Jettisoning of bombs. In recent months there's been a greater tonnage of bombs dropped on Britain by us and the Yanks than by the whole bloody Luftwaffe.' There was a pandemonium of whistling and catcalling. Jammy waved it down. 'Yeah, it's a real laugh at briefing, but when you are holding up a main-line train service or asking the poor buggers at Bomb Disposal to clear up your mess, it's not so funny. If you must jettison I want exact times, map reference and fusing details immediately after landing. It's easy to get away with it by saying nothing,' he smiled, 'and that's why I'll press for disciplinary action against the whole crew that doesn't report jettisoning.'

They were all in a good mood now. 'That's it Jammy, give 'em hell,' shouted someone. Again Jammy gave one of his sneeze-like laughs.

As the Intelligence Officer got up it was quiet enough to notice the sounds of the countryside: outside the window a chestnut tree moved abrasively, swifts called, a blackbird sang and thrushes were learning how to fly, the scent of newly cut hay came on the warm breeze. It was hard to believe that here in this pastoral backwater plans were being made to destroy a town.

Longfellow had been watching and listening to the briefing with the close attention of a journalist. The drama of the scene moved him. This was history being made. Last week he had sent these men out to destroy Cologne. Cologne, why it was beyond belief, a thousand years of history shattered into fragments in less than two hours by these young kids. Like a chapter he'd written for his second book: his criminals had sat around in easy chairs drinking brandy and discussing in matter-of-fact tones their plan to rob a bank. He'd rewrite that chapter, because now he knew that it hadn't been matter-of-fact enough! This was how it really should be: young fellows, some still in their teens, offering each other cigarettes and making notes about how many tons of high explosive they would plant in a city centre.

Longfellow got to his feet slowly to make sure he had their attention. He ran his hand through his thick black hair. 'Can you see me at the back?' he called. There was an affirmative murmur. 'I'm surprised to hear it, I can't see you through this damned fug.' There was some polite laughter. The room was blue with tobacco smoke and the yellow lights, he noticed, glowed through the swirling fumes like distant igneous planets. He made a note of 'distant igneous planets'. That would do for the book. Longfellow's clerk pinned up a bombing-pattern diagram headlined CREEP-BACK. It was a long blob of bomb-hits extending to meet an arrow marked 'Bomber Stream, Line of Flight'. Longfellow put on his spectacles and stared at the diagram. This made his whole audience look at it.

'Tonight,' pronounced Longfellow slowly and clearly, 'we are attacking Krefeld. The heavy industry . . .' He was unable to continue because of the noise, which was getting louder.

There was a shrill laugh from Kit Pepper – one of Sweet's gunners – and a sudden handclap from Roddy Peterson next to him. Longfellow held up his hand and then loudly corrected his error. 'Tonight, gentlemen, *you* are attacking Krefeld.' There was another sort of noise now; quieter and mollified. He decided to skip the build-up description of the target and go on to the matter of his real concern. The one that the Intelligence people at Group were complaining of so bitterly; in a word: creepback.

'Now, you Backer-Up crews,' said Longfellow, turning back to them. 'It's your job to drop your new flares into the centre of the existing flares. I've said this a thousand times but I will repeat it once again. When you see the marker pattern on your approach you are seeing it in perspective. That foreshortening is an optical illusion, so don't drop short of centre. Creepback is this tendency to fall short and then shorter still. So don't do it.' He paused long enough to give importance to his next few words. 'Now you chaps know as well as I do: there is another reason for creepback. One that people are reluctant to mention.' He paused again. 'Plain old-fashioned cold feet.'

The room was silent; no one coughed or murmured. Longfellow had their fearful attention. The Groupie looked towards the journalists but the smoke was too dense for him to see their reaction. Longfellow continued, 'When the flak is coming up hard and heavy, you get itchy fingers. What you want to do is to get rid of your bombs and get the hell out of there. Of course you do but if you are going to drop your bomb-load in a field of potatoes then what the hell are you going all the way to Germany for? That last few hundred yards to your aiming-point, gentlemen, is the difference between tearing the Hun's guts out and throwing in the towel.' He took off his horn-rimmed spectacles and replaced them in a theatrical gesture.

Longfellow had theories about briefings. The cold accusation of cowardice, followed by a manly understanding tone, a logical argument and the final sporting allusion, was calculated to shock, stimulate and reinforce the determination of his audience.

'Rule Britannia!' shouted someone at the back.

'These armchair warriors,' murmured Digby, 'they'll fight to the last drop of our blood.' Battersby giggled nervously.

Impulsively Flight Sergeant Lambert stood up. It was the first time he'd ever asked a question at a briefing.

'What are the guts of Krefeld?' asked Lambert. 'What are we aiming at in that city centre?' He had a target map in his hand; he waved it.

This wasn't so good, thought Longfellow. He ran his fingers down the back of his hand like a man adjusting the fit of a pair of chamois gloves. He peered forward to decide what sort of man this was. He tried to see his eyes but the ceiling lights threw the fellow's eye-sockets into darkness and masked his expression as efficiently as a pair of dark glasses. He smiled nervously at Lambert and remembered the standard answer he'd prepared for this sort of question. Sometimes the crews got fidgety about dropping their bombs right into the centre of crowded towns. It was natural that they occasionally needed bolstering up a little. Longfellow held up a target map of Krefeld and tapped the centre of it. 'A Gestapo headquarters and a poison-gas factory, that's your aiming-point. All right?'

He felt the mood of the room change as he said it; there was a suppressed muttering and a heightened excitement. The element of anger that a moment ago had been directed so unjustly at him was now turned upon the real enemy: Krefeld.

The Group Captain preferred not to wear his spectacles except in the privacy of his office. He didn't look at Lambert directly, he closed his eyes and nodded wisely, as though he had known about that city centre too.

Other technical officers continued the briefing. Sandy Sanderson, Squadron Engineer, was wearing an expensive blue lambswool roll-neck and as he spoke of the fuel-loads he kept peering to see if there were any women among the journalists. The Gunnery Leader said that Lancasters were still coming back with damage by .303-inch bullets. 'British bullets. That means trigger-happy gunners firing at shadows. Keep awake, keep alert and keep the turrets moving so that the oil stays warm and thin, but remember that there are two-motor bombers with us tonight, so don't open fire until you positively identify the night fighter.'

The Signals Leader gave details of the splasher frequencies – a rapid change of frequencies for bearings from beacons – and then the Met man gave them an outline of the weather situation. His curving line of cold front was in places two hundred miles in error and his prediction of its midnight frontal positions was even more inaccurate, but it would make no difference to these crews, who were going only as far as the Ruhr. There they would find anti-cyclonic weather as predicted.

'Moon full, rising 00.30 hours at target: one hour before zero. Sunrise is 05.46 hours, so you won't have to worry about sun-up. Now the cloud: along the enemy coast there'll be some well-broken layer cloud. The residual thundercloud will have followed the cold front and won't affect you. Over the target area you'll have a very thin layer of medium cloud between 1,000 and 20,000 feet. Sorry I can't be more precise than that, but it will probably have cleared by 01.00 hours.'

'Jesus!' said Digby without lowering his voice. 'We're going to be dancing naked in the full moon and he consoles us that we needn't worry about sun-up.' Loudly he said, 'Anyone want to buy my wristwatch?' There were a few laughs.

Even if the Met man didn't hear Digby's exact words he interpreted the sentiment without difficulty. Hurriedly he added, 'You'll have enough stratocumulus at 2,000 to 3,000 feet to give you some cover; visibility moderate. The bases will be the same: stratocumulus at 2,000 to 3,000 feet; visibility moderate. You've had your winds, navigators. North-west wind over target, remember. See me afterwards if there's anything else.'

The last man on his feet was Wing Commander Munro, the Squadron CO. Young 'Tapper' Collins wasn't the only man who was completing his tour of operations that night. John Munro was also embarking on his final trip of the tour, with the difference that this was Munro's second tour; tonight was his sixtieth bombing raid.

Munro spoke in the carefully modulated tones of the British upper class. 'Not much to say tonight, gentlemen. Flak concentrations: the map speaks for itself. You are routed to by-pass these unfriendly regions, so don't wander off or invent some new route that you believe to be better. Keep in the stream and you'll avoid most of these red patches.'

Sweet called out, 'What about a route that avoids that big red patch?' The big red patch was the Ruhr, so everyone laughed. The Wing Commander smiled as broadly as he knew how to. 'Keep in the stream, chaps, and watch your bombing heights. The only collision danger is over the target and if you keep to your height band it is almost eliminated. Don't run across the target except from the north-west where the datum marker is. It's rather like driving a car in traffic: keep on your side of the street and you are perfectly safe, but drive across the traffic stream and the chances of colliding are considerable.' His audience, few of whom had ever driven a car, nodded knowingly.

'And no evasive action over target. There'll be no night fighters there when the flak is firing. Once you're clear, keep to the return route and timing. This is a well-planned show, chaps. It's a big raid – about seven hundred aircraft – with Lancasters, Wellingtons, Halifaxes and Stirlings.'

'Hooray,' shouted a dozen old-timers from the back of the room. Munro looked up and smiled. On recent raids 12.9 per cent of the Stirlings had been lost compared to only 5.4 per cent of the Lancs. If it comforted them to know the poor old Stirlings would be with them, lumbering slowly along at their feeble ceiling and drawing the brunt of the flak, why should he spoil it? But his young brother was piloting a Stirling this night, and the smile was a mask.

When the briefing ended there was a clatter of boots and a buzz of conversation as the flyers shuffled out through the door and into the golden world of the afternoon sun where the air smelled of newly cut grass. Munro buttonholed Flight Lieutenant Sweet near the door. 'A word to the wise, Mr Sweet. These crew reshuffles: bad biz. If any of them want to change crews tell them to come and see me.'

'You mean Cohen and Digby?'

'I mean Cohen and Digby.'

Sweet smiled winningly. 'They were requests. Digby asked if . . .'

'Before you go on, old chap, let me tell you that this afternoon I had Flight Sergeant Digby, Royal Australian Air Force, on my neck, flushed with the exertion of hard-pedalling around the peri track, flatly refusing to leave Lambert's crew. These chaps get superstitious, you know.'

'We can't win a war on superstition.'

'Oh, I wouldn't go so far as that. Old Hitler's been using it pretty strenuously and gaining quite a bit of ground. The old torchlight processions and secret signs, eh? No, if these chaps get comfort from their toy bears and lucky lingerie hanging by the windscreen, let them have it, I say. That goes for crewing too.'

'But that's mutiny, isn't it? Surely Flight Sergeant Digby should have come to me in the usual way if he thinks he's running B Flight.'

'I can see you haven't had much experience of our Australian allies, Mr Sweet. I'm damned lucky he demeaned himself to mention it to me. There are quite a few of his countrymen who would have been on the blower to Australia House and done it via their Prime Minister and ours if they thought they were being victimized.'

'You're joking, sir.'

'I wish I were. Don't know how, in fact. My trouble, I suppose. Anyway, Mr Sweet, forget Digby going to your crew even if he is the best bomb aimer in the Squadron. And even if your bomb aimer is by far the worst . . .'

Sweet smiled again. 'Oh, it wasn't for that reason, sir . . .' Sweet touched Munro's arm in a gesture of reassurance. Munro shrank away. He had a horror of men patting his shoulder or grasping his arm.

'Whatever reason, Mr Sweet, forget it,' he said coldly.

'Take Cohen, forget Digby?'

'Take Cohen, forget Digby, that's the spirit.'

Ashamed of his reaction to Sweet's gesture, Munro leaned a little closer to him. 'Perhaps your idea is to pile all the B Flight duds into one crew in order to get them reassessed as unsuitable for pathfinders and transferred. But why, Sweet, why in the name of God, choose Lambert's crew? Lambert's one of the best pilots on the Squadron.'

Sweet smiled at Munro. He felt sure that he would be able to convincingly refute this unfair suggestion. 'All I'm interested in, sir, is flying maximum ops with maximum bomb-loads and killing maximum Huns.'

'Really?' said Munro.

'I just want to get the war over,' said Sweet.

'Quite a few of us feel like that,' said Munro and before Sweet could reply added, 'Another question, Sweet. Has Lambert had a portrait of Stalin painted on his aircraft?'

'Stalin, sir?'

'Stalin, that's it.'

'No sir, that's Sergeant Carter's aircraft: L Love.'

'Umm, that's what I thought. Group Captain came your way this PM to see the aircraft with the bomb-release malfunction. He saw the Comrade's portrait on it . . . he's fretting.'

'I'll have the riggers paint it out.'

'And have one of your chaps write to the *Daily Mirror*

about it? No, I wouldn't advise that. As you know, it's unserviceable tonight. Do nothing until the Group Captain mentions it to you directly. Then you will have a problem.'

'I'll think of a way to deal with it, sir.' Sweet smiled.

'I'm sure you will,' said Munro coldly. Who could say that youth was rebellious. Why, chaps like Sweet would do anything to avoid a harsh word. Munro sighed. After the war, he felt, the world might be full of Sweets, selling their vacuum cleaners, parrying political questions and entertaining millions on television. Eventually everyone in the world would become expert at the modest words, kind smiles and bland assurance that gloved the iron hand of ambition.

Man, frightened that machines might dominate him and overawed by mechanical performance, was becoming mechanical in his emotions and reactions, thought Munro. His gestures, jokes and obedience were robot-like. Lambert's foolish and provocative question, much as Munro deplored such behaviour, was at least human by the very nature of its error. That smiling little Flight Lieutenant Sweet would never do such a thing.

Sweet wasn't the only person to be buttonholed. All over the room men were giving last-minute warnings, greetings, advice and information to friends and strangers.

The chaplain was a member of the Socialist Party and secretly regarded himself as a rather dangerous reformer. In his opinion this was why his bishop had been so keen to get rid of him into the Air Force. Compulsory church parades, some articulate atheists in the Officers' Mess and an inherited stutter had made his task harder than he'd expected. Still, it was his duty to seek out the troubled and he found the man with the lined eyes who'd almost spoiled the whole briefing by disquieting his comrades.

'Are you troubled, Flight Sergeant?' he asked Lambert.

'Why doesn't the Church stop the war, Padre?'

The young chaplain had listened carefully to his archbishop, so, like the Intelligence Officer, he had the answer ready. 'The war is due to the sin of mankind, including our own. And so we have got to do it and be penitent while we do it.'

'So I'm the right hand of God, am I, Padre? I wonder if the Germans have padres telling them they are.'

For one moment the padre's resentment and anxiety almost betrayed him into praying that he would not stutter. He did stutter: 'I . . . I . . . I . . . hold the King's commission, Sergeant, and I'll ask you to treat me with the respect my u . . . u . . . u . . . uniform deserves.'

'Come on, Skip,' called Digby loudly. 'We've got some killing to do.' The padre glared at them both. Why should these men insult me, he thought; they know I can't stop the war?

'Pay no attention to them, Padre,' said Longfellow. 'They couldn't care less about decent people's feelings.' He wondered whether it was either of those two who had laughed at him when he made that slip of the tongue at the start of the briefing. Once Longfellow had hero-worshipped the young aircrew, but that was long ago during the Battle of Britain. That was before he encountered the arrogance that constant danger granted the young. 'Intrepid birdmen,' he said scornfully after all the birdmen were out of earshot.

CHAPTER FIFTEEN

Walter Ryessman often recalled the day when his name had been put forward for the job of Burgomaster. It was a job for life, but he anticipated that two hours a day would be more than sufficient to supervise the civic activities of such a small town. That was before the war, of course, when the world went at a slower pace. Decisions about slum clearance and extensions to the gasworks were referred to sub-committees and the answers were seldom in dispute. Walter Ryessman had been made Burgomaster because of his long and faithful membership of the Party. Now that the nation was at war his primary job was to ensure that Altgarten played its part in winning it, and that took him eight hours a day of paperwork and meetings, with frequent visits to anywhere and everywhere to be sure that the air-raid precautions were provided as the law demanded. At first the hospital authorities and the TENO engineers' commander had resented his sudden unannounced arrivals. Soon they realized that Ryessman had influence in the Party far greater than his post as Burgomaster of Altgarten would suggest. He also had an honorary rank in the SS. So they learned how to put on a show of welcome when the tall white-haired man appeared like a ghost in the middle of the night. It was part of the briefing of any new sentry, night-watchman or caretaker to be on the alert for the Burgomaster.

The Rathaus was a red-brick building that faced Altgarten

railway station across the grassy, tree-lined Bismarckplatz. From his office the Burgomaster looked down upon the war memorial. The fountain splashed brightly in the afternoon sunlight. On the face of it were the names of forty Altgarten men who had died in the First World War. Already the side panels were almost full with Second World War casualties and the Burgomaster wondered whether the base of the fountain would be suitable for carving more names. He decided it would have to be.

The Burgomaster had seen many changes in the Rathaus since he had taken office. The basement which had once housed the birth, marriage and death records had been turned into an air-raid control room. There was a gas curtain at the door, emergency lighting with its own generator, a large-scale map of the town and a smaller-scale one to show its position in the district. Phones connected the room to the police, fire, gas, electricity and water officials in various parts of the town and there were special lines to the rescue and repair service and to the senior air-raid precautions officials in Dortmund. Official visitors to Altgarten were always taken to see the Control Room and Herr Ryessman was very proud of it, although some of the ruder clerks called it 'the eagle's burrow'.

His office had been moved up to the top floor along with the marriages, births and deaths registry and the housing department. Artfully they had put benches in the corridor outside the marriage registry so they had been able to convert the waiting room into the office of the Burgomaster's clerk – Andi Niels, a solemn young man with a gastric ulcer which, together with a certain amount of string-pulling by the Burgomaster, had released him from Army service. Downstairs there were the tax, street-cleaning and ration-card offices, and the east wing of the building was given over to the police, although the Oberwachtmeister had his office on the same floor as the Burgomaster so that he was available for conference.

The Burgomaster went next door to his assistant's office, noting with satisfaction that in the corridor sandbags and a rope, axe and stirrup pump had been placed according to his most recent order.

His clerk's office was smaller than the Burgomaster's and was crammed full with filing cabinets, but he envied his clerk the view he commanded. From this window he could see the tall spire of the Liebefrau rising from the medieval roofs of the town centre. Beyond, where the open country began, there was the Wald Hotel tucked into a patch of dark woodland, and to the north, catching the sun, were four long glasshouses that were a part of Ryessman's own property.

He was still enjoying the view when his assistant came into the room. He was startled and to Ryessman's surprise he flushed.

'Herr Ryessman,' said the clerk politely. 'Is there something you require?'

'No,' said the Burgomaster, watching with amusement as the clerk hurriedly pushed the files he was holding into the nearest filing cabinet. By the time he turned back to the desk he was more collected.

'Today is my birthday, as you well know since you have been sending the invitations. I wanted to ask you to join our party this evening at Frenzel's.'

'The Herr Bürgermeister is very kind,' said Andi Niels. 'I shall be honoured.'

'It's a small affair,' said the Burgomaster. 'This is no time for ostentatious display, but there will be smoked eel to start and Frenzel's special roast duckling to follow.'

The Burgomaster was puzzled by the young man's behaviour. Usually a relaxed and self-composed fellow, today he seemed anxious and neurotic. He straightened a picture on the wall, wiped dust from a shelf and moved around the room. Perhaps his ulcer was playing up, thought Ryessman.

'If you will excuse me, Herr Bürgermeister,' he said. 'You have an appointment with your tailor and I have a meeting too.'

'I was forgetting the time,' said the Burgomaster. He nodded to Niels and left the room. Outside in the corridor there were five people. At first the dark clothes of the older people suggested that they had come to register a death. Probably, thought Ryessman, they have these same clothes for weddings, births and deaths. It was the young couple who showed that this was a wedding. There was no doubt about them. They were so clearly in love that they were oblivious of everyone and everything around them. The young man was dressed in a dark well-cut suit with a small spotted bow tie. He was a handsome boy with big eyes and a strong jaw. There were not so many young men like that still in civilian clothes, thought Ryessman. The girl was pretty. She did not have the wide pelvis, heavy bones and strong arms that were common to the local girls. She was petite with jet-black hair cut short and a heart-shaped face that was pale and doll-like. The parents shuffled uneasily as Ryessman walked down the corridor. Here in the country older people had never lost their fear of authority, thought Ryessman, and that perhaps was a good thing. Young people were less respectful and as he passed he heard someone whisper and the young man looked up and stared him straight in the face.

Perhaps if the Burgomaster had been busy that afternoon he would have never pursued the matter or come across it in the first place. But the afternoon was quiet and sunny as he sat at his desk idly turning over the carbons of letters passing between departments in the Rathaus.

Dear Sir,
    The Burgomaster thanks you for your letter of the twelfth of May and confirms that MEYER, Hans-Willy, of Rheinprovinz Altgarten Florastrasse 36 is now

officially down-classified to Jew of two-thirds Jewish blood.

Your department will ensure that his employer is informed and that any privileges that he had due to his former status as a Jew of one-third Jewish blood should now be withdrawn.

A. NIELS
for the Burgomaster

Niels had initialled the carbon as was his usual practice. Acting on impulse the Burgomaster phoned through to police records and asked them for their file on this man Hans-Willy Meyer.

'You have it already,' said the police constable.

'You are sure?'

'I am certain, Herr Bürgermeister. Herr Niels came down for it personally. He said you had asked for it.'

'Thank you.'

'Is everything in order?'

'Yes,' said the Burgomaster. He knew the man with whom he had spoken, an elderly constable who had been put in charge of records after being badly injured in a fight with two drunks at the beginning of the war. He was a man of experience and would have made no mistake. The Burgomaster picked up the phone but replaced it and walked along to Niels' office instead. The wedding party were still waiting in the corridor.

Niels was not in his office and although at first Ryessman was about to dismiss the matter from his mind he had second thoughts and went through the cabinet to find Meyer's police file. It was not there. There were in fact none of the grey-covered police files anywhere in the cabinet. It was then that he remembered that Niels had been carrying a grey file when he had come into the office and found Ryessman behind his desk. Yes, there it was, stuffed into a cabinet of purchase agreements so carelessly that its cover was bent double.

The Burgomaster read through the file of documents. Meyer was a twenty-one-year-old Jewish farmworker. He was not permitted to serve in the Wehrmacht. His file was a very ordinary one that could have been that of any of Altgarten's two dozen Jews. Ryessman had hoped that his data card with its identity photo and fingerprints would have been there, but it was not. Perhaps police records filed them separately.

Meyer had been down-graded because his grandfather, a butcher from Lübeck hitherto listed as an Aryan, had now been classified as purely Jewish. This made Meyer's father two-thirds Jewish like his mother, and, as everyone knew, the offspring of two such Jews was a two-thirds-Jewish son, not a one-third-Jewish son. What puzzled Ryessman was where the information had come from. Usually in cases of this sort one found in the file a short unpleasant note from a neighbour or fellow worker. Typed sometimes, or written in block capitals to conceal the writer's identity. Often they contained obscenities, sometimes they ended with Nazi slogans instead of a signature. This file had no such note. The grandfather had been dead since before the Party came into power and these documents had originated with the Lübeck police records office. It seemed unlikely that they would have made a mistake but then perhaps in 1933, the first year of Hitler's power, they had been overworked, for that was when all these Jewish files began. Before that the police had dealt only with criminals.

It was time to go for his fitting. He replaced the file as he had found it, even bending it as before. As he left his office he saw the wedding party again. They were no longer tense and the bridegroom held his wife's hand protectively. Herr Holländer, the registrar, brandished a huge bunch of keys and used them to unlock the cupboard on the landing. He reached for one of the hundreds of black-bound volumes that lined its shelves. The ceremony was not yet complete and Holländer looked the groom in the eye warningly. They were hushed and solemn as Holländer handed the official edition of *Mein Kampf* to the bride as was mandatory in all Reich weddings. The Burgomaster nodded approvingly at them as he passed.

The sun now shone from a clear blue sky and Ryessman enjoyed the walk up Dorfstrasse past the ruined windmill on the corner. As he crossed Vogelstrasse he could smell the sweet, freshly cut timber in the carpentry shops where as a young child he had lingered on his way to school. He tried to forget the business of Meyer but he could not. Even as the tailor – old Herr Voss himself – supervised the fitting of his fine Party uniform he remembered it again. What sort of spiteful motive was behind the reclassification? Not that Ryessman had much sympathy for Jews; it was simply a matter of procedure. If there was a reclassification, then the file should show the evidence for it. If the reclassification had been upwards instead of downwards then Ryessman would have suspected corruption. It did happen, it was useless to deny it. There were such large sums of money involved. Some of them would offer a fortune rather than go into a concentration camp. It wasn't fair that these Jews put that sort of temptation to loyal policemen and Party workers, but what could you expect from such people?

'Raise your arm,' said Herr Voss. 'Too tight?'

'Exactly right.'

'Bend forward and straighten up.'

The Burgomaster did so and Herr Voss fussed around the back of his collar, slashing at the soft brown cloth with his chalk. It was a smart uniform; he wished it had been ready this morning when the family had had its group photo taken. How fine his mother had looked even at eighty-six, and the children in their best suits had been transfixed and silent in case the photo should show them as having moved. For their parents had promised them dire punishments if this photograph for grandfather's birthday was less than perfect.

'Sit down. Clothes must look as well on a man seated as

upon him standing.' Again he applied the sharp edge of the chalk. It was an honour to be fitted by Voss himself. Voss was among the wealthiest men in the town. In 1930 in an upstairs room in this very building he had first tried his hand at making a uniform. It was for an old and valued customer who had just joined the SA. One of his fellow officers had admired it and by 1933 Voss uniforms had become famous for miles around. One wealthy SS officer came from Berlin and had previously been a customer of the famous Stechbarth, Göring's tailor. It made Voss very proud. Some people said things against them, but the Nazis had done wonders for the uniform business, whatever other faults they might have. There were so many part-time organizations that many Germans had two or three uniforms. Voss' greatest complaint against the Nazis was the way they had deprived him of his skilled Jewish staff. It was all very well, these arrogant young men complaining about stitching and the cut of the breeches. They didn't seem to understand that there were secrets to tailoring a pair of breeches that were known to very few cutters, and they were all Jewish.

'Stand up.'

It was almost as though the Burgomaster had read Voss' mind. He said, 'Are there many Jews still in the tailoring business?'

'Yes, Herr Bürgermeister,' said Voss. 'I still have one cutter downstairs and there are certain lining materials which can be obtained only from Jewish concerns in the Netherlands. Now take this lining in your tunic . . .'

'I don't wish to know about it,' said the Burgomaster hurriedly. 'I was asking in case you have heard of a person named Meyer: Hans-Willy Meyer.'

'I don't recall the name, Herr Bürgermeister, but my cutter Jakob might know. Shall I fetch him?'

'Yes,' said the Burgomaster.

Poor Jakob; he came into the room in answer to old Mr Voss' call and found the Burgomaster in his full Party uniform. For a moment he completely forgot that this was the very garment he had been handling only an hour before and went white with horror.

'There's nothing to fear, Jakob,' said Voss. 'There's nothing to fear, Herr Bürgermeister, is there?' he added.

'Nothing,' said the Burgomaster. 'I merely wondered whether you knew a young man named Hans-Willy Meyer. He lives in Florastrasse.'

'No, Herr Bürgermeister,' said Jakob.

'It will not mean trouble for him,' promised the Burgomaster. 'I promise it upon my word as a German officer.'

'You are sure, sir?'

Voss said, 'Of course, Jakob.' All these Jews were suspicious; why couldn't they behave like patriots.

'The fellow has been denounced,' declared the Burgomaster dramatically. 'Tell me what you know of him; it can only help.'

There were so few Jewish families left in Altgarten that it was foolish to deny that he knew young Meyer.

'He is a fine young man,' said Jakob. 'His family comes from Lübeck. He works on a farm. It means catching a bus at five-thirty A M.'

'When did you first know him?' The Burgomaster offered Jakob a cigarette. The Jews didn't get a tobacco ration – or a meat ration either – and Jakob dearly loved to smoke.

'I lived near his parents in Lübeck,' said the old tailor. He took a cigarette but stored it carefully away.

'His father's parents were Jewish?'

'No, both his father's parents were Aryan. It was just his mother's mother who was Jewish.'

'Are you quite sure?'

'I am quite sure, Herr Bürgermeister. There was so much talk about it.' Jakob gave a short laugh. 'His father was one of the most prosperous pork butchers in Lübeck.'

Ryessman smiled. 'So this fellow Meyer is only one-third Jewish.'

'For you perhaps, Herr Bürgermeister,' said the old tailor. 'For me, he is not Jewish at all.'

The thing that still puzzled the Burgomaster was the way in which this Jewish fool Meyer had signed the reclassification form. It was almost as if he wanted to be downclassified.

'See the shoulder, Jakob: high when the Herr Bürgermeister is seated, but straight when he stands.'

Ryessman was irritated that they should talk of him as though he was deformed. Like surgeons rather than tailors, and that's the way they looked at him too.

'Are you finished?'

'Yes, thank you, Herr Bürgermeister. The day after tomorrow for another fitting. We must have it exactly right.'

'My secretary will phone,' said Ryessman.

'Is he well?' asked Voss.

'Niels?' said Ryessman. He smiled. 'He was when I left him an hour ago.'

'I thought I saw him going into the front entrance of the hospital,' said Voss. 'I wondered whether he was sick or just visiting.'

'You were mistaken,' said the Burgomaster, but his voice lacked conviction. Young Niels had not been his usual self today, and there was the strange business of the hidden dossier. Perhaps he was sick, perhaps he was in hospital. From the window of Voss' office he could see the grey-brick St Antonius Hospital and beyond it the flat roof of the Annex building. For a moment he was tempted to use the phone and ask the reception if they had admitted Niels, but he decided that if Niels was in hospital the Rathaus would have phoned him here at the tailors to report it.

The Burgomaster was wrong on both items. At that moment Andi Niels, personal secretary to the Burgomaster of Altgarten, was occupying a bed in Room 28 on the top floor of the silent Annex building.

Originally the Annex had been intended as an overflow

225

for St Antonius solely to cater for Altgarten's increased population, but under the new hospital zoning arrangements it was used to receive air-raid casualties from badly bombed cities in the Ruhr. From here they were dispersed as soon as possible and the beds made ready for the next contingent of casualties. It was a stroke of genius to build the Training Centre for Samariter nursing assistants between the hospital and the amputee camp. The poor little girls worked until they dropped. Especially on those awful days when convoys of the new bus-like ambulances were jammed along Joachimstrasse so that air-raid victims from the Ruhr were lying in corridors for want of bed-space. Samariter with only a couple of weeks' training found themselves working in the operating rooms or casualty wards. On the days when there were no RAF raids the Samariter worked almost as hard in the Amputee Centre across the road. At any time of day or night the nurses' accommodation wing of the Training Centre was dark with a silence marred only by the snores and nightmares of the exhausted girls.

There were many young girls in Altgarten: Red Cross nurses, Frei sisters, Brown sisters and Samariter. The tea-rooms and hairdressers vibrated with their chatter and the inhabitants of Altgarten were never at loss for a story about their shameless activities. Once a month there were dances at the Training Centre. TENO officers, SS men from the Wald Hotel training camp and certain local residents received neatly penned invitations and displayed them like honours. All three of the town's hairdressers could be certain of one ticket; so could the haberdasher and an old man named Drews who regularly obtained bolts of silk and linen from some secret source over the border. For obvious reasons the senior staff at Kessel's brewery were asked and the Burgomaster's office received a ticket as a matter of courtesy. Andi Niels used that ticket.

Tonight there was to be a dance at the Training Centre. The girls had decorated the assembly hall with coloured papers and cardboard representations of Mount Fuji. On the tickets it had hopefully said 'fancy dress with a theme of old Japan' but only the most enthusiastic girls had sewn together a costume.

'The old fool invited me to his birthday dinner,' said Andi Niels. 'What the devil can I do?'

'Couldn't you get away early?' said the nurse. She was a short plump sexy girl who giggled readily at any situation. She giggled now.

'There'll be toasts to his father, the regiment, officers who fell in the first war. Then we'll listen to speeches and sing old war songs. You've no idea what it's like.'

'There'll be food at the dance. The girls have been saving their rations for three weeks.'

'No matter,' said Niels sadly. 'We'll go to Düsseldorf this weekend and stay in a fine hotel.'

'And share a room?' said the nurse. She giggled. 'They will ask for our papers.'

'I can fix that.'

'Have you inherited some money?'

'As a matter of fact, I have,' said Niels. He turned over in bed and reached down to her. 'You've left your stockings on,' he accused.

'Just in case.'

'The door's locked, and no one will come up to the top floor during the day.'

'I'll take them off,' said the girl. 'But I must be back on duty by five.' She climbed out of bed again.

'By five I must be in my office,' said Niels. 'I've left lots of work there.' He watched her take off her stockings and suspender belt. She knew he was watching her and she moved in a deliberately provocative way, knowing that his impatience would put an edge on his appetite.

Niels breathed heavily. 'My God,' he thought, 'I'm going to miss all this next week.'

* * *

After August Bach had driven away, Anna-Luisa busied herself in the house and garden. She scrubbed the kitchen floor, boiled down oddments of soap and cleaned out the chicken house. At four o'clock she met Hansl at the Volkschule and walked him past the fire station. Both of the Magirus fire engines were outside and he watched intently as the equipment and paintwork was shined to a high gloss. The firemen were accustomed to the Volkschule boys and Johannes Ilfa, the Gruppenführer on the number one engine, recognized Hansl and lifted him up to see the driver's seat. For months he had seen Anna-Luisa meeting the child from school. One of his friends had teased him about concealing a secret passion for the girl. He would be teased even more if seen speaking to her.

'My name is Johannes Ilfa,' said the fireman, offering Anna-Luisa a cigarette.

'My name is Johannes too,' said Hansl.

Anna-Luisa waved the cigarette aside. 'We call him Hansl,' she explained.

'We? . . .' said the fireman. 'He is your son? I thought you were the nurse.'

Anna-Luisa enjoyed his obvious discomfort. 'You mustn't jump to conclusions.'

'Do you never smoke?' he asked, the packet still open in his hand.

'Not in the street. Have one yourself.'

'It's forbidden.' He brushed his fine moustache with the back of his hand.

'Lift me up again,' called Hansl, and Johannes Ilfa did so. The little boy fingered the shiny steering-wheel and then looked at his hero in wonder.

'We mustn't be a nuisance.' said Anna-Luisa.

'You couldn't be a nuisance.' He looked at her for a long time trying to find something to say. Something that would make her delay and make her smile at him again.

'We must go.' She smiled at the fireman.

'Make *Mutti* bring you again, Hansl,' called the fireman.

'Yes,' said Hansl, and he gripped Anna-Luisa's fingers in his warm hand as though he was part of a conspiracy.

'Say goodbye to Herr Ilfa and thank you,' she told the child.

They both waved when they reached the corner. At Mauerstrasse they turned right. This was the main road that joined Kleve to Krefeld and followed the ancient walls that marked the edge of Altgarten. On the other side of Mauerstrasse a wide stream moved sluggishly southwards. Hansl liked to throw pieces of paper into the green water and run to each of the wooden bridges to see them move underneath.

Much of the wall still remained and Frau Birr's tea-room was built into the massive stones. From the second floor there was a view as far as the high ground upon which stood the Burgomaster's glasshouses near the waterworks. In the other direction there was a view of the Wald Hotel, now taken over by the SS and garlanded with tall barbed-wire fences and endlessly patrolled by guard dogs.

Smart *Hausfrauen* of Altgarten gathered in Frau Birr's tea-room each afternoon accompanied by their daughters in neat dark dresses and well-kept shoes. That's why TENO officers, Army doctors and administration officials from the Amputee Centre liked to have tea here. Sometimes cavalry officers and veterinary surgeons, complete with spurs and riding-crops, came all the way from their depot near Kempen and set the ladies' hearts aflutter.

Hansl and Anna-Luisa shared a slice of *Apfelstrudel*. The coffee wasn't too bad and Frau Birr could usually find a small glass of milk for the boy. The people in the big cities didn't live as well as this, thought Anna-Luisa. Life seemed unbelievably sweet. Soon she would be Frau Bach, and the ladies in the tea-shop with their fruit-filled hats would have to nod in a way different from the condescending smiles they gave to the RAD girl.

Frau Hinkelburg, the architect's wife, was just as conde-scending as any of them but at least she was affable. This day she sat with Anna-Luisa and Hansl and told them all her news.

There were always stories about the Russian prisoners of war in the disused factory beyond the brewery. The citizens of Altgarten were fascinated and a little afraid of these strange Bolshevik men from the far side of the world where so many young Germans were being sent.

'They put two fierce guard dogs to keep the Russians inside the fence at night. Even the dog-handlers were wearing thick protective gloves. By the next morning the dogs had been cooked and eaten. Only the bones remained, they say. And those they carved into crucifixes.'

Frau Hinkelburg paused long enough to cut a piece of cake and hurry it into her mouth. Anna-Luisa felt that she was expected to add something, but she kept her own wonderful news to herself to be gloated over and devoured slowly. Even before she'd swallowed her cake Frau Hinkel-burg smiled at Anna-Luisa and began again.

'Frau Kersten is going to put apple trees in the field behind the cemetery and she's bought the land she leased from Richter. The money she must make from the potatoes.' Frau Hinkelburg opened her fine new patent-leather hand-bag so that Anna-Luisa could clearly see its Paris label. From it she took a small lace handkerchief and brushed a cake-crumb from the corner of her mouth. 'I heard that Frau Kersten has a leather box full of money hidden in her bed-room. She can't bank it, they say, for fear of the tax department.'

'Her farmhouse is being replastered.'

'By the French prisoners of war,' added Frau Hinkelburg. 'Have you noticed the tall one with the tiny moustache?'

'The one giving orders?'

'He's giving more than that, my girl, if the stories about him and Frau Kersten are true.'

'But Frau Kersten is nearly fifty.'

'Many a fine tune is played upon an old violin.' Frau Hinkelburg laughed loudly and clamped her hand over her mouth in a gesture she believed refined. The diamonds on her hand caught the light. 'Before the Frenchman, they say she was casting her eyes farther afield.'

'What do you mean?' said Anna-Luisa.

'Your employer, my dear.'

Anna-Luisa laughed good-naturedly.

'You think that's funny?'

'But Herr Bach and that fat old Frau Kersten . . .'

'Yes, Frau Kersten would be a lucky woman to have Herr Bach as a husband,' admitted Frau Hinkelburg as she thought about it.

'Any woman would be a lucky woman.'

Frau Hinkelburg looked up sharply. Her ears were attuned to chance remarks and she never missed an innuendo. '*Ach so!*' was all she said, but Anna-Luisa knew that one part of her secret was a secret no longer. Frau Hinkelburg put a freckled bejewelled hand upon Anna-Luisa's thin white arm and smiled at her.

'You were not here when the Wald Hotel was really a hotel. What a wonderful place! The chef was French, from Monte Carlo. People came from all corners of Europe – and from America too – to dine there and stay in the suites that face on to the gardens and the forest. There were floodlit fountains and an orchestra outside in the summer. They used to dance until two or three o'clock in the morning and the sound of the music could be heard right across the town on a still summer's night. When I was a young girl I would open my bedroom windows and listen to the music and the voices of the fine people who left their motor-cars and chauffeurs waiting down there in Mauerstrasse. It will never be the same again.'

'When the war is ended, perhaps . . .'

'No, the world has changed since then. There is no place

for romance now. Why, look at what the Wald Hotel is now used for.'

'No one knows what it's used for.'

'I know,' said Frau Hinkelburg. 'My husband is an architect and he heard it from someone in the Burgomaster's office.' She leaned closer to emphasize the confidential nature of her theory. 'It's a human stud. Young carefully chosen Aryan girls are sent there to –' she hesitated – 'to have children by selected SS officers.'

'How awful,' said Anna-Luisa. She said it mechanically for she did not believe it.

'Awful,' agreed Frau Hinkelburg, 'and yet fascinating. Is it not?'

'There are so many stories about the men in the Wald Hotel.'

'Because they so seldom emerge from the place.'

'Probably,' agreed Anna-Luisa.

'Well, it's understandable,' said Frau Hinkelburg. 'They have everything they want there, don't they?' She laughed coarsely; Anna-Luisa smiled.

'Are you going anywhere tonight, Anna-Luisa?'

'I have so much ironing to do.'

'I thought you might be going to the Burgomaster's birthday party at Frenzel's. They are having Russian caviar and roast duckling. I am going.'

'Herr Bach scarcely knows the Burgomaster.'

'But his cousin Gerd knows him.' She watched the girl carefully. 'And you are a friend of Andi Niels, the Burgomaster's secretary.'

'He's no friend of mine,' said Anna-Luisa; 'he's horrid.'

'He has a reputation,' agreed Frau Hinkelburg, 'but he wields a great deal of influence in this town. The girls with extra clothing-ration coupons . . . you'd never believe.' She laughed again.

'I have heard stories about him,' said Anna-Luisa.

'There are stories about everyone in this town. Small

towns are always full of gossip. There are stories about you, even . . . you would laugh if you heard them.'

'About me?'

'It means nothing, child. A beautiful girl is bound to have stories told about her . . .'

'In connection with whom?' interrupted Anna-Luisa angrily.

The woman smiled and Anna-Luisa knew that she wanted her to be angry.

'Whom?' repeated Anna-Luisa. 'What lies are being spread?'

'I never listen to scandal,' said the old woman haughtily. 'It's all stupid nonsense. I have told you that.'

'With whom?'

'With everyone, child; you would have to be the most energetic courtesan since Pompadour.' She patted her arm again and the bejewelled rings flashed in the sunlight.

Fischer was a young man – twenty-four last birthday – but his bloodshot eyes and the black rings of tiredness around them made his appearance deceptive. Now that he had had a steaming hot bath and washed the Russian dust out of his hair he shook away some of his fatigue. He found a last clean set of underclothes and a reasonably clean shirt in his baggage. An orderly had just returned his boots to him brightly shining, although there were deep scratches that went right through the leather in places. His long leather overcoat hanging on the door was also beyond salvage. Its lapels were scuffed white and the sleeve seams had been ripped and resewn so many times that it was crookbacked. He put the Knight's Cross over his head and tucked the lady's garter to which it was attached under his collar out of sight.

In the front line no one any longer wore their conspicuous Leibstandarte cuffband but now Fischer put it on his sleeve. The words 'Adolf Hitler' shone bright and new compared

233

with the faded fabric of his jacket. Fischer stroked the armband. The number one SS division, and he was to join number twelve. Ugh! He feared it might be like this rundown SS training depot where even the sentries were improperly dressed and the slow-witted young officers only half trained. It depressed him to think about it.

He looked at himself in the mirror. A tall slim man with a yellowish complexion that never altered no matter how long he spent in the sunshine. His eyes were black, intelligent and attractive. His brows were bushy, meeting above his large hooked nose to make a straight line across his face. At school he had been chosen to play Julius Caesar when his teacher said that he looked exactly like a Roman emperor. Adolf Fischer liked that idea and even now he would sometimes have too many drinks and surprise the other officers, who knew him only as a zealous and consistently savage warrior, by long quotations from Shakespeare's play.

These rooms on the first floor with balconies overlooking the lake had once been the finest rooms in the hotel. The bridal suite, perhaps. Now they were used for officers in transit and they had been left unaltered even to the china jug and basin on the marble washstand with an enamel jug of boiling water delivered each morning to the rooms without baths. The pictures too remained: stag hunt, dawn in the mountains and Napoleon after Waterloo. There was a knock at the door.

'Come in,' bawled Fischer. He was surprised to find that his visitor was an old man who outranked him considerably. Embarrassed by the manner in which he had shouted, Fischer came to a stiff position of attention and waited with unseeing eyes until his visitor bid him relax.

'Standartenführer Wörth,' the old man introduced himself. His voice was quiet and his manner hesitant. Fischer had to watch his lips to understand his words. 'I'm the commanding officer. Please continue with whatever you were doing. I only wished to offer you my greetings as I shall not be dining in the Mess this evening. The Burgomaster here in Altgarten is an old Allgemeine SS officer and he's having a rather formal dinner party.'

It was frightening, thought Fischer. The German Cross medal on the old man's pocket showed that he had been a fighting soldier in this war and yet now he'd become a mere vegetable, wrinkled and bent like an old turnip and so pale that Fischer felt positively tanned beside him.

'I have acquaintances nearby, sir. It was my intention to call upon them this evening.'

'Splendid,' said the old man. 'You're going to this new "Hitler Jugend" Division.'

'The Division commander was with me in the Leibstandarte. He's asked for me.'

'Reich Germans?'

'Yes. All of them born in 1926, volunteers from the Hitler Jugend.'

'It will be an *élite* division.'

'Yes, my tame *Untermensch* will look out of place.'

'So I hear.'

Fischer felt obliged to answer the unspoken question. 'He's a first-class gunner and mechanic. I had him assigned as a personal servant only in order to keep him.'

'You're a tank man?'

'Tigers; I volunteered for the first tank company the LAH got.'

'Cavalry man myself.' He flinched from some secret pain. 'Left a hand behind in Rzhev, can't hold a rein and fight with one hand.' Fischer noticed the stiff glove. Cavalry; that explained everything. These old fogeys are from another world.

'Cavalry Brigade Fegelein?'

'Yes.'

'It's largely *Volksdeutsche* now.'

'In my time it was just Reich Germans. It was an *élite* unit then.'

'I know that, sir.'

Wörth looked at Fischer's cuffband and then again at the young man's face. He saw his own youth there. Wörth was with the Leibstandarte in 1937. What fine fellows we were! Our average age was eighteen years one month. *Liebchen aller Herzen* they called LAH in those days. Heart-breakers we were too. Handsome fellows. The volunteer ahead of Wörth at the medical was failed for having one filled tooth. He could scarcely believe it now, when he looked at some of the odds and ends they had sent him. Dutchmen some of them and Flemings too. Keen of course, but he couldn't understand a word they said. Somewhere nearby a guard dog barked and then another one. There were shouts and a yelp of pain before the dogs became quiet. 'Those damned dogs will drive me mad,' muttered Wörth.

'I can well believe it, sir,' said Fischer. 'Why don't you get rid of them?'

'Why indeed,' said Wörth and smiled as though Fischer had made a rather good joke.

Leibstandarte, this old man, was it possible? 'Rzhev?'

'January 'forty-two, the Rzhev pocket.' It was months since he'd last spoken of it. 'My company of cavalry were trying to find Ivan. Our artillery found us.' In the snow, horses and riders moved like ghosts, silent and invisible in their newly issued white smocks. Wörth was riding Rosenknospe, a lightfooted horse as fast as any other in the company and with a gentle disposition.

They were in the Valdai hills where the Volga rises, north of Rzhev. They had come over the rise cautiously; Hentschel first on the black mare that he'd had all the way from the training school in Warsaw. At the bottom of the rise there was a T34, its turret askew and a black circle round it. Hentschel waved them on and then went close to the sooty burned-out tank, but there was no sign of life there. It was snowing slightly and the horses were fidgety, tossing their heads and missing their footing as they encountered debris, bodies and goodness knows what under the snow. 'It was our artillery.' They must have had the old T34 zeroed in; by getting close to that we were asking for it really. 'A T34 might be very different from a Tiger tank but Russian cavalry looks just like us, eh?' Then there was the noise: deafening thuds and the screams of horses and men. Instead of a black and white silent film it became a noisy colour film. The black mare racing across the snow, dragging young Hentschel – his second-in-command – by his foot, with horse and rider spilling blood as they went. Hentschel, Hentschel. 'No horses survived, four men did.' Rosenknospe, his favourite, threw him and then kicked wildly. It was frightened, its eyes dilated and mouth open. Then he saw that its belly was split open and its kicking feet entangled in its own entrails. Damn you, Rös'chen. Get up! 'Crawled back three miles on hands and knees.' The pain. 'Took twenty-eight hours.' Why the devil should he remember it all today? He pushed it back again deep into a recess in his mind.

'You were all right?'

'Only survivor. The other three died of wounds in hospital. I was there for three months, discharged myself. But only on anti-partisan work after that.'

'That's important duty.' Must the fellow relate his adventures. That little scuffle wouldn't merit a mention nowadays.

'Strong stuff; a whole village sometimes. Old men, old women, and then there's the problem of one's own soldiers with the girls. You take a hundred villagers . . .' His voice faded before he described their fate. 'Strong stuff. I was glad to leave it.'

'Necessary stuff, sir. We must never let up on any of them,' said Fischer.

Wörth looked at him and nodded, confirming not Fischer's opinion but his own opinion of Fischer. Wörth grimaced involuntarily. 'Gangrene, pain recurs more frequently lately. My foot and hip too. Without the sunlamp I can't walk.'

'It was bad luck, sir.'

'Mustn't bore you with my stories.'

'No question of that, Herr Standartenführer.' Not much!

The old man suddenly became tired. 'Witting,' he called in a voice no louder than the rest of his conversation, and from behind the door came an NCO. 'Leave you now, Fischer. Don't see you again, luck.'

'Thank you, sir.' Fischer came rigidly to attention and averted his eyes as the bent old man was helped out through the door. Moving ever more slowly he inched his crippled feet forward. Witting closed the door gently.

> 'This is a slight unmeritable man,
> Meet to be sent on errands . . .'

quoted Fischer softly to himself. On the table there were the remains of his meal. He'd eaten two frankfurters and a dish of boiled potatoes but had left the dehydrated cabbage and powdered soup. German Army frankfurters, by some miracle of logistics, tasted the same in Danzig as they did in Paris. He wondered how his driver was managing the repairs on the Kübelwagen. It would be ready by ten PM he was sure of that. He'd ordered it for ten and his driver would have it in good order even if he hadn't eaten, bathed or slept and was still wearing the same stinking underwear. Still, you can't have everything.

From his pocket he took a small notebook. Written there was the name of Herr Voss the tailor followed by his private address. There were four other names and addresses in Münster and Dortmund but they had been ticked. Fischer went out on the balcony to have a cigarette and stare at the placid lake and the ducks. Soon he would phone.

Andi Niels, the Burgomaster's secretary, got back to his office at five-fifteen. There was a note waiting: the Burgomaster wanted to see him urgently. He sighed irritably;

already the doorman and the typist next door had given him the same message. He went to check that Meyer's file was still where he had hurriedly pushed it. Only when he was sure it was there did he go next door.

'Niels,' said the Burgomaster, 'you have been signing documents and borrowing police dockets in my name without proper authority.'

Herr Holländer from the marriage registry was standing in the corner with a look of satisfaction on his rat-like face. He had always been jealous of Niels, who he knew could win any argument by invoking the Burgomaster's name. Now he was delighted to be in at the young upstart's undoing.

Niels had not responded to the Burgomaster's statement, so he spoke again. 'This file on Meyer, Hans-Willy.'

Meyer, Hans-Willy, thought Niels, the old buffoon spoke like an official document.

'Explain the down-grading,' said the Burgomaster.

'It's all in order, Herr Bürgermeister,' said Niels, smiling in one final hope that Ryessman would let the matter drop.

'I didn't ask you that, Niels.'

'He wanted to be.'

'What do you mean?'

'He wanted to be.'

'Don't raise your voice to me, my boy. You know very well that what he wanted is nothing to do with it. You made entries on the documents, why?'

'So that he could be married.'

Ryessman remembered the dark-eyed boy and girl. 'Was he married this afternoon?'

'That was him,' said Niels. 'You frightened the life out of him.'

'I did?'

'He thought you were about to stop the ceremony. It can't be altered now, you know.'

'I still don't understand,' said the Burgomaster.

Herr Holländer said, 'I understand, Herr Bürgermeister.

Marriage between two persons with one-third Jewish blood is forbidden, but marriage between a person with one-third Jewish blood and a person with two-thirds Jewish blood is permitted under certain circumstances. The man Meyer wanted to be down-graded so that he could marry the girl.'

'But she must be mad,' said the Burgomaster, trying sincerely to comprehend it. 'A girl with only one-third Jewish blood could have married an Aryan.'

'They are like that,' said Herr Holländer. 'I get them coming into the registry for advice. It's hard to believe, but some of them would sooner marry one of their own kind than one of us.'

The Burgomaster shook his head in wonder. He looked up at Niels. 'What did they pay you?'

'Nothing, I did it to help. They were in love.'

'Must I hand this matter over to the Gestapo?'

'Three thousand marks.'

'When I think of what I did for you, Niels . . . It was my influence that secured your discharge from your regiment when your mother told me of your stomach ulcer.'

'Well, your influence didn't last long, Herr Bürgermeister. I didn't get a discharge. I was placed temporarily on the reserve. My papers came this morning. I rejoin the 15th Panzer-grenadier Division in Sicily next week. They are awaiting the invasion. I shall never come back.' That little bastard Holländer was smirking gleefully.

'You would do well not to come back, Niels. Give your mother a hero for a son, you at least owe her that.'

'More than I owe her money to pay the rent and keep her from starving?'

'I would rather starve than have a son like you. You are an enemy of the State, a thief and a liar.'

Niels stood waiting for the Burgomaster's wrath to diminish.

'Get out,' he said after a long silence. Niels was pleased to get away so lightly.

240

'And . . .' said the Burgomaster. Niels turned. 'You will pay the three thousand marks to the Winter Help Fund and show me the receipt. I shall not withdraw my invitation for dinner tonight, but I shall not be unhappy if you fail to turn up.'

'Yes, Herr Bürgermeister,' said Niels, trying to look sad. That was wonderful. He had far better things to do tonight: the dance, and providing the terror flyers stayed away perhaps a visit to the fourth floor of the Annex. There was a tall Viennese nurse whom he rather fancied. She would be tastier than the Burgomaster's roast duckling.

Niels had been responsible for the eighteen invitations to the Burgomaster's dinner at Frenzel's. He had done the job carefully, remembering all sorts of obscure cousins and business colleagues. In fact, only one invitation had gone astray; the one to Frau H. Pippert, widow of a building contractor, had been typed with the wrong street-name and the postman had guessed, wrongly, that it was intended for Fräulein G. Pippert, a teacher at the Volkschule.

Gerda Pippert knew from the moment she opened the envelope that the invitation was not intended for her. On the other hand she also knew, unlike the Burgomaster, that Hanna Pippert – Johanna really, of course, but no one called her that – had died over six months ago. Hadn't she received more than a dozen wrongly addressed letters of condolence from brick merchants, timber firms and manufacturers of stoves and boilers. And hadn't she forwarded them to the brother-in-law of the dead woman at some address in Krakow. Gerda Pippert deserved the invitation. In the circumstances surely no one would begrudge her honorary membership of the Burgomaster's family for one festive evening. It was over three years since she had eaten a meal at a fine restaurant and as for being recognized, if they didn't even know that old Hanna was dead, what chance was there that they would remember her face. Anyway, old ladies looked alike. She could put some new lace on her black dress. One of her ex-students – now an artillery officer – had sent her an antique lace tablecloth from Brussels. She had never risked a teapot on it, but as a collar for the black dress it would be most chic. She decided to gatecrash the dinner, or, as she rationalized it to herself, attend as a friend of the family.

She had written a brief acceptance, carefully smudging the initial. She looked at herself in the full-length mirror of the wardrobe. It made the dress look quite new. Her white hair was drawn tightly back and fastened with a black ribbon. She would wear just a touch of face powder – it was a special event, after all – and leave her spectacles off. Then she remembered the old lorgnette. It was in the bottom of her sewing box, a splendid device with an ivory handle and gold rims to the glasses. She could no longer see very well through the lenses but held up to her face it looked most distinguished. What's more, it would give her something to do with her hands. In the sewing box there was an old ivory cigarette holder too. She put it in her handbag. Tonight after the coffee and speeches and cognac she would try a cigarette again. If only her handbag were a little more elegant and the handle weren't so worn, but if she held it low against her skirt it didn't notice so much. She paraded up and down the bed-sitting-room practising wellborn gestures. The dress looked fine. Tonight Gerda Pippert, fifty-six-year-old spinster and schoolteacher, was to dine with the Burgomaster! It was the most exciting prospect she could remember since her holiday in Heidelberg in 1938.

Gerd Böll may have been the town wag but he was no fool. Sometimes he regretted that he had left the university, for the young people there had a sense of humour more nearly tuned to his than had the people of Altgarten. In spite of disapproving eyes Gerd continued to act the fool for he knew that it was his particular strength that he could endure the supercilious remarks of his neighbours without wishing them ill.

Of all the people of Altgarten, Gerd's best friends were among the TENO engineers who manned the camp on the Krefeld road. Many times Gerd had taken his van and gone with them into the Ruhr after a big RAF attack. He had seen the TENOs digging for hours into burning wreckage and finding only shrivelled corpses. He'd seen them lifting steel beams in their bare hands and he'd noticed that some of the most pugnacious and disreputable roughnecks among them could be the most gentle with the injured. None of them were young, for the young had all been screened off to provide TENO battalions for bridge-building and demolition with front-line fighting units. Each man had a technical skill and their easy discipline reflected this, for theirs was a job where a few minutes could mean a cellarful of people saved from flames or drowning. They were a strange breed of men, new to Gerd Böll. They took a drink when others would need a night's sleep, they settled for a cigarette instead of a meal and swore when lesser men would have wept.

In addition, Gerd liked their equipment: the tractors, lorries and mobile cranes, the pumps and generators, and the winches that could topple an office block.

It was five-forty, almost time for Gerd to report his movements to the Burgomaster's Control Room. This evening of all evenings it was scarcely necessary, for he would be at Frenzel's with the Burgomaster. For a birthday gift he had bought a small humidor, inlaid with ivory and mother of pearl. One of the Russian POWs had made it for him. He wondered if the Burgomaster would disapprove if he knew its origin. Perhaps he would recognize the style of work, for the madonnas they sold from door to door had the same design on the skirts as the humidor had round its lid.

Dark suit? Well, Gerd didn't have a dark suit. Apart from this green suit he didn't have one at all. And this one had long since ceased to fit him. He unfastened the jacket buttons and breathed out with a long sigh of relief. Well, he'd leave it open. It would never notice when he was sitting down. He sat down now at his antique desk and cleared aside the accounts and unanswered correspondence. From this window he had the ugliest view of Altgarten. The cramped slum tenements crowded together between brewery siding and gasworks as did the people inside them.

In the cobbled street a group of children, some of them in Hitler Youth uniform, were kicking a ball around. Gerd watched them with interest but eventually the moment he had been putting off arrived. He pulled a piece of paper towards him and sadly began a letter to his cousin August.

Rheinprovinz, Altgarten
Bahnhofstrasse 33

June 31st, 1943

My dear kind August,

Perhaps you will despise me when you have finished reading this letter and yet, try as I have, I can find no alternative to writing it. This afternoon when I met you with Anna-Luisa and you both looked so radiantly happy it seemed clearly my duty (and my joy) to keep silent. Now I once again think otherwise. Think of me and my predicament as I write this letter. As unhappy as you may be, spare a moment to remember that I too am as sad.

The test of friendship is the extent to which a man will expose the friendship to total destruction by doing something he believes is in the best interest of his comrade. The girl is beautiful and to be sure has been a loyal employee and a fine guardian of little Hansl. But a young girl like Anna-Luisa has a life different from us, different too from any style of life we can remember. Like any beautiful girl living alone in a town filled with young men, the temptations put to her are unreasonable, but it would be dishonest of me, and foolish of you, to pretend that she has not succumbed to those temptations in a way that has made her notorious.

As your housekeeper, her private life is of only limited importance to you, and of no importance to me. But when marriage is mentioned, my dear good cousin, how can I not speak? At first you will dismiss my letter as gossip. Perhaps you will be tempted to ask for details. Do not do that, August. It can only cause you deep and lasting pain. Again I repeat, August, it can only cause you more pain than you already know.

Your cousin,
GERD

CHAPTER SIXTEEN

Oberleutnant August Bach, who knew nothing of the letter his cousin had written to him and would in fact never know of it, walked along the soft beach in the evening light. One thousand suns bounced upon the wave-tops and the sound of the sea was harsh and constant.

It was the coldness of the sea that formed the water particles in the air – twenty thousand of them in every cubic inch – by cooling it to dew-point. So along the shoreline the incoming air became cloud and moved inland and became warm enough for the cloud to disappear. Patches of mist brooded in the cold trees and made the taller dunes into tiny desert islands. On the strand where August walked the mist was churned by the wind to reveal the golden horizon and then wrap him again in its cottonwool.

Deep-rooted yellow poppies and sea-sandwort struggled for life against the shifting sand that exposed their roots one day and buried their heads the next. Along the high-water mark nature's usual debris had collected: edible urchins like battered shaving-brushes, cuttlefish bones, channel wrack, some of it dried and blackened, the mussels pounded loose from the endless steel stakes that extended out into the ocean and pointed at England. There was other flotsam too: pieces of packing-case with cryptic stencil marks, a few dozen squashed oranges and a burned piece of yellow lifejacket. Over everything there was thick shiny oil that added a sour smell of decay to the brisk salt breeze.

Bach tapped the loose sand from his boots, climbed a short flight of wooden steps and opened the door of the shack in which he lived. At first his men had thought him mad for commandeering this ramshackle hut perched high upon the dunes. It had been an equipment store for the Dutchmen who had planted the dune grass and maintained the sea wall. Bach had had it lined with insulating material and supported on new metal beams to make it dry and free of rats. Inside there were books, a stove, a simple Luftwaffe bedstead, an old armchair and a table at which he worked. The few men under his command privileged to see the place at close quarters recognized now the wisdom of his choice. His Luftwaffe signals company numbered one hundred and fourteen men, with him their only officer. He was quite happy to live and eat with them, but men who obey orders need a chance to complain without an officer to overhear. His little hut, half a kilometre from the other buildings, gave them that chance. He unlocked the door and let himself in. His desk was placed near to the window from which he could see the beach and ocean when the weather was clear. Willi, his second-in-command, had lit the stove, for even on a summer's evening there was dampness in the air that made the bedding cold and edged the lenses of his binoculars with tiny spots of moisture. He filled a kettle from the tap at the washbasin. The pipe rattled like a machine gun and the water was warm from its journey through the hastily laid water pipe that went along the sunny dunes to the main building.

He treasured these few moments alone as he came to terms with this environment. He remembered Anna-Luisa and felt a warm contentment at his memory of her. He knew that once the Stabsfeldwebel arrived and work began he would no longer be able to give himself to these sentimental emotions. He wiped the lenses of his field-glasses and walked to the rear of the hut. From this window he could see back across the dunes to the radar buildings and, when it was not misty, all the way along the coast to the tip of the tall radar aerials of the next Himmelbett station.

He focused the glasses upon a clump of grass and waited for the mist to move. Just a fidget of wing and a stretch of long neck was for a moment higher than the edge of a nest. The grey herons were still there on the dune side. They usually stayed close to fresh water, especially in the summer, but since this coast had been made a prohibited area the wildlife had become more active. These had laid their eggs in May. Now it was almost time to go. He wondered whether they would return next winter. He felt that they were an omen.

Satisfied that all was well with the herons, he began to change from his uniform into old, more comfortable clothes. He pulled off his high boots, using the home-made wooden clamp behind the door. When the kettle began to hum gently he called Willi on the phone.

'A cup of chocolate, Willi,' he said.

'Thank you, Herr Oberleutnant,' said the man at the other end. August chopped the coarse chocolate pieces into chips, melted them in the boiling water and beat the mixture until it was frothy.

August was watching his Stabsfeldwebel marching along the dunes when the heron returned. It was a huge ungainly bird with curiously slow and mechanical wing movements that made it seem man-made. Its legs trailed behind it and from its beak there hung an eel. The bird in the nest gave a croak of pleasure and raised its head to look. Always one or other of them remained at the nest. 'Kroink'; it circled the main buildings. Perhaps the great radar aerials attracted the birds, thought August, as it flew across the face of the Freya. White mist wove through the intricate metalwork like skeins of soft raw wool through a comb and the aerial moved gently, scanning as far as, and farther than, the enemy coast. Sometimes it even detected RAF planes that never left the English sky.

Willi Reinecke knocked briefly and waited for permission before he entered. He carefully brushed the wet sand from his jackboots and stood correctly at attention. The steaming cup of chocolate waited for him on August's desk but first the two men enacted the ritual of salutes and greetings of rank that was a necessary prelude to all military intercourse.

Willi Reinecke was a tall thick-set man of indeterminate age. Born in Hessen-Nassau, the promise of work in the steel industry of the Ruhr had drawn him north as a young man, but, unemployed and desperate, he had finally joined the Army. He still had a lot of hair. It was greying at the sides in a distinguished way that would have looked right on a banker. As a youngster he had been quite a ladies' man, but a grenade had exploded on a parapet while Willi was still looking over it. His nose had split open, his cheek was a maze of scars, and one ear was missing altogether, which is why he grew his hair long. A veteran of the Moscow battles, August had guessed when he had first been posted here, but the Stabsfeldwebel had growled 'Verdun' and only then did August realize that his second-in-command was a lot older than he liked to admit.

They had disliked each other on sight. Reinecke was a senior NCO of the old school. Twice August had seen him kick a man who had dawdled and he would not hesitate to clobber anyone who looked as if he might argue. These incidents had made the first trouble between them. At first August had tried to explain that the personnel he commanded were Luftwaffe technicians, not cannon-fodder, but that had no effect. Finally August had decided to fight with Reinecke's weapons. He gave the amazed Reinecke a blistering dressing-down and ordered him to parade each shift an hour before their work commenced. At that time there were six shifts – manning the radar machinery was tiring for the plotters working in darkness and gruelling for the men exposed to the sea breeze – and so Reinecke found himself on parade six hours out of the twenty-four.

The lesson was not lost on the stubborn old man and, after a month of the new régime had convinced him that August was quite prepared to continue the same schedule for the war's duration, he called for a truce. He did this when August was away on a two-day course in electronics. The Oberleutnant returned to find that the draughty little hut in which he had elected to live had been completely remade. It had been equipped with furnishings stolen or borrowed from goodness knows where and a large double-glazed window had been fitted to facilitate August's bird-watching. From that moment the two of them had tried to work together, and in that curious way that happens sometimes to people with such contrasting beliefs and back-grounds they had become very close. When August Bach understood the man better he realized that his tyranny was matched by a concern for the welfare of his men. Willi Rein-ecke was not above stealing, lying and even falsifying docu-ments to ensure that his men were properly clothed and fed.

Even more surprising was the skill that Willi Reinecke had shown in the plotting-room. For the first week or so August had used one of the younger technicians to help him plot the bombers, but Reinecke always appeared whenever there were enemy planes in the sector and finally August worked with him one night. Incredibly it was that night that the thousand-bomber raid upon Cologne passed overhead. Willi Reinecke didn't have the lightness of touch for which the training school would give high marks. He stumbled up the steps of the ladder to the plotting-table and swore loudly when August needed silence. It was a rare night in which Willi didn't drop his Kneemeyer measure two or three times or kick the table as he hastily gauged the speed of the bomber that the radar held in its beam. Willi's value was in the way he could guess the intentions of the quarry. Some of them had a device that told them they were held in the invisible radar beam. These would jink and turn desperately. Willi would poise his marker over a point where he expected the bomber to go while August guided the fighter pilot on to it. It was surprising how often Willi outguessed the *Tommis*.

Willi Reinecke had a wife and two children. He didn't smoke, rarely drank alcohol and lately he had shown an interest in August's bird-watching. He was very proud of his first attempt at taxidermy and prouder still when August put it in a place of honour on his desk. In short, Willi Reinecke was a conundrum and that, more than any other thing, was what drew August close to him.

Willi removed his belt and special flak Service greatcoat with its wool lining and the stripes on both cuffs that, in the Wehrmacht, marked the company's senior NCO. He hung it behind the door. August remained in his armchair and Willi sat erect in the seat at the desk. He nodded his thanks as the chocolate was pushed towards him. He sipped it and held his scarred hands around the cup for a moment before giving his report. He unfolded a piece of paper and read the names.

'Two men sick since you left on Friday: one of the plotting-table orderlies – Gefreiter Path – said he had tonsillitis, but I took a look at him.' Willi looked up. 'He's running a slight temperature but it's only a sore throat. I've put him on light duties outdoors. That should do the trick and meanwhile he's not breathing sore-throat bugs all around the Seeburg table.' Again he referred to his paper. 'The other case was Gefreiter Kick – the cook with the handlebar moustache – he complained of stomach pains. Too tender for indigestion and the wrong side for appendicitis. Regular colicky stabs of pain. I sent him into Rotterdam with the ration lorry; the hospital are holding him for observation. Meanwhile Unteroffizier Zewlinski will work the last shift until Kick returns or we get a replacement. There's not much work on that shift except counting the stores.'

'And you think Zewlinski can count the stores unaided?'

'I'll be keeping an eye on him.'

'You are quite a physician, Willi. I'm very impressed.'

251

'I've had a lot of cavalry experience and men are just like horses. I could always tell the horse-pox or colic (which just needed isolation and a rest) from the lymph cases and the strangles that have to be sent back down the line as fast as possible.'

'To the slaughterhouse?'

'Sometimes, sir.'

'And you sent Kick back?' Bach grinned but Reinecke didn't.

'We shan't see him again,' pronounced the old man grimly. 'But I let Unteroffizier Zewlinski think he'd only be doing the extra duties for a day or two.'

'I understand, Willi.'

Willi peered at his piece of typed paper again. 'Two men to divisional signals course, three on the gas course, six men guarding the unoccupied gun site near the village with Rimm in charge of them. The cook that HQ borrowed is still there.' Willi looked up. 'He plays the accordion,' he added significantly.

'He wasn't much of a cook,' said Bach.

'We should try to write him off and ask for a replacement.' Bach nodded. 'Three in hospital in Rotterdam including Kick, ten on leave, four on day pass, three on ration detail: one hundred and fourteen men present and correct.'

Bach nodded.

'Two more bicycles stolen,' said Willi Reinecke.

'This time they are for it.'

'The men who lost them are on open arrest. I thought you'd probably sentence them tomorrow after the cashing-up is done. Then they can go into Rotterdam tomorrow afternoon as soon as the second shift go on.'

'You have informed the local civilian police? They got the last one back, didn't they?'

'Yes, sir, but riding a Wehrmacht bicycle is a risky business for a Dutch civilian. To get home one night after curfew perhaps . . .'

'Yes, if you spot one outside a bar, unlocked and waiting to be stolen. It's just carelessness.'

'Exactly, sir. Either that or they are going farther afield in the back of one of the wagons. I have informed the military police office in Rotterdam.'

'I will sentence them tomorrow. Air activity?'

'Little or nothing.'

'They are expected tonight.'

'We had the alert. I have assigned Lemmers' crew to the Freya and I have rearranged the shifts as you ordered. The best crews will take over their radars at midnight.'

'It's a short night for them. Let's hope it's to be the Ruhr, then they might cross this sector on the outward as well as the return.'

Suddenly August realized that Willi's family lived in the Ruhr. Confused and embarrassed, he searched for something else to say. 'Moonrise is . . .'; he tried to see the time from the chart.

'Moonrise tonight is 00.30, sir. Yes, it will be nice to get two cracks at them.'

'And sunrise is 05.46. They will have come and gone by 03.00, I would say.'

'I told the crews that if the target is in the Ruhr it will be a four-hour shift. If the *Tommis* go farther than that, the number two crews will stand them down for a break and we'll put them back on for the return.'

'Good, Willi. You out-think me every time.'

Willi smiled. They both knew it wasn't true, but it was nice to hear the Oberleutnant say it. They drank the hot chocolate. Willi knew that there was no more official business.

'A good weekend, sir?'

'Wonderful, Willi.'

'Your small son is well?'

'He runs me into the ground. I don't know where he finds the energy.'

'My two are the same. I'm glad to get back here for a rest.'

Willi looked round the Oberleutnant's room. He felt privileged to be allowed into it. Even the senior officers who came on visits to the radar station were seldom invited here. On the wall above a desk cluttered with glue, wire and soldering equipment there was a sheet of white card upon which August Bach had been reconstructing the bones of a gull's wing. Alongside it were pasted reproductions of Leonardo drawings of a wing and some photos of gulls, avocets and harriers in flight.

'The sparrowhawk came back.'

'Photo?'

'I'm not as quick as you are, sir.'

'It's just practice.'

'We got some interesting movements on the radar last night.'

'Birds?'

'No doubt.'

'Log it all, Willi. We're in a unique position that could make a real contribution. Until now the ornithologists didn't know that birds flew at night.'

'The operator made a note of the time.'

On the desk there was the blackheaded gull that Willi had wired and mounted. He hadn't mastered the trick of folding the wings and he wouldn't permit August to help, so like many an amateur taxidermist before him he had finally fixed them outstretched – gull at moment of alighting. Under the gull's red feet he had put a nest with three blue-green eggs. Whatever its faults, as August had told him, 'No one would guess it was a first attempt.' Willi turned it round proudly.

'You saw the heron just now?'

'I'm going to get married again, Willi.'

'That's good, sir.'

'To my housekeeper.'

'That's wise, sir. At our age a man wants a sensible woman, not a flashy piece of skirt.'

August smiled. 'I'm afraid that many of my friends might say that she is a flashy piece of skirt, Willi. She's an RAD girl, not much older than my son.'

It was Willi's turn to be embarrassed, but August didn't care about anything. He was enjoying the warm feeling of being in love. He opened a drawer of his desk and took out a bottle of German brandy. He poured a slug of it into the Stabsfeldwebel's chocolate.

'Drink up, Willi,' said August Bach. 'Let's think ourselves lucky that we are not flying with the *Tommis*. For tonight, I have a feeling, we shall have a remarkable success.'

'Success,' echoed Willi and drank his chocolate and brandy.

For some time they sat in silence, drinking and watching the shadows lengthen and the blurred sun drop towards the misty ocean.

'There was no mail?' He knew there was none. Had there been any, it would have been placed upon his desk-top as it always was. 'None,' said Willi.

'He's an inconsiderate little bastard.'

'He'll be all right: bright lad, lots of combat behind him. You know how quickly you'd hear.'

'He can look after himself; I was thinking only of his promotion. He's been a Sturmmann for over a year and the lowest ranks live like pigs in the front line.'

'Promotion is slow in the Waffen SS units.'

'I wish like hell he wasn't in an SS unit,' said August.

'I'd feel the same if it was my boy.'

'Only because they don't get enough rest between combat.'

'Of course,' said Willi. 'I understand.' He got to his feet and stood correctly at attention again. 'If the Oberleutnant permits . . . there are the personnel and ration returns.' The old NCO had moved from intimate chatter to the absurd third person of the Kaiser's army.

'Carry on, Willi. I'll be along soon.'

He spent a few minutes looking through a trayful of paperwork. It could all wait until tomorrow, he decided. He put on his long black leather overcoat. The wind whined gently as he opened the door.

The sea was blood-red by the time Oberleutnant Bach walked along the wet sand to start work. He walked as slowly as he could. He picked up pieces of seaweed and a tern, stiff with diesel oil. Once he thought he saw a hedgehog among the dunes and waited five minutes for it to reappear but it didn't.

From the sea's edge the futuristic shape of the radar aerials was awesome even to him. He could easily pretend that he had just emerged from this sea upon some Atlantis where the technics were a century ahead of anything he had known. The metal graticule, as big as a large house, that swung gently from side to side was codenamed Freya. August remembered that Freya was a Nordic goddess whose watchman could see one hundred miles in every direction by day and by night. It was a fair description of the Freya radar device and August reasoned that if he could work that out, then so could the British Intelligence. (In fact he was correct. Dr R. V. Jones worked it out and reported to the Chiefs of Staff accordingly.)

Not far away were the two shorter-range, but more precise, giant Würzburgs. They were like electric bowl fires as big as windmills. They too swung gently around the horizon but always returned – like the Freya – to point westwards to where in East Anglia the Allied bomber airfields were but half an hour's flying time away.

Gently August put the dead tern back on the sand. It was 22.00; the *Tommis* were not even in the air yet and when they were the Freya would give warning. The sand crunched underfoot. He kicked a hole in it and the sea appeared there as if by magic. Eggs for tea and a walk along the silent beach in the evening sunlight; Hansl and Anna-Luisa would love it here. After the war they would live somewhere remote. This was a fine rich country. Even with a hungry Wehrmacht gnawing at it for years there were still eggs and milk and sometimes cream. A few months ago Willi had come back from Zuidland with a whole sheep. August had checked the ration returns and the petrol sheets but had found no discrepancy.

From the tops of the dunes one could see fields of vegetables and greenhouses just like Altgarten. But here in the spring they had eaten them. The soups had been brimful of vegetables and meat and he had not complained, nor even investigated. He told himself he would have found nothing amiss anyway. The truth of it was that he was a bloody awful officer. That's why he had never risen above Oberleutnant. And that was why he was strolling along the strand with a pair of Zeiss 16 × 40s, soft shoes and an old sweater, instead of besieging Leningrad in full battle order.

Still, thought August, one war is enough for any man. In the first basinful also he had been happy. Flying his Albatros twice a day and living on good food and wine in a fairy-tale château on the Meuse. Wouldn't any spoiled young brat fresh from university give his life for a chance like that? That's just what a lot of them did give. Who knows why any survived, except that suddenly the brain feels anew the prick of self-preservation that deserts young men for a few years and so makes heroes possible and wars welcome.

He raised his glasses to the naval gun bunker. Upon it sat a tern. He flicked the binoculars into focus and watched with pleasure as it searched its wings and preened itself. Suddenly there was the rumble of the emergency generator being tested. The bird rose alarmed and flew out to sea until August lost sight of it.

The sea mist had thinned considerably but the light was going fast. Reluctantly he put his glasses into the case and entered the T-shaped hut and its plotting-room.

* * *

Had August been able to see eighty-five kilometres to the north he would have seen the coastal convoy and the anti-aircraft light cruiser *Held* continuing steadily on their course. The guns they had fired at Löwenherz and Himmel were long since cleaned and readied for action but there had been no other interruptions and, as 'Admiral' Pawlak had predicted, they were now halfway to the Hook. The convoy had moved closer to the coast here, for the danger from wrecks was lessened and the danger from Allied aircraft increased.

This piece of coast was still enveloped in a thin streak of mist but the sunset had turned it bright gold, 'like a Turner'.

'Like a what?'

'A painting by Turner, just a swirl of golds and reds and orange, a sort of land of ghosts.'

'You give me the creeps you do, Dikke. You know what your trouble is, you read too many books, and books will get you nowhere. Now come away from that porthole and listen to what I'm saying and we might get ourselves another ring round the gun.'

The plump boy from Königsberg went and sat on the bunk where 'Admiral' Pawlak with his mouth full of cheese was explaining about gunnery. On the wall of the storeroom there was a bright disc of light moving upwards as the sun sank lower and lower.

'It's rhythm – no one ever teaches you that but that's the secret of a high rate of fire – rhythm.' He broke off another piece of cheese and put it in his mouth. 'Now take that starboard number two gun, that loader waits for the breech to clear and then leans in with the next shell just like they teach you at gunnery school. That's all very well for demonstration work or target shooting but when you have a plane taking evasive action like this morning's one did you've got to anticipate.'

'When I was at training school, one of our crew caught his hand in the breech.'

'Well, he must have been a slow-witted fool, Dikke, like you.'

'That's right, he was. That's why I don't try these tricks of yours.'

'You're a fool, Dikke. Do you want to stay a K3 all your life? Tonight I'll take the loading. We'll be under control from the bridge so you can be number one, I don't care.'

'Thanks, Admiral.'

'Forget it, Dikke. If we are going to get our third *Tommi* tonight we'll have to get a lot of shells into the air.'

The ships in the convoy were lit by the sun like golden toys on a black velvet sea. Inside the cabin the light grew redder and redder.

'Put on the light, Dikke. I can't see to eat my cheese.'

The plump boy did as he was told.

'And close the port covers. You know the blackout regulations. Do you want to get us bombed?'

CHAPTER SEVENTEEN

The NAAFI closed at ten o'clock but the Salvation Army canteen was open until ten-thirty. By leaving the Station cinema early and sprinting across the parade ground it was possible to get a cup of tea before bedtime. Mrs Andrews who served in the Sally-Ann judged the films by the number of hot drinks she sold last thing at night. 'It's not a very good film; fourteen teas Monday and I had to make a second pot on Tuesday night.'

The previous week there had been a flying film. The hero made love with a sober intensity and flew with drunken abandon (the complete reversal of the activities of the RAF boys). A cowardly pilot ran amok, was ostracized and finally flew sobbing into an enemy plane. The CO ruled with his fists and cried glycerine tears each time one of his boys failed to return. The RAF greeted this film with jeers and catcalls. The projectionist had phoned the Orderly Officer about it.

'Shouting at the film, are they? And you want me to come over there so they can shout at me? Not Pygmalion likely. I saw it last night. It's about time you got some good films.'

They had no contact with this film or its makers. RAF selection boards had ensured that none of them ever experienced such extreme emotions. No one at Warley had ever publicly sworn vengeance upon the Germans (unless you counted the CO). No one here endured a crash so light-heartedly, took off into thick fog or swigged whisky round the Mess table, toasted absent friends with song and threw their glasses into the fireplace. Here grief was measured by what was paid for the auctioned, worthless personal effects of the casualties. Tears were for actors. Here cowardice was their common conceit and all had their own favourite acts of cowardice of which to boast. The flyers of Warley were men of even temperament who, for better or worse, did not react profoundly to the work they did.

Tonight there were no crews in the crowded cinema. No one left early nor did they make a noise. It was an old Charles Laughton film – *Rembrandt* – and so many turned up that they had been forced to get folding seats from the Operations Block and sit latecomers along the aisles.

The Music Circle meeting in the Education Hut had assembled nineteen assorted ranks to listen to Georg Kulenkampff and the Berlin Philharmonic play Beethoven's Violin Concerto. The performance was virtually faultless and their pleasure was marred only slightly by having to turn the records every few minutes. The Education Officer had the irritating habit of conducting, but when the music had finished and he produced a few bottles of beer all was forgiven. They were there until almost midnight talking about music. There were very few places on the aerodrome where all ranks could meet on a completely equal footing, let alone drink and smoke together.

The Station dance band had been in existence for six weeks but there had been only two rehearsals with every member present. Two of the band were working tonight. Sergeant Tommy Carter, a keen amateur saxophone player, was flying Joe for King, and a corporal who could play the piano relatively well was on duty in Flying Control. This night the fellow on the piano could only play from the singer's line and the trumpet player was all over the place. It wasn't his fault, for although he had studied music for two years, his instrument was the violin. The seven musicians practised together at the far end of the NAAFI, but when the canteen began to fill up they stopped playing and sat around drinking tea. The leader, an LAC clerk from South-ampton, said that if they couldn't do better than this they should tell the dance committee to bring in a civilian band for the Sergeants' Mess dance next month. By the time the NAAFI closed they were all a little depressed.

Musically, however, Warley Fen was dominated that summer by a simple but subtle melody. Erks whistled it as they bicycled to dispersals. Fitters hummed it as they replaced the sparking plugs on the Merlins and a big-breasted blonde NAAFI girl named Veronica played it on the piano with lots of improvised vamping. A slim-hipped MT corporal with a thin moustache impersonated Al Bowlly and sang it word-perfect with every inflection of that singer's voice. In the Officers' Mess there was a gramophone record of it that someone had brought back from London.

Every lunchtime of that hot summer the cadences floated across the even, bright green lawns of Warley Manor and made the tea-roses tremble. The Sergeants' Mess had the same record and it had become the custom for returning aircrew NCOs to call into the Mess for one last nightcap after leaving the tension and excitement of the debriefing. That record was always near the gramophone and usually the first arrivals would put it on. Sometimes after a grim night when there were a few missing faces they would play it repeatedly until dawn shone.

> Easy come, easy go. That's the way,
>   if love must have its day, then as
>   it came let it go.
> No remorse, no regrets. We should part,
>   exactly as we met; just easy come, easy go.
> We never dreamt of romantic dangers
> But now as it ends, let's be friends and not two
>   strangers.
> Easy come, easy go, here we are, so darling
>   au revoir, easy come, easy go.

A quarter of a century later, men who knew Warley Fen that summer when the bombers went out night after night remembered nothing more clearly than that little melody. It needed only the opening trumpet notes, the wire brushes and guitar to transport them back there again.

Not all spare-time occupations were musical. Flight Sergeant Bishop, the Station blacksmith, was Sergeant of the guard. He was sitting in the guardroom assembling a large picture of a galleon in full sail from sweet-wrappers and coloured paper. It was a painstaking hobby and the portrait of Joe Louis on the wall in his quarters represented nearly three hundred manhours of tearing, cutting and pasting. People who saw the pictures wondered that the clumsy muscular hands of the blacksmith could work in such meticulous detail.

Aircraftman First Class Albert Singleton, an Officers' Mess waiter, did that evening, with the help of Aircraftwoman Janet Marsden, motor-transport driver, steal from the aforesaid Mess one seven-pound tin of butter, three seven-pound tins of marmalade, eighteen pounds of bacon and twenty-eight eggs. These stores, the property of His Majesty King George the Sixth, were taken to Peterborough in an RAF Hillman van, also the property of His Majesty. The foodstuffs were delivered to a restaurant owner against payment of seven pounds ten shillings. By ten-thirty Singleton and Marsden had visited several public-houses and consumed a considerable amount of alcohol.

It was nearly eleven o'clock when they came down the blacked-out country lane from Ramsey and parked near the perimeter fence. It was warm in the front seat of the RAF van and the windows grew misty with their breath as they kissed and cuddled in the dark. After a few minutes one of the lorries carrying aircrew came past them along the peri track. They paused to watch it.

'It's a new driver we've got,' said ACW Marsden, nodding towards the crew bus. 'She's straight from the training school, talk about keen.'

'Not like you,' said Bert Singleton.

'I'm keen sometimes,' said the girl, and they kissed again. As the crew lorry got to the far corner they heard the crews shouting remarks about blackout to some house in the village but they didn't stop kissing.

Binty Jones folded up his comic and began speaking in his mock-American accent. 'Eleven o'clock, guys,' he said. 'Let's get this little old show on the road. I've got me some heavy petting in Peterborough before sun-up.'

Digby zipped his flying boots and looking up in surprise said, 'Are you still sleeping in Peterborough, you mad bastard?'

It had become fashionable among some of the crews to have their names written across the front of their flying helmets. A bottle of light-pink nail-varnish was going the rounds. Cohen was writing 'Kosher' on his.

'That I am, feller,' said Binty. 'A quarter of an hour from billet to bedroom. That's all it takes me on the motorbike.'

'Quarter of an hour,' said Lambert. 'I'd rather fly the operation twice than go that last ten miles on your banger.'

'Fifteen miles,' corrected Binty. 'Ah well, I'm a professional, you see.'

'Professional crumpet-chaser?' said Digby.

'Milkmen all are,' said Cohen, 'aren't they, Binty?'

'Some of them,' he grinned proudly. In spite of his carefully pressed clothes and shirt starched like card he was not much to look at: cropped hair, bad teeth, short stature and pockmarked face. None of which was an impediment to his frantic motorized sex-life, in pursuit of which he journeyed constantly across East Anglia. 'It's the bike that gets them, man, the rhythm, you see. They hear that in the middle of the night and they quiver like a jelly.'

'You still with that married sheila?' asked Digby. He knew the answer but he wanted to draw Flash Gordon into the discussion. He liked to hear them argue.

'She's a smashing piece of crackling, man.'

'Why don't you find yourself some piece of single skirt?' said Flash.

'You know why, man. All the best single crumpet in Peterborough has been taken over by the Yanks.'

'Well, I don't think it's right. Her old man fighting in the desert. I just don't think it's right.'

'I'm just keeping it warm for him, man.'

'I hope he comes back and knocks the daylights out of you.'

'No danger, I've seen his photo, a tiny fellow he is.'

'A judo instructor.'

'Sheet-metal worker with a REME unit in Alex.'

'He'll come back and clobber you,' warned Flash.

The conversation had taken the same lines that it always took and after it they were silent as they always were. Binty opened his comic again. 'What's the time now?' asked Digby.

'Three minutes later than the last time you asked,' said Cohen. Again he checked the contents of his green canvas bag: torch, rice-paper message pad, radio notes, protractor, dividers, coloured pencils, course and speed calculator, log book, target map, star tables and ruler. It was all there.

'That's quite a watch you've got there, sport,' said Digby.

'My uncle's. My ma gave it to me this morning.'

Cohen returned the nail-varnish to Digby who put it on the shelf of his locker and padlocked the door. 'Come on, Maisie,' said Digby quietly. They looked across to the far side of the room where a line of aircrew were waiting for Maisie Holroyd to issue them with flying rations. Batters was next.

'Four Bovrils, three coffees.'

'Four Bovrils, three coffees,' she said, and the clerk gave Batters the required vacuum flasks of hot drinks as well as seven packets of sandwiches, chewing-gum, boiled sweets and chocolate.

Sergeant Jimmy Grimm, the wireless operator and stand-by gunner, was a cheerful beardless man of twenty-three. He would have been acutely embarrassed to know that among Warley's WAAFs he was known as 'the blond bombshell' for although he was married with a two-year-old child he was absurdly shy in the presence of women and was easily shocked by the sort of jokes that the crews related with such proud maturity. Sometimes, balanced over his radio, he'd write long, long letters to his wife Mollie in large looping handwriting and always in green ink.

An average wireless operator, Grimm was a dedicated amateur photographer and the billet that he shared with Digby and Cohen was a disordered muddle of enamel trays, film tins and parts of his home-made enlarger. Often both bathrooms were full of prints, with others in the wash-basins. Once one had jammed in the drain and flooded four rooms.

These were group portraits of the whole crew that he was passing round. He had a little clockwork device that enabled him to rush and join them after starting the shutter. Handsome lads they all were. Relaxed and smiling like any one of a million young men. Looking at those prints now, it would be easy to say that it was the work of an amateur or that the materials were inferior or unsuitable because they were stolen from Air Ministry supplies. That wouldn't be true. The fact is that the boys were all like that: their faces were not out of focus or over-exposed, they were bland and smooth and as yet unformed. Those grinning cherubs awkwardly placed in that wartime snapshot are a high-definition portrait of the men who that night climbed into their flying boots, adjusted their parachute harness, borrowed clean shirts, reread old letters, lost a quick hand of cards, wrote IOUs for half a crown and watched the clock so carefully. And so often.

'Bloody good snap that, Jimmy.'

'Us with the old Door behind.'

'What a handsome group!'

'Enlarge it yourself, Jimmy? Bloody good shows.'

'Look at Dig, scowling. He's a card.'

'Pockets undone as usual, Kosh.'

'Good of the Skipper.'

'Too serious.'

'Well, he is more serious nowadays.'

'It's that bloody Sweet giving him the needle.'

'Sweet's all right. One of the boys. He's got a good sense of humour.'

'Sense of flipping arse-crawling, you mean.'

'Any more photos, Jim? Is that your garden?'

'Can I keep this, Jimmy?'

'Cost you one and threepence.'

'Bloody robber.'

'Here you are. I'll send it to my mum,' said Battersby.

'Me too,' said Binty. 'Four I'd better have. No, make it five.'

'Who's that bird with the pram?'

'What a smashing piece of crumble.'

'Shut up, you berk, it's Jimmy's missus.'

Crews were still arriving. There was an endless clang of locker doors, with occasional arguments when someone discovered their helmet missing or their boots borrowed and returned muddy. Flying gear was worn piecemeal according to personal taste and crew position. Usually the Lanc's heating system blew warm upon the wireless operator, roasted the bomb aimer and left the navigator to freeze. So most of the navigators were wearing the whole gear, from leather Irvin jackets to silk undersocks. So were the rear gunners. Most WOpAGs on the other hand had only the mandatory helmet, boots and Mae West over the same working blue and white rollneck sweater that they had worn at supper. Some flyers had brightly coloured silk scarves and even civilian shirts. Sandy Sanderson wore a fine leather jacket that he'd had made in Cairo.

It was a warm evening and now the blackout shutters were closed the changing-room became smelly as the crews crowded into it. Some of the early comers were playing cards for money while the late arrivals were grabbing their flying boots and filling their shoes with loose change, farewell letters and dirty pictures before pushing them into the back of their lockers. Few were pessimistic enough to leave a spare key behind and all the tin lockers bore scarred paintwork from being forced open many times.

Wing Commander Munro edged his way across the room.

'Mr Lambert.'

'Sir?'

'Last month after the cricket match you paid for both lots of beer. Will one pound ten see me out of debt?'

'It's only a pound, sir.'

'Here you are then, old chap.' He smiled, gave Lambert the money and was gone.

'Until now he's just paid alternately. That's the way we've done it since the season started,' said Kosher.

'He just wants to be out of debt,' said Lambert. Thoughtfully Kosher looked again at the Wing Commander, who was on the far side of the room giving an encouraging word to Fleming.

Fleming's crew felt that they were being scrutinized and they were careful to display no sign of excitement or nerves. Fleming had bent and dirtied his peaked cap to make it resemble those that had done a few thousand flying miles tucked behind a pilot's seat. Now he was wearing it at a rakish angle as he finished reading a copy of Routine Orders. He folded the paper up carefully to make a paper aeroplane.

'What's that, Mr Fleming, a Lanc Mark IV?' said Munro in an attempt to make a joke.

'That's it, sir,' agreed Fleming. He launched the paper wing. Everyone watched as it flew straight and level the length of the room. When it reached the tea urns, where the catering WAAFs were dispensing flasks of hot drinks, it hit a thermal. It nosed up until it stalled and fell like a dead bird to the floor.

'Back to the drawing-board,' shouted Binty Jones. Fleming smiled shyly.

Batters returned with a vacuum flask and a packet for each of them. Then complicated exchanges began. Binty liked gum – it was part of his Yank posture – so Digby exchanged his gum for Binty's barley sugar. Then Flash Gordon gave his gum to Binty for chocolate. Then Digby passed his extra barley sugar to Flash who took this, and a contribution from most of the crew, back to his brothers and sisters. There were nine of them. A few months before, Binty had taken him home on the motorbike. After returning he'd hinted that the spare rations from the boys would be the only treats those Gordon kids were likely to see.

All exchanges finished, Lambert gave them each a sealed escape kit containing a compass, counterfeit money, a silk map of Germany and some compressed dried fruit. Then they shuffled along the covered walkway to the next building. The parachute section was always clean and shiny, brightly lit and smelling of floor polish like a hospital for machines. Two bored WAAFs tugged parachutes and harnesses from the shelves behind them and threw them on to the counter with a clatter. Pilots' chutes had their parcel of silk fixed to the harness so that it formed a seat. The other crew members carried their silk canopies as a separate brown-canvas parcel which before use had to be fixed to their chests by metal clips. Until they returned, each crewman would carry the chute with him wherever he moved. The pilots didn't have to remember the life-saving parcel, but, on the other hand, moving about within the aeroplane's cramped interior with a pilot-style chute strapped behind one's thighs was difficult. So there were comparatively few bomber pilots in POW camps.

Joe for King's engineer, Ben Gallacher, was having a noisy argument with one of the WAAFs.

'So why wasn't it done while I was on leave?'

'I don't know anything about that,' said the girl. 'Your chute isn't repacked yet. You'll have to take this one instead.'

'I told your chiefie that I was going on leave.'

The LAC shrugged her shoulders indifferently. 'I just work here.'

'I want my own parachute. I've always flown with the same one. It's lucky. Don't you understand?' First he had lost his own reliable air-tested L Love and now they wanted to give him a strange chute.

'I don't know what you are making such a fuss about. This one is just as good as your one and it's just been checked and repacked.' Glad of a pause in her strenuous work, she patted her hair into place. 'You're holding up the whole queue, you know.'

'Get stuffed,' said Ben. 'I'll go without.'

'Don't be a fool, Ben,' said Lambert. 'Take it.' Lambert had been one of Gallacher's instructors at his Conversion Unit.

'Aw,' said Ben, walking away.

'Someone will notice,' said Lambert. 'How will you feel if you abort the trip for your whole crew?'

The boy made a rude noise and then took the parachute. 'Perhaps you're right, Chiefie,' he admitted. A line had formed by now and someone shouted, 'What's up?'

'Someone's brought one back,' replied Digby loudly. 'Says it didn't bloody work.'

Everyone smiled at the joke they had heard so many times. The line moved forward again and the two girls pushed the harnesses and packs across the counter with a mechanical indifference interrupted only when they saw some crewman they knew. Then there would be an exchange of smiles and a hurried 'Good luck'.

From the other room Ruth came and stood in the doorway watching her husband as he took his parachute.

At the door there was another holdup: two of the lorries

were late. Some of the boys went outside and watched the last glimmer of daylight. It was cold and some of them took a drink from their vacuum flasks or bit into the chocolate ration. Almost every crew had a mascot of some sort and teddy bears and rag dolls were cradled in their arms or stuffed into their webbing harness and silk stockings were worn as scarfs.

A muffled cheer went up as the missing lorries arrived. 'B Flight here,' called the WAAF driver. There was a sudden flurry of activity as some of the flyers punched each other playfully and vaulted up into the lorry. Lambert looked back and gave Ruth a brief thumbs-up sign. She nodded. He only just had time to climb aboard as the lorry lurched forward. The tailboard rattled loudly. The girl driver followed the blue lights that marked the peri track while twenty-eight crew in the back complained loudly about the slow journey and whistled. They bumped over the runway's edge and went across the black smears of rubber where the bombers' wheels first touched the runway on landing. The lights of Warley village were visible to the left. 'Blackout,' screamed the crews, 'pull a finger.' 'Put that light out.' There was little chance of their voices carrying all that way to the village even on a still summer's night but this was their chance to let off steam that had been building up since they had first read their names on the Battle Order that morning.

The lorry turned off the peri track on to the double pan where two aeroplanes were silhouetted against the dark sky.

'O for Orange and L for Love,' she shouted.

'Good luck, Skip,' whispered Micky Murphy.

'Good luck, Micky,' said Lambert. Lambert's crew and Carter's crew tumbled out of the back of the lorry, swearing and complaining as helmets were dropped and harness snagged on the tailboard. They waddled away to the two aircraft, the harness constricting their movements.

The eighteen-year-old WAAF driver had been a flutter of nerves since she had arrived late at the crewroom and faced a chorus of whistles and complaints. Now she leaned out of the cab and peered into the darkness. 'Is that Z Zebra?' she asked Digby.

'Sorry, luv,' said the uncaring Digby. 'I'm a stranger here myself.'

'What's up, miss?' said Battersby in his squeaky voice.

'It's the first time I've done this job. Is the next aeroplane Z Zebra?'

'After you are back on the peri track again, Zebra – The Volkswagen we call it – is on the left-hand pan. Sugar is on the right-hand one, near the hangar and B Flight office.'

'Thanks a lot,' said the girl. She hesitated for a moment. 'And good luck, Sergeant.'

'Ted Battersby; Batters they call me.'

There was a thunder of stamping from the impatient crews inside the lorry followed by loud whistles.

'Good luck, Batters,' said the WAAF, blowing him a kiss. She let in the clutch and the lorry jerked forward, throwing its passengers off balance. The girl shouted her name back at Battersby but there was so much noise from the crews that he couldn't hear it.

The ground staff of each aeroplane were standing quietly under the wing. One or two of them had special friends among the aircrews and sometimes a conversation would be taken up right from the point at which it had been interrupted.

'Do you ever have trouble with the ears?' asked Binty as he checked the mid-upper turret.

'No, mine have all been very good so far. But I never let them mix with the other dogs in the kennels. That's where all the troubles start.' The Corporal armourer and Binty went on discussing their whippets. Binty didn't have his own dogs but he had a financial stake in his uncle's and on the basis of his conversations with Corporal Hughes he was now able to return home with many suggestions and criticisms. 'You tell your bloody Air Force mate to stick his advice,'

Binty's uncle had told him on his last leave, 'or I'll come down there and help him with his bleeding aeroplanes.'

'Sternberg did *The Blue Angel*,' said Cohen, 'but *The Cabinet of Doctor Caligari* was directed by someone I've never heard of named Wiene.'

'I could have sworn it was Sternberg. Funny how the memory can play tricks. *The Last Command* was Sternberg?'

'Oh sure. You don't make many mistakes, Mike. I remember seeing that. It was almost a remake of *The Last Laugh* with Jannings.'

'A lot of those films were remakes of earlier European ones.'

'Ever see *The Salvation Hunters*?' asked Cohen.

'That was early Sternberg. They thought it was a masterpiece at the time. At my last station the Film Society got hold of a sixteen-millimetre print.'

'Pretty terrible, I thought,' said Cohen.

'It's a long time ago,' said the fitter. 'A lot has happened since then.'

'Yes,' said Cohen, who had seen the film in Vienna when he was a child. 'You're right.'

Flight Sergeant Worthington started another conversation without preamble. 'Two fuses and four wiring faults. We'll have to strip the wiring right out of it and renew every inch of it.'

'So Carter's taking a reserve kite?'

'It only arrived this afternoon, it's been a struggle to get it ready. Carter's furious and so is Gallacher. It's not my fault, Sam.' He kicked one of the tyres.

'Everyone knows that, Worthy.'

'Carter was bloody rude. There's no need to be rude.'

'Nerves, Worthy.'

'I suppose so. But we all worked our guts out on Joe for King. No one could have got it ready in time.'

'Forget it, Worthy. He'll be apologizing and buying you pints lunchtime tomorrow. You know old Tommy Carter;

he flares up but he doesn't mean it.' Worthington slapped Lambert's arm gently with the canvas pitot-head cover. He always did that to show it was removed. Lambert scribbled his signature on the RAF Form No 700. Creaking Door was now Lambert's.

'Your new kid knows his way around a wiring diagram, I must say,' said Worthington.

'Battersby?'

'Yes, he's a demon on theory. He worked out the position of the short circuit on paper, but it was enough to make a strong man weep, watching him trying to fix it: gentleman's fingers.'

'As the actress said to the bishop,' said Digby. The bomb-doors were open and now he came round to the front, where Lambert and Worthington were standing, to inspect the bombs. He jabbed a finger at each, murmuring to himself as he counted them, pulling each bomb trying to shift it within the jaws of the grip. He clasped a 2,000-lb bomb and lifted his feet off the ground so that the jaws took his weight too.

'I wish you'd come out and do that before we get here,' complained Lambert.

'Have a little faith,' said Digby..

Automatically Lambert took his wallet from his battle-dress blouse and folded into it the gold fountain pen that had been his twenty-first birthday present from his parents. It was an unspoken arrangement that if anything happened to him the wallet with all his letters and documents, and a last letter that he'd rewritten from time to time, should go to Ruth. The fountain pen was for Worthington to keep and the money was for drinks all round in the Sergeants' Mess. Worthington nodded and looked at Lambert with concern. It seemed to him a bloody awful sort of war. He'd seen a seemingly endless progression of young kids go to war and eventually not come back. Carefully he put the wallet into his inner pocket.

Lambert was just going to climb aboard to start the

motors when he saw the Group Captain's Humber coming round the peri track. It stopped beside the plane.

'O for Orange; Flight Sergeant Lambert,' murmured Flying Officer Griffith, the Admin Officer, into the Groupie's ear. Griffith ticked his piece of paper.

'Bloody cold, Lambert, what?' said the Groupie stamping the ground energetically.

'Yes, sir, freezing,' said Lambert. He pushed his battered rag doll into his tunic.

Lambert and the Group Captain looked at each other without knowing what to say and yet both were reluctant to turn away.

'Your lucky doll?'

'Yes,' said Lambert. Self-consciously he produced the rag doll: a cross-eyed figure in a black velvet suit.

'She's getting pretty old now,' said the Groupie.

'Yes, sir, it's the altitude,' joked Lambert.

'Really?' said the Groupie. At one time the aircrew were bright middle-class boys with style and a sense of fun. Now they were working-class lads with no proper schooling and accents he could scarcely understand. What did Lambert mean about the altitude? So many of these young scoundrels had got their sergeant's rank too easily and the result was a familiarity of manner that he didn't readily take to.

'Not the first trip you've done to the Ruhr, eh, Flight Sergeant?'

'That's right, sir.'

Usually the Group Captain listened to the BBC news broadcast at nine o'clock. That gave him something to talk about as he visited the planes.

'I missed the news tonight,' said the Groupie.

'I heard it,' said Lambert. 'An American fortress raid on the Channel ports. And there's a big new German attack upon Rokossovsky around Kursk from Orel and Byelgorod. In the first day's fighting alone the Red Army destroyed five hundred German tanks and over two hundred aircraft.'

'Splendid,' said the Groupie and turned on his heel and hurried back to his car. He wound up the window against the cold night air.

'Bloody Bolshie,' said the Group Captain.

'Pardon, sir,' said the Admin Officer who hadn't heard the conversation.

'Lambert, a bloody Bolshie I say.'

'Lambert, sir?'

'Why else would he have "Stalin for King" written on his aeroplane?'

'I don't think it's there now,' said the Admin Officer tactfully. He knew it was Carter's aeroplane to which the Groupie referred.

'I know it isn't there now,' said the Groupie sarcastically. 'He's had a fresh aircraft given to him today.'

The Admin Officer was about to correct the Group Captain but it seemed such a small matter to argue about. He'd be with the Groupie for most of the night. Why put him in a bad mood.

'I see, sir,' he said. He watched the red sparks fly as the Group Captain lit his pipe and puffed at it angrily.

'Just gave me a lecture about his glorious Red Army.'

'Really, sir?'

'Well, of course I'm not going to put up with that sort of thing. Take me to see that young officer who's on his first trip tonight.'

'Pilot Officer Fleming, sir. Z for Zebra. Parked near the trees, driver.'

The car turned and crossed the peri track. The Groupie seemed not to have heard. 'I'll get rid of him, Griffith.'

'Yes, sir.'

'Young Sweet was on about him only today.'

'Was he, sir?'

'Hinted that he was a Red.' The Groupie gave a short humourless laugh. 'Only I was too damned stupid to see what young Sweet was driving at.'

'He said that Lambert was a Red?' asked Pilot Officer Griffith in amazement.

'No, he didn't. Too loyal to his flight, too damned fine a young officer to even suspect a senior NCO of such a thing. No, Sweet just reported a piece of Lambert's bloody propagandizing Communist bilge in the Mess. As I say, young Sweet was so hesitant that it's not until I had the full force of it myself that I've tumbled to what's going on. What say you to that, Griffith?'

'Remarkable, sir.'

'Bloody remarkable, Griffith. If the AOC had got wind of it I'd have been remarkable on my bloody earhole, Griffith.' No sooner had the Group Captain got his pipe alight than he rapped it against the metal ashtray to empty it.

'Indeed you would, sir.'

'Who did you say this next one was?'

'Z for Zebra, sir. Three officers in the crew. The captain is Pilot Officer Fleming. His first operation.' The car stopped and Griffith ticked his list of names.

'Bloody cold, eh, Fleming?' boomed the Groupie striding across the tarmac. The Admin Officer prodded the smouldering tobacco to be sure it was quite extinguished. With all this petrol about smoking was strictly forbidden.

Voices carry a long way on an airfield, especially at night. Battersby had heard the WAAF driver stop at S Sweet on the far pan.

'All change,' she called. There were laughs and shouts and then he heard her say, 'Good luck, sir,' and knew she was talking to Sweet. Battersby felt a stab of jealousy. After all, she had blown him a kiss. He walked around, checking the exterior of his aircraft. Officers always got the pretty ones.

A Corporal rigger poured hot sweet tea for all of them. The enamel cups were chipped and smelled faintly of oil but it was hot and welcome. Digby was still leaning against the wheel and dreaming when he heard the distant voices of Joe for King's crew. They were standing around the door of their aeroplane arguing.

Their aeroplane smelled new and strange and the ladder still had protective grease on it.

'Why can't we have Joe?' Ben Gallacher said.

'Ask Himmler,' said Carter. 'You've asked me ten times. It's not the fuses, they can't trace the fault.'

'What am I, then?' said Gallacher. 'Am I the bloody Flight Engineer or the tea-boy? Why aren't I consulted?'

'Can't you get it into your thick head? The kite's duff. For Christ's sake stop binding, you're making me jumpy.'

'I want to fly in Joe for King,' said Gallacher.

Collins, the bomb aimer on his last operation, reached into the inside pocket of his battledress blouse and found a piece of chalk. He climbed up two rungs of the ladder and, leaning to one side, he wrote 'Joe for King' across the squadron letter. Under that he scribbled just a huge curling moustache.

'Now you are flying in Joe for King,' said Tommy Carter, 'get in and bloody well belt up.' Gallacher swung round and aimed a punch at his captain. The punch sounded very loud and it was followed by a shocked silence. Tommy didn't respond at all; he'd taken the blow on his thick harness and it hurt Gallacher's hand more than Tommy's chest.

Joe for King's navigator was Roland Pembroke, a public-school-educated twenty-year-old from Edinburgh. Watching the two men growling at each other he was filled with a despairing horror. The engineer and pilot had never got on well together; Gallacher had failed the pilot's course and was still jealous of the ones that hadn't. Tommy, on the other hand, had that exasperating calm rectitude that only policemen display. Roland Pembroke had done everything he could think of to bring the two men closer. He turned to the Corporal rigger and asked in a whisper, 'Did you get it?'

'It will be waiting; that bird Cynthia in the Bell is saving me a bottle.'

'And cups,' said Roland Pembroke in his soft lowland accent.

'Glasses,' said the Corporal. 'She's promised to wangle me some glasses.'

'Great,' said Roland.

'And I've got sausage rolls too.'

Roland pushed his navigational gear into the door of the plane and heaved a sigh of relief. Tomorrow was Sergeant Carter's twenty-first birthday and the completion of 'Tapper' Collins' final operation. Roland Pembroke had planned a surprise party right there on the pan so that the ground-staff boys and the crew could celebrate. It had started badly.

'Ten trips done, twenty to go,' said Pembroke as he disappeared into the aeroplane, crossing his fingers to stave off danger as he always did.

There are many ways in which the life history of an aircrew can be charted. There would be a simple graph of the odds that an insurance company would offer. The chances on this one began low – the first three trips were five times as dangerous as the average. But as skills and experience mounted so the chances of survival for each trip became better. Another graph, thirty trips with a five-per-cent casualty rate, would be a simple straight line: a mathematical proposition in which each trip held equal danger and the line ended at trip number twenty. There was yet another graph that could be drawn, a morale line charted by psychiatrists. Its curves recorded the effect of stress as men were asked to face repeatedly the mathematical probability of death. This graph – unlike the others – began at the highest point. Granted courage by ignorance and the inhibitory effect that curiosity has upon fear their morale was high for the first five operations, after which the line descended until a crack-up point was reached by the eleventh or twelfth trip. Perhaps it was the relief of surviving the thirteenth operation that made the graph turn upwards after it. Men had seen death at close quarters and were shocked to discover their own fear of it. But recognizing the same shameful fears in the eyes of their friends helped their morale, and after a slight recovery it remained constant until about the twenty-second trip, after which it sloped downwards without recovery.

The eleventh trip was not marked by crews asking to be taken off flying, getting drunk or running sobbing through the Mess. In fact few men asked to be grounded, and their reluctance was fortified by the RAF authorities who would stamp the words 'lack of moral fibre' across the man's documents, strip him of rank and brevet and send him away in disgrace with the bright unfaded blue patch of tunic proclaiming him an officially recognized coward.

No, the eleventh trip was marked by more subtle defensive changes in the crew: a fatalism, a brutalizing, a callousness about the deaths of friends and a marked change in demeanour. Noisy men became quiet and reflective while the shy ones often became clamorous. This was the time at which the case histories of ulcers, deafness, and other stress-induced nervous diseases that were to follow the survivors through their later years, actually began. The crew of Joe for King were on their eleventh trip.

The crew of The Volkswagen, on the other hand, were about to do their first trip. Like a young man with his first sports car they were keen and raring to go. They weren't tired in the way that Lambert was tired, their reflexes were sharp, their eyesight keen, and their hands itched to prove themselves. Lambert was like a weary old businessman climbing into his family saloon to do a trip that he had done all his working life. He was tired, dulled, slow of reflex, and frightened. And yet, as any insurance company will tell you, it's the old men in family saloons who pay the least insurance and the kids in new sports cars who die.

Pilot Officer Cornelius Fleming sat at the controls of The Volkswagen and tried to hide his pleasure and excitement. He heard the boys making nervous jokes but he was determined to put on a show of bored indifference for the ground crew. One of the riggers, a gruff-spoken cockney, came into the cockpit with a tin can.

'Here's your tin, sir,' he said.

'What's that for?' said Fleming. He closed his eyes in a mannerism that at medical school had affected concentration.

'To take a leak,' said the rigger.

Fleming suspected he was being made the butt of a joke and looked at the man suspiciously.

The rigger grinned. 'Do you want to put it under the seat?'

'Don't be ridiculous,' said Fleming and sighed.

'Suit yourself, guv,' said the rigger and walked back through the plane. He climbed down on to the ground and threw the can away under the ash trees. That was the trouble with officers, you could never tell them anything. That pansy-faced sprog officer had looked at him like he was offering dirty postcards to a bishop. The only crew here with three officers in it, and he had to be assigned to them. No matter, they wouldn't last long, the poor sods. Zebra was a real duff kite and no matter about cleaning it up and calling it some foreign name, it was just a matter of time before it fell apart at the seams.

Fleming knew that he'd upset the fellow and he cursed himself for his handling of the business, even if it had been a legpull. Becoming a good skipper was the most difficult thing in the world, and the most desirable. At one time all he'd sought of God was a pilot's brevet. Then he'd fastened his desire upon a commission. But it was all so difficult; a good skipper must be an expert pilot, a classless gentleman, a democratic commander and, most impossible of all, an intrepid leader who kept his men safe. Always there was this damned class business. That chap would merely have grinned if an NCO had called his bluff about the tin. It was all right for Lambert; these chaps with a gong and a tour behind them could do no wrong in the eyes of their crew.

'Bertie!' Fleming called his young Flight Engineer who before meeting Fleming had always been Bert.

'Sir?' The boy's flying gear was too large, so that he looked like a child dressed in his father's clothes.

'All OK?'

'Yeah, all okey dokey, sir.'

'We'll follow Lambert out, Bertie.' The engineer nodded. Okey dokey, thought Fleming, what strange things they say.

Lambert was the first of B Flight to start up. He slid open his window. 'Clear for starting, Worthy?' Twenty feet below him the trolley-ac was plugged in and ready.

'Clear.'

Lambert put his hand out of the window, pointed a finger at the port inner and then turned his thumb upwards. From the tarmac Worthy pointed his left hand at the same engine and revolved his right index finger as though to move the prop with it. Lambert pressed the starter button. There was the pitter-patter of the booster pump and a chuffing noise. Then came the opening bangs of the Merlin, an affront to the still countryside. It caught, and roared. Then the next one started, and the next, until the sound of thirty-two engines echoed back from the trees of The Warrens and the black tin side of the hangar, like a million frantic drummers marching off to war.

Sam Thatcher was awakened by it. He looked at the clock; it was 11.23 PM.

'They're off again,' said his wife.

'Third time this week,' said Sam. 'I'll have to get some sleeping pills or something.'

But there was an hour before take-off time and as suddenly as they had started the motors cut. Soon the night was quiet except for the muttered curses of men working by the light of torches and the murmured conversation of the crews.

Flash Gordon, the little Nottingham miner, his pockets bulging with confectionery for his brothers and sisters, was looking at his turret. He waited until the last engine cut and the silence was broken only by a few planes of A Flight from the far side of the airfield.

'You've done a good job there,' said Flash. The Sergeant armourer deserved the praise; it had been more difficult than it looked to remove a section of Perspex from the vision panel of the turret. 'I won't be firing at any more oil dribbles and thinking they are Junkers 88s,' said Flash, and he laughed.

'Did you ever do that, Flash?' asked the armourer.

'Never saw one,' said Flash. 'Fifteen trips I've done and I've never seen a night fighter.'

Binty Jones, the mid-upper gunner, walked past. The armourer called after him. 'I'll do your turret next, Binty.'

'Like bleeding hell, you will. I check my Perspex every day. There's not a speck or spot anywhere. And if there was, I wouldn't be such a bloody fool as to fire at it, man.'

'It was oil dribbles giving the trouble,' said Flash angrily, 'not scratches.'

'I don't care what it was, you won't get me in that rear turret again, so don't come asking me to swap when you get another one of your bloody head-colds, right?'

'Right,' Flash shouted after him, 'I won't, don't you worry.'

'You'll freeze if your electric suit goes u/s,' warned the armourer.

'I'm practically freezing now,' said Flash.

'It's cold tonight,' the armourer agreed and buttoned his Service overcoat up to the neck and wrapped his home-knitted scarf high around his ears. The motors of the A Flight planes had warmed and been switched off. The airfield was silent. There was nothing to do but wait.

In the aeroplanes men were making secret promises to God, performing superstitious rituals or finding excuses to say heartfelt truths. A fly buzzed drowsily on Tommy Carter's windscreen.

'Go home and get some sleep, you stupid bastard,' said Tommy. 'You don't know when you're well off.'

Lambert placed the doll named Flanagan behind his seat.

'He won't see anything from there,' said Digby. 'Throw him down here, I'll put him in the front turret.'

'He's seen it all before,' said Lambert. 'And he wouldn't find it hard to break the habit.'

Wing Commander Munro opened the side window to inhale the air. Then he placed his walking-stick under his seat. As his crew had already guessed, that stick was the CO's lucky charm, although wild horses would never drag the admission from him. Munro looked at the sky and breathed deeply. He noticed that cloud had eaten a piece of the Great Bear and was sniffing at Scorpio. From the trees at Witch Fen an owl hooted loudly.

'Hear that, sir?' said Jock Hamilton his navigator.

'Yes indeed. It's good luck,' he added hurriedly. Jock looked at him unconvinced. There was a silence then until he heard a train puffing and rattling northwards. Soon that train would be in Scotland near to his wife and the boy. He would be in Germany. Munro looked at the sky; it still wasn't quite dark. To the north it was a purplish colour, almost green.

The low that had caused the thunderstorms across Europe turned north as it neared the Swedish coast. The air pressure in the low was equalizing and soon it would die. The Met men were rubbing its Chinagraph image from their maps and marking in the progress of the high that had come marching behind it from the west. This mountain of air already pressed down upon England. Its outer layer slid towards Ireland and Biscay and Norway, where the pressure was less. The descending air became warmer and any clouds in its way evaporated. As it got closer to ground level this descending air brushed against the rotating earth and was deflected clockwise so as to form a gently whirling air mass that measured hundreds of miles across – an anticyclone.

284

It had brought the light-blue sky and diffused sunset that promised another fine day. But this starry night was cold, for with few clouds to trap the rising heat the ground became chilly underfoot and the airmen slapped their hands against their sides and complained of the long wait.

It was fifteen minutes past midnight, BDST, when the first of the Lancasters moved. Last-minute urination took place before the crews were buttoned into their clothes and settled into the seats they would occupy for several hours. A full bladder, or even worse, wind, could cause pain at high altitudes. Quickly gobbled beans on toast could have a man writhing with pain at a moment when he was most needed. Ponderously the bombers rumbled round the peri track. Some were in a hurry to beat the queue that would form at the southern end of the runway.

As soon as Lambert's Creaking Door moved, The Volkswagen followed. Fleming kept its tail in view as the planes crawled past the dim blue perimeter lights. What greater disaster could strike them now than that he should put a wheel into the soft-going beyond the lights and hold up the whole Squadron? He touched the brakes as they came to the corner by the Ramsey road. A Hillman van had parked there with its headlights on or else Fleming might well have turned too wide and clipped his wingtip against the fence. Lambert's tail-light moved again. Some of the other bomb aimers were shining a signalling lamp from the nose to help light the way but Lambert preferred to have his eyes accustomed to the darkness. Each Lancaster announced its arrival at the runway by flashing its code letter to Control. At the answering green light the take-off run commenced and the next plane crawled into position.

Lambert glanced towards the crowd of ground crew that were waving from the edge of the runway. Old hands, young girls, and even the NAAFI women were there. Even when it was raining they came to see the bombers away. Lambert felt grateful to them.

'Big crowd tonight,' said Binty.

'Your harem,' said Kosh.

'Ah,' said Binty.

John Munro had detailed the take-off pattern. Moving from their pans on to the peri track the bombers lined up on both sides of the runway's end. No sooner had one plane got a green than the next one was signalling its code letter. A bored officer in Flying Control logged each take-off and phoned them to the Operations Room where, on a wall-size blackboard divided into rectangles, was entered each pilot's name, code letter, take-off time, and time of return. There was also a space for remarks.

Each of the bombers was loaded far beyond peacetime safety limits and getting them into the air was no easy matter. Lambert drove up an invisible ramp as steady as a rock and as perfect as a theorem. Then came Fleming, a slight swerve before unsticking, for this was the first time he'd flown with a full bomb-load.

You could recognize any of Tommy Carter's take-offs: too much throttle, stick back too early, and undercarriage retracted before he was over Witch Fen. This night he swung badly too. Angry, and new to this factory-fresh aeroplane, he'd applied too much rudder. Halfway down the runway he was already askew, pointing at the Control Tower and travelling too fast to stop before the main road. He knew he was going off the hard runway only when its white marker lights came racing under him like tracer shells. Beyond that there was earth, damned soft earth after last night's rain. He heaved desperately on the stick with one hand and tried to push the starboard outer's throttle forward to correct the swing. He felt one wheel plop off the sharp edge of tarmac. Gallacher braced himself against the bulkhead and cursed.

Tommy wasn't flying the aircraft any longer, he was fighting it.

'Panic boost,' he shouted. They might have been his last words except that the propellers hung upon the cold air like fingertips to a crevice. For long seconds he gained no altitude but skimmed the grass with only inches clearing his tyres. Then slowly and dutifully Joe for King the Second sniffed the air.

In the Control Tower the Duty Officer, the Group Captain, and a Flying Control WAAF stood transfixed at the sight of a complex alloy parcel packed with high explosive, phosphorus, fuel, and magnesium being steered directly towards them at a hundred miles an hour. No one moved until the aeroplane roared across the top of the tower, clearing the railing by inches, shaking its foundations and taking an aerial with it.

Tapper Collins always stayed in the nose for take-offs and landings, even though it was against regulations.

'I saw the bloody bomb aimer,' whispered the Group Captain, scarcely able to believe it. 'I saw the bloody bomb aimer's face.'

And Tapper had seen them too: white petrified staring blobs flashing past not more than thirty feet under him.

'Jesus Christ,' said Tapper. 'I thought you'd left something behind.'

'Bit of a swing,' explained Tommy.

'Bit of a swing?' said Tapper. 'We've got the bleeding Groupie's hairpiece tangled in the undercart.'

'You don't have to bloody sit there,' snapped Tommy. 'It was your idea.'

'I could have touched him,' said Tapper. 'Could have reached out and tweaked the silly old blighter's hooter.'

One after another the giant planes climbed into the darkness and disappeared. The coloured wingtip lights thundered over the misty, alcohol-laden Hillman that Singleton and his girlfriend had borrowed for the evening. They stopped cuddling until the last plane – Munro's own D for Dog – took off. As the sound of it faded away the countryside became silent.

'It's funny when the planes are away. It's sort of lonely,' said the girl.

'What do you mean?'

'I don't know. You get used to those big planes everywhere you look. Last month when they were all diverted to Yorkshire because of the fog it seemed funny to see the aerodrome in daylight all empty. And there was hardly anyone around in the sections either.'

'I wouldn't mind them being diverted for a few days. It'd make my life a bit easier, I'll tell you,' said Singleton.

'I wonder if they'll all come back,' said the girl.

'It's a gamble, isn't it?'

'They've been lucky lately.'

'Able bought it last week, U Uncle the week before, and that Flight Sergeant Lambert brought back a dead navigator three trips ago.'

'I'm glad you ain't in one of 'em, Bert.'

'I could have been a gunner, but my feet let me down.'

'I couldn't bear it, Bert. Give me another kiss.'

They kissed for a few minutes then Singleton said, 'Were you frightened tonight?'

'No, of course not.'

'Go on, you were.'

'A bit.'

'It's exciting, isn't it, knowing you might get nicked. But I spend it too easy, that's my trouble.'

The girl laughed.

'You know what I'd like to do one night. Now this might surprise you, Beryl. I'd like to get hold of some tyres or petrol. That's where the real money is.'

'Or booze,' said the girl.

'You would think that, because you have no experience of crime,' said the Mess waiter. 'Booze is locked up and counted. Only a mug goes after booze.'

'Whatever you say, Bert.'

'I told you I was a villain, didn't I?' he warned. 'Don't keep giggling, Beryl.'

The girl was tempted to tell him how many times she had

been in trouble with the law and of the final house-breaking escapade that had sent her to Borstal, but wisely she smiled and said nothing.

Lambert knew the way from Warley to the coastal assembly points as he did the one from his billet to the Mess. Usually he flew straight to the assembly point using a course based upon the Met man's estimate of the wind. Cohen then faked in the Gee fixes from that point back to Warley. From there onwards Cohen did real Gee fixes. Tonight Lambert knew the wind was wrong from the moment he was airborne and he steered well to the south, allowing the wind to push him on to the track he required. 'Southwold,' announced Digby. He was lying in the nose of the plane looking down through the transparent bowl.

'OK,' said Cohen, who knew he was talking to him. This was the way they always did it.

Cohen took a fix from the Gee radar and marked the time at Southwold on his plotting map. 'There's quite a wind, Skipper,' he said.

'We'll see,' said Lambert. 'When we've got a bit of height we'll have a better idea. The high winds may be different.'

'Permission to test guns?' asked Binty.

'Yes, both of you,' said Lambert, knowing that Flash would ask immediately after. Digby tested his nose guns too. The sound of the guns rattled along the metal fuselage and from Digby's turret at the front there was a smell of cordite and scorching oil. Tracer sprayed in a gentle curve and splashed down into the sea.

Today's pressurized, high-speed, high-altitude, jet-propelled traveller might find it hard to imagine the very different experience that flying was to these men. The whole aeroplane rattled and vibrated with the power of the piston engines. The instruments shuddered and the figures on them blurred. Oxygen masks were mandatory and they needed microphones and earphones to even converse. At these altitudes their power-weight ratios made these planes very vulnerable to the condition of the air through which they flew. Although now, in the cool of night, the aircraft was steadier than it had been in the heated turbulence of afternoon, the air was still full of surprises. They hit hard walls of it and dropped sickeningly into deep pockets. They bucketed, rolled, and yawed constantly. Their degree of stability depended as much upon the pilot's strength as upon his skill, for the controls were not power-assisted and it required all of a man's energy to heave the control surfaces into the airstream. And all the time there was the vibration that hammered the temples, shook the teeth and played a tattoo upon the spine, so that even after an uneventful flight the crew were whipped into a condition of advanced fatigue.

Digby sat down next to Cohen. He had his own gadget, the H2S radar set, to operate. It looked down at the world below and gave an X-ray picture which distinguished between woodland, water, and houses. Often the set went wrong and even at its best the picture bore only a messy resemblance to a map. Cohen had warmed the set and they both watched the dull green screen.

'What do you know? It works,' said Digby.

Cohen pushed his map case to the back of the plotting-table and stood it on end. That obscured the neat metal patch. Flight Sergeant Worthington's riggers had riveted it over the jagged shrapnel hole. Through that had come the splinter that had entered a navigator's lung and killed him in this very seat four trips ago.

'Don't do that, sport,' said Digby. He pushed the map case aside. The little adjustable desk lamp hit the new metal at an angle that made it shine like a glass eye. 'I like to see that,' said Digby. 'I figure that lightning don't strike twice. You and me have got the safest seat in the kite here.'

Cohen looked at the metal plate and felt better about it.

'Is everybody happy?' asked Lambert.

To the tune of *Abdul the Bulbul-Amir* Flash Gordon in the rear turret sang tunelessly:

> 'Just an old-fashioned Avro with old-fashioned wings
> And a fabric all tattered and torn
> She's got old-fashioned Merlins all tied up with strings
> And a heater that never gets warm.
> But she's quite safe and sound, 'cos it won't leave the
>   ground
> And the crew are afraid of the chop.
> One day we will try to see if she'll fly
> While Mother looks after the shop.'

Flash waited for a word of appreciation or applause, but none came. Binty said, 'Man, is yo' jes' crazy wid rhythm.'

'Oh, shut up,' said Flash.

'When you've all finished singing and chatting,' said Lambert, 'perhaps I could say a word.'

'Gentlemen,' said Digby. 'It's my proud pleasure to introduce to you the captain of our aircraft, your genial host and raconteur, who has given up his eighty-first birthday to be with us here tonight. Gentlemen, your friend and mine, Flight Sergeant Samuel Lambert, DFM.'

'Now let's get ourselves organized,' said Lambert.

'For a change,' said Jimmy Grimm.

'For a change,' agreed Lambert.

Jimmy Grimm tuned his radio carefully. 'They've given us new winds, Skip. Do you want them?'

'Give them to Kosh,' said Lambert.

They flew higher and higher and for every thousand feet they gained the temperature dropped two and a half degrees centigrade. The crew buttoned themselves into their suits or moved closer to the hot-air blowers. At 8,000 feet they began to breathe the oxygen that they had brought with them. Lambert continued to climb. They entered a cloud bank. There is as yet no way to discover if ice awaits you in a cloud, except to fly into it with your fingers crossed. This cloud seemed unending. The cold chilled the aeroplane to its marrow and slowed its circulation. Door's port outer coughed not once but twice and then didn't fully recover.

'Fuel flow?'

'OK,' said Battersby.

'Give it some fully rich.'

'I have already.'

'Good boy.'

The motor, appreciative of its luxury diet, roared into full power.

'Carburettor icing.'

'Temperature looks OK now.'

'We'll be out of it in a moment.' Lambert put the aircraft into a steeper climb and Battersby adjusted the engines to give him more power.

'I hate cloud,' confided Lambert.

It pressed against the windows and made the cabin even darker than before. Battersby fussed over his instruments and was anxious to prove his expertise to Lambert. The engines had only just begun to unsynchronize when Battersby reported, 'Pressures and temperatures look all right.' The motor began a weary drone.

'Do you know why it's doing that?'

'Oil getting too cold and stiffening the pitch control?'

Lambert nodded and said, 'Can you synch them again?'

Battersby waggled his fingertips upon the levers. After choosing the wrong motor and then overcorrecting he finally had the engines back into their regular harmonized roar.

'Bang on,' said Lambert. 'Micky just can't get the hang of that.' Battersby had never felt so proud of himself.

One by one the stars pricked the roof of the cabin and they were above the cloud. Lambert's controls had become slack and mushy now, for Creaking Door had reached its normal ceiling and no amount of pulling on the stick would make it climb higher. This was the stage of the journey where

Lambert employed a technique that an old-timer had told him about, way back when he was flying Whitleys. By suddenly lowering the flaps fifteen degrees while flying at cruising speed, Lambert and Battersby caused the aeroplane to hit a wall of air. It shuddered with the impact and the whole aeroplane leaped 200 feet higher. Each time it did this it held its new altitude. By this method Lambert could add over 1,000 feet of height to his ceiling. The first of a series of spine-jarring thumps ran through the aircraft. 'We're going up the steps,' said Lambert. 'That's what I wanted to tell you.'

Flight Lieutenant Sweet stared out into the night. Beneath him he saw a tiny rectangle of flare path and guessed there was another squadron climbing to join the stream. He had above-average night vision and usually saw pinpoints before the bomb aimer saw them. There were no other aeroplanes in sight. It was odd that no matter what methods of timing were used to pack the bomber stream as tight as possible, the sky was still so immense that he sometimes did a whole trip without catching sight of another aeroplane. He supposed that fellows with below-average night vision went whole tours without seeing anything.

Ahead of him the front turret moved gently from left to right.

'Bomb aimer. Don't keep fidgeting about with that turret.'

'I'm searching, sir. That's orders.'

'Then swivel your neck.' Sweet's voice rose a tone.

'I'm keeping the hydraulic fluid warm, sir.'

'Must you always argue, Spekey?' Sweet made it into a joke; placatingly he added, 'Keep still, there's a good chap.'

'Pip' Speke, an eighteen-year-old with a big black moustache and a reputation as a lucky gambler, ducked out of the turret and got down on the floor behind his bomb-sight. Most crews had Sergeant pilots and some crews stuck together. Some went off boozing as a crew. Some had decent officers even. The easiest way for any of those lucky ones to make Sergeant Speke lose his temper was to tell him how fortunate he was to fly with such a fun-loving good sort as that modest Flight Lieutenant Sweet, DFC.

'Navigator,' said Sweet, 'how many miles to the coast?'

'About ten,' said the navigator.

'Let's not have too many "abouts" tonight, eh, Billy-boy,' said Sweet. 'Bomb aimer, let me know when you see the coastline.'

'OK.'

Sweet looked down. The countryside was dark but in spite of the blackout the faint shape of towns could be discerned. 'Navigator,' said Sweet, 'I can see Lowestoft below us. We're off course.'

'Are you sure, sir?'

'Am I sure, sir? Yes, I am sure, sir. Beyond it I can see a bit of a glim from Yarmouth. We're at least ten miles north of our track.'

There was a short silence while the navigator calculated their position on the Gee. 'Steer 120 degrees,' said the navigator. 'The winds are wonky.'

'That's just a correction. I want to join the stream at the assembly area over Southwold.'

'In that case, sir, turn almost due south, let's say 160 degrees.'

'That's more like it, old son.' Sweet realized he had upset the navigator and upsetting people was a luxury he seldom indulged in. 'This is the Flight commander's aeroplane, chaps. We must do things by the book. It's stupid, I know, but if we start cutting corners the other crews will do it.'

Sweet flew south humming to himself. Suddenly he said, 'Did I tell you the story about the WAAF officer and the sergeant? . . .'

'English coastline coming up, sir,' said Pip Speke. Now it was possible to see how good Britain's blackout was, for beyond the coast the world below them was truly dark.

CHAPTER EIGHTEEN

The huge Freya radar aerial swung gently, smelling the cold wind that blew from England. It stopped, began to swing back and stopped again. Willi Reinecke called to August Bach down the length of the dimly lit T hut. 'First contact, sir.'

And so the battle began: three groups of men using every device that science could invent began to grope around the blackness like gunmen in a sewer.

August hurried up the wooden steps to the plotting-table platform.

'Logged at 00.35 hours,' said the clerk.

'Near Lowestoft. An extreme-range contact,' said August. 'Congratulations, they are not even over the British coastline. The Freya is working well tonight.'

'They seem to have stopped the jamming lately,' said Willi.

'Since we made the wavelength band wider. They can't jam the whole width of it.'

'And it's the tuning.'

'"And it's the tuning,"' said August smiling. 'I said "Congratulations".'

'I've told the FLUKO,' said the telephonist. 'They hadn't had a previous contact.'

'Good,' muttered August. He put his protractor on the map. He knew all its bearings like the palm of his own hand but still he put his protractor on it as he gave his instructions. Willi admired that sort of thoroughness, especially in an officer.

'The red Würzburg to sweep from Ipswich to Yarmouth, 270 degrees to 290. Don't tell them the range or they won't try so hard.'

'Lowestoft,' said Willi, looking at the map. 'That's well north of the usual route. Perhaps they are going to Berlin.'

'Too early to say yet. Perhaps they are routed south and that one is a few miles off course. That would account for it. We'll have to wait and see, Willi.'

Soon Willi said, 'You're right, sir, you're right. He's turned almost due south.'

'They'll assemble over Southwold,' nodded August. 'They are creatures of habit, the British.'

Out in the cold among the windswept dunes the crew of the red Würzburg became newly alert. They knew that the Freya had twice the range of their equipment, but the Würzburg had a narrower beam and was therefore more precise. It could 'see' one aeroplane and tell its altitude and so bring the night fighters into contact with it. The Freya gave an early warning but the Würzburgs made the kill.

'The Nachtjagdführer is giving us two Ju88s from Kroonsdijk,' said Reinecke. He was still on the phone. August nodded.

'Let's hope it's a pilot we've worked with before,' said Willi.

'When that fool let the *Tommi* escape last Wednesday I could have killed him,' said August. 'He must have been right on top of him.'

'The blips superimposed,' said Reinecke disgustedly.

The T hut was the centre of the Himmelbett station which August commanded. Nearby there were other huts: billets, Mess hall, motor-transport garage and the radar machines themselves. As well as the Freya there were two identical Würzburgs: great bowls, seven metres across. One (blue) to record a night fighter and the other (red) to follow the passage of one of the RAF bombers. Inside the T hut two plotting-clerks sat hunched underneath the big wooden platform that dominated the interior. Each of them wore headphones and was in contact with a Würzburg. To show the progress of both planes, each plotter shone a spotlight upon the glass map that was his ceiling. From their position on the platform August and Willi Reinecke could see the two lightbeam spots through the Seeburg table in front of them. One was red, the other blue. Their job was to bring the two dots of light together. After that the German night fighter should be able to pick up the bomber ahead of him on his own radar detector. Or, on a brightly moonlit night, perhaps even see him.

The T hut was dark. There were no blips on the Seeburg table, for the enemy aircraft were not yet within range of the Würzburgs. August looked at the large-scale map on the wall and every few minutes Willi reported the progress of the RAF bomber stream as it flew across the North Sea straight towards them.

The phone buzzed quietly. 'Our two planes are airborne,' said Willi.

'Tell the blue Würzburg to sweep from 50 to 70 for them.'

Willi Reinecke was biting his fingernails. August smiled. This was the worst time of all. Many nights they picked up the *Tommis* as they assembled over their own coast, but often the bombers were headed elsewhere. Himmelbett Station Ermine was only one small sector of a long coastline and unless the bombers headed straight into the Ruhr they would pass by out of range. In that case they would spend all night gnawing their knuckles and cursing their luck. One thing Willi knew: the best crews were on duty; if the terror flyers came this way they would be certain to pick them up. After that it was up to the night fighters.

'Here comes the jamming,' said Willi. Then, more officially, 'Airborne jamming on the Freya, a wide band of it, averaging 290 degrees. Constant bearing, increasing in intensity.'

'The jamming aircraft must be coming straight for us.'

Willi said, 'I don't know why the Nachtjagdführer doesn't send some of our boys out to shoot them down.'

'How bad?'

'Not too bad. He's still getting a clear blip and if the tube grasses up more he can side-tune to improve it.'

'The Würzburg will have them soon.'

'Thank goodness they can't jam those.'

'Any night now, Willi my son.'

From where August stood he could watch the table and the wall beyond it. The map stretched from East Anglia to Frankfurt. The smaller one showed only Ermine's sector and the overlapping circles of the sectors surrounding it. Now that the early warning had been given the other sectors were alerted and lit up bright green on the glass map.

Willi tapped the table with his Kneemeyer measure as he listened to the messages. 'First night fighter overhead.'

'I want him right out to sea at the extreme range of the Würzburg. Let's see, if they are coming in from Southwold let's say code-square Heinz Emil Four. How high is he?'

'Fifteen thousand feet, still climbing.'

'As high as possible, Willi. Height is everything.'

CHAPTER NINETEEN

'That's eight million three hundred thousand and eighty marks you owe me,' said Löwenherz, setting up the chessboard again.

'It's in my other trousers,' said Kokke. On the radio a close harmony group was singing.

> *'Everything ends, everything passes,*
> *Upon every December follows a May.*
> *Everything ends, everything passes,*
> *But two who love always remain faithful.'*

The girls cooed to an end and were replaced by a men's chorus singing *Bomben auf England* with appropriate wire brushes and drums. There was a loud raspberry of displeasure and the man nearest to the radio turned the volume down before any missiles were thrown in his direction.

Löwenherz looked round the Alert Hut. The crews were sprawled around the place in the most remarkable poses: hair uncombed, ties loosened and feet resting on chairs. It was as if they were all dead, thought Löwenherz, as if fumes or gas had done for them all, and yet if the loudspeaker sounded the quiet double click that warned of an announcement they could all be on their feet, tugging their helmets on to their heads and draping their bodies with oxygen connectors and microphone and earphone leads that made them a part of their machines.

Klimke – Kokke's radar man – used to spend these hours in the Alert Hut writing interminable letters to his wife, but since she had been killed last Christmas he had taken up knitting. In spite of howls of derision and practical jokes he sat calmly producing endless scarves for everyone he knew. He couldn't master the knack of decreasing, so he could only knit rectangles. Alongside him Leutnant Beer jerked convulsively in his sleep. A mosquito was buzzing round his ear.

'What a Wagnerian body of men,' said Kokke, looking around at the dozing flyers. Klimke grinned but did not stop knitting. Kokke moved his piece and they began a new game.

'Not fool's mate, Kokke. You underestimate me.'

'Never, Herr Oberleutnant,' said Kokke, and Löwenherz lost a knight.

'Damn.'

'Experience is better bought than taught,' said Kokke, moving forward.

'You lose because you are too reckless,' said Löwenherz.

'But I have more fun,' said Kokke.

'Probably,' agreed Löwenherz.

'Double or nothing on what time the first plane is put up?'

'Very well,' said Löwenherz. 'Midnight.'

'Midnight?'

'Short summer night with full moon means a short trip, that means the Ruhr. To get back before first light and allow time for stragglers they will probably time the attack for two o'clock. A Lancaster does 225 miles per hour, so it will pass over the British coast at zero minus 50. A good Freya radar will pick it up then, but by the time they fiddle around talking to the FLUKO and the Nachtjagdführer it will be fifteen minutes past one.'

'That leaves us fifty minutes.' Kokke had to raise his voice a little, for the radio music was now much louder.

'It might leave us all night. Who knows if we shall be put up?'

'Such modesty, Oberleutnant.'

Löwenherz smiled. 'About fifty minutes, yes.'

'And how was "*die Wurst*" bearing up this afternoon?'

Among his close friends in the Officers' Mess the *gemütlich* Hans Furth was happy to answer to '*Hanswurst*' (clown). However, he took exception to Kokke calling him simply '*die Wurst*', perhaps because of its feminine gender. Kokke seldom referred to him otherwise.

'Bearing up remarkably well,' admitted Löwenherz. 'Everyone who gets into trouble is an exhibitionist and he's going pig-shooting to forget it. The Mess will make *Wurst* of his successes.'

'*Wurst wider wurst*,' said Kokke.

Löwenherz smiled; 'sausage against sausage' also meant 'tit for tat'. 'He knows you hate him.'

'And I'm sure he's very mature and forgiving about me.'

Löwenherz nodded. 'He is.'

'What a bedside manner! After the war he'll have an expensive Berlin clinic for old ladies who have too rich a diet.'

'I only hope that after the war it's Berlin where the old ladies are wealthy and diets are rich.'

Kokke shrugged. 'Then perhaps Moscow. Or even New York.'

'I was hoping he could help. About Himmel, I mean.'

'That *Stoppelhopper* is interested only in helping himself.' It was a favourite German nickname for Austrians who were said to be mercurial, untrustworthy people who leaped around mentally as a man running barefoot through stubble fields. 'He could have done something about the documents without calling in the SIPO, but he was pleased with an

301

opportunity to show what a loyal, laughing little Nazi he can be.'

'We'll get no help from him,' said Löwenherz.

Kokke looked at him, heartened by the plural. 'Suppose both of us opened our mouths for Himmel.'

'I beg your pardon.'

'Suppose both of us supported Himmel and his protest. You're a baron and an ace, I could perhaps swing the old man.'

'Redenbacher?'

'I might be able to.'

'A slim chance.'

'Too slim for you?'

'Look . . .' said Löwenherz; he laughed in protest and embarrassment. 'You can't just put this to me, here and now.'

'How much longer is there? By this time tomorrow the man who took you into battle when you were a duckling will be in a concentration camp.'

'A civilian prison. They will hold him for trial and investigation.'

'A nice distinction. And afterwards release him with a reprimand?'

'Can't we talk about it tomorrow?'

'Herr Oberleutnant, we can't put off everything until tomorrow.'

'That's what Himmel said.'

'Exactly.' The swarthy Kokke stroked his short beard reflectively.

There was a click as the Operations Room clerk switched on the microphone and a hum as the circuit came alive. Under his feet Bubi awoke, snorted, yawned and nibbled at Löwenherz's boot.

'You should have made your bet, Kokke. I was wrong, the *Tommis* are early.'

Kokke didn't answer. Löwenherz looked around the hut;

no one had moved but now their bodies were tense. There were only dim red lights glowing in the Alert Hut, not enough light to read, scarcely enough to play chess. At the far end of the hut there was a huge glass aquarium; inside it tropical fish moved in slow motion. Löwenherz remembered the day it had arrived: five men and a heavy lorry. They spent three days fixing it up; it had been supplied by order of the High Command. At the time the whole Geschwader had been desperately short of cannon shells and no amount of pleading would release the aquarium lorry to fetch some.

He remembered the winter battles before Moscow, the men clad in their thin summer uniforms. One of the last air lifts into Stalingrad had brought rubber contraceptives. He remembered too the fuss they had made about salvaging the motor of the ancient wrecked Junkers before finding that it was a British engine. The whole damned Luftwaffe was being mismanaged by political favouritism and political fanaticism. The Freezing Report that Himmel had shown him was just one step away from the aquarium.

I'll stand by Himmel, thought Löwenherz and suddenly realized he'd said it aloud. My God, he thought, that bloody aquarium!

'Thank you, Herr Oberleutnant,' said Kokke. 'I knew you would.'

'I'm a fool,' said Löwenherz, and he wondered if he could get out of it some way.

The microphone click came again and the dispatcher's voice said, '*Achtung! Achtung!* Oberleutnant Löwenherz, Major Redenbacher and Leutnant Kokke to instant readiness. Oberfeldwebel Himmel, Leutnant Beer and Feldwebel Schramm are now at alert.' The toneless voice ended with an electronic click.

'Thanks,' said Kokke as he zipped his flying overall. 'We'll beat them, Oberleutnant.'

'Why do you think that?' asked Löwenherz bitterly. They were both grabbing at their equipment and climbing over out-stretched legs as they moved to the door. Löwenherz saw his radar operator pulling on his boots and made sure that Mrosek, his observer, was also ready.

'Put away your knitting, Klimke,' Kokke shouted. He turned back to Löwenherz. 'Because we are such an unlikely combination,' said Kokke. He grinned.

Löwenherz nodded but was unconvinced. '*Hals- und Bein-bruch!*' he said. To express the wish that a friend will break his neck and leg was said to fool the devil and bring him back safe. Kokke waved a grateful response.

'Uniform hats,' called Löwenherz to his crewmen Sachs and Mrosek. They both waved their folding cloth caps at him and Löwenherz responded by clasping his white-topped cap under his arm. If their aeroplane should be diverted to another airfield, the military police would make the devil of a fuss if they were hatless.

Löwenherz always insisted that his crew carried all the items that regulations demanded. Laden under a signal pistol, a garterful of flares, dinghy, lifejacket, parachute, iron rations, Pervitin tablets and a flashlight, they all hobbled to their plane.

It was cold outside and the yeasty smell of the sea was on the wind. The aeroplanes were warm and ready to go, and their crews were glad of the comparative comfort of their cockpits. Löwenherz placed his peaked cap behind his seat and made sure that his radio leads were fixed to his flying suit, exactly as regulations prescribed. Then he plugged it in and connected his oxygen tube. After that he made sure that his crew had done the same. His hands went through the sixty consecutive hand movements that they had done blind-fold at training school. The green and red panel lamps came alight. The ground crews were fussing around the rudders and wheels.

He looked at his observer seated beside him: Mrosek, a nineteen-year-old Leutnant with long black hair. His pinched face and prominent incisors gave him a rodent-like appearance; a comparison endorsed by his narrow chest, small stature and wiry agility. After the cannons had been fired it was Mrosek's job to crawl head-first into the nose to wrestle full drums on to the guns. That was difficult enough on the ground, but many times Mrosek had done it while Löwenherz had the plane in a dizzying vertical bank coming around for a second attack.

Mrosek's father was a vineyard manager from Heidelberg. Perhaps the proximity of so much wine had helped to make his disposition cheerful. He gave Löwenherz his quick ratty grin and held up his binoculars before he could be asked if they were aboard.

'Is everything in order?' Löwenherz asked his radar operator formally. He twisted in his seat to look at him.

From the rear seat Sachs smiled a deferential smile and raised his thin white manicured hand. He was a nineteen-year-old Feldwebel from Hanover and, partly because of his *nouveau-riche* and ambitious father, he remained in awe of the noble Baron Victor von Löwenherz Grawiec and modelled himself upon his pilot's speech, manners, walk and bravery.

Sachs the Saxon; Löwenherz wondered why there were always jokes about their capacity for hard work; it was a commendable virtue.

And that accent: 'No, *Junge*. Grandfather's ashes will not go on the mantelpiece. They will go into the hour-glass. Grandfather must work, all we Saxons must work.'

Sachs' father had been a builder's labourer in 1935 but when the West Wall was started he had gone into business with his brother-in-law, supplying metal clamps for poured concrete structures. By 1940 the company was listed on the Hamburg Stock Exchange. On the day of issue several Todt Organization officials were given free shares in the thriving young company. In 1941 Britain's unwillingness to come to terms meant the beginning of the Atlantic Wall. The most extensive engineering project in the history of architecture

305

was to deface Europe's northern coasts. The project devoured endless tons of prestressed concrete and used countless clamps. Georg's wrist-watch was Swiss, gold and as thin as a Pfennig. His cufflinks were jade, his shoes hand-made and under his regulation NCO's uniform his under-clothes were silk. His trips into Amsterdam were made in a new sports car, except at weekends, when his father would send the chauffeur in the Mercedes with its Todt Organiza-tion pennant flying.

Georg Sachs, to his father's great disappointment, had become a radar operator after failing to meet the require-ments of the pilot's course. He had grown to like his job and was good at it, which is why Löwenherz had chosen him from all the others on the Staffel. During the final minutes of an interception Georg knew that the aircraft was under his command. As he told his father, at the moment of the kill Baron von Löwenherz was nothing more than a machine-minder.

'Everything is ready, Herr Oberleutnant,' said Georg Sachs.

Control came on the air.

'Major Redenbacher to Himmelbett Station Tiger, circle beacon at 5,000 metres. Leutnant Kokke to Himmelbett Station Ermine, circle beacon at 5,000 metres. Oberleutnant Löwenherz to Himmelbett Station Gorilla, circle beacon at 5,000 metres.'

Each of the pilots acknowledged the order.

'We're going on to oxygen now' said Löwenherz. Some of the crews waited until they were over 1,200 metres but Löwenherz knew that loss of night vision is one of the first symptoms of oxygen-lack.

The wreck of the old Junkers 34 was garlanded with red obstruction lights. They came past it round the perimeter track as fast as safety would allow. The ground was soft and he was careful not to cut corners. Across the aerodrome the Flying Control personnel saw his navigation lights, and as soon as he reached the end of the runway they switched the flarepath on.

'Clear to take off, Katze One,' said the Control Officer without waiting for him to ask. There were gusts coming from the IJsselmeer that made his plane falter as it passed over the dijk road. Löwenherz pulled the control column back and the variometer showed a steady climb while holding the air-speed. Now he extinguished the navigation lights on his wingtips. There was no light anywhere except from his instrument panel. The artificial horizon with its tiny green luminous aeroplane tilted as he came round on a course for Gorilla, almost due south of him – the long rectangle of runway lights passed under him getting smaller as it went.

Kokke was the next to go. Redenbacher was next behind him and perhaps that's why his take-off was a copybook example of flying skill. The forward window was hinged down the centre. Kokke pulled it closed but did not lock it. He left it slightly ajar, for like many flyers he liked to hear the note of the engines as clearly as possible. He enjoyed the sound of the airstream as it whistled through the gap. Gently the tail came up and they were airborne. Leutnant Klimke, the radar man, felt the wind round the back of his neck. He shivered, adjusted his hand-knitted scarf and watched the airport buildings tilt and drift under the port wing.

'It's freezing back here,' he said, 'close the . . .'

Until radar was discovered and manned by dedicated men, few people guessed how many flocks of birds moved after dark. This night nearly one hundred gulls, driven inland by the bad weather, were flying towards the fishing villages on the IJsselmeer where nets laden with juicy titbits had been hung out to dry. Only eight birds of the flock hit Katze Five. Two were bisected by the propeller blades and three struck the engine nacelles, were mangled and sucked into the air intakes. Two hit the leading edge of the wings and were cracked open like eggs.

It was the one that burst through the slightly opened front

window that did the worst damage. By the time it entered the cockpit it had no wings or head. It was little more than half a pound of bloody offal that hit Kokke in the face, plus of course a thousand feathers. But it came in at two hundred miles per hour, putting out both eyes, fracturing his skull (with multiple fractures of his right cheekbone and nose) and dislocating his jaw. It was impossible to distinguish where the bird's remains ended and Kokke's face began. He lost consciousness almost instantly, but somewhere a reflex had ordered his hands to pull on the control column and they pulled. Neither the observer nor Klimke realized what had happened even when the cockpit was white with shredded feathers. Kokke was dying, medically perhaps already dead, but his muscular arms strained at the control column with a live man's strength. It was no use. Kokke's radio line was not fastened to his back. The radio plug from his helmet had fallen into the gap in the floor through which the control column passed. To have got the control column back far enough to gain height he would have had to crush a solid metal plug to wafer-thinness.

The Ju88 hit the IJsselmeer at a shallow angle. Finishing his sentence as though everything depended upon it, Klimke gasped '. . . Window', and was dead. The waves were about a yard high and with a soft crunch the plane was swallowed like a gourmet's oyster. All the crew were dead by then, for the impact snapped their vertebrae. The black aeroplane slid into the dark water, banking and turning as it had in the sky, until with a gentle thud it struck the seabed. The tail broke off and the aircraft was enveloped in a cloud of muddy water.

With a thump the yellow life-raft, activated by a water-immersion switch, erupted from the compartment in front of the tail. There was a hiss of compressed air and a flurry of bubbles. It inflated, writhing like a demented monster, as the air entered each rubber compartment in turn. Finally it was a perfect yellow circle and it floated up until it was held

308

by the six feet of restraining cord. It stayed like that just under the surface of the sea: a sculpture-like yellow ring seemingly balanced upon the taut cord. The current sent it spinning gently like a hoop upon a conjurer's finger. For many months it remained there, turning in the sunlight and in the darkness and attracting foolhardy fish until, rotting compartment by compartment, it finally sank to the ocean bed and disappeared. By that time eels had eaten the three flyers.

'I've lost radio contact with Leutnant Kokke in Katze Five,' said the ground operator.

'Damn these bloody radios,' said the officer. 'He's only been on the air for two minutes. You'd better reassign Löwenherz to Ermine; they're getting fidgety out there. And tell Kokke to return to base. It's probably only his transmitter gone, in which case he'll still be receiving you.'

The operator nodded and tuned to Kokke's wavelength to tell him that his transmitter was not functioning. 'Announcing: I am deaf,' he said. 'Announcing: I am deaf.'

Löwenherz laughed when he heard the news. He could imagine Kokke cursing. So they had ordered him to return to Kroonsdijk. Not a chance of Kokke doing that; he would try and get into the stream and find a *Tommi* without radar aid. Löwenherz's radar operator tuned their radio to the controller at Ermine.

'Order: proceed to Heinz Emil Four,' said the new voice calling him from Himmelbett Ermine. Let's see, Heinz Emil Four was halfway to England. He'd probably be the first pilot into the bomber stream. Tonight was starting well.

CHAPTER TWENTY

The bombers were swimming upwards. Ignoring their assigned heights, most pilots that night kept their noses trimmed skywards and let the technical limitations of their machines decide the altitude at which they turned the trim wheels back to normal. Some of the older Stirlings could not get above 11,000 feet. Even the best ones at 18,000 were not above the extreme range of the 8.8-cm flak. The two-motor Wellingtons, however, of even older design, could all do better than this and the best of them, at nearly 24,000 feet, were flying higher than any other planes in the stream.

Lambert had pushed Door to nearly 21,000 feet. Now he trimmed the controls so that the plane was flying 'hands off' and turned on the automatic pilot. He felt the elevators kick as it engaged. He had corrected course for the changing wind, so they had crossed the British coast at the prescribed assembly point. In his curtained cabin Kosher watched the shape of the pulses on the scope of the Gee and calculated their position from its map. He pencilled a dot upon his plotting-chart and calculated how much longer it would take until they were over the target. 'Fifty minutes to TOT,' he announced. They had entered Luftwaffe fighter grid-square Heinz Emil Four although they had no way of knowing that. Now they were at the front of the bomber stream. That was no great navigational achievement; the stream was an unwieldy slab of bombers flying as much as fifteen miles to

310

either side of the pencilled route. It was timed to be nearly two hundred miles long. So while Creaking Door was over the North Sea the rearmost aircraft was only just taking to the air.

Tonight visibility was poor and only the sound of 2,800 high-performance engines marked their track. Each of those engines required the manufacturing capacity of forty simple car engines. The man-hours spent constructing each four-motor aeroplane would have built almost a mile of Auto-bahn. The radar and radio equipment alone equalled a million radio sets. The total of hard aluminium amounted to 5,000 tons, or about eleven million saucepans. In cash, at 1943 prices with profits pared to a minimum, each Lancaster cost £42,000. Crew-training averaged out at £10,000 each, at that time more than enough to send the entire crew to Oxford or Cambridge for three years. Add another £13,000 for bombs, fuel, servicing and ground-crew training at bargain prices and each bomber was a public investment of £120,000.

Without including the Oboe Mosquitoes, the nuisance raid on Berlin, the OTU planes dropping leaflets upon Ostend, training flights, transport jobs or any of Coastal Command's activities, this bombing fleet cost eighty-five million pounds.

Six bombers had already landed – the 'boomerangs'. Most aircrew hated to abort, for unless they bombed the target the trip didn't count towards their tour. One Lancaster had got as far as the coast when a radiator leak caused the port inner to disappear in a cloud of steam. A Stirling had a faulty radio and the pilot of a Wellington was suffering from stomach pains. The latter turned back just before the Dutch coast. One Lancaster taking off from an airfield near Lincoln bounced badly enough to smash the undercarriage – one wheel went through a barn roof – and was unable to retract its landing gear when in the air. Its fuel-jettison device failed too. It was still circling its base under orders from Flying

Control. When enough of its fuel had been used up to achieve Safe Landing Weight it would try a landing. At Warley Fen, John Munro managed a perfect take-off in spite of a tyre blow-out. He'd corrected the resultant swing effortlessly and two of the crew didn't notice anything unusual. His problem would arise on his return.

Creaking Door, S Sweet, The Volkswagen and Joe for King were all within half a mile of each other, with Lambert 2,000 feet above the others, although on this dark night the only person to know that was the radar operator at Ermine who watched the blips slide across his screen. Lambert was as high as the plane would go and the control column was mushy and insensitive in his hands.

High above him, almost touching the stratosphere, he could see long wispy cirrus clouds. At the moment they weren't lying along the wind direction, but the wind would continue to back until they were. They heralded rain, but Lambert's interest in the clouds was a more immediate one and warned of a more immediate danger. The clouds glowed white and luminous, spotlit by a bright moon that had not yet appeared over the horizon. Soon it would appear and the sky would lighten and the mantle of night would start to go at the elbows.

The Freya radar warned the smaller, more accurate, Würzburg of the stream's route. Its three-man crew complained of the cold, as they always did, and tilted the mirror until suddenly four blips – Door, Sweet, The Volkswagen and Joe for King – slid across the hooded radar scope. The number one operator missed three spots of light but held the fourth one and tuned to it. Inside the warm dark plotting-room August held his breath like an angler when the float twitches.

'Red Würzburg has a contact, sir,' said Willi Reinecke, 'in Heinz Emil Four.' It was as August had predicted. He compared the blue spot of light that marked Löwenherz's night fighter. It was about ten miles away from the red one. 'Question: your altitude and bearing, Katze One,' said August as a double check.

It was Sachs, the radar man in the back seat, who replied. Löwenherz, hearing the call, turned his instrument-panel illumination to minimum and leaned close to the black windscreen. He could hear the wind buffeting the hinges and fixtures.

'Order: Caruso ten left, Katze One,' said August. Löwenherz touched the rudder bar. He knew that he must comply with every instruction immediately it was given, for the heavy Junkers with its clumsy aerial array was not much faster than a Lancaster. For the same reason its stalling-speed was higher.

'It's a parallel head-on intercept,' said August. 'I'll bring him in slightly to the north of the *Tommi*.'

'Announcing: boring cinema,' said Löwenherz. It was code for poor visibility.

Willi Reinecke gave a little splutter of indignation. 'They are always complaining.' He followed the moving points of light across the frosted-glass table, marking their progress with a wax pencil so that the converging courses could be seen. In spite of the dimmed lights August could see that the plotting-room had begun to fill up with off-duty personnel who wanted to see the excitement.

'Prepare: 180-degree turn,' said August.

'That's clear,' crackled Löwenherz's acknowledgement.

'A starboard turn,' August explained to Willi. 'If he turns to port he'll pass close enough across his front for the *Tommi* to spot him.'

By now Löwenherz had become a part of the machinery; it was August who was flying the plane.

August looked round the plotting-room at the expectant faces. Some of the men were in overcoats thrown over pyjamas, their hair awry and faces stubbly. They watched him with the godlike and superior impartiality with which spectators judge card games. An orderly elbowed his way through them and came up the steps of the rostrum with a tray of coffee cups. The coffee soon disappeared and he went back to the kitchen for more. August drank his without tasting it. He watched the two coloured lights rushing towards each other. They represented a combined speed of six hundred miles per hour. He knew that a mistake in the timing of Katze One's turn could cause them to miss the contact. That wasn't an enjoyable thing for the commanding officer to do for an audience of subordinates.

'Skip, give me a bit of straight and level for a star shot.' Kosher Cohen stood under the Perspex astrodome fixing the stars through a sextant. Kosher was one of the few RAF navigators who was skilled in its use. At the navigation school he'd handled it better than his instructor. 'Where the devil did you learn how to handle one of these, son?'

'My father's yacht, sir.'

'And a bloody comedian to boot. Sit down. Next.'

There wasn't time for another shot, so he compared his readings with the Gee fix. Four shots with a four-mile-wide cocked hat to show their position. Not bad at all.

Cohen looked at his plotting-chart in the tiny circle of his desk light. To make good his track he drew the wind-speed and direction and calculated their ground-speed from the remaining side of the triangle thus formed. 'Eleven minutes to the Dutch coast,' he said. No one answered.

Lambert shifted his behind on the hard parachute pack. The heavy unpowered controls required a lot of physical strength to move them and already he had an ache in his shoulder and the usual pain in his spine. He sat upright to stretch his back and rolled his shoulders. 'We are within radar range,' he warned the crew. 'Keep your eyes peeled for fighters.'

Like all of the bomber stream's wireless operators, Jimmy Grimm, whose father had a radio shop in Highgate, was tuning his radio to the frequencies between 7050 and 7100 kilocycles trying to find an enemy voice. Then he could transmit a signal on the same frequency to blot out the conversation between controller and fighter pilots. A microphone was fitted into an engine of each bomber especially for this purpose. Suddenly he heard August's voice.

'Order: start turning . . . now.'

'Turning,' said Löwenherz.

Jimmy Grimm was excited. 'I've found one of their controllers and a night fighter.'

August Bach's voice came over the headphones with the same clarity that Löwenherz heard it. 'Order: steer 097 degrees,' said August. 'Announcing: enemy range ten kilometres.'

'The plane he's following is on our heading,' said Cohen.

'Every plane in the stream is on our heading,' said Digby. He was full-length in the nose trying to see the Dutch coast.

'I wish I could understand German better,' said Jimmy Grimm. 'That's the trouble with being a radio ham; in peacetime I used to pick up all sorts of stations and only speak a few words of everything.'

'While you types are sodding about, some poor bastard is going to get the chop,' said Digby. 'Why don't you jam him?'

'Perhaps it's us he's after,' said Binty from the mid-upper turret.

'Can we steer on to 080 degrees just to be sure, Skipper?' said Cohen.

'You're the navigator,' said Lambert and put the plane into a shallow banking turn.

'He's still a long way behind the bomber,' said Cohen, 'and the Controller keeps telling him to lose height.'

'You are still well above him,' August told Löwenherz; 'lose another five hundred metres.'

Again Löwenherz touched the control column and the fighter dipped. Beside him the observer had his field-glasses on his lap; the bomber was too far away and the night too dark for there to be a chance of visual contact yet. Behind

Löwenherz, facing rearwards, the radar operator was boxed in with so much equipment that he was scarcely able to move. His three radar screens that showed range, altitude position and lateral position were tucked under his right elbow and to see them he had to cock his head on one side like a sparrow. It was useless to look at them yet, for the equipment wouldn't show the target until they were three thousand metres away.

'Order: hold it,' warned August. Löwenherz throttled back.

Flash Gordon was staring through the newly open part of his rear turret. God, it was cold, but he could see better than he had ever done before. If he bent forward he could almost get his head outside the aircraft. When he rotated the turret the slipstream passing across the barrels of the four Brownings made a gentle screaming sound, like high wind through telephone wires. He kept the turret moving, making the gun muzzles describe little circles as he had practised at gunnery school with pencils in the muzzles. A good gunner could write his name like that. It was a lonely position in the rear turret, especially when night fighters were about, for then chatter on the intercom was forbidden. Flash Gordon and Löwenherz were staring towards each other with all the concentration they could muster, but the night was too dark for either of them to see anything.

Flash heard Cohen order a change of course and watched the clouds slide past the tail.

August watched the red blip change direction on the Seeburg table. Willi marked it with the pencil. 'He's turned to port,' said August. 'Order: steer fifteen degrees left. He's very close now.'

'I think it is us,' said Cohen. 'He's told him to change direction.'

'Jam him,' said Lambert urgently. Jimmy Grimm tuned his 1154 transmitter to the 1155 receiver, heard its whistle, sought the silent 'dead space' and switched on the microphone that was fixed inside the engine. Lambert banked steeply to change course again.

In the night fighter they were silent. Löwenherz had turned as directed; Mrosek the observer had his field-glasses to his eyes and was scanning each side of the aircraft where the radar did not point. Suddenly Sachs' radar tube lit up at the end of the range circle: a *Tommi* at extreme range.

'We've got him,' said Sachs, trying hard to keep the excitement out of his voice. Suddenly jamming deafened them, so near were they to Jimmy Grimm's radio transmitter.

'Just in time,' said Löwenherz and they tuned the noise to minimum. Löwenherz switched the gun safety-catches to 'fire' and a line of red lights appeared on the instrument panel. Suddenly the whole Junkers hit a patch of turbulence. The plane dipped steeply like a horse refusing a fence. A wingtip fell and Löwenherz had to use all his strength to correct the plane's heading.

'The *Tommi*'s slipstream,' said Löwenherz, but the others knew what it was. The force of it showed how close they were behind the speeding bomber.

'He's turning right,' said Sachs as the blip on his screen started travelling along its base line. 'He's turning, keep turning.' He watched the tube.

'Level out but keep turning, range still closing. Straighten out, range still closing too fast. Twelve hundred metres.' Löwenherz followed the turn until when heading almost due south the bomber straightened out and Löwenherz did too. 'Where do you want him?' asked Sachs.

'Slightly starboard.'

'He's about seven degrees starboard.'

'That's enough, read off the range.'

'Under one thousand metres, closing slowly.'

Löwenherz wanted to move on to the bomber as slowly as possible, for that would give him the maximum duration of gunfire. 'Bring me in level with him. I'll lose height when we get a visual.'

'It's still very dark; you'd do better to have him against that bright cirrus.'

'Very well, bring me in a little below him.'

'Nine hundred, left a touch. We're coming in too quickly, Herr Oberleutnant.'

'I can't see him.'

'Still too fast.'

'Damn, why is he throttling right back?' Löwenherz reduced his speed until Sachs grunted, 'That's in order, Herr Oberleutnant.'

'Still can't see him.'

'We're very close, five hundred metres.'

'Got him,' said Löwenherz, and at the same time Mrosek also gave a yell. Eight yellow dots of exhaust flame pin-pricked a horizon across the darkness.

And because all primitive rituals, especially those concerned with death, have their own vocabulary, Löwenherz reported his sighting to Bach with the words 'Kettle drums, kettle drums'.

'Lancaster bomber,' said Mrosek, whose task it was to identify the targets before an attack.

'You beauty,' said Löwenherz.

Flash Gordon was a mild man, small in stature, humble in origin and quiet of voice and yet within him was growing a hatred of Binty Jones that he wouldn't have thought possible. Hardly a day went by without a jibe or a word of sarcasm and now most recent and hurtful of all was Binty's scorn of his turret modification. If Binty had publicly recognized what a fine idea it was, then the Gunnery Officer might have ordered the turrets of all Squadron planes to be similarly altered. Who knows, it might have been called the 'Gordon panel'. Invented by a gunner named Gordon, people say he was one of the greatest gunnery experts the Air Force ever had.

Although Flash Gordon never told real lies, he had come to realize that sometimes a white lie can be necessary for the sake of mankind's progress. If telling a lie was the only way of having an excellent modification incorporated into Warley Fen's aeroplanes then a lie wouldn't stand in his way. In ten minutes I'll do it, he thought, but changed his mind. There would never come a quieter time than now: that fighter scare was over and they were quite alone in the sky.

'Fighter, fighter. Corkscrew port, go!' said Flash Gordon. Without bothering to use the sights, he opened fire into the blank darkness. Lambert, obeying instinctively the command that any crew member was empowered to give, flung Creaking Door into a vertical bank and let it drop through the air like a slate.

Binty Jones, not to be outdone by his colleague, also fired his guns. Curves of tracer hosepiped across the sky as Door fell faster than its turrets could turn.

'My God,' said Löwenherz as the tracer came towards him. Instinctively he shied away, while Door's eight exhaust flames tipped vertical and slid out of sight under his nose. The little .303 bullets that the *Tommis* fired were seldom fatal against the solidly built Junkers, but still Löwenherz found it impossible to fly through them.

'He's seen us,' said Mrosek. Löwenherz swore. He followed the bomber down, trying to bring the flame spots up past the windscreen again, but now that he was higher than the bomber he no longer had the advantage of the moonlit clouds.

Lambert was following the classic manoeuvre of the corkscrew and chanting its litany as he went, to warn the crew: diving port, climbing port, roll, climbing starboard, diving starboard, roll, diving port, climbing port . . .

Many times Löwenherz had seen such an evasive pattern. Four or five times he had been able to execute identical manoeuvres in formation with his victim and kill him while they danced together. He could not do it this time. For a corkscrew can be executed in such a leisurely fashion that it occupies ten miles of air-space (some pilots corkscrewed like this the whole journey) or it can be the brutal wing-wrenching, back-breaking manoeuvre that Lambert now put into effect.

'Lost contact,' said Sachs.

'My fault,' said Löwenherz.

The night fighter's Li C1 airborne radar projected only a narrow cone of signals straight ahead (between 60 and 30 degrees to be precise). Löwenherz waggled his aircraft through a horizon-searching series of manoeuvres. It was no use. He switched on the radio transmitter.

'Announcement,' said Löwenherz. 'Katze One, contact lost.'

'Katze One,' said August, his voice still badly marred by the jamming, 'Order: steer 200 degrees.' August looked at the plotting-table and saw that the blip that was Creaking Door was at the extreme edge of his sector. 'He has luck, that *Tommi*,' said August. 'If he'd turned the other way we'd still be able to go after him.'

'There are plenty more where he came from,' said Willi.

In Creaking Door Lambert had stopped corkscrewing. His hands were trembling; so that Battersby would not notice he kept a tight grip on the controls. Suddenly the pain in his back and shoulder, unnoticed during the time of danger, returned with new ferocity. 'Give me a course for Noordwijk, Kos,' said Lambert.

'086, Skip,' said Cohen. Always the perfect navigator, he had been keeping the calculation fresh while waiting for the question.

'Now do you believe in my clear-vision panel?' Flash Gordon asked the world at large. He had waited long enough for a word of congratulation or thanks.

'Bloody good show,' said Lambert.

'I don't believe you saw anything,' accused Binty Jones.

'A damn great night fighter, man. In fact, I think I may have hit him.'

'Balls,' said Binty. 'There was nothing there.'

'Then why were you firing?' asked Flash. There was no reply. 'The Gordon clear-view panel, I'm going to call it.'

'Just an old-fashioned liar with old . . .' Binty began the fourth verse of the song.

'For Christ's sake belt up, everyone,' said Lambert.

S Sweet had lost headway by the wind error back at Lowestoft and Door had been turning and corkscrewing over the ocean so that by midnight, German Time, while both Sweet and Lambert were eight miles short of the coast-line, Tommy Carter in Joe for King and Fleming in The Volkswagen had reached Noordwijk, turned and were four miles along their final leg for the target. About midway between them – two miles off Noordwijk – Löwenherz was moving back over the sea. Twice he had passed within one hundred yards of Joe for King. For a few seconds his wingtip was only twenty feet from the tailplane of a Halifax but none of the crews had spotted these near-misses and to them the sky seemed vast and empty.

Noordwijk-aan-zee is a holiday resort on the coast of Holland. In 1943 the sand was criss-crossed with barbed wire, and steel spears were hidden in the sea. The hotels had become convalescent homes and military offices and the wide sea-front that in peacetime was crowded with holiday-makers was guarded by armed sentries. The lighthouse stands on the modern esplanade and now its shaded light was switched on while the convoy moved past. The flak-cruiser *Held* was leading the line of ships and it located the bomber stream as they passed overhead. Each time the *Held* fired, the sound rattled every window in Noordwijk and flashes lit up the whole sea-front. The red fire of one salvo burst uncomfortably close to Löwenherz's Junkers and he climbed away from the flashes. It was the second time within twelve hours that 'Admiral' Pawlak had fired at Löwenherz but there was, of course, no way in which either of them would ever know that.

'How nice of them,' said Lambert, 'they've got the Noord-wijk lighthouse switched on for us.' He asked Cohen for a course that would take him well short of the nearby town of Leiden with its notorious flak concentrations. Even while Lambert, and Digby in the nose, were looking at the pulsating glimmer of the lighthouse, the whole esplanade suddenly lit up as if the sun had selected that town for a private dawn. Two pathfinder Lancasters had dropped flares to mark it as the turning-point for the bomber stream. The lighthouse keeper peered out of the window at the blinding yellow Christmas trees of flares that inched slowly downward, crackling loudly and sending up snakes of white smoke. Illuminated by the flares the smoke looked yellow. So did all the hotels and the faces of the sentries and the Luftwaffe aircrew staring out of the windows of the convalescent home.

'Kos,' said Lambert, 'turning-point markers at Noordwijk.'

Cohen pulled aside the curtain that screened his chart table. The light from his desk was briefly reflected in Lambert's windscreen before Cohen switched it off. It took him a moment to adjust his eyes to the dark. Then he leaned across to the window and saw the strip of coastline with its hotels and lighthouse lit by the flares.

'That would be about right,' said Cohen and stood staring for a moment before going back to his charts.

Löwenherz, two miles to the north, also saw the flares. 'Ermine Control from Katze One,' he said. 'Turning-point markers going down on Noordwijk. I'll head towards them until you give me a contact.'

At Ermine Willi Reinecke quickly wiped the wax pencil marks off the frosted glass as the kitchen orderly returned with more coffee. The wide-eyed young man served Willi and August and then gave one each to the blip operators who sat under the table. He gave one to the telephone man too. Outside, the orderly had seen a big glow in the sky. 'Big fires to the north of here,' he confided. 'Leiden's getting it, I should think.'

Scornfully the telephonist said, 'Nonsense. That's just the *Tommis* dropping their marker flares to help the bombers find the way. The raid hasn't begun yet, *Junge*.' He took the hot coffee and put in three sugars. It was going to be a long night if they came back this way.

Very, very high in the sky above Noordwijk a fast RAF Mosquito also saw the flares. The 8.8-cm flak could not reach the Mosquitoes because they flew so high; the Würzburgs had difficulty tracking them because they were made of wood, and the night fighters had not been able to catch them because they were so fast. This one was flying to Ahaus where he would turn south for fifty miles and, flying under electronic guidance, would lay four red markers upon Krefeld for the heavy bombers to pound. That, at any rate, was the plan.

Meanwhile it was exactly one minute past one o'clock when the flares went down on Noordwijk. Within seconds, reports of them were being phoned to the Opera House at Deelen where they were marked in on the giant screen. Sentries in coastal watchtowers saw them and so did air-raid volunteers on factory roofs. The Control Room of the flak-cruiser *Held* gave their bearing and the Hitler Jugend gunners at Ahaus reported their glow.

In the Flugwachkommando at Duisburg the experts waited to see whether the planes would really turn at Noordwijk. It was an RAF trick to drop TP markers, having briefed their crews to ignore them. This had sometimes caused the FLUKO to warn the wrong district, and workers lost sleep sitting in damp cellars cursing the Luftwaffe. Still worse, the defences and people in the real target were left unprepared.

Within two minutes there were enough other reports to persuade them that the stream was turning. Warnzentral's commander needed only to nod to his attentive deputy. PAZs (pre-alert zones) became AZRs (alert zones) as the bombers moved eastwards. The country over which the bombers moved blacked-out completely. Railways stopped, stations went dark, factory workers took shelter.

'AD 30 for the whole Ruhr.'

Air Danger 30: cities, towns and villages as far as Cologne and Dortmund were told to prepare for an attack in thirty minutes. At the flak sites cigarettes were doused and coffee abandoned as men came grumbling, laughing and yawning out of the rest huts, buttoning their greatcoats against the chilly night. The barrels were elevated, searchlights tilted, radar warmed and shells fused. Civil-defence workers, police, fire services and hospitals were warned too. Shelters were unlocked and the Nazi Party organization through which bombed-out civilians were cared for began to prepare. Fires were lit under vats of soup, blankets were sorted, shrouds made ready, ration cards endorsed and bundles of second-hand clothing untied. Altgarten was now in the PAZ.

CHAPTER TWENTY-ONE

'Did you see the sunset this evening?' asked Gerda Pippert of the man sitting on her left. She had gained confidence by now. No one had guessed that she was not the Frau Pippert on the invitation list, and nowadays everyone was far too concerned with his own life to inquire into hers.

'Ah,' said her companion, 'we should have been out in Koller Meadow, you and me, holding hands and catching pneumonia on the damp grass.'

Gerda Pippert blushed. He was frightful, this bald-headed little man with whom she had sat through dinner, and yet everyone else took his jibes in good spirits, so she was reluctant to object. Although, goodness knows, Koller Meadow behind the hospital and Nurses' Training Centre had become truly notorious on these summer nights. There was a joke going around town: whenever someone had a bruise or cut they said they had fallen over a nurse while crossing Koller Meadow in the blackout.

The architect's wife, who even on this warm evening had insisted upon sitting through dinner in her fur cape, leaned across and said, 'I heard they were going to have caviar.'

'I've never had caviar,' said Gerda Pippert.

'It's horrible,' said Gerd Böll. 'I'll take smoked eel every time.'

'How lucky you are, to have a taste for the common things,' said Frau Hinkelburg. She was watching her architect husband at the far end of the table as he talked with a redheaded young cousin of the Burgomaster. Once before she'd had trouble with her husband over a redhead.

'There are certainly enough common things about,' agreed Gerd Böll cheerfully. As he reached for a second helping of tart he winked at Gerda and she smiled at him. He didn't care what he said to anyone and she admired that in a man, she always had.

She looked around the table at all the guests, especially the ladies. There was the Burgomaster's mother, what a dignified lady: eighty-six years old with a lace blouse boned high under her chin and freckled white hands glittering with rings. There was the Burgomaster's wife, her white hair drawn back in the severe earphone style that was now considered patriotic. A handsome woman of great charm and kindness, neither of which virtues could truly be attributed to her husband.

'And the lady with the diamond tiara?' asked Gerda Pippert.

'Gräfin von Linck.'

'The astrologer?'

'None other,' said Gerd.

'People say Reichsführer Himmler consults her. She says victory will come next year.'

'Yes, she does, she says that every year.'

Gerda Pippert scrutinized Gerd's face in alarm and Frau Hinkelburg tutted her disapproval.

All the waiters were busy attending to the curtains, so Gerd reached to the ice bucket and served both ladies with a little more French champagne. He noticed that the 1937 label saying 'For export to England' had been overprinted with 'Réservé pour le Wehrmacht'. He wondered if that labelling department had already prepared similar ones for the Americans or even the Russians. To drown the thought he served himself an extra measure.

The windows of the Frenzel Stube's private room gave all

the Burgomaster's guests an extensive view of the town, which is why the waiters had waited so long before closing the curtains and putting on the lights, but once that was done a different atmosphere came to the party. More intimate and seemingly more private too, the guests – merry with the Burgomaster's carefully chosen and generously supplied wine – settled into their chairs and made ready for the speeches and toasts that would occupy the rest of the evening. Some speech-makers already had their notes before them on the table.

Gerd Böll timed his exit nicely. A second helping of Frenzel's apple tart marked the end of the evening as far as he was concerned. He knew the drill from now on: coffee cups were standing by on the trolley and even before the spoons were in the saucers the first of the speech-makers would be on his hind legs mouthing a diligently assembled collection of sycophantic and patriotic clichés. Each would bring lengthy if unenthusiastic applause. It was a damn shame about the cigars – bluntended *Stumpen* from Holland – that had long since disappeared from any sources that Gerd Böll knew, but even they didn't tempt him to stay. He had explained to the Burgomaster that this evening he would have to leave early in case of air-raid duties.

'Duty comes first,' the Burgomaster had said. Many years ago he'd been complimented on his fine speaking voice and he always pronounced his careful *Hochdeutsch* as though speaking to an imbecilic foreign child.

Actually Gerd Böll was going down to the railway-station buffet for a game of skat with his TENO friends. He'd promised to be there before eleven-thirty and he whispered his excuses to the garrulous wife of the architect and to the simple old schoolteacher woman seated next to him.

'Goodbye, Frau Pippert,' said Gerd. 'So nice to see you again, and I'm glad to see your foot is so much better.'

Frau Pippert smiled uneasily. So the real Frau Pippert had a bad foot. 'Yes,' she said tentatively, 'it's much better now.'

327

She decided to embellish it a bit. 'The toes give a stab of pain from time to time.'

'Well, we can't complain about that,' said Gerd cheerfully. 'After all there are not many people these days who can grow a complete new leg after an amputation.'

Gerd smiled and kissed her hand. 'Have a wonderful evening, Frau Pippert,' he said. 'A grocer has to be most careful about confusing the bills for two ladies of the same name, but luckily there are no other grocers here this evening.'

Oberwachtmeister Müller was on his feet as soon as the coffee appeared, but by fast footwork Gerd just made it to the door. Müller pulled at the skirt of his blue uniform jacket and cleared his throat nervously. It was an honour to speak first and yet it was difficult too. The waiters were still serving the coffee and he noticed more than one guest looking enviously at that fellow Böll as he practically ran to the door. Someone rapped upon the table with a spoon and then, as he began to speak, they gave him their undivided attention.

The police chief related the Burgomaster's achievements and Altgarten's role as a war-winning and law-abiding part of the Third Reich. If it was a story that also reflected the police chief's successes, then that was exactly as it should be. Other officials added their praise; the Gasmeister and the Kreisleiter gave brief speeches.

Some speakers saw this as an occasion upon which they could once again relate Germany's progress from the demoralized nation that emerged defeated from the First World War to the mighty fear-inspiring master of Europe in 1943. Schott – the electricity chief – had known the Burgomaster for the greater part of this time. In 1933 they had worked side by side at a bench in one of the factories that were secretly rearming the newly planned Wehrmacht. Schott spoke of those times. It was not a period of his life about which the Burgomaster cared to be reminded.

'An old man in the paint shed stole one piece of perambulator each day. When he had all the parts he tried to reassemble one in his living-room. Funny thing, he told me, every time I try it I end up with a machine gun.'

There was laughter and applause and even the Burgomaster smiled primly.

Most of the men were in uniform. A stuttering Party official from Berlin had come in an SA uniform complete with ceremonial dagger, commemorative armband 'Horst Wessel' and a display of medals and ribbons. He presented an engraved plaque to mark the Burgomaster's service on the committee of a local Adolf Hitler school.

Obersturmführer Berger, senior full-time SS official of Altgarten, then stood up. He straightened the knot of his black tie and flicked at his sleeve as if to remove a piece of lint from his grey tunic. Satisfied with his appearance, Berger smiled upon his neighbours. He announced the Burgomaster's promotion to honorary SS Obersturmführer and made a witty speech describing the lengths to which the Allgemeine office had gone to arrange that the promotion be announced on this the Burgomaster's birthday. He also made a little joke that the Burgomaster had caught up with his own rank and he thought he should now turn the tables upon him by becoming honorary Burgomaster. It wasn't much of a joke, but there were so few jokes made that evening that the guests took that opportunity of having a side-splitting laugh and a cough.

The evening sped past, thanks in some measure to the way in which Frenzel's waiters enthusiastically complied with the Burgomaster's order to 'keep the champagne coming until everyone has had enough or I tell you otherwise'. The old room smelled of roast duckling, schnapps, candles and good cigars. Smells that went deep into the oak panelling and joined memories of other dinners in other times.

The rehearsed speeches came to an end at five past midnight when the tiniest Jungvolk boy in Altgarten presented the Burgomaster with a huge bunch of flowers on behalf of all of the Nazi Youth organizations in the district. There were still some impromptu addresses and the old songs.

'A memorable evening,' said Berger, who had taken off his SS jacket and was leading a chorus in a voice as powerful as it was discordant.

SS Standartenführer Wörth – CO of the SS unit at the Wald Hotel – smiled indulgently at Berger as he sang the old Party songs. He joined him in a chorus of one that he remembered from his days as an ensign, although the old man's voice was scarcely audible. At twenty to one he declared that it was his bedtime and got to his feet. He was like an overbred Borzoi dog, his limbs thin and spindly and his face the same, with sad grey eyes that looked round anxiously as though fearing unprovoked attack. The old SS officer moved slowly, prodding the floor with his stick before committing his weight to it. He gave a nod to the other guests and edged through the door. Behind him Dieter Witting, a burly NCO, was ready to support an elbow or pull a chair for him or signal a person from his path in a courteous and unobtrusive way that would not mark Wörth as the desperately sick man that he was.

The car was close to the entrance and the driver wrapped blankets across his commander's knees before closing the door with a considerate click. Wörth sank back into the leather seat and closed his eyes to meet the pain. His missing left hand still tormented him more than did his injured knees or feet.

It was a few minutes after one when a messenger arrived from the Rathaus and whispered in the Burgomaster's ear. Until that young fellow arrived with his steel helmet, heavy-duty gloves and official overalls it had been perfectly possible to forget that there was a war on.

'Can I have your attention,' said the Burgomaster, and the whole room was alert. The waiters stood at attention, the way they did each morning when Herr Frenzel inspected their hands and nails.

330

'I have official notification that there is a heavy force of RAF planes in the air tonight. Our FLUKO in Duisberg has given us the preliminary warning. They predict that the Ruhr will be attacked. My guests will no doubt wish to answer the call of duty at the earliest possible moment. I will therefore bid everyone goodnight. Heil Hitler!'

'Heil Hitler,' repeated the guests soberly. The Burgomaster kissed his wife and mother and bowed to his guests. The first ones to leave saw searchlights to the north-west. Soon after that the early warning sounded.

Altgarten railway station was noted more for the liveliness of its buffet than for the liveliness of its train schedules. The Bahnhofecke had become a favourite hang-out for policemen from the Rathaus across Bismarckplatz and for TENO engineers, as well as the brewery manager and his foreman and of course the railway people who were there all the time.

It was smoky and noisy all day every day and it smelled of thin beer, cheap tobacco and synthetic sausage. Sometimes it didn't close until three AM even though the one o'clock train was the last one. Many times when the main line was bombed troop trains had been shunted into Altgarten and the two old ladies who ran the Bahnhofecke had served beer, coffee and sandwiches until the supplies were exhausted.

The buffet was furnished like a Victorian parlour. There were dozens of plants, glass-fronted cases full of polished glasses, a bust of Beethoven and a drawing of Wagner, a coloured reproduction of the Führer and an old piano. On the top shelf of the bar there were school caps donated by high-school students when they went off to the war. It had become a ritual, and now there were twenty-eight dusty caps untouched since the day they were flung there. On that same top shelf there were four ancient empty Scotch whisky bottles. Never a week passed without some joker ordering a White Horse or a Black and White but still old Frau Klein was able to smile as if the joke was new.

The three tables near the piano were the best ones. From the counter one of the two old ladies could lean over with bread, beer, sausage and potatoes, but on a crowded evening customers near the door could shout all evening and still not be served. The three best tables were marked with *Stammtisch* flags, so that only regulars would dare to sit there. This evening the centre one was taken by a group of men playing skat for small money stakes and a little crowd had collected to watch the card players: Gerd Böll and his two TENO friends.

Fuchs Ueberall was talking. His TENO jacket was hung upon his chair. The two stars on its collar-patch showed him to be a Zugwachtmeister, which is a grand title for an NCO. His Army braces supported ill-fitting grey trousers that almost covered his chest. He had a strong Saxon accent. It seemed especially comical here where the local people spoke a high-speed dialect like Dutch, but no one smiled. It would be fool-hardy to annoy this amiable giant.

'You'll never get them bowling here in Altgarten,' said Fuchs. 'It's too near the Dutch border for the *Tommis* to risk it.'

'If you mean bombing say bombing. I hate these slang words,' said Peter Reuter, a TENO officer. He asked for another card. That rumour was resurrected every now and again. 'It's a comforting thought.'

'They are forbidden under pain of execution to bomb targets within twenty kilometres of any frontier of their ex-Allies,' said Fuchs Ueberall. He put emphasis on the word 'bomb'.

'How do you know that?' asked Peter Reuter. 'I hear the Americans and British never execute their soldiers.'

'We are eleven kilometres from the Dutch border here. Do you know of any bombs dropping as close as that to the border?'

'Yes,' said Gerd. He won the trick and piled the cards in front of him.

'Oh, I know about the plane that jettisoned its bombs on Frau Kersten's place. That doesn't count.'

'You'd better explain that to Frau Kersten,' said Gerd. Some of the men laughed.

'Play on,' said Bodo. Fuchs was a rumour-monger.

'She's too busy learning French to let me prove anything to her,' said Fuchs, and there was a louder laugh.

The one o'clock train was almost due when Jürgen Löwe, one of the Hitler Youth bicycle messengers, came into the Ecke. He wouldn't sit down because he had an urgent message for Andi Niels and had been unable to find him.

The HJ messenger said, 'The Ruhr is going to get pasted tonight; over seven hundred *Terrorflieger*, the FLUKO message said.'

One of the men playing cards said, 'That will be the second heavy raid in a week.'

Two brewery workers were playing chess in the corner. They had their French Army helmets and gloves ready and were wearing their civil-defence overalls. 'Lie-in tomorrow morning,' said one of them, for if the alarm went at night they were paid a two-Reichsmark bonus and allowed two hours off in the morning.

'Loser of this game goes back to phone the Rathaus.'

'Suits me,' said the second one and he brought his bishop to threaten the king's knight.

Herr Holländer, the marriage registrar, was one of the local Blockwarte. He swallowed the last of his beer and hurriedly got to his feet when he heard that a raid was imminent. It was his job to open the shelter and collect front-door keys from local residents in case of fire bombs. He also must make sure that old deaf Frau Klietmann was properly awakened when the alarm sounded. Not all the people from his block would go down into the shelter, in spite of the regulations. Most of them worked in the brewery and no one who had to clock-on at a quarter to seven wanted to interrupt his sleep and go into the cold cellar. Blockwart Holländer slipped out quietly.

The one o'clock train came in exactly on time with a whistle, a groan and a hissing of steam. Six TENO engineers who were going on leave left the Ecke to derisory cheers. The doors had hardly stopped swinging when one of the TENO men put his head back round it. 'Come and look at the *Tommi* flares going down – somewhere near Neukirchen I'd guess.'

The words were hardly out of his mouth when the Public Warning began. The warbling notes echoed eerily across the town. Even then not everyone left the Ecke. The Public Warning was only a preliminary caution for people in the street or a long way from shelter. And even if the more serious General Warning sounded it was purely academic out here in Altgarten; the bombs were destined for one of the big cities of the Ruhr.

Gerd Böll still had his playing-cards in his hand when he went out to look at the flares. They were a long way away, sputtering little pinpoints of intense light like that of the old-fashioned acetylene cycle lamps. Gerd decided it was time for him to report with his van to the Rathaus Control Room. Once the FLUKO let them know where the attack was being centred he would head into the bombed town to help. That was the advantage of being single, thought Gerd. He'd never be able to do such a thing if he had a wife and children to look after. That's what led him to think of Hansl and the girl. If the attack was going to be a heavy one – over seven hundred, the messenger had said – then perhaps he had better call in at August's place and make sure the child and the girl took shelter tonight. They'd object, of course, but he would insist upon it. He sat down again and took a last look at his cards. Then he raised his eyebrows to ask what Reuter thought would happen.

Bodo Reuter played a famous game of skat. He'd played

334

it when as a fifteen-year-old he'd falsified his age to go to the first war. He'd played it in the Merchant Navy and now after many evenings in the Bahnhofecke playing Gerd Böll and old Fuchs for Pfennig bets he'd almost regained his former skill. After a few glasses of Gerd's home-made schnapps he'd tell stories: around the Cape in a floating dock, the Grand Banks in a Spanish trawler, the trenches in the winter of 1917, Paris in the summer of 1940, brawls in Boston, brothels in Shanghai. Oberzugführer Reuter had done it all, and, as he said, some of it twice.

He was from Hamburg, a quick-spoken man, thin, tall, with light-blue eyes deeply set into their sockets, drawn face, high cheekbones and a big forehead with receding soft fair hair. He looked more like an art critic than a pioneer officer; most of Altgarten's TENO battalion were, like Fuchs, brawny fellows with a noisy sense of humour.

Some of the regulars at the Ecke found it hard to believe that this quiet-spoken man had done the things of which he told, but he had a chestful of medals to prove it and, as he had once told a crowd of angry Bolsheviks, his hands told the story of his life. Knobbly red angry hands they now were, shiny with scar tissue and criss-crossed with corns from a windjammer's lines.

Bodo threw his hand of cards upon the table to indicate that the game could not continue. Gerd lined up the edges of his cards with a neurotic care and Fuchs Ueberall sadly assembled the whole pack together and put it into its box. For an hour Fuchs had become a civilian again, but now that Altgarten had come under attack he was jerked back into the world of harsh military reality.

'Take my grocery van,' Gerd told Bodo. 'I will borrow a bicycle and be with you before you are ordered out.'

There was no time for the courtesy of argument. Bodo caught the keys that were thrown to him and, nodding to the other men in the bar, hurried out. Fuchs sat in the front seat alongside his officer and a few minutes later it was Fuchs who shouted in time for them to avoid driving into a big crater near the railway crossing.

Gerd borrowed a woman's bicycle from Frau Klein behind the bar. The tiny slotted blue street-lights had been extinguished but the luminous paint on the trees and lamp-posts helped him find his way through the darkened town.

As he passed the Nazi Party HQ, he popped in to tell them there was a big raid tonight, but one glance told him that he needn't have bothered. The NSV kitchens were bust-ling with voluntary workers in aprons and Party officials in their fine uniforms. Shrewdly it was a matter of policy that compensation, clothing, soup kitchens and emergency aid for the homeless were all provided by Nazi Party workers. Gerd picked his way past mountains of potatoes. The raw smell of the freshly peeled ones was strong. Gerd hated that smell. There were blue fantailed gas flames under the soup vats and more potatoes were being tipped into the peeling-machines.

'Some coffee, Herr Böll?' said Frau Grundel.

'I mustn't interrupt the good work,' said Böll. The woman smiled. Many years ago they had held hands under the trees and on summer evenings like this had walked along the stream as far as the Kersten windmill, long since broken and demolished. Now she was nearly fifty, widowed with three grown-up daughters and a soldier son. She ran her baker's shop and still volunteered long hours for the Frauenschaft. Frau Grundel reached for a chipped enamel mug from the shelf of mugs that stood ready by the stove. She poured the hot dark coffee and passed it to him.

'For the Hilfzug?' asked Gerd Böll.

'That's it,' said the woman. 'The lorries are waiting. It's strange to think that within three hours poor bombed-out people in the Ruhr will be drinking our good hot potato soup.' She smoothed the starched white apron of her uniform.

'We've a lot to thank God for.'

'God and the Führer, Gerd,' said the woman.

'There are flares dropping to the north,' said Gerd. 'And searchlights.'

'You are the third one to tell us,' said Frau Grundel. 'But there's no need to be alarmed about the *Terrorflieger*; our brave boys will be in the air after them.'

'I must be getting along,' said Gerd Böll. He swallowed his coffee and pursed his lips at the bitter after-taste. Frau Grundel noticed his grimace.

'You've nothing to worry about; our anti-aircraft defences in the Ruhr are the most formidable in the world.'

'Goodbye, Frau Grundel,' said Gerd. She turned away and switched on the peeling-machine which made a noise like thunder.

Anna-Luisa was brushing her hair carefully, three hundred times as she did every night, when she heard the voice of little Hansl from the next room.

'Fräulein, Fräulein.'

'Yes, Hansl. But you must get back into bed.' He had pulled back the curtains.

'The pretty lights, Fräulein. Such pretty lights. Like Christmas trees in the sky.'

Anna-Luisa went to the window. 'Yes,' she said. 'Exactly like Christmas trees, Hansl.'

'Is Daddy doing it?'

'No, Liebchen.' The coloured lights were close; very close. She picked him up. 'You're a weight, Hansl. Soon you will be too heavy for me to lift.'

'When I am a man I will lift you, Fräulein.'

'That will be splendid,' said Anna-Luisa and kissed the boy.

When the knock came at the door she went to it still carrying Hansl.

'Herr Böll, is something wrong?'

'Good, you are dressed.'

'Why?'

'I want you to take shelter this night.'

'Shelter?'

'Next door with Herr Voss. Last month he told August that he wanted you and the child to shelter there if the air raids came. His shelter is reinforced and has fans for air. Suffocation is the great danger, you see.'

'Tonight?'

'The flares are dropping already. They are target markers. You must hurry.'

'But they will not bomb Altgarten.'

'Please hurry.'

'I must get my shoes and a coat for Hansl.'

'I can't wait, Fräulein,' said Gerd. 'Hurry, and knock loudly on Herr Voss' door. I know he's in because his black-out always has chinks in it, but he plays the gramophone and he may not hear you.'

'It was kind of you, Herr Böll.'

'I promised August,' said Gerd coldly. He swung his leg over the saddle of Frau Klein's bicycle and pedalled away towards the TENO camp.

When the first bombs fell it was a sound new to Anna-Luisa: a slippery, shuffling half-whistle, like a heavy parcel sliding down a metal chute. Each ended with a bang. Not the sort of bang that a firecracker or a pistol makes. This was as different from those bangs as a tuba is from a piccolo. These were big brassy bangs that slapped ears, shook the ground underfoot and kicked urgently at the windows.

'We must hurry, my darling Hansl.'

CHAPTER TWENTY-TWO

The lights of the final Lancaster disappeared over the hedge of Warley Fen airfield. The sound of that last one became fainter until it too was gone. For a few minutes there always remained an unnatural quiet that made even insensitive people speak in whispers. The Group Captain was not an insensitive person. He stopped signing papers and turned out the desk lamp before drawing the blackout curtains and opening the window. A cold wind made the papers on his desk flap noisily. The flare path was switched off and except for the shielded lights on the corners of each building and a careless blackout in the Operations Block the night was dark and still.

It was always the same for him when the aeroplanes had gone; the Group Captain felt remote. He had a secret fear that one night none of them would come back and he would sit alone on the airfield for ever after. This was the twelfth raid this month. It was too many. His men were tired and so was he. He'd pulled every string he knew to be used as a pathfinder squadron, but if he faced the truth they weren't up to it. They were very ordinary airmen and he was an unexceptional commander.

He wished he could manage on four hours' sleep a night like so many of the young ones could, but missing sleep made him tired, forgetful and easily irritated. In spite of that he always waited until the planes returned. It would be unthinkable to go back to the house and try to sleep. He hated the place; it was far too large and empty for one man. Warley's previous Station commander had a wife and three children and so much furniture that he'd been pleased to leave half of it behind when he'd heard that Jarman had no furniture of his own to bring.

He wished Helen had lived long enough to see him get his scrambled egg and a station of his own. Some of his comrades and their wives felt sorry for him in that there had been no children. Laurie and Daphne had even said so. That was because they had no idea of the relationship between a commander and his men on a proper combat station. An operational station: how often they had dreamed of it and joked of it when he was a young acting Flight Lieutenant in the tiny peacetime Air Force. Then it had seemed that promotion would never come. 'Roll on death, promotion is too slow,' they used to joke in the Mess. Now, my God, it was sometimes too fast. They had kids of air commodores throwing their weight about; kids!

As his eyes became accustomed to the darkness he could see as far as B Flight dispersal. In the tin huts, where men would keep vigil through the cold night, tiny temperamental stoves were being coaxed into flame. The Group Captain sniffed the wood smoke and remembered his seven days in the front line in the spring of 1917; it was his whole leave. Those brave gods had thought him crazy but they had no idea what it did to a young infantry officer to incarcerate him in a supply depot for the entire war. And at a time when at the front the average life of a subaltern was three weeks!

His aircrews were even more stringently selected than Haig's young officers and yet in this month alone he'd lost three crews on their first trip. One crew had been here only eight days. They had the courage of a thousand lions and no one would be allowed to mar the honour he felt at being in the front line with them. He sniffed loudly, closed the blackout curtains and turned on the desk light again. The adjutant had left a pile of papers for signing and he continued through them mechanically without reading the contents. It was like being the mayor of a little town. Nowadays he scarcely saw his aeroplanes.

Again he picked up the note from Laurie at Besteridge.

Dear Jar,

What price Saturday now? Still no matter, I never said, 'Sports results are the acid test of skilled command.' But you might be able to convert me to your point of view over a pint.

LAURIE

Attached to the hastily scrawled note there was a newspaper clipping showing a famous cricketer in Air Force uniform with a Wellington bomber behind him and Laurie grinning alongside. The caption said that the batsman was now knocking bombs into German boundaries and was proud to be a member of the finest team of all – the RAF.

Group Captain Jarman grunted. He'd never regretted anything more than the much-quoted remark he'd made after his cricket side had won the cup, but that was years before the war, when he was a young kid, commanding a small unit for the first time.

It was only since Laurie had got this damned professional posted there that he'd suddenly taken an interest in cricket and started to borrow good players from all over the Command. The AOC loved it, of course. He and Laurie were as thick as thieves lately. Laurie had a devastating memory for indiscretions. Not his own of course, but his rivals'. God knows what else he'd be saying in the Mess on Saturday after they'd wiped the floor with Warley's keen but amateurish eleven. Sweet had taken over as captain this season and had done a pretty good job with them, except that this slow bowler – he looked down at his notebook – Lambert hadn't

341

even put in an appearance for the last few games. The Group Captain filled his pipe carefully and lit it.

There was a knock at the door and his clerk came in.

'Corporal Taylor,' she announced. She was just going off duty.

'Hello, Corporal Taylor. That's all right, stand at ease. I don't think we've met before.' He smiled. 'But you've probably seen me about. You're in Safety Equipment, aren't you?'

'Yes, sir.'

'And now you are probably wondering why I sent for you.'

Corporal Taylor said nothing.

'Sit down, Corporal. As perhaps you know we have a tradition in the RAF that on certain occasions officers and men talk what we call "man to man". You probably know what I mean by that.'

Corporal Taylor still didn't speak.

'It means that what we say to each other is informal. It means that you no longer have to weigh each word you say in case it might be what we call "conduct to the prejudice of good order".' He smiled paternally. 'At times I've had fellows cut up frightfully rough when I've let them do that. Of course they've regretted it afterwards, I've made sure of that but meanwhile I've been able to get to the bottom of something that's troubled them. Smoke, Corporal?'

'No thank you, sir.'

'Now how long have you been married to Flight Sergeant Lambert?'

'Three months, sir.'

'Are you happy here, Corporal?'

'Why aren't you happy there, my girl? What's so different about that aerodrome?' The Group Captain was so like her father.

How could anyone describe it? Low-power bulbs at dead of night, iron beds, dirty linen, damp walls, and a door banging desolately. Behind it some bereaved girl is taking an

342

unendurably hot bath and drinking gin. 'It's the war, Dad.'

'I'm near to my husband.'

'Exactly, and meanwhile you've continued to use your single name for WAAF records.'

'Yes, sir. I've been meaning to do something about it but . . .'

'But Section Officer Holroyd hasn't chased you up about it and you're frightened that you'll be posted elsewhere if Records hear.'

'Yes, sir.'

'Well, I've spoken to Miss Holroyd about you and she tells me you're a conscientious worker and she feels that on an operational station efficiency is the main thing.'

'Yes, sir.'

'Yes, there's nothing more important than efficiency in this day and age. There's nothing more important than killing Huns. The RAF has no Colonel Blimps. It's a young Service with young ideas and it's not hidebound by rules and regulations, but there must be a matter of give and take. You know what I mean.'

'Perhaps I will have a cigarette, sir.'

'Here we are, matches on the desk. But give and take means that the Air Force expects people to have a similar goodwill in return, Mrs Lambert, and that's what I want to talk to you about.'

'Yes, sir,' said Ruth.

'Your husband, Mrs Lambert, is one of my most experienced captains. There are not many people on this station who were flying in 1937: myself of course, Wing Commander Munro . . .' The Group Captain felt that it was not a good line to pursue. 'Anyway, when we've got a chap – a regular RAF aircrew bod – painting Communist slogans across his aircraft what will people think, eh?'

'Communist slogans?'

'Communist slogans, Mrs Lambert. "Joe Stalin for King." You would call that a Communist slogan, I take it?'

343

'I would call it a joke, sir. When people say that, they don't intend it to be taken literally. I mean everyone is saying it. I've even heard it on the wireless.'

'And that's exactly what we've got to be careful about.'

'But that's not painted on my husband's aircraft. That's painted on Sergeant Carter's L for Love.'

'Allow me to know my own aeroplanes, Mrs Lambert. You'll have to allow me that.' He smiled, pitying her feminine limitations.

'Is that what you wanted me for, sir?'

'No, it isn't, Corporal. I've sent for you to see if we can't get to the bottom of what's troubling your husband. Mrs Lambert, he seems determined to challenge authority. And on this aerodrome' – he smiled – 'well, I'm authority.'

'Challenged you, sir?'

He leaned back in his chair, not sure of how to continue. When he began to speak again it was with a new tone of voice as though he had decided to reveal everything to her in a sudden attempt at reason. 'As you might know, Mrs Lambert, I'm a committee man. Can't help it, always have been, always will be. You get a reputation for helping with one set of chaps and each of them will be off trying to get you on some other committee. But if there's one darned committee I'm pleased to be on it's the cricket committee. It was my idea to appeal to the public for used cricket gear. Last year we staged parades, we flew a Lancaster over Peterborough dropping leaflets about it and had collections at the local cinemas whenever there was a flying film running. Got a trainload of cricket gear too. Well, that's good stuff, Mrs Lambert. Keeps the chaps fit and amused. Cricket's a little like flying in combat, I always say: long leisurely time in the pavilion followed by brief moments when a chap faces some fast bowling. Damned like cricket, saving your presence, Mrs Lambert. Understand?'

'I don't think I do, sir.'

'The cricket match on Saturday, RAF Warley Fen versus

RAF Little Besteridge. I want Warley to win, Mrs Lambert. That's natural enough, isn't it?'

Ruth smiled. It seemed so childish to go to all this trouble about a game. 'And you want my husband in the team?'

'Well, of course. We all know he's the finest slow bowler in the Group. With him we'll knock spots off them but without him we've got no bowler worth the name.'

'And this match is special? I mean, you haven't minded that he hasn't played much recently.'

'Trust you to see right through me, Mrs Lambert. As my mother once said, there's not a woman in the world who can't see right through me. Yes, the Station commander at Little Besteridge is a chap I've known for years. He once played for 3 Group. If his dotty little Maintenance Unit at Besteridge beats us he's going to make life hell for me on every committee meeting afterwards.' He laughed and puffed at his pipe.

'You flatter me by suggesting that I can influence my husband, sir. And even if I could, I'm not sure that it would be wise.'

'Come, come, Mrs Lambert, I'm not that naïve, and neither are you. Give and take, take and give. That's the Air Force. You are living unofficially with your husband in the village when it's strictly against regulations, but your Section Officer and I don't want to be unreasonable . . .'

Ruth looked round the room as if seeking a way of escape. It was dark and inhospitable and the air was charged with the herbal scent of the CO's tobacco. Over his desk lamp there was a fly-paper, its gum shiny in the yellow glare. There were a dozen flies on it and not all of them were dead. She knew she'd not been brought here to be consulted or even commanded. Nor did his intimate confessions of frailty convince her that he was anything but devious. She had been brought to bear witness that the CO was a man of infinite compassion and wisdom, a man devoid of personal ambition or prejudice, reluctant to see her husband punished for his intractable behaviour. Ruth's father was like this. She remembered the way in which he'd humiliated her very first boyfriend and afterwards pretended to be unaware of having done so.

Ruth put one of her fingernails into the back of her hand until it almost bled; she wanted to be oblivious of everything except that little pain and she knew that if she were stoical about it this frightening old man and his clever questions would disappear. When she looked up he had not disappeared. 'I don't know what you want of me,' she said. She hoped he would reply, 'Nothing.'

'All I'm asking of you, Corporal, is to convey an unofficial message to your husband.' He tapped his pipe into the ashtray. 'I'm even thinking of taking him off flying duties.' He watched Ruth during this slow and studied declaration but he saw no change in her calm face. He was growing impatient of this foolish girl. A loyal wife would have immediately perceived the trouble that was in store for her husband. Her silliness was almost funny and he permitted himself a trace of a smile. 'You know what being taken off flying duties will involve, Mrs Lambert?'

Ruth had been frightened that the Group Captain would see her hands trembling, so nervous was she, but his smile changed all that. It was the brief smile that some men kept ready for women, babies and respectful beggars. Both patronizing and complacent, it triggered in her a righteous wrath. She tried to keep her voice low and calm as she replied but the anger in her voice could not be concealed. 'I know what it will involve, sir. That's the ultimate punishment in the Air Force. But it doesn't frighten me. How do you think I feel when I watch his plane take off at night? I'm lying awake full of sleeping pills that have no effect, waiting for a ring at the bell instead of the sound of his key in the lock. When they are diverted because of bad weather it's worse. I stay near a phone all the time waiting in case one of the girls from Flying Control might have heard something about the casualties. Take him off flying, if that's your decision, and then I'll have a husband who will live to see the war over.'

He pretended to concern himself with the papers on his desk. 'I don't think you understand the disgrace that will go with him being grounded. Have you? . . .'

She was determined not to raise her voice again. 'Disgrace is only for men. Save talk of that for your schools and your clubs and your old comrades' dinners. Save talk of disgrace until you lose your cricket match, or for the next hesitant hero.'

He looked up. 'Is that the way you will bring up your children, Mrs Lambert, without pride and without honour?' He said it as though he thought it most likely.

'Ask the widows of your dead aircrews how they explain honour to their fatherless children. Or to the rent collector.'

She twisted her wedding-ring nervously and looked into the old man's eyes to see what effect her words were having. Like her father, he refused to reveal his discomposure even when, as now, she was promising to stop. Oh well, she would continue: 'If you really want to know what I mean by disgrace, it's to hear you talking about killing Huns as though it was a manly duel instead of blowing people and their homes to pieces.' How could this old man ever understand, she thought, he has no wife, no children, no home?

'Just make sure your husband knows what's involved, Corporal.'

'Don't worry, sir, everyone on this station knows what's involved. We are all playing in your cricket match, aren't we? I wonder what your team will score over Krefeld tonight. And I wonder if my husband will be run out.'

The Group Captain said, 'I think that will be all, Corporal. We shall be rectifying your present position *vis-à-vis* your marriage.'

'You can decide between making my husband very unhappy or me very unhappy. But one of us will be quite content.'

'You are dismissed, Corporal.' She stood up slowly and gave a salute of insolent perfection. Level with her eyes a fly buzzed frantically but could not escape from the sticky paper.

One had these hysterical women to deal with and yet there was a limit to the disciplinary action possible. If an airman had even thought those things he would have stripped him of his rank and put him into the glasshouse, but these women couldn't be treated like that. They were just uniformed civilians really and in any case they'd always think of some womanly ailment to excuse themselves. Or else they'd go off and get themselves pregnant. What's the use?

He'd been a damned fool to speak to her in these circumstances, especially at night. A Groupie in Coastal had reprimanded a WAAF sergeant for losing some stores whereupon she'd cried her eyes out and practically yelled rape. It had finished up with the Groupie apologizing. Apologizing!

When she'd gone he rang the buzzer on his desk. 'In the morning I shall want to speak to Section Officer Holroyd.'

'Shall I pencil in the subject?' said his clerk.

'No, I shan't forget what I'm going to talk to her about.'

He could, of course, be elsewhere when Laurie brought his damned cricket team here on Saturday. It was damned disgraceful: that hysterical girl going on like that at the very moment when his lads were risking their brave young bodies.

CHAPTER TWENTY-THREE

'*Levator labii superioris aloequae nasi*': for no reason at all Pilot Officer Fleming, at the controls of The Volkswagen, intoned the words like grace. He had in fact once said it as grace in the Officers' Mess and had got by unchallenged, but he'd taken care not to do it when the Medical Officer was at table.

'What's that, sir?' said Bertie the Flight Engineer, who thought it might be a technical matter he'd neglected.

Fleming closed his eyes and tilted his head. 'It's the longest name of any muscle in the human body.'

'What's the name of the shortest one?' said the mid-upper gunner and was promptly answered insultingly, accusingly and unscientifically by the wireless operator.

'OK, chaps,' said Fleming. 'Let's have a bit of hush.'

Four of the Leiden searchlights had been on for some time but now another six were switched on. 'Look at that,' said Fleming.

'Searchlights,' said the Flight Engineer. In every group of lights there was one that remained vertical. That one was controlled by a Würzburg radar; it was called the master searchlight.

'I'm going to steer a bit to the north, Mac,' Fleming told his navigator. 'No sense in heading straight towards that muck.'

'Don't let's even head for the fringe of it,' said the Flight Engineer.

349

Fleming laughed; perhaps the boy wasn't such an idiot after all. It was a bad system, training an engineer apart from the crew. Fleming had known the rest of them for weeks, but he'd flown only a few hours with this child, his assistant pilot. Fleming wondered if the boy could handle the controls sufficiently well for him to go back to the lavatory. Next trip he would take that tin can he'd been offered and be grateful for it. Was it fear that did it? He'd noticed that the engineer and the bomb aimer had already been back there. It was easy for them, but he was strapped into the pilot's seat and getting out of it was a struggle.

Fear should tighten the rectum and bladder, not loosen them, or so his medical training told him. In the Briefing Room he had watched his fellow men grow pale as fear diverted their newly thinned blood from the skin and the viscera to the brain. That's why so many had been unable to eat their supper. He'd felt his own heart begin to beat faster as his blood – now red-corpuscle dominated, sugar-rich and laden with adrenalin – rose in pressure. He handled the heavy controls with newly found strength and knew that fear had supplied blood to his muscles and his liver had released carbohydrate into his veins. His lungs benefited too, taking more oxygen in breaths that were both deeper and faster.

The first sight of the searchlights had provided him with further physiological evidence of his fear: loss of peristalsis and gastric juice had turned his supper into a hard knot and his saliva had gone, so that his tongue was rough against his mouth. Lastly, his scrotum had constricted tight against his belly. Resulting from these changes Fleming believed he could detect a rise in body temperature as a result of the increased basal metabolic rate. To confirm his theory a trickle of sweat rolled down his spine. His father – a truly dedicated physician – would be interested to hear of these observations.

'Keep this course, Skip,' said the navigator. 'We'll turn

five miles inland instead of over Noordwijk. That should keep us well clear of Leiden.'

'Okey-dokey,' said Fleming and for the first time felt truly like a skipper.

Robin, fellow officer and bomb aimer, had been sitting at the navigator's table filling in his log. He collected up his parachute, target map, log and Thermos flask, disconnected his oxygen supply and came forward. He pushed the Flight Engineer gently to one side and, waving a greeting to Fleming at the controls, bent double to put his foot downwards until it reached the step formed by the glycol tank. Carefully he ducked his head under the traversing ring of the front gun turret with its twin Browning guns. This was his world. It was quieter here. He spread the map out and lay full-length, with his belly on the exit hatch and his head in the clear-view bowl that formed the nose of the aeroplane. Outside the night was growing lighter; the moon was coming out. He looked round with interest but not surprise; he had always known it would be like this.

To the right, one of the searchlight beams was shorter than the others and instead of tapering its beam ended in a blunt hammerhead. 'Look,' said Robin, 'they've got someone in the searchlights.'

'Poor swine,' said Fleming as he watched more searchlights affix their beams to the aeroplane.

The trapped plane was tilting and twisting like a tormented animal, but, although it broke clear of some of the beams, always at least one of them hung on to it. The flak had started now; some of the bursts were so close to it that the smoke obscured their view for a second or two but still the plane flew on.

'We have him on our set now,' said Löwenherz.

'Where do you want him?'

'Just starboard and level.'

'Let me put him a trifle high, Herr Oberleutnant.'

'Very well.'

351

'We're closing too fast again.'

In the searchlights everything was white. Two more had him now and they were fixing him to the sky like gleaming hatpins holding a fluttering white moth in a black velvet box. There was a brief flicker under the plane and it shivered slightly.

'He's hit.'

'It's B Beer, the Navigation Leader.'

'The immortal Lud.'

The navigator couldn't see. 'Are they getting out?'

'No, he's jettisoning his bombs.'

As they watched it the bomber seemed to swell up very gently with a soft 'whoomp' that was audible far across the sky. It became a ball of burning petrol, oil and pyrotechnic compounds. The yellow datum marker, that should have marked the approach to Krefeld, burned brightly as it fell away, leaving thin trails of sparks. The fireball changed from red to light pink as its rising temperature enabled it to devour new substances from hydraulic fluid and human fat to engine components of manganese, vanadium, and copper. Finally even the airframe burned. Ten tons of magnesium alloy flared with a strange greenish-blue light. It lit up the country-side beneath it like a slow flash of lightning and was gone. For a moment a cloud of dust illuminated by the searchlights floated in the sky and then even that disappeared.

'Jee–sus!' exclaimed Pilot Officer Cornelius Fleming in horror.

'No parachutes,' pronounced Robin from the nose. The searchlights began moving again.

'Flak did it,' said the mid-upper gunner, who had the best view of all.

Far away near Utrecht, Fleming saw another master searchlight tilt from the vertical position at which it rested. The top of its beam seemed to explode as it moved across cloud patches. Between the patches it reached seven miles into the sky. Unfalteringly it found a victim.

'The stream isn't routed over Leiden,' said Fleming to his crew. 'All of those aircraft are off course.' It sounded not only prim but callous, but before he could modify the sentiment the mid-upper gunner said, 'I don't give a bugger who they are; it takes the heat off us and for that I am truly grateful. Amen.'

'Kettle drums, kettle drums,' said Löwenherz.

'Lancaster,' said the observer, putting away his field-glasses.

Löwenherz hardly increased speed at all; he inched underneath the huge aeroplane very very slowly. He looked up through the top of his cabin and he could see every detail of it. He let its red-hot exhaust pipes pass back overhead until he was exactly underneath the bomber. The two planes roared through the sky in close formation until, in the classic manoeuvre of the night fighter, Löwenherz pulled the control column back with all his strength. His nose went up closer and closer to the great bomber. The fighter shuddered as it neared stalling-point, hanging on its propellers, thrashing like a drowning man but suspended and stationary for a moment. Over him came the bomber. 'Horrido,' said Löwenherz to tell Bach what he was about to do, and he pressed his gun-buttons and raked its belly from nose to tail. The gunfire lit both aircraft with a gentle greenish light. Löwenherz squinted to preserve his night vision as much as possible. These Richards were nothing but high-powered gun platforms and the demented hammering of the big cannons deafened the flyers even through their closely fitting helmets – just as the smell of cordite got into their nostrils in spite of their oxygen masks. Working exactly by the instruction book Löwenherz kept his guns going even after the nose of the Junkers began to fall back towards earth. Suddenly the gunfire ended. The drums were empty.

Three 20-mm MG FF cannons were fitted in the nose of Löwenherz's Junkers 88R. In sequence of threes there was a thin-cased shell containing 19.5 grammes of Hexogen Al high-explosive filling, an explosive armour-piercing shell with a reinforced point and an incendiary that burned at a temperature between 2,000 and 3,000 degrees centigrade for nearly one second. Each cannon was firing at the rate of 520 rounds per minute and was fed by a drum containing 60 rounds. So in seven seconds all of the cannon drums were empty and 180 shells had been fired at The Volkswagen. The target measured 300 square feet, and 38 struck the aeroplane. Theoretically 20 shells would have constituted an average lethal blow.

'My legs,' screamed Fleming. 'God! Help me, Mother Mother Mother!'

The first shell that penetrated the aircraft came through the forward hatch. Missing the bomb aimer by only an inch, it exploded on contact with the front turrent mounting-ring. It dislocated the turret, severed the throttle and rudder controls, burst the compressed-air tank and broke open the window-spray glycol container. In the airstream the coolant atomized into a cloud of white mist. One twenty-sixth of a second later the second shell came through the bomb compartment and exploded under the floor of the navigator's position. In the mysterious manner of explosions, it sucked the navigator downwards, while blowing the astrodome, and the wireless operator standing under it, out into the night unharmed. Although without his parachute.

Three shells – one HE, one AP and one incendiary – exploded in glancing contact with the starboard fuselage exterior immediately to the rear of the mid-upper turret. Apart from mortally harming the gunner the explosion of the HE shell fractured the metal formers at a place where, after manufacture, the rear part of the fuselage is bolted on. The incendiary shell completed the severance. A structural bisection of The Volkswagen occurred one and a half minutes later and two thousand feet lower. Long before this, another HE shell passed through the elevator hinge-bracket on the tail and blew part of the servo trim tab assembly into the rear turret with such force that it decapitated the rear gunner. Those six hits were the most telling ones, but there were thirty-two others. Some ricocheted off the engines and wings and penetrated the fuselage almost horizontally.

He couldn't hold her, he couldn't. Oh dear God, his arms and legs! Dropping through the night like the paper aeroplane. 'I'm sorry, chaps,' he shouted, for he felt a terrible sense of guilt. Involuntarily his bowels and bladder relaxed and he felt himself befouled. 'I'm sorry.'

It was no use for Fleming to scream apologies; there was no one aboard to hear him. He outlived any of his crew, for from 16,000 feet the wireless operator falling at 120 mph (the terminal velocity for his weight) reached the ground ninety seconds later. He made an indentation twelve inches deep. This represented a deceleration equivalent to 450 times the force of gravity. He split open like a slaughtered animal and died instantly. Fleming, still strapped into the pilot's seat and aghast at his incontinence, hit the earth (along with the front of the fuselage, two Rolls-Royce engines and most of the main spar) some four minutes after that. To him it seemed like four hours.

The air-conditioning in Ermine's plotting-room wasn't intended to cope with so many off-duty personnel standing round as spectators. In addition, the tension seemed to raise a man's body temperature as does a meal. August mopped his brow and heard Löwenherz give the traditional victory cry, 'Sieg Heil!'

'Sieg Heil!' said August. Willi came to attention and gave August a formal salute of congratulation in a situation where most men would have shaken him by the hand. There were shuffles and coughs from the onlookers and murmurs of congratulation. The loudspeaker crackled.

'He's breaking up,' said Löwenherz. 'The main spar has snapped and the fuselage is doubling back like a hairpin.'

Willi wiped the wax marks off the table.

'Order: go to Heinz Gustav One,' said August.

'Please: via Noordwijk?'

'Announcement: yes, Katze One.' To Willi, August said, 'He might get a visual contact if they are still putting flares down but I can't call the flak to a stop just because he is overflying them.'

'He won't hang around,' said Willi, 'he's a bright fellow.'

'We're all smart fellows,' said August. Willi smiled at August, his ruddy battered face twisted like a freshly squeezed orange.

Löwenherz let the Junkers fall from its vertical position and after gaining speed he eased the antlers back and began climbing to fly back through the stream. Mrosek took off his seat straps, lit his torch and crawled down into the nose to change the sixty-round cannon magazines on the Oerlikons. Löwenherz held the same shallow climb, but a patch of turbulent air caused Mrosek to blister his hand upon the breech. Changing the drums was an awkward job even on the ground in daytime, but Mrosek never complained. They flew on past Noordwijk without spotting any bombers, although there was lots of flak including even some brightly coloured 3.7-cm stuff from Valkenburg aerodrome. The Junkers continued right out to the western extreme end of Ermine's range. Those two interceptions had been quick and easy, but next time he might need to traverse the whole sector under August's guidance before he made a contact.

In Joe for King, Roland Pembroke the young Scots navigator had overcompensated for the wind error. His Gee was unusable owing to German jamming. Now his mistake had brought Joe for King to the Dutch coast five miles south of the turning-point. Ahead of him, flying through flak and searchlights, there were others who had made the same error of reckoning.

'We'll go south of it,' said Tommy Carter.

'South of Leiden?' said Roland, who had worked out his plot carefully and rather objected to abandoning the Flight Plan.

'South of that muck,' said Tommy, waving towards the flak and lights ahead of them.

'OK, boss,' said Roland.

The brand-new aeroplane had a strong smell of fresh paint and varnish. The controls were hard and stiff under Tommy Carter's hands and as he turned the wheel it made brittle cracking sounds. On the other hand, everything worked properly. On his previous aeroplane two or three of the instruments were suspect and would stick and lag behind the others. In some ways he liked having this nice new aeroplane. He wondered whether they'd be allowed to keep it.

Tommy knew it was a bad idea as soon as he changed on to the new heading. It wasn't only Leiden that was alive with flak, it was this whole coast; The Hague under the starboard wing was damn nearly as bad as Leiden. There were Grossbatterien of dozens of guns and searchlights working under radar control. The whole land was asparkle with gunfire. Tommy fixed his eyes upon a black region of countryside beyond the gunfire and pushed the throttles forward.

'Close your eyes and swallow,' said Tommy; 'it will soon be gone.' The motors screamed loudly.

There was an explosion rather nearer than the previous ones. It rocked the wings and made an acrid smell.

'There's light stuff too,' said Tapper Collins, the bomb aimer. He was in the nose watching ropes of red and yellow tracer curve towards them and fall away at what he knew to be thousands of feet below but which looked close enough to touch. 'Lots of light stuff now, from directly below us.'

'That must be the aerodrome at Valkenburg,' said Roland Pembroke.

'Jesus,' said Tommy. 'Leiden to the left of us, Hague to the right of us and now we are doing a straight and level over a bloody Hun aerodrome. What do you think you're on, charge of the flipping Light Brigade?'

'Sorry, Tommy,' said Roland politely. He didn't point out that the change of route was Tommy's idea.

Tommy Carter didn't answer, for at that moment all of his attention was taken with a searchlight that, having remained vertical and immobile for some time, had tilted and now moved towards them.

'It's coming at us,' said Collins from his position at the bombsight.

'You berk, Tommy!' said Ben Gallacher, and Tommy Carter was outraged that he should be blamed for something so obviously beyond his control and not of his liking.

'Sideslip down the beam,' said Collins. He was a veteran and Tommy respected his experience. This new aeroplane required extra strength to move its controls. He heaved at them and banked until the light was blinding bright. It had them. The cockpit was so brightly lit that it made his eyes ache and he could only see by almost closing them.

The theory was that by sideslipping down the beam the searchlight would (by continuing to move along) lose you. This searchlight crew seemed to have seen the trick before, although in fact Tommy Carter's sideslip was not nearly violent enough to test the theory.

'Fire into the light,' Tommy called.

'Turn more, I can't reach, I'm full traverse and I can't reach,' replied the gunner.

Suddenly the light went out. Tommy and Ben tugged at the controls and the bomber eased out of its steep bank. The flak and searchlight had gone and the night was agreeably dark and silent. He began to climb again. It was more than a minute before anyone spoke and then everyone spoke, chattering hysterically and trying to make jokes.

'Everyone shut up,' said Tommy Carter in the tone he used when he didn't want an argument – what his crew called his copper's voice.

'Navigator,' said Tommy with unusual formality of address, 'give me a course so that we'll join the stream beyond Leiden.'

'085,' said Roland in his prim public-school accent.

They flew on in a silence broken only by the drone of the motors. 'Sorry, boys,' said Tommy finally, intimidated by the silence of his crew. 'Bloody stupid of me to go south of Leiden.'

'That was a master searchlight,' said Collins the expert. 'The blue ones are always radar-controlled.' Because arc lamps seem more blue when angled towards the viewer, RAF crews believed that the ones pointing at them (the bluish ones) were the most accurate, ie, radar-controlled. Luftwaffe crews over Britain believed the same thing, but there were no blue searchlights.

'Then why did the flaming thing go off?' said Ben Gallacher.

'We were a bit small,' said Tommy. 'They decided to throw us back and wait for a Stirling.'

'I'd like to know why,' said Ben.

'It's a secret new weapon that some of our planes carry,' theorized Collins.

'We'll never know for certain,' said Tommy, 'so belt up and be grateful.'

At that moment on the ground near Valkenburg a young Indian Feldwebel was shouting abuse in Hindustani, which is well suited for that purpose. He watched three phlegmatic signals-regiment mechanics remove the front of his searchlight. In the British Army, before capture, they had been separated by caste. The Wehrmacht, however, had mixed their new volunteers together, with only these brightly coloured turbans – lilac, ochre, green, and even pink and white with blue spots – to show the difference between himself and the lowest of the pariahs. Again he swore an ancient oath at the mechanics. One of the fools proclaimed it to be an ill-omen. It was difficult to contradict him, for today they had been told that the local Dutch civilians had protested at the presence of *kaffers* and they were to be moved to France with all their new flak equipment.

This was one of the first of the new high-performance

200-cm lights to be delivered. A beauty – 2.7 million candle-power. Damn! He kicked the cable angrily. It was just his luck that, after a first-class contact on the Würzburg and a *Tommi* in the beam, just then the carbons should go. Some-times he wished he was back home in Delhi.

In the potato fields a few miles to the west of Ahaus the young Leutnant who had spoken to August and Max during their delay on the road surveyed his Grossbatterie. The two Hitler Jugend guns were manned and ready; those boys were always the keenest. Some of the other guns were not com-pletely jacked up and some were not even uncoupled from their prime movers. It had been a long hard day, with many delays on the road and his Oberst complaining every step of the journey.

The Leutnant sniffed the air and detected a faint smell of soot and smoke. Whenever the wind was from the south it brought the aroma of the Ruhr with it. During last month's raids the air had also carried the smell of fouled earth, brick dust, cordite and burning buildings.

The sound of aircraft engines came suddenly. He phoned to his Control Room and when the phone was in his hands he looked up and saw the glint of moonlight upon a wing. He saw it for only a moment and it was too high to be more than a speck of light but it was leaving a condensation trail that glowed in the moonlight. Even had his 8.8-cm guns been ready to fire they couldn't reach that height.

The information was passed to Deelen but already it was superfluous. Other reports showed that the aircraft were two Mosquitoes at 32,000 feet.

'They are turning at Ahaus,' said the Plot Officer.

The Operations Officer moved his hand to make an arc southwards from Ahaus, pivoting upon the Oboe transmitter at Dover. His thumb swivelled across the open country until it encountered the shaded pattern of a large town in the Ruhr. He looked then at the bomber stream's reported position. The heading of the bombers would bring them over the same place.

'Krefeld,' he said. 'I'll bet a week's pay on it.'

The other officer nodded. He didn't take up the wager.

The plan was now clear. On their present heading the bomber stream would pass over Krefeld at half past midnight. Moving a hundred miles an hour faster and turning to approach from the north, the Mosquitoes – with their secret Oboe device – would pass over Krefeld three minutes earlier. That would be exactly enough time for the coloured indicator bombs to mark the target for the heavy bombers.

The routes were converging like the rays of light through a burning-glass and tonight attention was focusing on one town. The leaflet raids over Northern France, the lone Mosquito that was causing the alarms to sound all the way to Berlin, and the dog-leg course that had taken the stream to Noordwijk before turning, were all clearly seen for the ruses they were; the target for tonight was Krefeld. Deelen Control and Duisberg FLUKO began to arrange the defences of the Reich accordingly.

In peacetime a complicated electronic device like Oboe would have spent six months more on the test bench and four or five in prototype, and anything up to a year would have passed before they were sold, installed and in use. But this was war and Oboe was in production. It needed nursing all the way to the target and even then it was no surprise to Flying Officer MacIntosh when the set went dead twenty-five miles short of Krefeld.

'Not a sausage. What a nuisance, the signals were clear as a bell – then it went dead.'

'We'll turn back, then.'

'Might as well. We're on the curve but we'll never find the target with a dud set.'

'Bloody thing. I cancelled a date tonight.'

'You shouldn't have joined.'

The Mosquito turned abruptly until it faced west to England. There was no sense in going a yard nearer to the Ruhr than was absolutely essential.

'Let's get out of here, Mac.'

There were two radio transmitting stations in England from which the signals went to activate Oboe. The stations could handle only two Mosquitoes every ten minutes. The two planes that should mark the target for the very first bombers to arrive were now reduced to one plane. That one was piloted by Pilot Officer Alan Hill; his observer was Peter Hutchinson.

They had done everything according to the book. They had flown at 32,000 feet, for only at this height were the signals able to reach over the radar horizon. At a point fifty miles north of Krefeld they had turned southwards. Keeping the steady beat of the signals in his ears the pilot had banked his wing to fly a gentle curve that would – at the moment the signal from the second transmitter reached him – bring him at the right distance from Krefeld to allow for the forward movement through the air of the 250-lb target-indicator bombs.

They did not know that the accompanying Mosquito had turned away with its Oboe device out of action. Nor did they know that they were accompanied by a German aeroplane up in this region of the sky that was almost the stratosphere. It was a specially equipped Ju88S in which the GM1 system injected nitrous oxide into the superchargers and thus provided oxygen that boosted its performance by nearly twenty per cent. Its endurance was measured in minutes and a few nights previously it had used up its Ha-ha device just as it caught sight of the Mosquito. Tonight there had been no miscalculation. Tonight the moonlight had made the upper reaches of the sky into a floodlit arena.

'Bombs armed,' reported the observer. At the speed they were going, Krefeld was only two minutes away. There was suddenly a thumping sound and the controls were wrenched from the pilot's grasp. The panel was bent and torn and the glass from its instruments flew in all directions. Two Perspex panels had suddenly gone white and the sky was no longer to be seen through them. Even when the bangs stopped, the engines were screaming an octave above their normal tone. The Mosquito performed a flick roll, steadied itself for a moment and then put its nose up and stalled. As he dived the aircraft to regain control they saw the Ju88 far away on the port beam. Its wings shone in the moonlight as it turned to find them for a second attack.

'Fire!' said Peter Hutchinson.

'What with?' said Alan Hill angrily, until he noticed that the port engine was coughing blue flame and spitting orange sparks and his few remaining instrument needles were collapsing. He wrenched at the tiny jettison box by his side and tore a nail as he broke the safety wires. There was a lurch as two 250-lb target-indicator bombs – each almost as big as a man – fell out of the bomb-bay, and then he struggled with the box for what seemed like hours until the other two went. Relieved of the weight of its bomb-load the aeroplane responded more readily to its controls. He kept the nose down and headed desperately for the cloud bank but it was still two thousand feet below him as the Ju88 came in again. More pieces of wing disappeared as the cannon shells punched holes through the wood.

'To hear you two young fellows talk you'd think the Germans had no fighter planes.'

'They don't as far as we're concerned, Dad. We're too high for them.'

'Well, I didn't say this in front of your mother, Alan, but mark my words, your Jerry is a damn good engineer and if he wants to get up to you one of these nights he'll do it.'

'Drink up, Dad, we've two more days of leave yet.'

'And change the subject, I know. Your job's too hush–hush to talk to your father about.'

'Peter, Peter, jump! She's coming to pieces.' Peter didn't

move. That last attack must have done it. Please God, don't let that Junkers come round again!

In the Junkers the fuel warning lights were on. He'd had his forty-five minutes' fun and now the nitrous oxide was used. He turned away from the Mosquito. It was done for, he could see that. He wondered if Luftwaffe High Command would let him claim it; they were so keen to keep the Ha-ha secret.

Alan Hill held the stick with one hand and shook Peter frantically with the other. There was no sign of life. He grabbed at the flying helmet and turned the head to look into his friend's glassy eyes. As he shook him the oxygen mask fell aside and he had difficulty in refixing it. Peter's face was covered with fresh blood.

Down where the bomber stream was flying it was cold – colder than the coldest of domestic freezers – but up here it was even colder. Sixty degrees below zero and the air was rarefied and its pressure fatally low for a human lung. Alan undid his safety belt and Peter's too before he put the stick over. When the Mosquito was upside down he fell out of his seat. He tried to pull his observer with him but Peter's leg was caught under the bent instrument panel. He tugged at Peter's arm but that too became bloody even as he watched.

Alan took one last gulp of oxygen and then holding his breath he let himself fall. He dropped a long, long way before pulling the rip-cord but even so he had slight frostbite and lost the joint of an index finger that stuck to the metal handle. Perfectly, the canopy bloomed above him. He landed in a ploughed field two miles from the Dutch border. His only other injury was a bad cut on his right hand that must have happened during the first attack. He realized then that the blood on Peter's face and arm was from this cut. He asked himself if he could have saved Peter's life. Alan was interned together with other bomber crews and was thus not interrogated in the way he would have been had they guessed him to be an Oboe pilot. He spent the rest of the war in a prison camp and died aged forty-nine in a motor-car accident in Liverpool, and yet there was not a day when he did not ask himself that same question.

A layer of cold air lay close upon the great district of the Ruhr, untroubled by any wind. This cold still air trapped smoke from the furnaces and factories and held it like a grey woollen blanket. Water droplets had built up against this layer and formed a roof as dense and flat and smooth as a sheet of grey aspic: what today we call smog. One target indicator jettisoned by the Oboe Mosquito went into this layer near the Rhine at Duisburg. The second went into the Rhine. One and a half minutes and nine miles later the second two landed on the south-east edge of Altgarten.

Detonated by barometric pressure at one thousand feet, each marker bomb spewed benzol, rubber and phosphorus for a hundred yards in all directions, so that there were two pools of red-coloured fire easily seen by the bomber stream four miles above the earth. It was Altgarten's fate to be on the track of the bombers as they flew from the coast towards Krefeld. Had the bombers passed a few more miles to one side or the other then the stream might not have seen the burning TIs waiting to be bombed. It was an extra misfortune for the town that the markers dropped on its far side, for the creepback would start to bring the bombing right across the town towards the approaching stream. Each crew would bomb as early as they could do so without shame. Then they would turn away before the concentration of guns and searchlights that guarded the Ruhr on Altgarten's far side. Perhaps some of the more experienced crews would not have been deceived by the markers into bombing the little town, except that to the H2S radar the acres of glasshouses that were Altgarten's special pride appeared on the radar screen like enormous factories.

The first Finder circled twice before putting flares down to the south-east of the markers, trying to get a visual confirmation. Then a Supporter – on his first trip – put a string of high explosive between the flares and the red TIs and a second Supporter did the same. The last of these bombs hit the Venlo road and set fire to a gas main.

Tommy Carter in Joe for King the Second was a Backer-up. He arrived five minutes early and put his four green markers on to the reds. One thousand feet above Altgarten sixty pyrotechnic candles were ejected from each marker. Each was suspended under a tiny parachute. Falling in close proximity and according to wind and weight they assumed the shape of a bunch of fiery grapes or, if bottom-heavy, a Christmas tree.

Within ten minutes dozens of Supporters and Finders had dumped their flares and HE upon Altgarten and inevitably the release points were creeping back north-west across the town.

Meanwhile, at zero plus three minutes, an Oboe Mosquito arrived exactly on time over Krefeld and marked the real target with four perfectly placed reds. They burned unseen by the bombing force. By now attention had been centred upon Altgarten and the plan had begun to go terribly wrong.

CHAPTER TWENTY-FOUR

Afterwards there were those who said that the Burgomaster was pleased when the first flares dropped near Altgarten. Karl Keller, one of the waiters from the Stube, said that he'd left there with a smile on his face after the warning had been delivered to him. But, as one of the civil-defence messengers said, it was his birthday and he had just finished a banquet in his honour, why shouldn't he be smiling?

An official car was waiting outside Frenzel's and the Burgomaster was taken at high speed through the empty streets to the Rathaus where a policeman saluted him smartly as he descended the steps to the heavily sandbagged Control Room. Inside, three civil-defence girls were at their desks and two Hitler Jugend cyclists were uniformed and at attention in the anteroom.

'Red Christmas-tree flares one mile to the south-east: 01.29.' The girl smiled. 'That's probably somewhere in Frau Kersten's fields.'

'Mark it in on the map, Fräulein.'

The telephonist said, 'FLUKO reports red markers near Duisburg 01.30. The same aircraft, probably.'

'Mark that in too,' said the Burgomaster calmly. 'We must know which way the aircraft are approaching.'

The Burgomaster hung up his hat and sat behind his desk. The yellow desk lamp made a rim around his profile. He passed his long white fingers over the three phones, blotter, pad and sharpened pencils as if to reassure himself that all was arranged to his orders. He had never been under air attack before. He was determined to work by the rules. For many months he had studied the instruction books and reports; tonight he would use his store of knowledge. Suddenly he stood up. It was the first Supporter aircraft putting down his stick of HE. Six 500-lb medium-capacity bombs fell in a line about seventy yards apart. Had there been an eighth bomb it would have fallen upon the Rathaus.

'What are they bombing out there?' asked the Burgomaster, looking at the wall of his office as though some mystic force might allow him to see through it and thus solve the problem.

'Frau Kersten's potatoes,' said the telephonist. 'Perhaps they are trying to starve us out.'

The Burgomaster froze her smile with a look. The First World War had left him with the belief that jokes under fire were only one step away from hysteria.

There was a rattle at the door-handle and another Hitler Jugend boy appeared. He was excited and flushed with the exertion of pedalling. 'The road is on fire, Herr Bürgermeister.'

'What do you mean, the road?'

'A thin white flame as tall as a house,' said the boy.

'Fräulein Eva, tell the Gasmeister. *Junge*, give the exact position of the fire. Fräulein Bertha, prop something under that door to hold it open so that there is free access to the Control Room. Tomorrow I want that door-handle mended properly. It's nearly a week since I asked for it to be done.'

'Yes, Herr Bürgermeister,' said the girl.

Tommy Carter's Joe for King came steadily across Altgarten and released a bomb-load which included the green TIs.

'And connect me to the waterworks master too.'

The telephonist pushed the key continuously but the phone was unanswered.

* * *

The waterworks master had hurried away from the Burgo-master's birthday party keen to prove that he knew his duty as well as the next man, but he'd forgotten the keys of his office. He walked across to the filter beds and the great water tank. There was nothing for him to do. He found the half-finished cigar in his top pocket and relit it and began a gentle stroll. There were red flashes in the sky. It seemed very close, but he knew such appearances could be deceptive. The sound of aeroplanes grew louder. He often watched them pass over on their way to the Ruhr. Sometimes he had seen them hit and burning in the sky like comets.

The waterworks master was Altgarten's first victim. When coloured marker bombs came down he began to run but he was swamped by cascading pools of green fire. And then came high explosive and his body was thrown into the air and buried in the churned soil amongst potato roots and splinters of tree.

The raid was no novelty for the Technische-Nothilfe Bataillon. They came out of their huts completely equipped before the first stick of flares had guttered and died. Their heavy trucks, with the wide white identifying band painted round them and the white bicycles strapped to the tailboards, were drawn up in convoy order and the men swung aboard in the darkness as they had done a thousand times before. This was just another air raid for the TENOs, with the subtle distinction that this time they did not have to go to it; it had come to them.

First the car decelerates and moves slowly enough for the driver to see the house numbers. Finally it stops. The men's voices are low in tone and volume and their rhythms imply orders and assent. Doors slam gently and metal-studded boots click loudly in the night air. The door-knocker rat-a-tats.

All over Europe in 1943, ears had become sensitive to such a sequence of sounds. At eleven forty-five on the night of June 31st old Herr Voss the tailor cocked his head and listened fearfully.

Herr Voss was a short plump man of fifty-nine. The crown of his head was bald, but a natural wave gave him curls across the ears and over his collar. He was a talented amateur baritone and as recently as 1940 he had performed at a local concert. His wife had once been a noted Lieder singer. They liked music of all kinds and had a large collection of records ranging from American jazz to Beethoven quartets and of course many choral works. Each evening he dressed in his black velvet jacket and tasselled smoking-hat. His daily housekeeper left them a simple cold meal and after finishing it he smoked his pipe and he and his wife listened to music, often until one or two o'clock in the morning. At present his wife was visiting their only daughter and son-in-law in Freiburg. Although alone in the house he kept to the usual ritual.

Voss turned down the music on the radio. For a moment he stood listening, then he shuffled down the hall in his carpet slippers to open the front door. Even before he got there the knocker sounded again. 'All right, all right,' called the old man irritably. 'Everyone is in such a hurry.' It was dark outside and he could just make out the silhouette of a steel helmet. 'It's the front-room curtain again, is it?' said old Voss, his voice changing into a soft apology. 'It's the cat that moves it.'

'Voss?' said the man. And now old Voss looked at him a second time. By the shaded light he could see that it was a Wehrmacht steel helmet the man was wearing, not a Luftschütz pattern.

'Voss?' repeated the soldier. His voice was strange.

'Yes,' said Herr Voss. He tried to say it doubtfully, so as to retain the option of denying it.

'This is the house, sir,' called the soldier in the thick throaty Russian of the Caucasian mountains. Another man came out of the darkness.

370

'Get the bundle,' he said in halting Russian. He was taller and slimmer than the HIWI, with a leather overcoat that was badly damaged on the elbows and lapels. 'I'm the one who telephoned,' said the tall one. His voice had the sing-song lilt of the Rhineland.

'Come in,' said Voss.

They both came into his sitting-room. The Hilfsfreiwilliger – auxiliary volunteer – was loaded under three long sacking bundles. He had them upon his shoulder and they sagged with their own weight.

'On the floor,' said the tall one. He was a pale-faced young man with tired eyes and a hooked nose. Like an owl, thought Voss. The man opened his coat to search for cigarettes and revealed the black SS rank patches on his collar. The foreign volunteer was a Feldwebel; his uniform was at least a size too small for him. On his sleeve there was a yellow dragon on a bright blue shield. 'Galician – 14th SS, eh?' said Voss.

'How do you know?' asked Fischer, taking off his coat.

'I tailor uniforms. I probably know more about Army insignia than you do. And you're Leibstandarte, eh?' The old man smiled, noticing the LAH epaulettes and new cuffband on Fischer's arm. He thought them the trappings of a poseur. Now he looked more closely at Fischer's Knight's Cross.

'We're posted to Hitler Jugend Division,' said Fischer angrily. He threw his leather coat over a chair. He hadn't wanted the old man to know which unit they belonged to, but lying was complicated. Still, there wasn't much danger that this little crook would dare complain about an SS officer.

The HIWI dumped the bundles on the floor, unsheathed a bayonet and neatly sliced one open. He unrolled it with the toe of his boot.

'From the National Museum in Kharkov,' said Fischer.

'Caucasian?'

371

'Kuba,' nodded the officer. 'Nearly three hundred years old. It could tell a few stories.'

The HIWI flipped back the corner like a professional carpet dealer. 'Look at it,' said Fischer. 'Notice the warp threads on two different levels. Look at the border.'

'Kufic,' said Voss.

'Exactly,' said Fischer. 'You know a thing or two about carpets.'

'I've bought them before.'

'So I heard,' said Fischer drily. 'You'll be a fool not to buy this one. It's a museum-piece.'

'Everyone says they've got a museum-piece,' said Voss, rubbing a corner of the carpet.

'Yes,' said Fischer, 'but not everyone takes it out of a Russkie museum at the point of a gun.' The HIWI watched them carefully as they spoke, trying to understand Voss' fast guttural *Platt-deutsch*, as much like Dutch as German. Suddenly comprehending, the HIWI laughed and revealed a set of bad teeth.

Fischer watched Voss' face as he examined the stitches. 'See how thick the base is.'

'How much?'

'Ten thousand.'

'Reichsmark?'

'No, Pfennig,' said Fischer sarcastically.

Voss ran his fingers across the flowers and birds. Soft reds and greens. The colours shone in the electric light. 'It's worth it,' admitted Voss.

'Worth twice as much,' said Fischer. He went to a silver box on the coffee table. 'I'll take a cigarette,' he announced.

'Please do,' said Voss. He looked at the other bundles. 'What are the others?'

'Modern Shirvans. They won't interest you, you know too much about carpets.'

The old man smiled at the compliment but the smile was frozen on his face as the first stick of bombs came down.

Immediately after that they heard the second bomb-load go. The farthest one was a quarter of a mile behind Frau Kersten's but the last one was upon the slum housing behind the gas-works. Voss and the two soldiers hurried to the door. Outside the night was as bright as day. Tommy Carter's green marker flares were hanging in the sky, each cluster spread out towards its base like a Christmas tree. There were other Christmas trees, one over the brewery and another near the church. To the south-east the sky was still glowing red from the Mosquito's TIs.

'Markers,' said Fischer. 'Those green flares form the corners of a square into which the other planes will drop their bombs.'

It was a common mistake, made because people on the ground didn't realize the big margins of error within which the bombers operated. Actually Tapper Collins was trying to put all of the green Christmas trees on to the same aiming-point.

Fischer had no sooner spoken than a salvo struck the northern side of the town. Amongst the 500-lb bombs there was a 4,000-lb cookie that made the ground rock. The echoes rolled through the narrow streets of the old town and Voss and the two soldiers found themselves full-length on the road without remembering how they got there. Another Lancaster started its bomb-run. Voss saw the two soldiers holding their hands over their ears to protect their eardrums. He did the same. They waited until the next ear-splitting explosions had rocked the earth.

'Have you got a cellar?' called Fischer.

'Yes,' said Voss.

'Let's get into it.'

Voss eyed their Kübelwagen parked at the kerb. He had half hoped that they would decide to hasten away but on the other hand he coveted the carpet. He had never seen one quite so fine. Except in museums.

The window of the next-door house rattled open. 'Herr Voss, is that you?'

'Yes, it is,' said Voss.

'Are they bombing us?' asked Anna-Luisa. The officer laughed.

'They are, my dear,' said the old man. 'You'd better bring the child into my cellar.'

'Thank you, Herr Voss.'

'And hurry,' called Fischer. They scrambled to their feet and hurried indoors. The Lancaster of Sandy Sanderson, Engineer Leader and Squadron dandy, released ten canisters of incendiary bombs exactly at the aiming-point. From each canister tumbled ninety magnesium sticks. For a moment nine hundred incendiary bombs hung together in the gaping bomb-doors like a cluster of iron filings dangling from a magnet. Then the air-stream punched into them and they sprinkled out over the town all the way from Mauerstrasse to Party HQ near the church.

Each 4-lb incendiary struck the ground with a sound like the crack of a whip and a white flash. Then they burned and flared fiercely. The three men watched from the door. One of the incendiaries hit the ground only a yard ahead of the Kübelwagen and the HIWI Feldwebel ran back to kick the bomb along the gutter and then kicked after it the red and white fragments of burning magnesium that it had scattered.

'Where's the cellar, Herr Voss?' said the officer and old Voss produced a heavy ring of keys and unlocked the cellar door, his keys jangling in his nervous fingers. The three men ushered the girl and the little boy down the stone steps. Once they were there the soldiers could see why the old man had been reluctant to allow them to see his air-raid shelter. It was a treasure house. There was a glass-fronted case full of silver and a box full of glassware, all wrapped carefully in newspaper. Squeezed among the antiques and boxes of goodness-knows-what there were four comfortable old chairs, and even a telephone extension. Calling it his air-raid shelter was a convenient rationalization for arranging a room in which the old man could survey his loot in privacy and comfort. Voss lit the oil lamp but the electric lights were bright enough to make it unnecessary.

Anna-Luisa laid the child Hansl upon an armchair. He was sleepy and she arranged a blanket round his head to muffle the noise.

It was the 2,000-lb high-explosive bomb from Tommy Carter's plane that hit the corner of Mönchenstrasse and Postgasse only a block away from Voss' house. In the cellar it shook the dust from the shelves. Old Voss coughed and the HIWI sneezed and then laughed uproariously. Outside, the dark street was clouded in brick-dust. The bomb had sliced thirty yards from the apartment block like a segment of cake, leaving brightly coloured layers of wallpapered rooms exposed. Sloping up to the second floor there was a mound of rubble with bricks, broken furniture, an upturned bath and slabs of unbroken wall poking out of it. There were freak escapes: a mirror on the wall, pictures unscathed and a parlourmaid found stark naked but quite unharmed in the garden at the rear. She had been asleep on the top floor.

Old Storp, the Blockwart, an overcoat over his pyjamas, came wide-eyed through the dust and darkness to meet the TENO engineers. He had a scrap of paper in his hands and he shouted loudly to make himself heard above the explosions.

'Eighteen people altogether. All of them sheltering in the cellar.'

The TENO man eyed the tall mound of bricks and rubbish. 'We'll never get them out,' he said briefly. With a terrible finality he chalked 18 on a piece of masonry and turned away.

'You must,' shouted the Blockwart. 'My wife's in there.'

'It's no use,' shouted the TENO man. A bomb exploded nearby and he crouched down. 'It's the water pipe that we must fix.'

The Blockwart started to lift one of the heavy wooden beams aside but finding it unmovable he grabbed at loose bricks. 'I'm coming, Bertha,' he shouted. 'Don't be frightened, my love.' He seemed no longer to hear the bombs dropping. He worked feverishly to clear a way to the cellar, but inside it they were all dead.

It was the sound of that same high-explosive bomb that brought Herr Voss back up from his cellar. Its blast distorted the nine-inch spun-iron water pipe that ran past his house and its lead-wool caulking had cracked badly enough for a steady flow of water to run into the Voss cellar. At first the flow was no faster than a kitchen tap but the water pressure opened the gap and did further damage to the caulking so that soon the water had formed a large pool and ran in streams under the easy chairs and wetted the bottoms of the wooden boxes. There was no drain in the cellar and Voss knew that unless the engineers got to the pipe soon it would be completely flooded. He hurried up the steps, anxious about the damage the water might do to his paintings and carpets.

The two soldiers remained in the cellar with Anna-Luisa for ten more minutes. Above them the bombs were shaking the house to its foundations. Hansl awoke and began to cry gently.

'We'll go soon,' said the officer. He got to his feet and began to unwrap some silver and glass that was packed into one of the boxes. He selected three Georgian silver teapots and a cream jug and placed them carefully on the armchair. Although not a word passed between them, the Feldwebel found a sack and put the silver into it. The officer selected an ancient flintlock pistol from the wall and found a red silk Kashan rug wrapped in newspaper on the shelf. He rolled it into the bundle of carpets they had brought with them.

'What are you doing?' asked Anna-Luisa. She smiled as she said it, hoping that they were only joking.

'We are old friends of Herr Voss,' said the officer. 'These are things we have bought from him.'

'I don't believe you,' said Anna-Luisa. She walked across

the cellar to the steps and called to Herr Voss, but no answer came.

'He's probably dead,' said the officer.

'Let's wait for him,' suggested Anna-Luisa, standing in his path and holding up her arm to prevent him passing. Fischer drew back his fist and punched her in the face as hard as he could.

She knew he had broken her front teeth even before she felt the pain of the blow. The force of it threw her back against the wooden boxes. She twisted her ankle and an antique decanter fell and smashed on the stone floor. She moaned in pain and holding her face in her hands she rocked to and fro trying to comfort herself. When Hansl began to cry loudly she gradually opened her eyes. The men had gone and so had the sackful of silver and the carpet. She pulled Hansl close to her. 'It's all right, baby, everything will be all right.' Her mouth was swollen and her voice was strange because of her broken teeth, but she went on saying it in order to comfort herself. The water was still gurgling into the cellar, but she no longer cared. No one did.

Upstairs the two soldiers moved briskly through the house. There was a moment's pause in the gunfire and bombs after the first bombers passed over. It was dark and there was a foul smell of brick-dust and disturbed sewage. They put the bundles into the back of the Kübelwagen and drove away. In the gutter only a few yards from the house was the body of Herr Voss. The soldiers didn't recognize him. There were other bodies in the street too; they hardly glanced at them. They had seen many dead bodies.

CHAPTER TWENTY-FIVE

Descended from Norsemen, the Munros of the Isle of Nichuish were a fierce God-fearing tribe of fighting men. It was said that they'd never sat down to a meal without thanking the Lord and opening the gates to the hungry, but they'd done so with their swords close to hand. Old Andrew's purse and sword never left his side from the day he first strapped them on until he died on the far-off battlefield of Lützen commanding one of Gustavus Adolphus' Scottish brigades. There, a silver damascened wheel-lock pistol pushed under his breastplate opened purse and belly and spread guts and gold across the battlefield. His brother Ian fled from Cromwell after Dunbar wearing the clothes of a crofter. Another Munro Americans buried – in four separate parts – under the cold soil of Lookout Mountain before the battle of Chattanooga had properly begun.

Andrew, a captain in the Scots Fusiliers, was in 1704 at Blenheim the first Munro to fight on the same side as the English. Since then there had always been one of the men of Nichuish in the British Army. The history of the Munros reads like battle honours on a dusty standard: Fontenoy, Waterloo, Inkerman, Aboukir, Koodoosberg.

In 1918 John's uncle had fought the Turks from Basra to Kirkuk and his father had spent four long years in France and collected a DSO at Ypres. They had both come back to the estate at the war's end. Uncle Ian had attended to the paperwork right up until the week he had died of some unidentified tropical disease. His father on the other hand had delighted in working on the land and with the livestock. So many times, arriving on vacation with his friends from school, they had mistaken his father for a cowherd. Now they were both gone, and with John and his young brother Ian both in the RAF the whole place was being run by Sarah. This is where the family's military tradition might end, thought John Munro.

He would advise his son against going into military service of any kind. Last week two airmen had come before him for creating a disturbance in the Airmen's Mess. One was reported to have said, 'After this lot you wouldn't get me to join a Christmas Club.' It was alleged that the other replied, 'You won't get me to bloody well join hands even.' Munro had given them three days' jankers for 'conduct to the prejudice of good order' but the sentiments were his exactly. Perhaps some day after the war he would see them on the street and tell them how much he had agreed. Although deep in his heart Munro felt sure that there would be no 'after the war' for him. He'd never before had such a premonition of death. He told himself it was merely because this was his last trip, but he could not convince himself of that. Last night he had written cheques for his tailor, his dentist and the Mess, written a letter to his wife and the child and propped it on his pillow, and revised his will. Everything was done except this; he corrected the course with a touch of rudder.

Munro looked calmly down upon the dark landscape. Although for the newer crews the searchlights and explosions were a confusing maze of danger, for the old hands the flak concentrations provided a grim series of familiar navigational pinpoints.

'Some silly blighter's drifted off over Nijmegen,' said Munro, watching the twinkling flak to port.

'Arnhem's pretty active too, sir,' said the bomb aimer. 'But not so many searchlights as there used to be.'

'The Jerries are pulling back into the Ruhr. I suspect they're letting their night fighters have a go over the target nowadays and using the lights to help them spot the stream.'

'It makes the navigator's job easier,' said the engineer. Jock Hamilton the navigator was always fair game but this time he pretended that he had not heard them.

'There's a buzz going round that they are going to do away with them,' said the bomb aimer. 'We'll be taking extra incendiaries instead.'

'You'll no' bluidy get back then,' Jock warned them.

The others grinned, but for Munro the threat reawakened his fears. He watched and noted the changing patterns of the air defences. It was amazing how far one could see from this height. On other, clearer nights he'd been this close to the Ruhr and still been able to see the English coastline. Tonight, thank God, he couldn't, but the cloud was breaking up as they got farther inland. He didn't like that. There was no sign of searchlights or gunfire ahead of him where the target should lie. He called the navigator. 'Are you getting a picture on the H2S, Jock?'

'It's no' so bad.'

'Can you see the River Maas?'

'Aye, sir. Just about. I make us level with Kleve.' The landscape was dark and featureless except that Munro could see the river far below them. The Maas curved gently away.

'Big bugger that one to port, sir.'

'Yes, that's what I call a searchlight. Makes the others look like a Toc H lamp.'

It wasn't far now.

Keeping a proper all-round watch in a top turret was a tiring procedure. It meant rotating the head in a manner for which human anatomy was not designed.

Lofty, Munro's gunner, did his series of horizon searches and ended each with two visual sweeps overhead. That's when he saw the shape. One piece of darkness with a horrifying slowness detached itself from the night sky and reached out to grab them in its black grasp. A man can't scream into an oxygen mask but, not knowing this, the gunner did scream. He almost choked, gasping for air with a force that gave him chest pains. He switched his microphone on to tell Munro what had happened but had difficulty in speaking. In a shaky voice he reported, 'A Lancaster just about parted my hair, sir.'

'Direction?' asked Munro.

'Same bearing as us, sir, but only a few feet overhead. How we missed him I don't know.'

'So long as the stream are keeping on course,' said Munro. Jock grinned to himself. It was typical of Munro that so close to a mid-air collision he should be concerned whether the other plane was on the correct course. 'Sure it was a fourmotor job, Lofty?'

'Yes, sir.'

'Good, but keep your eyes peeled.'

No one aboard Lancaster Q for Queen had seen Munro's Lanc come so close to them. The only crew member who might have seen it – Jammy Giles the bomb aimer – wasn't full-length in the nose looking down; he was sitting in the pilot's seat grappling with the controls. He'd never taken over the controls on an operational flight before. He was reluctant to do it this time until the pilot – a Canadian flying officer named Peterson, known to his friends as Roddy – made it an order. In spite of Jammy's superior rank the pilot, a taxi-driver from Montreal, was the captain. Jammy said, 'OK, you drunken Canadian bum, but I should be couchant by now.'

'Bum' and 'couchant' were two of Jammy's very favourite words, and just as the former was applied to his crew and his sex-life so was the latter applied to his job and his sex-life. It wasn't as easy to change pilots as they both thought. A stray boot hit the control column and for a time there were no feet on the rudder bar, both of which put the bomber into some unusual flying attitudes.

At first it had been a bit of a joke. Jammy had been sympathetic about Roddy's diarrhoea because it was undoubtedly the result of a drinking party that Jammy had insisted he joined. Closer to the target, however, Jammy was getting more and more anxious. 'Roddy, do you know what's got an IQ of one hundred?'

'No, what?'

'Ten Canadians. All right. Now get your flaming arse off that thunderbox, Roddy, and come back here and start driving.'

'I'm ill.'

'Canadian twit.'

'Limey berk.'

'I'm serious.'

'I'm serious too.'

'I'm the Bombing Leader, Roddy.'

'And I'm goddamn ill, feller.'

'All right. How long are you going to be on your bum?'

'You take her over target, Jammy.'

'And who will be couchant, you transatlantic twit?'

'Let Al bomb, he was always better than you.' The incapacitated pilot scored a shrewd blow with that suggestion, for Alun Davies the navigator had remustered from observer and knew almost as much as Jammy about bombsights, drift, markers and selector switches.

It was Jammy's strict instruction that the target should be identified both on radar and visually before bombing. 'Can someone hold Queenie straight and level while I do the couchant bit?' asked Jammy desperately.

Whoever was at the controls would suffer Jammy's wrath as they tried to comply with his steering directions over target. They all knew this and no one volunteered.

Jammy sighed, 'All right. Alun, forget the H2S, have a go at the bombsight, will you?'

'Certainly, sir,' said Alun, ex-public-school, ex-cinema-manager from Ffestiniog. He gathered together the maps under his lamp and took a closer look at them.

When Alun had last bombed, the target maps had been gaily coloured, fully detailed ones of the sort that a hiker would take on a cross-country stroll. Now the target maps were sombre things: inflammable forest and built-up areas defined as grey blocks and shaded angular shapes. The only white marks were the thin rivers and blobs of lake. The roads were purple veins so that the whole thing was like a badly bruised torso. On the old ones the rivers were bright blue and the trees green and hospitals were marked with a neat red cross. But now the urban conglomerations were just shapes like the ill-defined blurs that passed across the H2S radar tube. That, of course, was the whole idea. The old maps were as ancient as the idea of looking over the side of the cockpit to see the enemy you bombed. The new grey faceless maps were just one aspect of a new kind of war.

Alun Davies switched off the H2S radar set. That was Jammy's toy; Alun had never liked it. He gathered his maps and notes together and moved forward. It was dark. He saw Jammy's helmeted head rigid and silhouetted against the Perspex and groped for handholds as the plane lurched to Jammy's inexpert touch. As he passed the pilot's seat Jammy spared a hand long enough to pat his arm in encouragement. 'Don't forget the fuse switch, Al, and look for the red Oboe TIs first, then the greens. All right?'

'Very well, sir.'

'How are you back there, Roddy?'

'Goddamn miserable, Jammy.' It had taken the pilot several agonizing minutes to undo his flying clothes in order to use the Elsan chemical closet. Whoever decided that the flying meal should include beans had never suffered from wind at high altitude. The distension of the stomach and bowel that at ground level is merely painful becomes agony at 16,000 feet. Roddy Peterson had the added pain of an inflamed intestine. Originally he'd wanted to vomit and then a wave of shivering had hit him, followed by an urgent looseness of the bowels. Here at the back he'd plugged in his intercom and oxygen, but at 16,000 feet, with his trousers round his ankles, he was very cold indeed. In spite of being chilled to the bone he was sweating and could feel the perspiration trickling down his neck and back. He still felt sick and inside him there was an empty feeling of misery. Back here in the tail every trace of Jammy's inexpert piloting was magnified into rolling motion and sickening drops through space.

He'd never realized before how dark and lonely it was for the rest of the crew. Looking forward from the Elsan all he could see was the feet of the mid-upper gunner as the turret traversed with sudden purrs. When they flew near cloud there was enough reflection for him to see the gunner's arms too. Beyond that the tunnel of aluminium formers and ammunition runways seemed to extend for miles. Sometimes, like day at the end of a railway tunnel, he saw a pinpoint of yellow from the navigator's desk lamp. It was noisy here too. The roar of the engines was much louder from behind and the wind buffeting the tail bumped and groaned and curious little clinks came from the girders around him. Now and again there was the explosion of a flak shell nearby and once there was the pitter-patter of spent shrapnel knocking upon the metal skin. All the time he felt a desperate frustration at not knowing what was going on.

'You left your parachute on the seat here, Roddy,' said Jammy Giles over the intercom. 'One of the boys will bring my harness down to you. The chute is in the rear stowage. All right?' Roddy nodded.

'Hear me, Roddy?' Roddy was racked by another awful pain and a bowel movement that drained the life out of him. He groaned and scarcely summoned the energy to switch his microphone. 'I don't want a chute. I just want to die.'

At the controls Jammy saw an extra big searchlight

moving across the sky towards them. It looked very blue, as he'd been told the master searchlights were, and he pushed the rudder bar urgently. Without any bank the plane simply yawed sideways, skidding through the sky and lurching as the propellers tried to renew their grip upon the air.

'Yes. All right, hold on to your Elsan,' said Jammy. 'This might be your big chance.' Jammy gave a characteristic mirthless guffaw modified by the oxygen mask he was wearing.

Himmel saw the same big searchlights. As they swept across a patch of cloud they lit it like frosted glass. Conspicuous upon that white patch, like a cockroach on a counterpane, was the black silhouette of an aeroplane, and then came a second bomber slightly smaller.

'Announcement: kettle drums, kettle drums' – he thus dispensed with his radar station's services. Himmel had already followed one contact right across the zone of the Würzburg without success and was about to fly back along the stream and begin again. He switched on the Revi sight and an engraved cross and circle lit up on the glass before him. He put the Junkers into a steep dive, turning on to the same course as his quarry. The bomber had been at least a thousand feet below him when he'd spotted it and he watched the next patch of cloud hoping that he'd see it again closer to. At 15,000 feet he levelled off but continued on the same bearing. He'd only seen the bomber for a second or two and he might have misjudged its heading. Then the observer saw it again. One hundred yards away, much larger and just above the starboard horizon. 'There he is.' Himmel stole a glance at it. Too fast.

The speed of the dive was still affecting their forward motion and even throttling back drastically didn't help much. It was damned near. Himmel pulled the nose up. They slowed. It would put them above the horizon for a moment or two but it was better than showing them his exhausts.

'Corkscrew port go,' shouted Lofty Lee from his upper

turret and began firing as Munro slammed the stick over and stood the bomber on its wingtip. Lofty's machine guns tilted high above him as he tried to keep the night fighter in his sights while his own plane banked vertically and slid down. It was impossible. Munro grabbed the throttles and reduced the forward speed (and exhaust flame) to minimum and had the satisfaction of seeing the Junkers pass rapidly over him. Its exhausts glowed brighter and brighter as the angle narrowed and he was right ahead of them.

'Don't fire, anyone,' said Munro. 'He's lost us.' He'd seen his bomb aimer dodging under the ring of the front turret. It was tempting, of course, for now positions were reversed: Himmel's Junkers was silhouetted against sky and moon-lit high clouds. Munro kept in the blind spot behind the Junkers' tail and vanished against the dark background of earth. Himmel banked for a better view around him. Munro watched the plane ahead as it searched for them and held his breath lest they heard him.

'Everyone all right?' asked Himmel.

'One bullet starred the cockpit glass,' said the observer.

'Those piddling things don't do much damage,' said the radar man.

'Not to you, buried under all that machinery,' grumbled the observer.

'Keep looking for him,' said Himmel.

'We'll never see him in that muck,' said the observer.

'He knew what he was doing,' said the radar operator.

'My fault,' admitted Himmel. 'It's so seldom the *Tommis* spot us that I've grown complacent. I climbed. I should have dived and circled behind him.'

'They're lucky, those *Tommis*. Not many get away as easily as that.'

'Probably old-timers.'

'Someone else will get them,' said Himmel. 'Keep looking.' They kept looking, but finally Himmel had to tell his Controller that he had lost contact.

'Good work, Lofty,' Munro said to the tiny upper gunner who had warned them of Himmel's approach.

'I thought he was a Wellington in the stream at first. Then he went a little higher and I got a good silhouette of the bastard.'

'It was good work,' said Munro. 'Keep your eyes peeled, everyone. They'll put up every night fighter they have on a night like this.'

Cautiously Munro put the nose up and began to climb to his assigned bombing height.

Some bomb aimers were seeing a town under attack for the first time. In Jammy's plane, his navigator Alun Davies had done so many operations hidden behind his curtain that he'd almost forgotten what a target looked like. Battersby, in Creaking Door, stared down at the fires and flashes and for a moment forgot his duties. He'd expected the fires and markers to look much bigger, as they had in the training films he'd seen, but they had been photographed with telephoto lenses. From four miles high even a whole city block on fire was nothing more than a pimple of red in a vast bowl of darkness. A tiny red glow-worm was all that could be seen of fires that stretched from the gasworks to the brewery sidings. It was such a muddle, too. At the briefing the plan was so clear: red markers, then greens and yellows accompanied by the HE Illuminators scheduled to arrive before the Finders. Now, looking down, only the most experienced crews knew what was happening. Battersby couldn't distinguish a fire from a descending marker, or the flicker of an exploding bomb from the slower photoflash.

Wrong wind predictions had thrown the weight of the stream northwards and would have made the timings wrong even if they hadn't mistaken the target. Altgarten was nine miles closer than Krefeld and the immortal Lud's yellow had marked neither. Main Force Stirlings were arriving even before Illuminators. Some Primary Markers had had doubts about the correctness of the markers and had circled several times looking at H2S, thus making themselves late. Altgarten now was a meaningless chaos of greens and yellows, fires, photoflashes and explosions.

'The H2S is acting up, sir. I'm going to bomb the central fire,' said Munro's bomb aimer.

'OK, bomb aimer,' said Munro. 'She's all yours.'

'Left, left, and a bit more. Now we're nice. Steady. Left, left.'

The fires were like little furry animals, their edges softened by the smoke. And like animals they seemed to breathe, expanding and contracting as the flames inhaled the surrounding air-currents. Sometimes it was possible to see the tiny flicker of dozens of incendiaries as they landed and glowed pink. Much larger, the HE bombs flashed and were gone. From each aircraft came a photoflash bomb which exploded above the target with seven million candlepower of light that lasted longer than the bombs and threw enough light upwards to illuminate the bombers. One of these was going off every three or four seconds. Munro, listening carefully to his bomb aimer's instructions, saw by the light of one photoflash eight aeroplanes close around him and was so frightened that he made himself stare at his instrument panel.

'Left, left, steady.' There was no mistaking the instructions since the word 'left' was always said twice. Adding 'steady' without pausing was his way of telling Munro to only touch the left rudder. 'Steady, steady.' Plenty of flak now; the row of tiny fires crept along the bombsight wire with agonizing slowness. The Volkschule fire, the gasworks fire, the Nehringstrasse fire, the Altmarkt fire pulsated like red embers on a sooty fireplace. The bomb aimer waited for the largest one – the hospital annex – left, left, steady. The wire crossed the edge of it. 'Bombs gone.' The selector was at salvo. The whole bomb-load dropped away so that the Lancaster leapt into the air. Munro let the nose come up. For thirty seconds more they flew on straight and level, waiting for the photoflash to explode and the F24 camera shutter to turn over to record the accuracy of their bombing.

'OK.' Munro turned gently. 'Let's go home.'

Only a hundred yards behind him Jammy Giles was doing his best to follow his bomb aimer's instructions but he consistently overcorrected.

'Left, left,' said Alun. 'Right. Too far, left, left. Steady. No, too late. Right. Steady. Yes, that's good. Hold her like that. Steady. Left, left. Jammy, left, left, more.' The plane yawed across the target. The yellow markers slid past, well to the left of his bombsight mark. Under him came the Liebefrau church. The control column kicked against Jammy's sweaty grasp.

'Bombs gone, Jammy. Jettison bars across. It wasn't awfully good, I'm afraid.'

'Let's get out of here,' said Jammy. He tipped the wing down and with the engineer's help increased the air-speed.

'Wait for the photoflash,' shouted Roddy as the plane tilted.

'Bugger,' said Jammy, 'I forgot. Oh well, give me a course for home, Alun.'

Alun was looking back through the clear-view panel into the bomb-bay to make sure that the racks were empty. The 2,000-lb HE, the incendiaries and the 1,000-lb HEs had all gone. He tried to visualize the plot in his memory. 'Steer 280 for exactly four minutes, Jammy. By that time I'll have got a new course for home.'

'Close your bomb-doors, clot.'

'I forgot that.'

'But that you really forgot,' said Roddy archly.

'Now listen, Roddy, you bum. I didn't turn off like that to avoid getting a photo.'

'Flannelling limey bastard.'

'Deserter.'

'Have you been drinking, Jammy?' said Roddy.

There was a moment of hesitation. 'Only a couple,' said

Jammy guiltily, and suddenly his crew had discovered an awful secret about Jammy's lively indifference to danger. No one spoke for nearly five minutes; they were all silently vowing that no one else on the Squadron should know. It was now a family secret. In the pilot's seat the first red flush of embarrassment had faded from Jammy's cheeks. It was better that they knew.

CHAPTER TWENTY-SIX

In the Rathaus the Burgomaster's telephones were ringing continually: '01.39. Florastrasse. High explosive. Fifteen wounded, two dead. Mains intact. Road blocked.'

The telephonist bit her lip as she impaled her written message upon the spike with the others. She lived in Florastrasse.

'01.40. Railway line near brewery. High explosive. No casualties. Railway blocked.'

'01.41. St Antonius Hospital. High explosive. Unknown casualties. Mains intact. Road blocked.'

Munro's cookie hit the St Antonius Hospital. It landed squarely upon the front steps of its neo-classical façade. The fine columns and the great pediment collapsed and some of the girders followed it. Luckily the front of the hospital consisted of offices, the main staircase, the lift, the inquiry desk and storerooms. One of the operating theatres was severely damaged too, although the boiler house below ground escaped. The heating system and hot-water supply were in full working order as soon as the broken pipes had been cut out of the system by screwing up the valves. The doorman lost one of his legs and a doctor suffered bad scalds on his upper body from the broken central heating. Two theatre nurses had to be treated for shock and small multiple injuries. Four patients were cut by flying glass. At the time it seemed a miracle that so little damage had been done to the hospital by such an enormous bomb.

On the other hand the raid had scarcely started yet and the damage to the steelwork had made the whole structure unsafe. More immediately, since the sloping ramps and the big – bed-size – lift shaft had gone, it meant that there was no way of evacuating the bedridden patients from the upper floors. In the wards the flashes of bombs and guns were lighting up the frightened faces of the trapped patients. The markers painted the sheets bright green and yellow and the shadows moved eerily across the floor and up the walls as the flares floated down upon the town. Everyone wanted attention: bed-pans, sleeping tablets, a drink of water or just a word of comfort. The ones that could walk insisted upon going to the toilet even though that was forbidden once the night shift began. They huddled at the window, these frightened, privileged, mobile few. One of the A Flight Lancs dropped a salvo near the Liebefrau church. Then Jammy Giles came across the town. 'Bombs gone, Jammy. It wasn't awfully good, I'm afraid.' The explosion shattered more of the hospital windows and threw a dozen patients full-length to the floor. The far end of Dorfstrasse was just hot rubble.

'Get two dozen nurses from the dance,' ordered Matron.

'They are in the shelter,' said the ward sister.

'We need them here,' said Matron.

Throughout Altgarten a special burden of responsibility had fallen upon men of experience. Luftschütz officials, transport workers, gas engineers, electrical fitters and telephone linesmen had all begun to take their orders from the men who had experienced in other towns air raids of this ferocity. The fire chief, for instance, was depending upon Johannes Ilfa's eighteen months' duty in Cologne to provide solutions to the problems that arose this night, but Ilfa knew that for many of the problems there were no solutions.

Altgarten's population was about 5,000. For each person

there was 30 gallons of water per day. A sum based upon a 15-hour day shows a total need for 10,000 gallons per hour. A town's fire capacity was the margin of extra water for its fire brigades and for Altgarten this was calculated as double the normal rate. So Altgarten could produce 20,000 gallons of water per hour through its arteries until high-explosive bombs sliced those arteries and incendiary bombs by the thousand produced fires on a nightmare scale. To supply its water most of the town's pipes were of 25-cm diameter, but the expensive new houses along Dorfstrasse and Mönchenstrasse all had bathrooms and so the next size of pipe had been fitted in those streets, and the next size was 35 cm. Small by big-city standards but tonight the large-capacity pipes along Mönchenstrasse and Dorfstrasse had become a vital defence in the battle of Altgarten.

As soon as the 2,000-lb high-capacity bombs fell on Mönchenstrasse at the Postgasse junction it was the Burgomaster's strict order that the water pipes must be attended to before casualties or trapped survivors. The TENOs had arrived within four minutes and decided that the eighteen persons in the cellar were too near the centre of the explosion to have survived and they immediately brought out the large-girth canvas pipe sections. They kept a thin supply going until a bomb on Liebefrauplatz severed the junction. Still they continued with the repairs, working down the deep hole in shifts of four, each only being able to stand the work for five minutes at a time. They had dug down beneath the cracked pipe, slipped supports under it and hoisted it into position and then bound it with tape and glue. The men had been virtually immersed in liquid mud created by the water flow, for it would have taken the turncock half an hour of walking in a tight circle to close the main. Since water was coming from the pipe during the work the mud became more and more liquid and only by the quick-witted action of the winch operator on the stand-by lorry was Gerd Böll pulled out of the mud into which he had gone up to the armpits.

It was 01.46 when Jürgen Löwe, a Hitler Jugend messenger boy, arrived at the Rathaus. He carried his bicycle down the steps and propped it inside the sandbagged entrance.

'The Mönchenstrasse water pipe has now been repaired.'

The Burgomaster nodded.

'Heil Hitler,' said the boy.

'Heil Hitler,' said the Burgomaster.

The waterworks master was dead. Now that the main pipeline was repaired the Burgomaster had to make a decision for which he had no training. The city stream passed near to the waterworks and then curved back to become what had once been the inner moat of the old town. Nowadays it was one of Altgarten's most decorative features. Swans on the stream came majestically past the old timbered houses and a patient photographer could be rewarded by one of the most beautiful tourist views in the whole region. In summer the stream dwindled to little more than a gutter and in the last few rainless weeks there had been little more than damp weed there. But at least the stone canal was intact, if his most recent reports were to be believed. What was more, the irrigation valves could isolate the town section of it. If the Burgomaster deliberately pumped the water supply into the moat then the firemen would have a meandering supply of water right in the heart of the old town where the fire hazards were greatest. Each pump could take from the part of the stream nearest to the fire.

He looked at the map. There were so many fires: the Liebefrau church, the houses near the gasworks, the Volkschule, Nehringstrasse, the old market and the hospital Annex. Most of them would benefit from the stream being flooded. Now that the Mönchenstrasse pipe had been repaired they could take water out of the moat at one end of that street, pump it through the large-capacity Mönchenstrasse pipe and use it at the other end where the hospitals were.

On the other hand, the stream water was not fit for drinking and if he pumped it into the clean pipes of the town supply at Mönchenstrasse he would have to order all drinking water to be boiled for twenty minutes before use. That would be a great encumbrance to the hospital, soup kitchens and every living person in Altgarten. Furthermore, the water pipes would have to be cleaned next week and he would be called to account.

That was just one of the problems. He shuffled the memo slips on his desk. The Gasmeister had stopped sending messages by now. The gas was turned off at the gas holder. The oldest parts of the town, where they still used gas lighting, were in darkness. Here and there pockets of gas in the broken pipes were still blazing fiercely, but they would soon burn out. There would probably be no gas in the town for three days. Four times the NSV had phoned to tell him the vats of potato soup could not be ready because of the gas cut. 'Then let them have cold soup,' he finally snapped at them.

Ryessman called Schott, the electricity chief, whose report was brief and unequivocal. If the Florastrasse fires didn't spread towards him and if the hospital generators kept going, the supply on the central net, ie, the city blocks to each side of Dorfstrasse from the hospital to the brewery, would be working. The rest of the town would stay dark except for the Wald Hotel and the TENO camp, which had their own generator. 'At least that will guarantee the blackout for eighty per cent of the town,' added the electricity master facetiously.

'I don't know when you last ascended from your cellar,' said the Burgomaster coldly, 'but half of the town is on fire. You could read a newspaper by its light, even as far away as Frau Förster's sheds.'

'If you would prefer me to be reading a newspaper at Förster's sheds, Herr Bürgermeister, I will go there. But at present I am trying to keep the electricity supply of this town going in spite of losing my senior engineer and my most experienced foreman.'

'Continue to do that, Herr Schott,' said Ryessman angrily.

Actually Schott was being most restrained in his answer, for his chief engineer and foreman were laid out in his office. To get to his plans-chest he had to step over them. They had both been killed by the blast from one of Jammy Giles' 1,000-lb medium-capacity bombs. They had fallen backwards and landed in a heap in the doorway of his room. With only a Hitler Jugend boy to help him, Schott hadn't been able to get them up the steep cellar steps. So he had pulled the bodies into his office until a stretcher party could be spared.

In the Rathaus the Burgomaster ran his fingers along the course of the city stream: a blue mark on the map. A Luft-schutzpolizei girl marked the map with a wax pencil as the reports came in: the southern part of the Nurses' Training Centre was alight and they had had no reports from the Amputee Centre for some time. He suspected that the phone connection had gone and hoped the TENOs would be stringing an emergency line. If the fire jumped to the old buildings, then the St Antonius Hospital would be alight and that was packed with sick people. Some of them would be very difficult to move. He remembered that the electricity chief had made the hospital generator a condition upon which the supply of the central net would depend. Also he had said that the fire must not approach closer to the electricity station.

Electricity was still reaching the most vital sections of town: his Control Room at the Rathaus, the police station, the Emergency TENO Command Post they had set up next door, Party HQ with its soup, ration cards, blankets, money, etc, for the homeless. As long as the electricity on the central net worked, the phones would work, and there would be a chance for his town to survive.

He turned to the girl. 'Put the city stream into the Mönch-enstrasse pipes,' he said. 'And pump from the waterworks to keep the pressure going.' The TENOs were at the waterworks. He was confident they could manage.

The Luftschutzpolizei girl at the phone nodded. She had never expected him to do otherwise. So many decisions were like that. She was talking to the TENOs almost before he'd finished saying it. They had already sealed off the junctions at Mönchenstrasse and Zillestrasse where the mains were severed. Now they began to pump the water into the moat. The surface started to move the way it did in winter. One TENO man was stationed up near the cemetery to watch in case the flow began to reverse. That would be dangerous, for from that point the sewage effluent was in the stream. An HJ cyclist went to tell the firemen at the hospital to run out more hose. Then he told the men near the cinema that they too could use a hydrant. Until now it had remained unused so that the hospital complex should get the pressure.

For nearly one minute they were rewarded with a high-pressure jet that reached far into the fires of the Nurses' Training Centre through the third-storey window. A muffled cheer went up from the firemen and police but it turned into a groan. What the Burgomaster could not have known was that the 2,000-lb bomb from Tommy Carter's plane, which had landed on the corner near Voss, had caused concussion all along Mönchenstrasse. The cobbles made it difficult to see how much the camber of the street had increased. It was always a curved and bumpy surface but now some of the stones had been squeezed from the street like pips from a lemon. Under those cobbles at seven places the water pipes had opened at the caulking joints. These splits were now being made larger by the water from the city stream. Without a sign to show its going, Altgarten's precious water was soaking into its sewers and draining away. The hoses went soft, limp and finally flat.

Even as the newly found water supply was failing and a fire messenger was running back to halt the pumps, HJ boys were pasting up typhoid warnings on the lamp-posts. All citizens must boil their tap water and milk before drinking it.

Now for the first time the sweet smell of the newly dead perfumed the warm streets. Few of Altgarten's residents recognized it and some thought it might be a new sort of disinfectant, but old soldiers and TENO men glanced at each other and prepared the drums of chlorinated lime.

CHAPTER TWENTY-SEVEN

Altgarten was an awe-inspiring display that could be seen by airmen a hundred miles away. A flare crackled loudly and left a crooked trail of white smoke. It painted one side of the Liebefrau's steeple gleaming white and made a knife-like shadow across the Platz. Five of Jammy's 4-lb incendiaries had gone through the church roof and twelve others had straddled Frenzel's Stube opposite, some falling harmlessly in the roadway and others burning insidiously in neighbouring attics. Seen from the air all the fires were soft elongated red blobs. They were shaped by the direction of the speeding bombers from whose bellies hundreds of incendiary sticks tumbled, ignited and burned until the fires joined. Once there was a great mauve flash as an electricity line short-circuited.

In spite of the flak, Redenbacher followed the stream, judging its direction from the shape of the fires. He knew the Radar Controller would be annoyed with him for not keeping to his assigned Würzburg zone, but if he bagged a *Tommi* there would be no complaint. There, and another. Fast, very fast. He was in the stream. They were all around him: plump brown *Tommis*, full of fuel and explosive.

Major Redenbacher turned slightly to starboard to bring himself under and behind the nearest of them. A thump and a judder told him that he'd passed through its slipstream turbulence. A Stirling. He was so close that he decided to attack horizontally from behind and low instead of attacking under it. Here over the target the Stirling's rear gunners would mistake him for another *Tommi*. Redenbacher reached back with his left hand and switched on the Revi sight. He turned the illumination low. He had modified the sight with strips of gummed paper so that the range-estimator ring surmounted with a cross was merely four dull red T shapes pointing inwards. He was so close that two of the Ts cut the wingtips off the plane ahead. Skilfully he adjusted his speed to that of his target and switched his guns to 'fire'. He pressed the gun-button and the cannons and machine guns hammered away like road drills, their trails scratching the sooty night sky.

Redenbacher watched the shells entering the bomber with a detached interest that frightened even himself. The light from his gunfire illuminated the tail of the Stirling. The rear turret revolved and a piece of it became dislodged. It sped towards him, growing larger at a frightening speed until it filled his windscreen and with a terrible thump that shook the Junkers it turned the windscreen glass black. Unable to see, Redenbacher's flyer's instinct took control. He climbed steeply up through the stream. More shapes, that might have been bombers, were seen as dim blurs through the dark dribbling fog that eclipsed his forward vision. 'Oh my God!' said Redenbacher.

There were several thumps and a vibration from the prop and a rattle against the fuselage. The engine-temperature needle crept towards the danger mark. That was the trouble with the air-cooled BMWs.

In the Stirling, Flying Officer Ian Munro, on his fourth operation, pulled the bomb-jettison lever. The port outer was vibrating and it felt as though an aileron had been ripped up. Coolly he pulled back the pitch control, closed the throttle and pushed the feathering button. The broken propeller blades turned until they were edge-on to the air-stream and thus wouldn't be forcibly revolved by it. The propeller stopped. If they got back that engine would be salvageable. He called up the crew. There was no reply from the rear gunner.

'Captain to rear gunner. I repeat, are you OK?'

'This is Monty, sir. I'm back at the rear turret now. It's been rotated and is empty.'

'You mean Chris fell out?'

'Baled out, I'd guess, sir.'

'Bad show, I thought he was a bit edgy tonight. Can you get into the turret?'

'Afraid not, sir. It's fully rotated with the rear doors flapping open. I can see into it but I can't move it.'

'Leave it Monty. We'll just have to keep our fingers crossed, chaps.'

Not far away Flight Lieutenant Sweet's Lancaster began its bombing run.

'Left, left. Steady. Steady. Steady.' Sweet put his head into the transparent blister that enabled him to see the ground below. 'I don't want them there, bomb aimer. I want them in the dark patch to the west. Let's shake up his fire fighters. You know the drill.'

'Very good, sir,' said the bomb aimer hurriedly. 'I think I can still make it. Right?'

'Nothing doing. We'll go round again. We've come all this way, now let's do it according to the book, eh?'

Sweet put the plane into a steep bank. 'And don't let's have any moaning, chaps. Moaning gets me down. Do the job properly and then we can go home and not come back to this one again.'

Sweet cautiously watched the Lancaster ahead of him as he pulled across the stream to go round in a circle. There was enough light from the fires and photoflashes exploding below them to see other aircraft quite clearly; flickering like an old silent film.

Enviously Pip Speke, Sweet's bomb aimer, watched the exhausts of other planes now going home. Sweet continued a flat turn across the farmland to the south of the fires. It was silent and dark here, but a few miles away he could still see the fires and sticks of bombs flashing, one after the other, in little straight lines like some prize-winning score on a pin-table. The light threw shadows of Pip's head upon the inside formers of the aircraft. He watched anxiously as the explosions and fires came round to the front, levelled off and began to creep towards him like lava. None of the other crewmen realized how much more vulnerable a man felt lying full-length, watching the gunfire come slicing at his belly. Speke moved his parachute pack so that it covered his genitals. It was stupid, he knew that, but he always did it.

'You know where I mean now?' Sweet asked him.

'Yes, sir, the dark patch to the west.'

'Exactly. Fuse switches on? Salvo selected? We're coming in from the west this time.'

'Yes, sir.'

'Very well, bomb aimer. See if you can't do a very good job this time.'

The compressed air, released by electro-pneumatic valves, made a noise like a sharp intake of breath and there was a slight jar as the breech blocks of three Oerlikon cannons and the three MG17 machine guns retracted and cocked.

He turned the safety switch to select 'All guns'. The red panel lights winked.

'Kettle drums,' said Himmel. There ahead of him was an aeroplane.

The hammering of cannon shells interrupted Sweet's conversation. Himmel had placed himself beautifully. His assigned Würzburg patrol area came right up to Altgarten and a sharp Controller seeing Sweet's blip had guessed he was going round again to bomb.

Sweet's rear gunner fired only 146 machine-gun bullets before the power supply to the turret ceased. A damaged engine supplied its power. Slowly the gunner began to turn it, using the hand control. He tried to see the Junkers through the glare from the incendiary bullets and shells coming at him. The turret's Perspex shattered into sharp angular pieces and sparks flew from the gun barrels. The rear gunner was the first to die.

Himmel's incendiary shells also hit S Sweet's port outer engine and its coolant burst into flame with an audible spasm. Sweet flipped the throttle forward and then fully back. 'Close mastercock for port outer,' he told Murphy.

'It's off,' said Murphy.

Sweet pushed the control column forward to maintain airspeed but there was no response. He pressed the feathering button and closed the radiator. They waited for the propeller to stop turning. There was enough light from the fire to see it clearly.

Sweet struggled with the controls. The ailerons were badly shredded, which tipped the Lancaster fifteen degrees from level, and bent rudders caused it to steer to port. All the while there was an awful vibration threatening to shake the plane apart. Sweet joggled each of the throttles and found that the vibration slowed with the starboard outer's one.

'Close master fuelcock for starboard outer,' ordered Sweet.

'Starboard outer off,' said Murphy. The vibration slowed but only a little.

'It won't feather and I can't get her to fly level.'

'We're losing fuel from the port tanks. That's unbalancing the trim,' said Murphy. 'A broken blade is causing the vibration.' The two men looked out at the fire. It began in a perfectly straight line along the wing near the trailing edge and ended in a wispy ragged edge far behind. So far only the petrol spray leaking from the broken fuel tank was alight. Sweet pushed the button to operate the Graviner extinguishers but there was no visible difference.

Sweet leaned forward on the control column and gradually the nose dropped. 'Don't dive, Skipper,' said Murphy, but Sweet had heard too many pilots boast of dousing an engine fire by diving to be persuaded against it.

Unfortunately many pilots had found that increased speed only fanned the flames and sometimes the metal itself caught fire. But these pilots did not return to the Mess to relate their stories.

Micky Murphy stared at the blazing engine with a fearful attention. He'd seen alloy burn and now he watched for the intense white glare that heralded it. Using the toe of his boot he pulled his parachute bundle nearer to him. The airstream, speeded up by the dive, was spreading the fire from the exhausts smoothly across the upper surface of the wing in a fantail that flicked sometimes towards the cockpit.

It was a steep dive: the air-speed needle jumped to 390 mph without warning. Sweet wound the elevator tab control back and heaved at the stick but only managed to move it after Murphy added his weight. The aeroplane gradually flattened out and then rose a little. The air-speed needle fell back drunkenly to a dangerous 100 mph and then flicked between 80 and 120.

'I'd not be trusting the air-speed. The pitot tube is likely bent or perhaps its heater's gone and it's icing.'

'The heater's gone,' grunted Sweet, 'that's a laugh.' There was so much noise from the engines that, now they could spare a hand, they were both pressing their phones to their ears to converse. The altimeter showed a height loss of two thousand feet but Murphy no longer believed any of the dials. The bottom of the 'turn and bank' was fixed to one side and did not move.

Sweet had got her straight and level now but at the lower speed the vibration increased. The engine cowling glowed dull red. The alloy weld on a clip gave way and the cowling began to bounce violently in the slipstream. Each bounce gave them a chance to glimpse the bright yellow furnace inside. The gap provided a superfast channel of air that fanned the flames to a lighter colour until a second clip-weld gave way. For a terrible moment the whole cowling flapped above the burning engine like the bright red wings of a bird of prey. It bent backwards, slammed against the leading edge of the wing three times, broke free, lifted, slammed down heavily upon the upper surface of the wing and then, lifted clear by the aerodynamics of the airflow, it flew off over the tail flapping gently.

'A piece of wing. Jesus, it's fallen off. It just went past me like a vampire,' called the wireless operator.

'Calm down, everyone,' said Sweet. 'I can handle it.' To Murphy he calmly said, 'Cowlings are your check, engineer. Did you inspect that one before take-off?'

Murphy looked at him. There was plenty of bright yellow light in the cockpit and Murphy could see Sweet's face glistening with sweat as he fought the controls. 'It was fine, sir,' answered Murphy, 'and the port outer wasn't afire either.'

'I don't want any of your damned sarcasm,' said Sweet. Now that the cowling had gone the engine flames had lessened a fraction but the missing cowling caused a braking and spoiling effect upon the airflow which made the Lancaster buffet and bounce. Sweet had both feet on one rudder bar trying to prevent it yawing sideways across the sky.

There was a sharp crack, a whine and a smell of cordite as a shell burst nearby. They were attracting flak now. 'The flame on the trailing edge is looking very nasty, Mr Sweet, sir. She might explode her tanks.'

'Scientifically impossible, engineer,' said Sweet smiling. 'Even in an empty tank the fuel-air mixture is too rich to ignite and explode.'

'I've seen it happen,' persisted Murphy.

Sweet looked back over his shoulder and then gave Murphy a prim shake of the head to calm him. He was holding her now and, although the flames were just as bad, they weren't getting worse as far as he could decide.

'And Murphy,' said Sweet. 'You'll remove that name from your helmet. My crew don't steal each other's equipment.'

Murphy called to the rear gunner to ask if the night fighter was still there. 'See him, rear gunner?' Murphy asked.

'David's dead,' said the Canadian upper gunner.

'Can you see him from your turret, Kit?'

'The fire's so bright I can see the tail all right but bugger-all beyond it. It's dazzling from here. But how the Christ could he miss us, Micky? We're blazing like a bonfire. Both rudders are shot up and the port one is leaning sideways.'

'We are going in to bomb,' said Sweet. 'Bomb-doors open.'

'You mad berk,' said Kit Pepper the mid-upper gunner, 'haven't you jettisoned those bloody eggs yet?'

'Bombs gone,' said Speke. The aircraft lurched to confirm his words.

'You stupid fool,' said Sweet. 'Who told you to jettison?'

Murphy watched the feathered airscrew blade come to a stop. 'Port outer ignition off, sir.'

'It won't count towards your tour,' warned Sweet primly. 'Jettison is the same as an abort trip.'

'Who said we jettisoned?' said Kit Pepper.

'I aimed at the target,' said the bomb aimer obligingly.

'Liar,' said Sweet. 'We're miles off target.' There was no reply. 'That was sabotage and I'm going to put you on a charge when we get back.'

'If we get bloody back,' said Speke, 'I'll not complain.'

'Bomb-doors closed,' announced Sweet.

'Navigator, give me a course for Warley. Since you're all too frightened to do your job properly, we may as well go home.'

'Steer 283, sir,' said Billy Pace, the quiet ex-architect who was their navigator.

'The compass is dead, sir,' said Micky Murphy.

Sweet noticed that for the first time. 'I'll steer by the stars then.' He leaned over for a better view of the bomb aimer. 'What the devil are you doing down there, bomb aimer?'

'Getting bloody out,' replied Speke, struggling to undo the forward escape hatch. 'They may give the Victoria bleeding Cross to pilots who press on in flaming Lancasters, but not to bomb-aimers they don't.'

'You'll be court-martialled.'

'And you'll be dead,' said Speke. Murphy watched him. Once hit, these Lancs had a bad reputation for escaping crews: only eleven per cent of aircrew survived compared with twenty-nine per cent of escaping Halifax crewmen. Pip Speke got the hatch open and, as if frightened that Sweet might leave the controls and grab him, he dived head-first through the hatch. There was a thump as his legs hit the side of it and one flying boot remained inside the nose. A rush of wind coming through the hatch jolted Sweet.

Towards the rear of the Lancaster the wireless operator and Kit Pepper the upper gunner were unable to open the entrance door. Bravely they had struggled to dump hot flares and signal cartridges down the flare chute. One of Himmel's cannon shells had bent the door-lock but they hammered at it with the fire axe and kicked it open a little. Axe blows vibrated through the fuselage. Sweet had felt the weight of the two men move back towards the tail and had revolved the trim wheel to compensate. He guessed what they might be doing. 'No one leaves the aircraft, and that's an order. I don't care if I court-martial all of you.'

'OK, Cap,' said Kit Pepper, but he didn't pause in his efforts to open the fuselage door. Kit signalled to the wireless operator that he was going to squeeze himself out through the bent door. The other boy nodded agreement. The plane lurched under his feet so that he grabbed at the nearby turret to steady himself while he carefully clipped his chute to the chest of his harness.

'We are going to make it, chaps,' said Sweet. There were sparks from the starboard outer as he spoke. 'I'm holding it on 283.'

'The compass is u/s,' said Murphy. 'We are going round in circles. That's the target coming up to starboard. The rudders are warped. We'll never get her home. She's well alight too. Can't you see.' They were lower now and the Altgarten fires seemed both fiercer and larger. Most were lemon or pink in colour, but now there were deep red ones too where the fire had got out of control.

Himmel came in for another pass. The explosions of the cannon shells echoed inside the Lancaster's metal fuselage like a cricket ball in a biscuit tin. Three of Sweet's windows starred and the engine fire was seen through them as only a pink glow. Near Murphy's feet there were three black discs like bent gramophone records. Wondering what they were, Murphy saw a searchlight beam pass each in succession and realized they were gaping cannon-shell holes in the aircraft's stressed metal side.

Still the shells were exploding. Murphy heard someone scream and there was a whine of flying metal fragments. To the starboard side, high, at about four o'clock he saw another Lancaster flying straight and level. The flaming port outer of S Sweet illuminated the other bomber from underneath in an unnatural way that made it like a model used in a film. It kept too still and flew too perfectly straight to be real, thought Murphy. The flames shone on its propeller blades like four silver discs and Murphy could see the little white patch that was the nose and eyes of its pilot and he knew he was saying, 'It's them that are about to die and not us and I thank you truly O Mother of God.'

Murphy tapped the oil gauges: eighty-nine degrees, not too bad, and seventy-pounds-per-square-inch pressure was normal. The temperature and pressure readings for the wind-milling outer starboard was almost normal too, but that was just a momentary mechanical freak. He expected it to seize up very soon and that would put even more strain on Sweet's abilities, both physical and mental. Bang, bang. There were more hits; he could feel each one shake the metal floor. He decided it was hopeless, but he'd always had this petrifying terror of parachuting and even now it didn't leave him.

Fighter pilots either made a kill soon after being assigned to a squadron (as Himmel had downed a Polish bomber near Lodz) and then went on chalking up kill after kill, or else they never even damaged the paint on an enemy plane, no matter how often they went into combat. For this second sort of flyer just staying alive for fifty sorties was a notable achievement.

The *Experten* were easily recognized: they were alert and had remarkable reaction speeds. They were excellent gunners who were able to aim off correctly for deflection shots, estimating the enemy's speed and predicting his course. An *Experte* could control his aircraft to get very, very close to the enemy and hold that gun platform rock-steady long enough to kill. Three seconds could be enough.

Himmel was an *Experte*, while pilots like Beer would never make it. Driving his racing car had called for boldness but not this degree of judgement. Beer hosepiped his fire all over the sky while his plane was yawing and skidding. By the time he'd corrected his flying, the enemy was already into another evasive manoeuvre. Given an enemy flying straight and level ahead of him, then Beer might have shot him down, except that he probably wouldn't allow his plane to get close enough for more than ten per cent of his gunfire to strike home. But unfortunately for Sweet and Murphy it wasn't Beer who was attacking them, it was Himmel.

He watched the Lancaster growing in his gunsight as he came in as steady as a freight train. As if seeking its own destruction the target's wingtips reached out for the range-rings.

Bang. Bang. Bang. During the four-second burst forty-seven pounds of steel and high explosive left Himmel's guns and much of it hit S for Sugar.

Both the men levering at the exit door saw Himmel's Junkers closing upon them from the starboard quarter for his third pass. Kit switched on his microphone to warn Sweet, but all anyone heard was the beginning of a scream. A shell hit his belly and blew his shoulders from his legs. It atomized his trunk into a spray of red foam that covered the inside of the fuselage as far as the rear spar. The wireless operator standing beside him regained a brief consciousness drifting through the air under a parachute canopy. He felt cold and sleepy and a little drunk. His femoral artery was severed and he was losing blood as fast as his wildly beating heart could pump it into the night air. He died four thousand feet above Altgarten.

The plane gave an agonizing lurch. Until that moment Billy Pace the navigator had not been frightened, but, having survived Himmel's third pass, he urgently needed the reassurance of a solid, earth-like, well-built platform under his feet. But Sugar sagged and dropped fifty terrifying feet through space before regaining stability in a sickening groan of straining metal. The rear part of the fuselage was being wrenched from side to side by the airstream over the badly bent rudder. Each waggle made more rivets ping loose. Air rushing across the torn metal edges of two dozen holes in the fuselage made a loud and constant flute-like scream.

Billy Pace tried to climb out through the escape hatch on the roof above the main spar even before he had consciously decided to jump. He had clipped his parachute to the metal clips on the chest of his harness but could not get through the small hatch. Patiently Pace eased his shoulders back inside the aircraft and unclipped the parachute. Then he climbed out through the roof holding the parachute bundle in his hand. The airstream hit him like a hammer. It smashed against his face and chest at 230 mph and pinned his legs against the edge of the hatch. Inch by inch he dragged himself into its overwhelming force. It crushed his body and prevented him from inhaling properly. Suddenly the airstream overcame the strength of his arms and threw his upper body hard against the fuselage, twisting his knees in doing so. Then it plucked him out of the hatch.

The fire from the port outer enabled him to see as if it were daylight. He grabbed for a handhold but there was none. The slipstream slid him along the rough paintwork like a shove-ha'penny. He hit the upper turret hard and grazed both knees badly before tumbling off the fuselage top with his parachute bundle still in his hand. Beyond there was just space and into that he fell. He dropped, bowling over and over, and saw the aeroplane, and then the moon, pass over him. The tail wheel was only a yard away from his face, and because for a moment his speed was almost equal to that of the aeroplane, it seemed to move very slowly. He knew that his parachute was useless unless fixed on to the clips and cried tears of desperate rage as he fumbled for the metal rings. He had fallen four thousand five hundred feet before he realized that he could look down at his hands to see what he was doing. Then he was able to affix one hook with no difficulty, but he could not get the other one fastened. He did not dare look towards the ground but out of the corner of his eye he noticed the searchlights and the Altgarten fires circling slowly around his feet and growing bigger every second. He decided to hold the parachute across his body with one hand and pull the rip-cord, depending upon the single clip. When he pulled it there was a jerk that spun him sideways suspended from one strap. The canopy opened with a slap of air and Billy Pace, whole and unharmed, drifted gently into the zephyr-like warm winds of Altgarten.

Only Sweet and Murphy remained alive in the aircraft now. After the bomb aimer went, a gale of great intensity blew through the open hatch into the cockpit.

'Abandon,' said Sweet. 'Clear off, Murphy. I know you are only waiting for me to say it.'

Micky Murphy nodded. Sweet said, 'Use the forward hatch. Wait for my command.'

Murphy took an oxygen bottle and edged his way forward. He gripped the underside of the pilot's instrument panel and swung himself under it. He had to use all his strength to move against the 200-mph wind coming in. He got down on to the step and then straddled the open hatch. Through it he saw fires and searchlights. He plugged into the intercom and said, 'I'm ready to go, sir.' Sweet grunted.

The aircraft rolled alarmingly as the starboard-side aileron trim cable snapped and wrapped itself round the aileron hinge, locking it in a tangle of shredded wire. She kept rolling now until the starboard wing was tilted upward at forty degrees. Uncertain whether to jump, and devoid of his intercom, Murphy poked his head low and saw Sweet with his shoulders against the fuselage side red-faced and straining at the control column. It was only after he gave up the struggle that the coiled trim wire fell from the released aileron to droop in the slipstream. The controls were free again. Aware that some miracle had saved the plane from rolling over and over all the way to the ground, Sweet corrected the bank. Infinitely slowly the Lancaster came back to straight and level flight.

Murphy slammed his intercom plug into the bomb aimer's station and said, 'Aren't you going too, sir?'

'I took it up and I'm taking it down.'

'Not to Warley?'

'On to the deck somewhere.'

'You'll not do it alone.'

Sweet grunted again. 'You might be of use, I suppose.'

Murphy was frightened to jump out through the hatch. The burning aeroplane was almost like home to him. 'Better the devil you know . . .' said Murphy. He turned to climb up on the step and the airstream blew him back to his engineer's position. He clamped his huge hand around a metal girder 'Use the hand trim.'

'I was just going to,' said Sweet.

'And bring the revs up. We'll not be trying to save fuel.'

'Shall I detonate the secret gear?'

'I've done that,' said Murphy.

'What shall I do now?'

'Can you remember what the wind was?'

'No, I'm sorry. It's that bloody navigator. He's gone, I suppose. He was always bloody useless.'

'Never mind him, there's just the two of us left.'

'What about the night fighter?' asked Sweet nervously.

'Ah, I was forgetting him,' said Murphy drily. 'Yes, there's three of us really.'

Himmel was very close to them, watching the blazing bomber with a fear and fascination. 'Poor fellows,' said the observer. It was clear that the crew were struggling to keep her flying.

'They burn our cities and bury our people alive,' said Himmel. He moved into position for the *coup de grâce*. He had come up a few points to starboard now and was dazzled by the burning engine. A flak shell burst near the Lanc's starboard wingtip and both aeroplanes jolted.

'The flak will probably claim her,' said the observer.

'They claim everything,' said Himmel. He still did not open fire on the stricken bomber. He throttled back and suddenly there were bright blue-and-yellow flashes from his own exhaust.

Himmel knew the revs were dropping before he looked down at the gauge. Perhaps it was the vibration through the control column or a slight modulation of the engine's sound as the plugs began to oil up. Just the starboard motor: boost and oil pressure too. The valve was seating badly and again the mixture ignited in the exhaust manifold and gushed flame. That damned motor, if Kugel had changed the engine instead of trying to save Luftwaffe money by fobbing him off with a new set of piston rings there would be another *Tommi* downed.

'Tighten your straps,' said Himmel. 'It's a piano out of the fifth floor.' So as not to alarm his crew he used the slang term for a forced landing. Neither of them replied, but he saw the observer touch his parachute as if he could not depend upon his eyes to tell him it was to hand. She would cut at any moment. And when she does, that radar array will grant her the aerodynamic perfection of a broken brick. He put the nose down steeply, for he needed every bit of air-speed he could muster if he was to get them down in one

413

piece. The variometer needle sank. Above them the blazing *Tommi* was straightening out and flying level again.

'Butterbrot from Katze Nine. Butterbrot from Katze Nine. SOS engine failure. Map reference . . .'

'Ludwig Nordpol Six,' supplied Himmel's radar operator hurriedly from the rear seat.

'Ludwig Nordpol Six,' said Himmel.

'Order: steer 180,' came the reply. Himmel was already heading that way; he knew they would want to take him as far away from the route of the enemy as they could. Anxiously he watched the cloud patches. To port the Ruhr was under its usual blanket of smog, although here and there he could see the dull red smudge of a steel furnace. He steered away towards the flat, open country.

The Liaison Officer at Deelen was referring to his distress map. On it airfields with blind-landing apparatus were distinguished from emergency strips. High ground, obstacles and high-tension cables that would prove a hazard to a crippled plane were all indicated. Quickly he chose an airfield. Selected searchlights over which Himmel was flying tipped their beams almost flat along the surface of the ground. From 15,000 feet they were like grey roads, all of them pointing to the distress airfield.

'I can see them now,' said Himmel.

'Announcement: radishes and shroud too,' promised the Liaison Officer.

'Yes,' said the observer.

'We see it,' said Himmel. The starboard engine coughed twice and cut. Himmel feathered it and switched it off. Ahead of him a searchlight beam held upon a piece of cloud. That was the promised shroud, then came the radishes: white rockets and red rockets exploding above an airfield where ambulances and fitters, fuel bowsers and ammunition supply lorries were waiting for him.

'Shall I fire a red?' asked the observer.

'Why not?' said Himmel. 'We'd better contribute something to the party.' He tuned in to the blind-landing frequency and heard a single high note. They were exactly on course. Himmel was about to lower his flaps but on impulse he defeathered the propeller and switched on the ignition. The airstream spun the blades and it fired and roared into life.

'You bastard,' said Himmel. Neither of his crew spoke; they could almost taste the hot coffee that was awaiting them. He pulled the stick back and turned towards the bombing to look for the aeroplane he had half killed.

CHAPTER TWENTY-EIGHT

When the water supply dried up, Bodo Reuter – the TENO officer – took an HJ boy's bicycle and cycled through the bombs and shrapnel to report to the Burgomaster at the Rathaus. He hurried through the sandbagged entrance and pushed past the police chief. Impatiently he waited while a messenger from Frenzel's Stube completed his report. A bomb there had killed twenty-five people including eight of the Burgomaster's guests who had been having a few final drinks in the bar. The ground floor of the Stube had been converted into an emergency mortuary.

'Next,' said the Burgomaster, turning his blank eyes to Bodo Reuter. It was as if he had not heard the report, thought Bodo, and perhaps he hadn't. Perhaps he was waiting until tomorrow before coming to terms with such news.

'Why didn't you phone?'

'The phones have gone, Herr Bürgermeister. The western half of the power net is out of action. I could have phoned you from Party HQ, but that journey was almost as long as coming here directly.'

'The Western side?' said the Burgomaster. He looked at his telephonist; she nodded. In the part of town near the old market the electricity supply was carried on overhead wires from building to building. Some of those streets were now tangled with broken wiring, impeding pedestrians, blocking traffic and injuring cyclists.

'Report,' commanded the Burgomaster.

'The city stream is flowing well, Herr Bürgermeister. And the broken pipe on Mönchenstrasse has been repaired but there is hardly any water coming through it.'

'Why?'

'They have had four or five bombs on Mönchenstrasse. Only the first bomb made a crater in the road and severed the pipes but the others have cracked the joints. There might be a dozen leaks along the length of the street; it would take many hours to dig down to repair them.'

The Burgomaster listened to Bodo with an almost inhuman calm. He turned back to his map. At first he had placed a big red pin into the site of each bomb but it was ten minutes since he had run out of red pins. He fingered Mönchenstrasse and without turning round said, 'Voss' house was hit?'

'Voss is dead, Herr Bürgermeister. He was putting sand upon an incendiary bomb when he was killed by blast. Some of them contain an explosive charge.'

'The fool,' said the Burgomaster. Outside there was no respite from the bombing. 'Run hose the whole length of Mönchenstrasse. Take your water directly from the city stream.'

'Do you realize how much hose that is?' objected Bodo Reuter. 'And what will it give us? One single branch. We may as well pee on the fire.'

'There's no alternative,' said the Burgomaster. His hair was standing up from his head. His stiff wing collar had come unclipped from his collar-stud and it waggled in the air, making him look like a music-hall comic.

Reuter turned to leave but the Burgomaster took his arm and dragged him roughly towards the map of the town. There was a tremendous explosion nearby and although the others in the room ducked these two men seemed not to hear it.

'Where?' said the Burgomaster. 'Show me where.' His

voice was not his natural one, and for a moment the fireman was afraid of this comical-looking wretch with the scarecrow evening suit and white brick-dust down his waistcoat.

'We'll string out the hose, Herr Bürgermeister,' said the fireman.

'No alternative,' said the Burgomaster. He said it as though it was a little dictum that he lived by, and indeed for the last half-hour he had.

A Luftschütz girl finished typing a short note and passed it to the Burgomaster for signature. He called an HJ messenger. It was little Jürgen Löwe, the barber's son.

'Cycle quickly to Nehringstrasse, the fire at the bakery. They must demolish the houses behind it to create a fire break. The senior TENO officer will need this written order.'

'I've no bicycle, sir.'

'How dare you come here without it? The safety of the town depends upon a good messenger service.'

Jürgen was only fourteen. This was his first week of official duty and he was downcast by the Burgomaster's scolding.

'You'll run all the way. And next time you come on duty, don't dare forget your bicycle.'

'I didn't forget it, sir,' said the child. 'I was blown off it at the corner of Dorfstrasse and Zillestrasse. I could only find a wheel and that was badly bent.'

'Get along with you,' said the Burgomaster. 'And be careful.' The little boy ran out of the room clasping his blue-painted messenger's helmet as though it was an Iron Cross.

'It's finished,' said the telephonist. 'The bombers have gone.' She logged the call from the observer post on the Venlo road and soon there were more calls confirming the report.

Scarcely believing it, the Burgomaster climbed the steps from his Control Room like a man whose joints had aged overnight. The others followed him and as they emerged through the sandbagged entrance the glare made them half close their eyes. The fires were dragging the air across the flat farmland and creating a warm breeze. The more air consumed at ground level the higher were the flames and the greater was the heat at the fire's centre and the lighter its colour. Apart from the spectacular sight of the gas-holder the highest flames were from the Nurses' Training Centre. Thank God that, at least, was evacuated without casualties. They could feel the heat of the fires and hear the roar of them, but the hum of the aircraft had all but disappeared. Suddenly from the Liebefrau church there was a tremendous crash. A sheet of flame rose and sprinkled white-hot sparks across the roofs of the town.

The firemen had been expecting it. Half of a canister of incendiaries jettisoned by Munro's young brother Ian had been the deciding factor. Molten lead had been dripping on to the firemen below for some minutes. As soon as the men on the church roof saw the trusses buckling they hurried back down to the ground. The bells fell soon after that with a monstrous din. The stonework of the outer walls was expanding and it made angry growls and sudden cracks. The nave of the church was ablaze and the great stained-glass window had never shone more beautifully than it did in the Liebefrau's final agony. A buttress fell with an awful crash. The stonework continued to expand until, with an earth-shaking roar, it released the roof upon the burning interior. Sparks flew into the air for a thousand feet and the windows flashed red.

The fifteenth-century altarpiece, the carved pulpit and the painting of the martyrs that was said to be a Van der Weyden were gone for ever. The firemen turned away from the church. For some time their hoses had been directed upon the old houses and Frenzel's Stube on the far side of the Platz. One of the priests had become almost violent when the firemen refused to put their hoses upon the church. He had refused to believe that it was too late.

That sly fool Frenzel had stored five barrels of black-market schnapps and fifteen sacks of sugar in his apartment above the restaurant. The heat had fired the sugar and was exploding the schnapps barrels like high-explosive bombs, squirting burning alcohol on to TENOs and firemen in the street and as far as the neighbouring houses. In the cellar sat the Frenzels and their three young daughters. The firemen urged them to go to the shelter round the corner in Studentenacker, but the girls would not leave their mother. Frau Frenzel in turn would not leave her husband and Herr Frenzel would under no circumstances leave his cellarful of French wines. It was bad enough to sit there with the smell of his black-market Westphalian hams scorching. He cut another slice of Frau Frenzel's *Schlumperwerk* and bit into the sweet apple filling. It was always like this when he was worried; he ate without even being hungry. The firemen hoisted another hose up the face of the building to a second-storey window and tried to prevent the fire moving downwards. Frenzel's restaurant had become an emergency mortuary and the firemen were picking their way between rows of corpses laid out on the floor of the bar and awash with water from the hoses.

The hardware store on the other side of Liebefrauplatz was a similar fire hazard. Eight drums of paint had caught fire and were pouring down the staircase like molten lava, trapping and endangering twenty people in the cellar. The TENOs were digging towards them through hot masonry.

Near the gasworks a crowd of over a hundred civilians had formed a human cordon across the road and beaten up the crew of a fire engine who were on their way to the hospital and would not attend to their blazing homes.

In Florastrasse Herr and Frau Meyer who had been married that afternoon were sitting in a cellar under their parents' house together with a dozen guests. A Romanian cantor was singing the ancient songs of the wedding feast.

Herr Holländer, the man who had married the couple that afternoon, was at that moment opening the heavy door of a deep shelter in Kaiserin-Augustastrasse. He looked in every few minutes. It was a grimy street, not far enough away from the gasworks to be disassociated from the slums that surrounded it. Correctly garbed and with dimmed torch to hand, he looked around and then noted the time. Most of the occupants were brewery workers who on account of their early rising resented bitterly being told to take shelter. It was the law, as Holländer told them this night. It wasn't a decision of his, it was the law.

Most of them were snoring and there was a smell of stale breath and unwashed bodies. None of them would thank him for his concern. Holländer believed that they all hated him. He believed that they thought him a rodent-faced bureaucrat who used his job as Blockwart to interfere and pry into the business of his neighbours with the full backing of authority. Holländer's wife was a meek little creature – the rat and the mouse, someone had once called them. She did not believe that anyone could think such things of her husband, let alone say them. She was wrong and he was exactly right.

He closed the door behind him and hurried up the stairs. He had the keys of all of their apartments in his bag. Perhaps he should make sure that no fire-bombs had fallen into any of them. His was a grave responsibility and he met it with diligence and thoroughness. Perhaps the first apartment should be old Frau Klietmann's.

Andi Niels had succeeded in persuading the tall Viennese nurse to leave the dance hall 'for a breath of fresh air', but she wouldn't go to the Annex with him. So they had gone out across Koller Meadow and had been lying on the grass in a state of semi-undress when Tommy Carter's Lancaster arrived. One of his TIs splashed fire upon them so that they had assumed the strange boxer's pose that burned bodies take up. Both of them had shrunk to four-and-a-half-foot lengths of carbon.

For all the people in Altgarten the departure of the bombers brought a merciful quiet for which they had almost ceased to hope. Although warm winds roared through the narrow streets to feed the fires and carry away the cries of the injured, dying and trapped, at least most of the town was still intact.

Two hundred and sixty bombers had attacked Altgarten in the twenty-eight minutes between 01.24 and 01.52, which is an average of 9:3 aircraft per minute. Of these aircraft, one hundred and fifty-six bombed within three miles of their aiming-point. Only eight aircraft ignored the Altgarten fires and passed over them to bomb Krefeld by means of the H2S apparatus.

Most of the aircraft had a bomb-load of 14,000 lb and although twenty-five per cent of the RAF's high-explosive bombs were duds, it still meant that for several minutes at a time in Altgarten it was no easier to distinguish between the explosions of individual bombs than it is to identify those of a fast-revving car engine. Now that the bombers had gone the silence was curiously oppressive. When the Burgomaster spoke his voice seemed unnecessarily loud.

'Thank God,' said the Burgomaster. The others turned to look at him. It was not a National Socialist sentiment. The Burgomaster did not care. 'Thank God,' he said again.

There were clouds across the moon: cirrostratus thickening to become altostratus. Half an hour ago the moon had been a sharp-edged disc with a halo, but now it had become a soft white blob. For a moment the moon darkened behind the thickening cloud. There were chunks of fractostratus too, scudding across the town so close to the rooftops that they glowed bright red and flickered like little private hells in the sky.

'Filthy swine,' said Oberzugführer Bodo Reuter.

'The Mönchenstrasse pipes,' said the Burgomaster.

'Immediately, Herr Bürgermeister,' snapped Reuter. He took his small bicycle and found it difficult to ride. Odd that he had had no difficulty riding it when the bombs were falling. 'All of your hose to Mönchenstrasse,' shouted the

Burgomaster after him. Miles to the west there was the rumble of anti-aircraft fire as the returning bombers passed over the massed batteries near the Dutch frontier.

The diesel pump in the TENO yard had been destroyed and the tank below it was afire. A thin snake of black smoke crawled through the back streets near the railway, bringing oily smears, motes of soot, reddened eyes and a taste that reached into the back of Bodo's throat. He bit into the wet handkerchief tied across his face and pedalled faster. At the corner of Neustrasse he stopped and stared.

A curtain of dust, eddying and swirling in the air currents, moved towards the fires on Dorfstrasse. Those fires – Schmitt the butcher's, the old insurance building and Becker's dress shop – shone through the smoke as a fairy ballet through a theatrical gauze. By their light Reuter could see shop-window dummies – broken, stiff and denuded by blast – scattered among the debris on the pavement. Except that where the fires burned most brightly it was clear that they were not dummies.

But it was not the fires or the bodies that made Reuter stare: it was the absence of the entire city block that until tonight had separated Dorfstrasse from this corner. Over one hundred yards square and four storeys high, it was now a tangled mess that, apart from a couple of chimney breasts, stood nowhere taller than a man. The 2,000-lb bomb from Jammy's aircraft had exploded there. Yet elsewhere this night there fell bombs four times as heavy as that one.

Bodo climbed back on to his tiny bicycle and hurried to Gerd Böll near what was once the house of Voss.

'You keep looking across there,' said Bodo Reuter.

'It's Voss' place. My cousin's housekeeper is in the cellar.' Bodo noticed that his friend's eyebrows had been scorched and he could feel that his own were too, and his lips were cracked and raw.

They both looked at the pile of rubble where another 1,000-lb MC had demolished Voss' house. Neither of the men spoke; there was nothing they could do. Finally they walked to the hole in the road. Their torches probed around the crater with the deft professional touch of surgeons examining an open belly.

It had been neatly done. The gas pipes were plugged with wedges and, farther along, the twisted, brightly coloured electricity cables were roughly clamped across the charred ends as if with artery forceps. The special fire and police phone lines had also been given first-aid.

Lower than those, so that the water could not leak and cause a short circuit, there were the small-capacity street water-supply pipes, but the torches did not linger upon that side of the crater. The problems were all in the centre of the street. A layer of cobblestones had been scattered for yards and the paving and broken stone under it had collapsed into the crater. There the gas pipes bent drunkenly and the 35-cm water pipe was leaking at its joints. Deepest of all, and along the very centre of the street, just exposed at the bottom of the crater was the main sewer. It received the street's strong (ie, domestic) sewage as well as weak sewage from gutterings and rainstorm water from the street drains. The sewer pipe was lower than the water pipes so that it would receive any water that might leak from them. This, like many of the main sewers through the oldest part of town, was simply the medieval gully. Now water from the broken mains was coursing through it, moving south-west towards the sewage works. 'A few sandbags would do it,' said Gerd.

'It's worth trying,' agreed Bodo.

'Find the sewage manhole on Dorfstrasse, block up the outlet with a few sandbags, wait for the water to fill the sewer and then use the manhole as a sump from which to pump water.'

'Suppose the water level gets high enough for the sewage to get into the town water supply,' said Bodo. 'It will be the devil of a job to clean.'

'Then you can blame me,' said Gerd.

For a moment Reuter was silent. Then he said, 'Very well, Gerd, you are the doctor of engineering.' The group of TENOs were waiting for their next orders. Meanwhile they had been giving the distracted Blockwart Storp a hand to dig down towards his cellar.

Reuter said, 'Find the Dorfstrasse sewer inspection manhole and block the outlet with sandbags. Then tell the senior fireman at the hospital that he can take water from there.'

''*Raus!*' shouted Reuter, and his men leaped aboard their lorry. The Blockwart called upon them to come back. 'There are eighteen people under here,' he shouted. The lorry lurched forward.

'There are three hundred people in the hospital,' said Gerd gently. 'Your wife will be all right until we put that fire out.'

The Blockwart nodded. Under the ground the water from the mains was still splashing away.

Just a few yards away from where Gerd Böll and Reuter were standing, Anna-Luisa and little Hansl were trapped in old Herr Voss' cellar. The bomb had exploded above them at the third floor. Like most of the thin-walled HC bombs it had spread its shockwave sideways. In the cellar it had not sounded as loud, or made as much disturbance, as the earlier medium capacity had done, for that one had penetrated the road before exploding.

Anna-Luisa was not frightened when she was unable to open the cellar door. She suspected that the Waffen SS officer who had stolen Herr Voss' carpet and silver had locked it to prevent her giving the alarm. She pushed against it but it would not move. It was a solidly built door that Voss had selected specially to guard his subterranean storehouse. Anna-Luisa did not suspect that there was a couple of hundred tons of shattered masonry piled upon it.

It was very quiet there, apart from the gurgle of water. She didn't move around much. There was only the glow of the oil lamp now that the electricity had gone off. The light glinted upon the water that at the lowest part of the ancient stone floor was three or four inches deep. This didn't worry her either, for at its present rate the damaged pipe would take a couple of weeks to fill the cellar deep enough to drown them.

It wasn't until the TENO men had blocked up the Dorfstrasse sewer outlet that she became alarmed. For soon the combined sewer in the street outside began to fill. Half a dozen leaks along the whole length of the street were draining into it and the level backed up until it crept along the sewage pipe to the house. At Voss' house it reached the broken pipes above the cellar and then these too added to the flooding. For ten minutes she was horrified by the amount of water coming in. One side of the cellar was six inches deep in water but after that it virtually stopped.

It stopped because the firemen began to pump water from the Dorfstrasse manhole which by now had formed a sump. At last the firemen at the hospital had a reasonable supply of water to fight the fire. For them the fire had become a live enemy. With their newly found supply of water they were able to take their revenge upon it. Six branches were in operation on the Dorfstrasse side of the hospital. Now that the patients had been moved along to the intact wing of the building it could only be a matter of a couple of hours before the blaze was completely under control, ie, surrounded and reducing in area.

Of course it was uncomfortable for the patients. At first they had been close to panic and there was a time when the Oberstarzt from the Amputee Centre had brought ten armed soldiers to the hospital and told them to be ready to restore order in the wards at pistol-point. The turning-point in hospital morale was when Frau Thorn had thrown the contents of her bed-pan over a burning chair in the surgical ward. The story had gone through the hospital like lightning. Everyone knew Frau Thorn and everyone had laughed. It seemed to have restored the stoic German calm. The beds were crowded, with hardly an inch between them. Patients were mixed up, women and men were crowded together into corridors and storerooms, but no one complained. In one ward they were singing.

Across the road at the Amputee Rehabilitation Centre the Oberstarzt gave a sigh of relief when the bombing stopped. Already the hut nearest to the hospital fire had burst into flame. The radiation had heated the flimsy woodwork to a temperature where sparks falling upon the roof set it alight. There was no panic; there were enough soldiers among his patients to quell the spoken fears of the civilians. The nurses, helped by patients with only arm amputations, wheeled the beds out of the huts just before the walls ignited. Unfortunately those patients had to be left out in the open fields and already metal fragments had injured three of them and this had caused the others to become uneasy. But, as the Oberstarzt said, some of the patients in the huts were also being injured by fragments of broken glass.

It had been a trying time for the Oberst and he was no longer young. It was natural that people should think that the trainees in nurse's uniform were skilled enough to handle casualties, but many of them were shopgirls and domestic servants with only a few days' training behind them. Even the fully trained girls were really only to be trusted with dispensing hot drinks and emptying bed-pans. Goodness knows what damage the trainees had done this night!

'Put all the patients out on the field,' said the Oberst. 'We'll cool the huts off with buckets of water.'

Meanwhile on the other side of town at the Wald Hotel a crisis of another kind had occurred. It was a fine Edwardian building set in two and a half acres of parkland. Because of the high walls and the barbed wire, as well as the constant howls of fierce dogs, it was widely believed that the Wald Hotel was a secret SS centre of considerable importance. One rumour said that it housed Jewish millionaires who had bribed the SS to get them out of concentration camps and now lived here in luxury. There were stories about it being a stud farm for SS men on leave, as Frau Hinkelburg had suggested. Another rumour said that Stalin's son, captured on the East Front, was held prisoner here. In reality it was simply a Waffen SS dog-training centre and the screams heard at night were the yelps of hungry dogs.

The dogs began to bark from the moment that the first HE bombs fell near the waterworks and the excitement of the sentries communicated itself to the dogs, for they were trained to respond to human intentions. Ian Munro's Stirling had jettisoned its bombs when Redenbacher opened fire. Then it came low from the south across the bomber stream. Only two of its motors were still functioning; one of the others had run away and the crippled engine was tearing itself to pieces and screaming like a dental drill. It disappeared over the rise in the ground beyond the waterworks, still trying to gain height. The eager Heimatflak boys from the brewery had a go at it with their 2-cm batteries and the sky above the trees was criss-crossed with tracers and the smell of the firing drifted through the dog cages. The sounds and smells added to the excitement of the dogs and the barking increased until the dogs were running up and down their compounds in great agitation.

It was the 8,000-lb HC Blockbuster – the largest size of bomb dropped that night – that demolished a row of new houses near the cemetery and sent the dogs berserk. In one compound the dogs threw their bodies against the wire netting of their compounds, uncaring of the pain and blood. The netting tore open and the dogs ran through the hotel garden. Mausi Scheske was on guard duty; he shot one dog but was set upon by the rest of them and badly savaged. His brother opened fire and killed two of the dogs, but galvanized by fear five other dogs escaped over the gates. Poor little Mausi died of his wounds twenty minutes later, whereupon Hannes visited each of the dog compounds and shot the dogs. In twenty-five minutes he killed eighty-seven dogs, some of them fully trained and already assigned to a mountain regiment in Yugoslavia. Hannes was arrested by the guard sergeant, disarmed and locked in the old wine cellar. There was no wine there.

Standartenführer Wörth cursed the noisy dogs, but as the bombing stopped he returned to a pile of paperwork. He was sitting at a writing-table in his suite on the first floor. He had chosen this room not because of its proximity to the lake but because it had thick walls and was as far from the dog compound as he could live. His orderly entered the room at 02.00, bringing with him a young NCO with torn trousers and a bleeding leg wound. The NCO delivered a report about the Scheske brothers and the maddened dogs.

'Tell Hentschel,' said the Standartenführer.

The NCO knew no one of that name. He exchanged a quick glance with the orderly, who nodded and moved his head to indicate that they should leave. 'Heil Hitler,' said the wounded boy.

'Heil Hitler,' said the Standartenführer without looking up from his desk. It was ten minutes later when the orderly came to tell him about the horse and he hurried downstairs and out into the chilly winter's night to see if it could possibly be true.

'Rosenknospe,' he said. There were sugar cubes in his pocket. He'd never ceased to carry one or two since he was a child. 'Rose.' If only young Hentschel could have also been sewn up and put together again like the horse. Who in the regiment remembered him and had recognized the horse? Someone assigned to a veterinary farm, perhaps. 'Rosenknospe. You're not as young as you used to be, old girl.' The horse whinnied, the smell and the voice had helped her recognize him. How long since he'd ridden? Such a fine horse. She'd be well cared for now.

Dieter Witting, the Standartenführer's orderly, dozed for a few minutes after the last bombs. He was awakened by the bell and looked at the clock. It was a closely guarded secret that the CO could not go to the toilet without the assistance of his orderly. Witting put his overcoat over his pyjamas and took the case containing the syringe and tablets just in case they were needed. He went in without knocking, as was his usual practice when answering a summons. Wörth was sitting upright in his chair staring straight at the door. Witting wasn't frightened. Wörth tried to speak and his orderly bent close to his mouth.

'Rosenknospe,' whispered Wörth.

'Rosebud'; Witting had seen many men die and often their last words were incomprehensible.

'It's going to be all right now, sir,' said Witting. 'Yes,' said Standartenführer Wörth, and died of frostbite and wounds suffered eighteen months before.

The Burgomaster did not return to his Control Room. The planes had passed over and anyway all of his phones were out of order. From now on the air-raid services must work on their own initiative. He took one of the portable stirrup pumps from the entrance and walked towards the red glow of the old town.

He walked through his town in horrified disbelief. By the lights of the big fires near the gasworks he could see a whole row of slum housing that was simply a one-wall façade like a film set; the houses themselves had disappeared. Alongside the railway station a locomotive had jumped its tracks and was now several feet away from the railway lines. As he turned north on to Nehringstrasse the whole street was a blizzard of flying sparks. The first time he saw a body – just beyond Tornow the printer's – he stopped to look at it. It was Tornow's son, dressed in his naval officer's uniform. Quite dead. He recognized the body of a girl clerk too. After he'd passed fifty bodies he no longer glanced at them.

Only three minutes after he'd left his Control Room an NSKK motorcycle messenger arrived. The FLUKO at Duisburg had tried to get through by means of every official phone in Altgarten but when none of them could connect to the Burgomaster's Control Room they ordered that a messenger should go from Party HQ. The message simply said that the second wave of RAF aircraft numbering approximately four hundred planes was approaching Altgarten. All fires must be extinguished and non-essential personnel ordered to take shelter.

CHAPTER TWENTY-NINE

Lambert had seen six bombers since leaving Warley but he'd only had a glimpse of them. So far the trip had been uneventful. Sometimes he'd returned from trips to find other crews describing all manner of pyrotechnics and mayhem while he had seen little or nothing the whole trip. Other sorties had proved to be the very reverse.

'Changing tanks,' said Battersby.

'OK,' said Lambert.

The Flight Engineer let the tank drain to the final empty cough before changing over. That was the most efficient way to log the fuel consumption and avoid airlocks.

'Look to port,' said Binty. 'The searchlights have coned some poor bastard and the flak is coming up like confetti.'

Instinctively Lambert touched the rudder to steer away from the flak.

Digby was still in the nose. The target was full of coloured lights flickering and winking as the heat rose. There was smoke too. The flares and fires under it made it glow and the heat and blast made it ripple and bubble like milk boiling out of a saucepan. There was black smoke too from where the TENOs' diesel tank had been hit. Once Digby saw a shockwave expand across the brightest fire and wobble it like a redcurrant jelly. 'I'd like to bomb those flak bastards. What say, Skip, that I save a couple of thousand-pounders for the flak? We could . . .'

'Fighter, fighter, port beam,' said Flash Gordon. His four machine guns were joined an instant later by the upper turret's two guns.

'He's attacking someone else,' said Binty. Just a couple of hundred yards to port the thin line of incendiary shells turned like the sweep second hand of a clock as the night fighter closed upon his victim changing his angle of attack and then climbed away into the dark.

'Bomb-doors open.'

It had begun. They were fixed on the tramline course that would take them across the centre of the target's fires and into its flak. It looked like a child's birthday cake, half a dozen yellow candles flickering in a darkened room. A kid's birthday cake. Left, left. Steady.

The plane ahead was on fire. Its propeller blades slowed as they feathered, but the flames were getting brighter by the second. Steady. Right, hold that, nicely, nicely, hold that steady. The night fighter would come in again as sure as God made little apples and when he did Creaking Door would be brightly illuminated by those damned flames. Brighter still. Its cowling is breaking apart. Steady, left, left. Please God make him go down! He doesn't have to crash, if he'll just go down. Please God, just a thousand feet! Right. Steady. Five hundred, then.

A crash of flak made the wing lift. There was a patter of shrapnel. 'Come in,' said Jimmy.

You're veering, Skip. Left, left quite a bit. Even if it's Micky Murphy. Make him go down! That night fighter must be behind us at this very moment. Steady. Even if it's my mother. The light from the burning Lancaster was worse. They'll never save it now. Jesus Christ, that's another pass! That's the night fighter's cannon shells punching those pieces out of him. Get out. Jump, Jump, Jump. You bloody fools. The rear turret is hanging in shreds like a bundle of bent wire. So where are the parachutes? She's leaping about like a punch-drunk boxer. The propeller blades must have broken on the other side. Left, left. Smoke everywhere, Skipper, I can't bloody see. OK, hold her like that.

The pilot in the burning plane was throttling back. The distance between them narrowed and the tips of the flames seemed to be trying to get into their own airstream. Closer. So don't look. Look at the instruments and look at your engineer. Battersby was staring at him in horror. Lambert nodded encouragingly and Battersby turned back to his panel. He thinks I can save him. They all do. Why the hell should they pick on me? Steady, left just a fraction. Steady. That's good. 'She's well alight,' said Digby calmly. He was only speaking of the target. Target; I'd forgotten the target. They're having trouble to hold that blazing coffin and in a moment it's going to stall and we'll fly into it. Steady. God, it's coming closer still!

'Drop the bastard bombs,' someone shouted. It was a high-pitched anxious voice, not recognizable as any one of the crew until the cry was repeated and Digby identified it.

'Here she comes, Skip. Keep your hair on,' Digby told him calmly.

Is he so glued to that bombsight that he can't see that the whole sky is ablaze with this bloody great dying Lancaster almost touching our wingtip? Make it go down. Shoot it down. Anything but just darkness, please. Just darkness. Nothing should hold on like that, it's obscene. Perhaps they're all dead in there and it's on auto pilot and it will fly in the stream on auto pilot all the way to England with us. Who says you'll get that far, Lambert? Perhaps this is it, goodnight, Nurse. Blow out the candles.

'Bombs gone,' said Digby. His voice was completely relaxed, until he too saw the bomber losing height alongside them. 'My flaming oath.'

The other Lancaster's fuel was atomizing as it left the trailing edge of the wing and burning like a gas flame. A flare caught fire as it fell out of its flare chute. So white it seemed almost blue in a world coloured yellow and pink and red.

'Hold her steady, Skip, for the photo,' said Digby.

Lambert saw green-and-red pistol flares make a string of brightly coloured beads as they were jettisoned, already alight. He looked at Battersby who was occupied at his panel. The cockpit was golden with the light of the flames while thirty of the longest seconds in the history of the world ticked past.

'You cow. Flare chute's bent, Skip. The bloody flash is jammed in it.' Jimmy's voice.

'Kick it out,' said Lambert. 'I'm not holding this for ever.'

'It won't budge.'

'Make it bloody budge,' said Lambert. All that and they hadn't even got a picture for the Photo Ladder. He sighed as he banked the bomber over and slid into the darkness, away from the fiery aeroplane that Murphy and Sweet were trying to coax back to earth.

'That aged me ten years,' said Jimmy Grimm, who had been watching the burning bomber.

'Any luck with the flash, Jimmy?'

'Still trying, Skip.'

Grimm had echoed his thoughts but captains just don't say that kind of thing. That would be the second time this month he'd come back without a photo. On the Intelligence Officer's board the three rows of target photos arranged in chronological order would include one print that was merely a shiny blank card. Nor would there be caption detail either. It would be as if Creaking Door and its crew and its bomb-load did not exist.

'Watch for night fighters, everyone,' warned Lambert.

''Kay, Skip,' the gunners acknowledged dutifully, although they had not ceased searching the sky for one instant.

Lambert tasted the stink of rubber in his oxygen mask and knew that he had broken into a flush-sweat of fear. He unclipped his mask and wiped his face. His jaw was stiff and his chin was stubbly.

'Only one HE. All the rest were incendiaries and phosphorus tonight,' said Digby.

'Glad I didn't know that on the run in,' said Battersby.

'Concentrate, chaps,' said Lambert. Here was the moment of maximum peril. The tension of the target was suddenly replaced with a relaxed relief and a surprise at being still alive on the far side of the flak. Now came a terrible tiredness and with it a lack of fear, an inability to concentrate and an almost overwhelming desire for sleep. Men had returned to tell stories of crewmen – even pilots – who fell completely asleep on the return journey. Other crews did not return to tell the same story.

'Concentrate,' repeated Lambert. 'There are fifty million dedicated Germans trying to kill us. Concentrate.'

Lambert always said that or something similar. Jimmy Grimm nodded over his radio set and to help him stay awake he poured a cup of coffee from his Thermos flask and sipped it. It was scalding hot. From his rear turret Flash watched the target burning: a scattering of pink blobs. Suddenly one blob swelled and went white for a moment. It was the roof of the Liebefrau collapsing.

Lambert's head ached. He slipped an aspirin into his mouth. Binty took his Benzedrine. Battersby entered up the fuel change in his log book. In his navigator's log Kosher wrote 'Unidentified four-motor aircraft on fire over target'.

By now the moon was high. It wasn't the golden orb that dust particles colour for men on the ground. From here they saw it as it really was: a cold blue cipher in the sky. The landscape was blue and black and it was possible to distinguish dark patches that were towns and the edges of fields and trees. He saw the River Maas glint in the moonlight and then on the river a dark patch that was Venlo winked as its flak opened fire. The ground was often obscured by greyish-blue patches of cloud that drifted past only 500 feet below.

'Steer 271,' said Kosher. 'That will take us a shade south

of the stream, with Eindhoven to port and Tilburg and Breda to starboard. That OK?'

'If Eindhoven turns nasty, you must steer me farther north of it.'

'Wilco, Skip. I'll come up and watch if I may.'

'Bring a friend.'

Eindhoven – a notorious flak concentration – was quiet as they flew across the outskirts. It wasn't until they neared Tilburg that they saw intense flak again.

'The coloured-light stuff is Gilze-Rijn airfield. Breda beyond it. Fifty miles to the Dutch coast . . . with this wind, say sixteen minutes.'

'I'm going to start losing height,' said Lambert. 'We'll put on a bit of speed if we put our nose down.'

North of Breda the flak was concentrating upon one section of sky while the searchlights moved busily through the flashes. Suddenly there was a reddish flash. Larger than the others, it stayed bright longer too. 'Scarecrow shell,' said Digby. Everyone in Bomber Command knew about scarecrow shells; they were designed by a German flak expert to look like an aircraft exploding in mid-air. Still today survivors swear they could tell the difference between them and the real thing. But there were no scarecrow shells, only exploding planes.

'Yes, scarecrow shell,' said Lambert.

Satisfied with his identification of Breda, Kosher went back to his navigator's table behind the curtain. Battersby watched Lambert's hands as he kept the compass steady. Battersby had been trained to hold a Lancaster upon an even course, although landing one had actually been one of his recurring nightmares while he was training. The controls were tremendously heavy to move and yet Lambert seemed to use only his fingertips. Now he watched him ease the controls forward.

'Beginning descent, Skip?' asked Battersby.

'I want the cloud on my belly,' said Lambert.

Battersby nodded blankly. Lambert said, 'Nothing can get under our backside then.'

'What about radar?' asked Battersby.

'No, they need a final visual,' said Lambert. 'All OK, gunners?'

'Sure thing, boss,' said Binty.

'This clear-vision panel is fantastic, Skip,' said Flash.

'Good boys,' said Lambert. They were all good boys; Lambert was lucky. He let the Lancaster settle gently until it hit the greyish-blue bank of cumulus. Shreds of it poured across the wings and tufts made the windscreen opaque. He let the aeroplane wallow in the cloud, churning it up and sliding under it like a child hiding in bedclothes. Make the most of it, thought Lambert, ahead there was the Dutch coast. There this ragged cloud, like the land below it, ended. A vast plain of inert black treacle stretched below them glinting in the moonlight. That was the North Sea.

CHAPTER THIRTY

When the second and much larger wave of bombers began to attack Altgarten it wasn't fear that dominated the minds of its citizens. Nor, although this was in many minds, was it simple anger or a feeling of being victimized by fate. It was a neurosis of a kind that comes from being asked to do something beyond one's mental and physical capability. Life had got out of control. For the professionals, their jobs had got out of control. The fire-service officers had spent their lives handling one fire at a time with a plentiful supply of water and the telephones in working order. Tonight they faced over a hundred fires, many of them large and out of control. They were hampered by broken water mains, disconnected phones and exploding bombs. Now, just as they had the emergency power and phone lines almost complete and the water was pumping from the Mönchenstrasse sewer, it was going to start all over again.

There were many symptoms of this neurosis, and for some survivors it was the beginning of a mental breakdown from which they would never recover. One senior fireman was singing an old music-hall ditty over and over again as he worked at the pump. Several of the firemen at the hoses were speaking to the fire, swearing at it in a confused obscene mumble. At the Volkschule a Blockwart, after warning a group of people of the dangers of throwing water on to a burning incendiary bomb, had picked it up as though it was the demonstration dummy and inflicted upon himself very severe burns.

When the second wave of bombers began their attack, both Gerd Böll and his friend Bodo Reuter knew that it was going to be even bigger than the first wave. This was the way the *Tommis* worked and the fast-revving British engines were as loud as a swarm of hornets. Salvoes of bombs were centring on the fires. The noise hammered their eardrums and the blast plucked at their bodies. They both knew that a sensible man would take cover, but they moved up Mönchenstrasse towards the hospital fire in leaps and runs punctuated by long waits flat on their faces. There were several damaged lorries in the street; one – an Army lorry – was on fire. They passed it cautiously and then kept close to the walls until the last block before Dorfstrasse, where conscientious civil-defence men were throwing burning bedclothes and furniture into the street from a fire on the top floor.

Even before they turned the corner into Dorfstrasse they could see the fire at the hospital reflected in the wet roadway. The main street seemed to be running in blood as the brightly lit water rippled along the gutter. The air was full of sparks and the ground so littered with burning wreckage and incendiary bombs left to burn themselves out that Reuter trod into a patch of phosphorus. The goo burst into flame as he tried to scrape it from his boot. It was an evil, frightening substance that clung like glue. Reuter put his boot into the water-filled gutter, which extinguished the flame, but immediately afterwards it ignited again in the air. Finally Gerd used a piece of broken brick to scrape it away. Then they resumed their journey. Now they were stepping more carefully around the burning timber and white-hot magnesium fragments from the incendiaries.

They passed more than a hundred fires on their short journey and seven times threw themselves full-length to the ground as high-explosive bombs dropped nearby. Five times they were implored to give assistance in rescuing trapped people, but they refused, and even the angriest of civilians knew better than to argue with a TENO officer. Some of them, seeing Bodo's high collar, cuffband and black rank-patches, thought he was in the Waffen SS.

During the second wave's attack the fires got out of control. Even the most heroic fireman cannot survive a barrage of high-explosive bombs and the bomb-loads of the second-wave bombers had been planned with this in mind. Even after the last of the bombers had departed the effectiveness of the fire-fighting and salvage teams would be hampered by the delayed-action bombs. They would continue to explode for two more days.

Gerd Böll and Bodo Reuter always stayed together. They had de-fused bombs and tunnelled under masonry and walked across planks high in the air, each confident that the other would never let him down. Gerd Böll stayed with Reuter and Reuter's place was with his men at the hospital.

'Two hundred at least, sir,' said Reuter's Hauptwach-meister. 'Perhaps more, and that doesn't include the nurses who are up there with them.'

'And the basement?' asked Gerd.

'Another hundred. They can get out but there's nowhere to take them and they aren't exactly mobile. Some can hardly walk, let alone run.'

'No one on the top floor?'

'That's gone, it's just ashes up there.'

'What's that sound, like singing?' said Reuter.

'Screaming,' said the old NCO. 'When there's an explosion nearby or they see an incendiary they call out together. There's no panic, but being bedridden up there with a view across the city must be rather sobering tonight.' He gave a grim smile.

'The structure?' asked Reuter.

'All the front has gone and the steel went with it. The top floor is tilting according to one of the men who've just come down.'

'You've been up?'

'Half an hour ago, Herr Oberzugführer.'

'Let's go up and take another look. Bring a couple of messengers and a couple of strong fellows with ropes and axes.'

The journey up to the fourth floor was slow and circuitous but not dangerous. They used the service staircase as far as the second floor and although it was pitch-dark and littered with large pieces of debris it was intact. They passed through a crowded children's ward on the second floor and down a corridor littered with wet burned blankets. Through an office door on the left they glimpsed a surgeon carrying out an operation. Rembrandt-like lighting was provided by two oil lamps, an electric torch and five candles. They went through the broken doors to the old building and up the winding staircase. That was tricky, for in places the cantilevered stone steps had broken, leaving only broken stumps for toeholds, with a nasty view downwards that included sharp stonework projections.

Now and again they were splashed. Jets of water were striking the top of the stairwell and falling upon them in a fine spray. They waited patiently while another squad of TENO men and firemen lowered a door down the staircase shaft. As the door twisted Gerd saw the white face of an old man strapped tight against the board. His arms were slightly extended like those of a wooden doll. In short jerks he was lowered past them without a sound. Revolving gently, his face transfixed, eyes wide and mouth open, he was trying to remember how to scream.

Since Bodo's NCO had last visited the top floor, the roof had collapsed on one room, killing four radiographers. The floor tilted more now and there were cracks in the wall large enough to see through. Every minute or two the whole building groaned like an old man who has sat too long in one position, and like an old man it leaned a little more to one side. Always to the same side.

'Stay close to this wall,' Reuter ordered his men.

The floor lurched under them. The walls were bulging as the bricks expanded. The metal girders expanded too; pressed against the ceiling, writhing in the heat, they fired hot rivets across the room like bullets.

'How fast are they getting these people down?' asked Bodo.

'One team down the staircase, one by the airshaft. They are each taking about seven minutes.'

'Get the nurses out of here,' said Bodo.

'And the patients?'

'Get the nurses out.'

His Hauptwachmeister gave a perfunctory salute and turned to bellow at the men. 'You heard what the Oberzug-führer said, evacuate all nurses to ground level. We will start on this floor.' Without delay the TENOs hurried after the NCO, rounding up the nursing staff and ordering them to leave their patients. The nurses began to argue, but orders are orders.

'How long do you think, Bodo?'

'Not more than ten minutes, Gerd.'

Neither Bodo nor Gerd saw the first row of beds go. One of the TENO messengers swore and a nurse screamed and then the far end of the ward was empty. The light of the fire lit the ceiling, for there was no longer any wall, it had exploded out into the courtyard along with the beds and people. The second row of beds screeched as they slid across the tilted lino, for the wheels had the safety brakes on, but gravity was too much for that device. The beds collided and interlocked. Thrashing blanketed bundles grabbed at pillars and lost their fingernails. A nurse overbalanced and she toppled over. She slid on her bottom across the highly polished floor, trying to hold her flying skirts down all the way until she fell off the edge and into the courtyard two storeys below.

They were screaming now. Hysterical screaming which

neither alerts nor implores. Fatalistic yells and high-pitched cries were the final denunciation of an unjust world.

The TENOs linked hands. Gerd, Bodo and one of the TENO men had each grabbed a patient out of bed and, sharing the weight of their limp bodies, the six TENOs and Gerd inched their way from one handhold to the next along the hot bulging wall. Outside the bombs were exploding and flares were lighting the streets as bright as day. Shadows moved drunkenly and there was the continuous whine of shell fragments. The building was creaking and groaning now that the far end of the steel structure had collapsed. They felt the whole building sway with each explosion like a house of cards being blown upon. Each time dust and plaster fell noisily from the ceiling and sent up clouds of dirt. The abandoned patients were making more noise now, but the TENOs tried to close their minds to the distant cries.

They roped each of the three patients at the top of the circular staircase and two of the men went down to receive the lowered bodies. The stairwell was dark. The heat was coming up it like a chimney and there were bits of charred cloth and paper whisked skywards past them as they searched with their boots for the stone toeholds. For a moment a green flare directly above them lit the stairs like daylight – for there was no longer any roof – and then it drifted past, leaving them in an even more baffling darkness.

'Let me die,' one white-haired old man said repeatedly as they passed the rope under his arms. The stone was hot to his bare feet and he danced painfully upon the top step. 'Let me die, just let me die.'

'Shut up, you old fool,' Bodo shouted finally. 'I'll tell you when you can die.'

'*Jawohl*, Herr Leutnant,' said the old man in a clipped obedient voice that he hadn't used since 1918.

The TENOs worked without haste, testing each knot and examining each handhold, but their faces were flushed and sweat dripped off their chins. One of them took off his steel helmet and tried to clip it to his belt but in the darkness he fumbled and the helmet fell down the stairwell, ringing like a cracked bell as it hit the broken steps and bounced from wall to wall.

One by one the nurses from the top floor were coaxed, helped and handled down the stairwell. Then the patients were lowered on ropes. At last it was time to lower the last of the survivors. It was a woman scarcely conscious and whimpering softly as they fastened the rope around her. 'Soon have you down, mother,' Gerd encouraged her. She smiled in friendly disbelief. The steadying rope burned through when she was halfway down and she spun slowly round as the support ropes shrank with the heat. Gerd was halfway down the staircase, his steel-tipped boots wedged against the remaining inch or two of broken stair and his hands searching for a handhold. He spared a hand to grab at her spinning body and managed to slow the dizzying movement as she was lowered past him. She was still smiling. 'Nearly there,' said Gerd.

It was the TENO at the bottom who called up that she was dead. His voice echoed in the slim stone stairwell like some gatekeeper of the Lower World. That was when the whole of the old building collapsed, throwing beds and bed-ridden into the courtyard in one great heap of broken people.

'Six minutes,' said Gerd.

'Yes,' admitted Bodo. 'Damn them, we could have cleared those wards in another fifteen.'

On the ground floor one of the storage rooms for X-ray plates was on fire. Thick smoke was rolling down the stairs into the basement and many of the nurses were wearing wet masks.

In the courtyard torches flashed over the bent iron bed-steads and bloody blankets that were heaped upon the stone flags. It was senseless to worry about the blackout when the whole town was burning bright and visible for a hundred miles. Here and there the nurses and men were extricating a still-living body. 'Stretcher party,' they called, but it wasn't easy for a stretcher party to pick its way through the heap of two hundred bodies without treading on others that were still moving and groaning.

'Bombs gone,' said Digby, his voice completely relaxed.

When the two 250-lb phosphorus bombs from Creaking Door hit the old building the quick dropped flat upon the dead. The phosphorus bombs threw their showers of white sparks sixty feet into the air and they came down as pretty as fireworks with large fragments of burning phosphorus. A cluster of fragments struck Johannes Ilfa's legs. He knifed it away from the fabric and flesh but some were deeply embedded. Around him men screamed and fought and burned and sometimes survived. They wriggled like live bait and a few regained their feet like ghosts arising from a mass grave. Water had no effect upon phosphorus. The official instructions were to cover it in sand. Can you put sand upon a man's face?

Already Ilfa was finding it easier to reject the pleas of those too far gone to be saved. It was right to do so and logical too, but Ilfa told himself that it was one more step on the journey to inhumanity.

Ilfa, with most of the phosphorus splashes cut away, came coughing and spluttering through the smoke and heavy phosphorus fumes. The trim young fireman looked at the elderly TENO officer before saluting.

'Have your people got breathing apparatus, Herr Ober-zugführer?'

'It's ten minutes away,' said Bodo. His false teeth hurt him and he bit hard on his knuckle.

'Then, with your permission, we'll put my fellows in to sort through the bodies.' Ilfa coughed again.

'If only we could damp them down.'

'There's not enough water for that unless we abandoned the post office,' said Johannes Ilfa.

'What about the swimming baths?'

Ilfa wiped his moustache which, like his face, was glistening with water from the hoses. He'd used all the water from the municipal baths when they first ran short. Now he looked at the thin old TENO man and grinned.

'Sorry,' said Bodo Reuter. Like members of a secret society the two men recognized in each other the skills and judgement that were in such short supply this night. They looked up to the building opposite, upon which most of the water was being sprayed in an effort to prevent the fire spreading to that block. 'It's quite a mess,' said Ilfa tentatively.

'It bloody well is,' said Bodo. 'I don't envy you trying to sort out that heap if the bodies ignite.'

'My firemen are only kids,' said Ilfa.

Bodo nodded, but how old could this fireman be? His middle twenties perhaps, and yet now he walked across a dozen bodies without a trace of hesitation in his step as limbs flaked underfoot like charcoal logs.

There was a hesitant cough. Fuchs Ueberall was at Bodo's elbow; his flushed face and dilated eyes gave a clue to his suppressed hysteria. His voice was comically high-pitched.

'I can't go on, Bodo. Can't. I picked up a child and it came to pieces in my hands, Bodo. Can I go and give a hand with the digging? I'll send one of the boys back here. He came to pieces.'

Bodo Reuter grabbed his drinking-companion by the collar and turned it to squeeze his throat. 'I'm not Bodo, you *Narr*. I'm Oberzugführer Reuter and you'll call me sir, and you'll stand with your feet together and salute. And you'll do what you're told without argument and discussion or hesitation because, Ueberall, I swear to you by anything you can find to hold sacred right now that I will take a gun and blow your brains out if I so much as see you pause long enough to wipe the sweat off your big fat face. Now go.' He threw the man back towards the heap of bodies. Ueberall

447

stumbled and fell and as he got to his feet Reuter screamed, 'Understand?'

Like some young recruit, Ueberall sprang to attention and yelled, 'Yes, Herr Oberzugführer. Heil Hitler.'

'Heil Hitler,' said Bodo Reuter and to himself he said, 'They're not bowling, my friend.'

'No, they're not bowling,' said Gerd Böll.

Everywhere there were pieces of phosphorus. It lit up the whole place and gave off enough heat to ignite body-fat. Dead and dying were exploding with the same surprising flash with which a frying-pan ignites in the hands of a careless chef. Hair burned even more readily and the phosphorus and burning hair and flesh produced dense black smoke that attacked the eyes and mucus of the nostrils and made men choke and splutter. The heat was unimaginable and even the veterans were daunted by it. The largest pile of bodies was now blazing and no one could approach it.

'Breathing apparatus,' said Johannes Ilfa. He put his own on and it hurt him as he knew it would. He needed to inhale deeply to bring the air through the filters and each breath hurt his damaged lung.

The fire squad with its breathing apparatus moved slowly, like deep-sea divers. The nurses and the TENO men and the medical students and the fire-watchers, the policemen and the Blockwarten and the soldiers and the cripples who had tried to help the dying, withdrew. They climbed over the hot debris: a fabric woven of wood, brick and bodies. Their steps were lit by pieces of blazing phosphorus. Still chunks of brickwork and liquid roof-lead fell into the courtyard, but all the rescue workers reached the road except for eight nurses and seven men who were near the west wall of the old building when the chimney complex of the Annex collapsed upon them.

Johannes Ilfa had manned hoses, operated pumps and climbed over burning roofs. Splashes of phosphorus mottled his legs and, in spite of his knife-work, were eating deep into his flesh, burning with a foul smell. One of the youngest trainees reported Ilfa's wounds and he was ordered to a dressing-station.

Neither Gerd nor Bodo spoke of the two hundred men and women who had died in the courtyard. It was a taboo subject not subsequently mentioned except perhaps to a new recruit by someone who was there. Even then it was only after too many drinks and men spoke of it in whispers.

What was left of the old wing of the hospital had been pressed into use as a treatment centre. Here the dim lights of the emergency generator threw the scene into extremes of light and dark. Most of the patients were known to the doctors as they were wheeled in for surgery.

'Hello, Doktor Maurer,' said a girl who had been brought into the hospital for tonsillitis.

'We're going to have to take that arm off, Fräulein. You'll feel much better then, believe me.'

The out-patients' waiting-room had been converted into a multiple operating theatre in which eight doctors worked at once. A policeman with a bucket and pump hosed down the blood from the lino and a garbage can for severed limbs was wheeled through the ward on a tea-trolley.

In the corridor Johannes Ilfa, still cherishing his secret passion for Anna-Luisa, was ignoring his pain. He had been arguing stubbornly with a nurse who wanted to cut away his trousers to examine the phosphorus burns on his thighs. Now that he had rested for a while he began to realize how weak he had become. His lung hurt him more than ever. The nurse was a young trainee and she had no idea why the fireman was making such a fuss until a middle-aged ward sister came along. She had a piratical array of surgical instruments stuck into her belt and her hair had been frizzled by fire. She pulled her face mask down. 'Don't be so stupid,' she said angrily. 'Do you think you're the only one here who has soiled underwear?' Many had involuntarily emptied their bowels that night, but for Johannes Ilfa his decorum was to prove fatal. By the time his trousers and underpants were cut away he had died.

Along the corridor came two nurses in fancy dress: home-made kimonos and coloured sashes. One of them had been badly splashed with blood. Bodo Reuter watched the nurse tip Ilfa's slim body off the bench to make room for the living. Bodo took it by the hand as if to say goodbye and heaved it over his shoulder in a fireman's lift. 'We'll put him some-where,' said Bodo.

'Yes, let's get out of here,' said Gerd. 'It gives me the creeps.'

Outside in Dorfstrasse they put the body on the front seat of his Magirus fire engine before walking back along the hose lines.

'He knew his job,' said Bodo.

'Yes,' said Gerd. That accolade served as his epitaph for he got no other.

The sump constructed by blocking the sewer was still the main supply, but paper and sewage continually clogged the filters and the firemen had to pick them clean every few minutes, which left the hoses squelching air until the filters went back into the stinking water again.

The night air was hot but the men handling the hoses were shivering with cold and their hands were white, numb and stiff. A group of TENOs had three hoses on the far side of the courtyard dousing the neighbouring buildings that were not on fire. They soaked the walls of the post office and killed the deadly sparks. But the pump's five hundred gallons per minute was falling in shallow curves short of the post office roof.

'Disconnect two of those hoses,' said Bodo, 'or you'll never reach the next roof.' The men hurried to obey. 'And bring the pressure up to ten kilograms.' Gerd and Bodo waited while they disconnected the junction. This was diffi-cult to do while the water was pumping but a young fireman from the town fire service helped them. As the new pressure moved through the hose it bulged like a maddened snake, lashing from side to side in a frenzy that needed four TENOs to control. The new jet of water made a freezing draught that punched a hole through the black smoke and the firemen ducked their heads close to the nozzle of the hose to see through the tunnel of fast-moving clear air that fanned their faces.

The air was full of flying sparks like luminous locusts, with larger red embers floating gently downwards from the nearby fires. Each flash of light from the bombers' photoflash bombs, or from the explosions, illuminated the airborne flotsam. Some of the citizens of Altgarten were to survive to tell a story that the RAF dropped leaflets that night. Stories circulated of dire and ugly warnings of more raids to come, but, although leaflets were dropped upon Northern France that night, Altgarten got only bombs. The air was full of charred paper, some of it a thousand feet in the sky, but it had all come from the town itself. There were bills, wills, manifests, invoices, handbills, bonds, shares, love letters, warrants, carbon, dockets, leases, passes, deeds and misdeeds. Their scorched shapes floated on the warm wind and fell back upon the town like black snow.

Filing cabinets, deed tins, safes and post boxes were among the night's casualties, and one letter that journeyed a quarter of a mile into the air upon the thermal of the Nehringstrasse bakery fire had been posted by Gerd Böll that afternoon. His letter to August Bach came down in Liebefrauplatz and was run over by a TENO lorry, ripped by a fireman's boot and floated down a gutter into a drain and was lost in the sewer. It reappeared in pieces and was plucked off the hose filter several times until it softened and shredded and went through the wire mesh. It was only tiny specks of grey pulp when it came out of the hose nozzle and was sprayed into the heart of the fires that, in spite of all efforts, had started on the post office roof.

'Look!' shouted someone from the darkness as, high in

the black air above them, a Lancaster was hit and exploded in a red oily ball of flame. There was another bomber on fire too, but it kept steadily on its bombing run. Four spots of radar-controlled flak burst in a line under and beside it and finally, as its bombs fell away, the flak blew it to pieces right over the target.

It is impossible to forget the smell of a bombarded town. Under the sudden strange whiff of spilled perfume, chemicals or food, there is the constant stale aroma of wet cloth, charred wood and spent explosive. But dominating all else there is the smell of the compacted earth that has cradled the sewer pipes and the acrid stink of the dust from ancient bricks. Many of the rescue workers had tied wet handkerchiefs across their faces and had to drag them away in order to speak. 'Don't take the child away. He must tell us where his family were sheltering or we'll be sifting through this rubble for weeks.'

Herr Holländer had a busy night. He'd visited twenty apartments to be sure that no fire bombs were burning there. Between times he had put his head into the dark cellar where his flock were sheltering. He logged each visit and on the last one he had seen the bomber in flames above the city. As usual he called, 'Raid is still continuing but our brave fighters are giving the swine something to remember,' and as usual no one replied. The bombing was heavy enough to persuade him to stay there for a few moments. It was dark and fetid and since the 4,000-lb cookie had dropped across the road the fans were no longer working. Not that anyone had complained about that. They were automata, these local people, thought Holländer. They made good money in the brewery, for the Wehrmacht would buy all the beer that could be brewed. On overtime even a labourer had a fat pay-packet at the week's end. Some even had more pay than him. It was disgraceful. Now they were not even polite enough to make room for him to sit down.

He looked at their coarse hands and dull bovine faces and

452

the way their thick bodies had slumped against the support beams or fallen upon their neighbour's shoulders. One young girl had her head thrown back and her mouth wide open in a most unattractive manner. Sometimes he wished he could find a house in the Altmarkt or Mönchenstrasse – the nice end – or even the new estate. On the other hand his place in Kaiserin-Augustastrasse was so near his place of work, and so cheap.

The electricity had gone off and the oil lamps were spluttering in the foul air. He flashed his torch around to be sure that no one was smoking; that was strongly forbidden. It was as silent as a tomb. When Holländer realized exactly what had happened he let out a little yelp of fear. Or was it pain? Or perhaps compassion? Everyone in the shelter with him was dead, and had been for a long time. He had been visiting corpses. Eighty-six men, women and children with ruptured lungs had died without so much as gasping for breath. The human lung is a delicate device; even a pressure of seventy pounds per square inch will damage it beyond repair. The cookie near the brewery had done it, one of the first bombs that dropped.

Terrified, Holländer backed towards the door and tripped over some sandbags. He fell heavily. He was an old man; his brittle thigh bone fractured and the torch went out. The shadows from the oil lamps flickered eerily, but Holländer knew enough first-aid to realize that dragging himself to the door could tear a jagged edge of bone across the femoral artery and bleed him to death. He remained where he was. The rescue workers said he had a narrow escape. Two days later an astounded doctor made an X-ray of Holländer's lungs and sent it to a medical school in Cologne.

Firemen with breathing apparatus were salvaging the living from the mountain of dead in the courtyard. Now there was enough water to spray the hoses upon the workers. Their clothes were so hot that the water hissed and steamed as it fell upon them.

At Kaiserin-Augustastrasse 94 a man had insisted upon re-entering his blazing home to get his insurance papers and had burned to death. At one o'clock on the northern section of Dorfstrasse three men found with suitcases full of new shirts and sausages were summarily executed by a policeman. It was glass splinters in the sausage that made him certain they were looters. Frenzel's Stube had proved impossible to save and although the Frenzel family were finally forced to evacuate the place, forty-three bodies laid out there were incinerated when French brandy in the cellar exploded.

Frau Pippert, who had walked home along Nehringstrasse, helped to extricate a young policeman from a burning building and held him while a medical student amputated his trapped arm with a penknife. The policeman later recovered.

Four 4-lb incendiary bombs had hit the police station next door to the Rathaus and had been discovered and extinguished – although not before a senior fireman, who should have known better, had directed his hose on to a high-voltage cable and killed himself and rendered two other firemen unconscious for fifteen minutes. The shock shredded their trousers into rags and for the rest of the night they worked bare-legged.

It was a police motorcyclist who picked his way through the littered streets looking for Bodo.

'Herr Oberzugführer Reuter?' He saluted, and almost before Bodo returned the salute he was relaying his message and already eyeing the debris, deciding where there was sufficient space to turn his motorcycle combination.

'A *Tommi* has landed on Frau Kersten's farm. It is of vital importance that the crew do not destroy their aircraft before it can be examined.' Bodo nodded. He knew that certain parts must be sent to the special electronics laboratory that the Luftwaffe had set up in Dachau concentration camp. Jewish scientists were trying to discover the RAF's most cherished secret: the magnetron valve of the centimetric radar. 'Immediately,' he acknowledged.

'I shan't go with you,' said Gerd Böll. 'I'll get back to my cousin's house. His child and the housekeeper are in the cellar.'

'This is important,' urged Bodo. They both knew that Gerd would say, 'Not to me it isn't.'

Gerd nodded. 'A moment, please,' Bodo called to the policeman. 'Take this man to Mönchenstrasse.'

'Yes, Herr Oberzugführer,' said the policeman. Gerd climbed into the Zeppelin-like sidecar and using his powerful torch he helped the driver around the piles of timber and bricks. He looked back to Bodo and impulsively gave him a simian wave and pulled a face. Bodo waved and turned away.

In the centre of the street outside the hospital annex there was a TENO lorry on fire. The fire inside the building was so strong that the flames from the lorry were drawn horizontally towards the building. The motorcyclist drove round the lorry and by the light of it could see fifty yards down the road. As they reached Zillestrasse the lorry's fuel tank exploded with a tremendous boom.

Entombed in the cellar Anna-Luisa heard the lorry explode but was still not afraid. She had the child to comfort and in doing so she stilled her own fears. This basement had once been a kitchen and near the steps she found a small service lift. Its shaft was filled with rubble but alongside it on the wall there was a speaking-tube. She shouted into the tube too, but there was no answer. She could still hear explosions and she decided that most people would be sheltering from the bombs. 'We're safest where we are, Hansl,' she said. 'There is no hurry to go anywhere.' She fingered the fine silver and Meissen figures but without coveting them.

'I shall always love your father, Hansl.'

The little boy smiled. Everyone loved Daddy.

CHAPTER THIRTY-ONE

Had Sweet been able to inspect his own complexion at close quarters at that moment, he would have detected the faint bluish skin-pallor that warns of anoxia. His connexion had torn and he was getting very little oxygen into his face mask. The symptoms are an ebullient feeling of well-being and optimism far beyond that warranted by circumstances. Anoxia is a little like being cosily intoxicated.

Theoretically Sweet was right about the burning wing: at normal temperatures the fuel-air mixture in any partially full fuel tank is too rich to ignite. But the port outer tank of his Lancaster was not at normal temperature. At 20,000 feet, this summer's night was very cold and so too were the air-craft and its fuel-load.

The ragged edge of vapour fire trailing aft of the tank had done nothing to raise its temperature. Inside the tank the less volatile particles of fuel had condensed and thus weakened the fuel-air mixture. This is where the theory went wrong: the fuel was not only inflammable but highly explosive.

The rubber seal at the damaged aft edge of the tank had been on fire for several minutes. As it melted, burning rubber dribbled through the broken seam. The petrol splashing about inside (in spite of the baffles) doused the first few smouldering dribbles but finally an extra large one was sucked in by the vibrating seam. It produced the perfect conditions for an explosion.

Sweet thought that it was a direct hit by a flak shell. He would never change his mind. The concussion smashed much of the canopy Perspex and threw him sideways against his harness. The control column and rudder bar were momentarily wrenched out of his hands. Sweet was not sure what damage had been done, but Murphy, who had been expecting such an explosion, guessed exactly what had happened.

When the 114-gallon fuel tank exploded this broke the wing at the port outer engine. At the same time it fractured that engine's main girder at its point of attachment under the wing and partially severed a support at the wing's leading edge. Lacking that support, the burning engine began to buffet violently and within fifteen seconds it too tore itself away from what remained of the main plane. When the section of wing broke away the Lancaster continued for half a minute in an only slightly curving line. Then, its engine gone, the balance changed drastically. Lightened by the loss of the great twelve-cylinder Merlin the port wing tilted upwards. Gathering momentum, the huge bomber was beginning a roll. Sweet and Murphy put all their weight behind the control column but the port aileron and the section of wing attached to it had floated off into the darkness. The starboard aileron was little more than rags. Without ailerons to correct its antics Sweet and Murphy watched thunderstruck while half a dozen tiny orange spiders crawled up the starboard window and continued their movement over the clear Perspex roof and, faster now, hurried down the port window. That was Altgarten on fire. Each spider was half a city block blazing furiously. The huge aeroplane had rolled completely over.

Murphy had grabbed for his parachute and clipped it on as the plane began its roll. He knew that it must continue now. It would roll faster until centrifugal force made it impossible to escape from the bomber. Already his knees had buckled and he felt his whole weight pressing against

457

the cockpit floor and forcing him down towards the step in the nose position several feet below. Gripping the edge of the trunking around the throttle controls and projecting formers and metal edges, he dragged himself towards the black rectangle of night, kicking the fixtures of the folding seat to help him along. Once his broad shoulders were pinned over the edge of the bomb-bay housing, centrifugal force threw him head-first into the bomb aimer's position. His oxygen tube and microphone lead were throttling him. He tore them off his head but not before hearing Sweet say, 'No need to panic, I've got her.'

Already the Lancaster, with engines roaring, was beginning its second roll. It was moving faster now. The coloured lights and flames came nearer the transparent nose; she was tipping over into a spin. Frantically he bent his knees to get his boot-heel against the flat front of the bomb-bay. Panic-stricken, he kicked himself against the stiff airstream that smashed at him like an invisible sledge-hammer. Inch by inch and using every ounce of strength his leg muscles could give, he forced his body lower. The edge of the hatch bit into his body and caught every belt and buckle of his harness. Sweating and almost exhausted, his last kick got him into the black cold night. The centrifugal force threw him in a curve. As the curving fall flattened he found that he himself was spinning head over heels in a crouching position, his face close against his knees. He knew that he must not open his parachute until the spinning body stopped, but it did not stop. He waited for what seemed like an hour, until the lights flashing past him were dangerously close, and then he pulled the rip-cord anyway. The canopy and lines tumbled out of the brown-canvas cover, striking him in the face. He recoiled with the shock of the blow so that on the next revolution his feet did not go right through the support straps. Instead he was caught up in the harness by one boot. He kicked at it again but was unable to get free. He was frightened to kick too energetically in case he fouled the lines of the parachute and 'candled'. Cradled in his tangled harness like a baby in a stork's bill, Murphy floated gently down towards the stricken town. Once a searchlight passed across him and for a moment the silk canopy was blinding white. Murphy remembered a childhood prayer and said it aloud.

Sweet saw no reason for the engineer to go grovelling across the floor in abject panic. Sweet had been in plenty of spins. At elementary flying school it was a mandatory exercise. He didn't worry that the rate of spins was increasing, for he knew that the faster the spin the more air-speed he had and therefore the easier it was to regain control. He let the orange spiders come round again. By now they were dancing across the windscreen and he knew that his dive was almost vertical. Calmly he put his weight on one side of the rudder bar with both feet. He guessed it would need a lot of muscle, so he jabbed hard. There were no port ailerons and precious little port wing by now. Sweet fell forward, barked his knees and cut his knuckle. 'Damn,' he said mildly. He knew now beyond a shadow of a doubt that he must get out. The huge aeroplane was spiralling earthwards, its structure rattling and screaming. There were sounds of snapping metal. The altimeter needle was revolving backwards at a frightening speed. His hands were heavy weights that pressed upon his chest but he managed to remove his torn gloves to get at his harness and slowly he undid the strap. He checked that his parachute was correctly fastened and decided to get out by the nose-hatch. Statistically the nose-hatch was safest.

It was bloody silly, but he couldn't get up. He pushed and pulled and wriggled, but he couldn't get up. The force of gravity was pressing him to his seat so that his weight was beyond his strength to lift. There was a weight upon his head that gave him a double chin and made him feel sick. His blood, pressed downward out of his brain, dimmed his vision. Ridiculous. He had so much to live for: fit and handsome, he had a medal, two girlfriends (one with a flat in London), a little private income (his shares were doing nicely), promotion due in August, lots of good friends among the chaps. Why couldn't he get up out of his seat? His vision grew even darker as the increasing gravitational force of the spin drained his brain of its blood.

When Lancaster 'S Sugar' hit Frau Kersten's farm it made a crater thirty feet across and in places eight feet deep. The largest remaining part of it was the tail section that landed two hundred yards away. The rear gunner – killed in the initial attack – was still in his turret, which broke off before the impact. The forward part of the fuselage had hit the side wall of the farmhouse and demolished the whole building. Broken bricks and chunks of plaster almost covered torn and scorched paper money and coins that glinted in the light of torches. Saucepans were mixed with altimeters, bedheads with fuel lines, and pieces of Frau Kersten and her French soldier were intimately mingled with Flight Lieutenant Sweet. There were tattered ailerons, bent flaps. One hot twelve-cylinder engine had drawn a scorched furrow across the grass and lopped a tree. Another had turned the cowshed into a butcher's shop. There was a stink of burned oil and hot carbon and the red-hot metal pieces tinkled like sleigh bells. Among the personal effects found in the wreckage there were an ivory-handled knife with a cigar-cutting device, a warm bunch of keys, the bomb aimer's left boot and a torn flying helmet with 'Murphy' written on it in nail-varnish.

Bodo Reuter and his lorryful of TENO men arrived on the scene of the crash fifteen minutes after it had happened. He organized a search to be sure that no diaries, log books or radio equipment had fallen clear of the main impact points. Fuchs Ueberall and another TENO man found an RAF flyer tangled into a tree only a hundred and fifty yards from the crash. He was a burly figure who smiled nervously when challenged. The two TENO men killed him with their spades.

CHAPTER THIRTY-TWO

When the illuminated glass map had been in use for an hour the lightbulbs, warm varnish and painted metal gave off a smell that mingled with that of floor polish and tense bodies. All Luftwaffe T huts had this same smell when the air battles were at their peak. The smell, the tension and the glare from the Seeburg table combined to give August Bach a dull headache. It always did. When the raids ended early, or when the bomber stream's return route was over some other sector, he liked to stand outside the door, sniff at the ocean and let the night breeze refresh his tiredness and the darkness rest his eyes. The red blip turned gently and headed towards Utrecht. That was at the extreme eastern range of this sector. August corrected the fighter's course.

'He's getting away,' said Willi Reinecke. He followed the light dots with his wax pencil. He had traced a twisting record of inexpert attempts to intercept wherever the two lines intertwined. Now the two lines were converging once more and Willi's pencil hovered, trying to will the fighter on to its quarry.

'Order: increase speed, Katze Eight,' urged August.

In the darkness Leutnant Beer was staring ahead, trying to see the target. He glanced enviously to the north where the sky was lighter. If he had them that way he might be able to see them but heading eastwards towards the banks of cumulus that made the horizon ragged and ugly there was little chance of getting the *Tommi* silhouetted. If any of those fellows had ever been in an aeroplane at night they would have more sympathy than this edgy bad-tempered fool who, just because he could see the red blip clearly upon the table, thought that it must shine clear and visible up here in the sky. It was so lonely here, almost like being at the bottom of the sea with only a distant flicker of light to indicate that the world is awake – or even alive.

On the port quarter there was a battery of ten searchlights that moved aimlessly, slowly changing their abstract patterns from vertical bars to a grey ghost of a pyramid that even as soon as it was built was demolished and became Vs and Xs. A lot of help they were! Beer knew that should he wander near those beams they would try to kill him.

On the starboard quarter, eighty miles away, he could see the target being attacked. Distance had drained all colour from the flares and explosions and from here they were just a steady flickering grey pinpoint.

'He'll never catch him now,' said August in a long-suffering voice. 'Order: orbit beacon at 6,000 metres.'

He switched Beer off and connected himself to the red Würzburg operator. 'Give me another *Tommi*.'

'Very good, sir. There are still plenty coming.'

Willi Reinecke had long since taken off his jacket and tie and now he stretched his arms in great circling movements that relieved the aches in his limbs. With his battered face, shaggy hair and huge shoulders he looked like a clown acting up for a circus audience. But no one laughed.

'Is everything all right, Willi?'

Willi nodded, but August knew that all was not well. 'There's something wrong?' Anxiously August looked back at the table and across at the altitude charts. Had he made a fool of himself in front of them all? Had he put that last one in at the wrong altitude and then blamed him for failing to contact? He could see nothing wrong.

'Don't act up, Reinecke,' said August coldly. He knew

that something was wrong, but he would not be made a fool of by a subordinate. Not even his second-in-command. Unterfeldwebel Tschol, the senior messenger – a white-haired old man from Innsbruck – was also looking at August in a way that was quite unlike his usual demeanour.

Willi tried to pull his fingers off his hands and made loud clicks with their joints. 'It's the target,' said Willi finally.

'The target? . . .'

'They marked it precisely as far as we know, although some markers went down over Duisburg. The mist of the Ruhr would make a difference. Perhaps there's a reason, but could there really be?'

'What target?'

'The *Tommis* are carrying out a precision bombing attack upon Altgarten, sir.' Now he'd said it.

'That's impossible.'

'An error . . . winds wrong . . . a marker aircraft destroyed . . . equipment damaged.'

'Altgarten? The whole stream?'

'I'm afraid so, Herr Oberleutnant.'

August tried to visualize the scene there and for a minute he did not speak. 'Take over the table, Reinecke.'

'Sir.'

'Tschol, tell the telephone switchboard to connect my office phone to this number.'

Tschol took the scrap of paper but stood for a long time before acting upon the instruction. They both knew that he was giving August plenty of time to change his mind about the call. Such a thing was strictly forbidden.

'In your office?' said the messenger finally.

'Yes,' said August, 'and they must try the other numbers if there's no answer from the first one.'

'It's a court-martial offence,' said Gefreiter Orth the telephone operator when he was told to connect the CO to a private phone number in Altgarten. His cunning little eyes glinting as he watched Tschol's reaction.

'It had better not be,' said Unterfeldwebel Tschol.

'I'll fiddle it somehow,' said the operator. 'I wouldn't drop the old man into the dirt.'

'You'd better not,' said Tschol. 'If we lost him we might get that old bastard from my last station. You'd be sitting there in best uniform, pressed and clean with a cropped head, just in case some high-ranking snooper called by.'

The telephonist, dressed in vest, shorts and sandals, rubbed his stubbly chin and shuddered at the thought. He looked round at his little sanctum. Pasted upon the wall above the PBX there were a dozen nudes, a pair of baby's shoes, a crucifix and a warning notice, '*Feind hört mit!*' With a caricature of a big-eared Winston Churchill.

Orth was not only the most unsoldierlike man at Ermine, he was its most notorious black-marketeer. It was a well-known fact that when Orth hung the enemy-listening sign on the door it meant that the police were tapping the phones for security purposes.

'Rotterdam? This is Luftwaffe Signals, Ermine. I want a top-priority connexion to Altgarten, Rheinprovinz. It's by order of General Christiansen and should not be recorded in the log. If you want details ask Stabsfeldwebel Braun for a written authority. Yes, I'll wait, but only for a moment.'

The white-haired Tschol bit his lip anxiously. 'Is he asking this fellow Braun?'

Orth winked. 'Braun's one of our people for eggs,' he explained.

When the phone rang in the cellar Anna-Luisa was half asleep, for the ventilation fans had stopped and the shelter had grown warm and airless.

'Krefeld exchange here. Will you take an official call routed via Luftwaffe Signals Rotterdam?'

464

Before she could answer and even amid the crackling of the damaged phone lines she recognized August's voice. 'Anna-Luisa. Are you all right?'

'Perfectly all right, Herr Oberleutnant,' said Anna-Luisa. She was by now wide awake and guessed that August was running a great risk by calling her. 'I . . . that is, Hans and myself are in the shelter of Herr Voss. Work is going on as usual,' she added to make it sound more official.

'Work?' said August. 'What are you talking about?'

She had been about to say, the air raid is going on but we are safe, but she remembered that it was a punishable offence to reveal that a place had been under air attack until three days afterwards. She knew too that security officials might be monitoring the call.

'All is in order,' she said. 'Everything exactly as I promised you this afternoon.'

'It will be as we decided,' agreed August, cautious for the same reasons.

The noise of Sweet's aeroplane coming across the town at rooftop height was loud enough for Anna-Luisa to hear it even in the depths of Voss' cellar. There was a great roar as it struck the ground. It fractured into pieces of metal, each one the size and weight of a motor-car, and the pieces bounced across the fields, shaking the ground at each impact.

'I can't hear you, Herr Oberleutnant. There's a scratching noise and your voice is so faint.'

'It will be as we planned it would.'

'Will what?'

'Nothing,' said August.

'What did you say after "planned"? You said "It will be as we planned . . ." then what did you say?'

'I love you,' said August desperately and rang off. 'Thank God,' he said quietly to himself and he returned to the See-burg table.

'We have another,' said Willi.

August took the microphone and spoke to Beer. 'Katze

Eight. Order: steer 270 for parallel head-on interception. Question: height.'

'Announcing: height, 4,500 metres,' said Beer.

August turned to Willi. 'When will the *Tommi* start to lose height, Willi?'

'Any minute,' said Willi. 'This one won't wait for the coast; I feel it.'

'The coloured-light stuff is Gilze-Riju airfield. Breda beyond it. Fifty miles to the Dutch coast . . . with this wind, say sixteen minutes.'

'I'm going to start losing height,' said Lambert. 'We'll put on a bit of speed if we do that.'

Kosher leaned forward and arranged Flanagan the cross-eyed doll more comfortably against the windscreen. 'Can't have Flan falling over,' he said.

Lambert had been given the doll before his very first operational trip and it had travelled with him on every sortie. All of the crew firmly believed that to fly without Flanagan would lessen their chances of survival and Lambert had put him under lock and key between trips ever since a gunner from A Flight had borrowed him without asking permission. Lambert noticed that all of the crew would touch the battered doll at some time or other during the trip, although Cohen and Jimmy Grimm would find some rational excuse for doing so rather than admit to being superstitious. Jimmy's wife had darned Flan's foot last month and was making him blue velvet trousers.

Kosher returned to his navigation table and Lambert nosed down gently towards the cloud bank.

Willi Reinecke spat loudly upon his hands. August sincerely wished he would not do that – or at least not so loudly – but Reinecke's father had also done so for luck before starting any job, and in medieval times it had been a necessary defence against the devil. What chance did August stand of preventing Reinecke from doing it? Anyway they could do with some luck, from any source available. Willi pressed the soft tip of his wax pencil upon the light blip to begin the trace. For the second time that night, Creaking Door was to begin a journey across Ermine's plotting-table.

In the shelter a spellbound Anna-Luisa replaced the phone. Softly she sang her favourite song of the moment. It contained a promise of magic. And love, she knew, was magic.

> 'I know that some time there will be a miracle
> And then a thousand fairytales will come true.
> I know that no love so big and wonderful can pass
>   quickly. We both have the same star
> And your fate is also mine;
> You are far away and yet so far
> Because our souls are one;
> And that is why there will be a miracle some time
> And I know that we'll see each other again.'

CHAPTER THIRTY-THREE

Gerd Böll was an expert in the strange new craft of bombed buildings. He knew that they could be divided into three main types. There were the ones that disintegrated into rubble and formed a pyramid of impenetrable debris. Then there were buildings that collapsed only at one side, so that all the floors on that side fell to the ground. The hospital had done that. Then there was this sort of ruin: the most difficult and treacherous of all. The floors had collapsed in the centre of the building so that they now formed several V shapes, jammed one upon the other and waiting for an excuse to settle lower upon a careless rescuer.

Gerd knew some of the ways of debris. He knew that a flimsy chair could support several tons of brickwork or lock with another piece of furniture to produce a miraculous cavern in the very centre of the wreckage. He knew that gas could collect in airless pockets and be dense enough to ignite a spark or overpower a man who put his head there. He knew the dangers of dripping water and he knew that a panicky person needed twice the diameter of a careful, calm one and because of that some rescue crews had been unable to return along their own tunnels. He knew the added strength of curving or crooked tunneling. In short, he was an expert.

'No smoking,' he told a soldier.

There was no one way to tunnel into the heap of debris

468

which covered Voss' cellar. Gerd Böll surveyed the whole heap of it. He peered at the piles of bricks and bits of wood. He lifted doors and mattresses to study the shape of the pile and to decide where the lines of thrust were. The top of the pile was twenty feet above street level and flattened abruptly into a plateau that had a slight bowl of subsidence. Normally he would have begun to dig as close to the ground as possible, but here at the top an old sofa and kitchen table seemed to form the entrance to a natural cavern through the rubbish. He tested it with his feet and when only a toy dog and some shattered plaster moved he decided that it was firm enough to burrow into.

He was able to get his whole body inside the wreckage by moving only a few bits of batten and breaking a chair-leg and passing it back to the men behind him.

'Herr Böll is on his way' he heard a soldier say. He imagined that Anna-Luisa would be taking it very calmly. She was a remarkably placid girl, Gerd thought, a schemer or a saint. No, saint certainly wasn't the word. 'Often debris provides a natural course for the tunneller and if possible he is well advised to use it.' Even though he was now crawling at a more shallow angle he continued to move along the line of least resistance. He was deep inside the pile of debris when he stopped for a moment to listen to it. There were a few creaks and cracks and the shuffle of powdered plaster, but no danger signals. When he was a child he had had slight claustrophobia. The doctor had told his parents to leave his bedroom door open. 'He'll grow out of it.' Gerd had overcome his fears and was proud of having done so.

'Saw,' he whispered. Cocking his hand back over his shoulder, he took the handle of it and working with his elbows against his chest and with the blade moving only three or four inches he was able to saw through the bookcase in ten minutes. Beyond it there were books and these he could only deal with one by one. Heine, Schiller, *The Treasure of Silver Lake* by Karl May, *Love's Labour's Lost,*

Home Medicine, One Man's Journey Through German West Africa, Memoirs of an Infantry General, Hay-box Cooking were all passed back to the TENO who was at his heels, and each permitted Gerd to crawl forward another inch. A pile of gramophone records cracked loudly under his elbow and a piece of fireplace cut his leg.

'Silence,' said Gerd, and the word was repeated back to the men at the entrance to the tunnel and then a whistle was sounded to tell passers-by to listen for the cries of the buried. But Gerd had been mistaken.

Anna-Luisa was not crying; she was sitting in an armchair with little Hansl held close to her, rocking him gently and smoothing his hair. He was asleep now, for something of the girl's calm had reassured him. Since she had spoken with August she had played the musical box a dozen times, examined the Meissen and the silver and walked round the storehouse until she had seen it all. Now, with the oil-lamp flame turned very low – for she knew it would not get light here in the morning – she waited patiently to be rescued.

Gerd Böll made excellent progress, taking under an hour to reach ground level. Progress slowed as he went on, for Gerd preferred to jam a piece of wood or brick tightly against the tunnel's roof to hold the wrecked house intact. When he came back he would remove his pit-props one by one. However, this made passing debris back difficult and whenever he could he packed it flat instead. There was still enough room for him to progress through the wreckage by removing only a minimum of obstructions. It was the easiest tunnel he had ever made, almost as if someone else had made it for him.

Like an archaeologist Gerd recognized the compressed layers that had once been storeys: through bathroom tiles into stair carpet and on through pieces of kitchen sink. The kitchen floor was stone and Gerd anticipated a long hard dig there, but it was simple enough. The flagstones had shattered and there was a wide pit in the soft earth. Gerd moved through the hole carefully but still he scraped his shins on the broken stone. He was at an angle of forty-five degrees now with his head downwards and it was an effort to prevent his legs sliding upon him while his hands were occupied with the blockages in front of him. Twice he did slide forward and had to use all his strength to stretch his legs out behind him to get purchase on the bricks and timber.

He was almost into the cellar when he reached the end of his easy tunnelling. In front of him there was a green metal barrier. It was two and a half feet across and circular in shape. It fitted close against the house debris, as the circular door of a safe fits into a wall. Gerd stroked the metal door and wondered what sort of household equipment it could possibly be. A water tank perhaps, but had ever a water tank been as sturdily made as this? Thick steel fixed together with massive bolts that could . . . A bomb, my God!

Gerd decided that it was the end of a medium-capacity bomb. A six-foot steel canister that had been dropped set for long delay with a celluloid heart full of acid eating its way through to detonate the Amatol.

It had dropped upon the wreckage and torn a passage through the rubble, which was why Gerd had found the natural path so easy to move along. He'd followed the bomb. Long delay, but how long: one minute, two minutes, twenty-four hours? Gerd went hot and cold and could hear his heart beating like a drum. A 1,000-lb cookie would obliterate half the street, and he was cuddling it. He felt the bomb and fancied that it was hot, although he knew it was probably the temperature of his nervous hands that deceived him. He thought he could detect the sharp odour of British paint and varnish that he'd smelled on other RAF bombs.

From now on he was tunnelling in earnest. He worked along the side of the metal, using the strength of the canister to support one side of his tunnel and building bits of broken stone and wood from it where necessary. It seemed as though his trip past the cookie would never end. He moved past the smooth steel shape and was six feet lower at the far end of it. Suddenly a piece of bedstead gave way under his elbow, the cellar wall buckled and collapsed, and he found himself sliding forward into space. He fell because, with remarkable self-discipline, he refrained from grasping at the bomb to steady himself. He landed heavily.

'Herr Böll,' said Anna-Luisa, opening her eyes to find the agile little man crouching on the wet floor, having appeared with the suddenness of a Demon King in a pantomime. He was covered in brick-dust and rubbing a sore elbow.

'That's a bomb,' he said, awkwardly pointing at the dark smooth shape that was only just visible through the gap in the cellar ceiling.

'It looks like a water tank,' said Anna-Luisa. She came closer to stare at the metal shape.

'No, I think it's a bomb,' said Gerd Böll, but now he had an uneasy suspicion that she was right. He smiled awkwardly at her and then asked, 'Did you get the ring?'

'Yes,' she said. 'It's in my handbag. Do you want to see it?'

'I think we'd better try and get you out,' he said.

'I love Herr Bach.' She took the oil lamp and turned the wick on full and Gerd shone his torch too.

'It's thicker than any water tank I've ever seen.'

'Herr Bach's hot-water tank in the apartment in Krefeld was just like that.'

'Have you got everything?'

'There are some wonderful treasures here, Herr Böll. Did you know that Herr Voss had such wonderful things?'

Gerd switched off his torch. There were lots of things he hadn't known before, he thought; like young Anna-Luisa having false teeth. Perhaps she'd forgotten that she hadn't put them in. He tried to think of some way of reminding her without causing embarrassment. 'Voss is a wealthy man,' he said.

'I like him,' said Anna-Luisa. 'We might be dead now if he hadn't made us take shelter.'

'I'll help you climb up to the tunnel,' said Gerd, shifting an armchair upon which she could climb. 'Leave the child. It will be easier for me to bring him, I've done it before.'

'I'm glad it was you who came, Herr Böll.'

'Why?'

'I always had the feeling that you disliked me.'

'I don't dislike you,' said Gerd blushing. 'About the marriage I'm not so sure, but I don't dislike you.'

'But I would make Herr Bach a good wife, Herr Böll. I promise you, I promise you.' The intensity of the girl's words and the simplicity of her emotions showed Gerd a side of her he never knew existed. He patted her arm awkwardly and feared she would weep. He wanted to tell her about the letter he'd written. So that she would not see his face he picked up the child.

'I promise,' said Anna-Luisa again, and suddenly Gerd was happy for the two of them. He knew that his letter would have no effect upon two people really in love. It was August who'd been right. What did it matter what the girl had done or had been? The chances of happiness were too rare and too fleeting to be put under a microscope. He himself had been a rake in his young days and yet that had not prevented him becoming a loyal and loving husband. Why should it not be true of this girl?

AC McDonald, RAF armourer, whose father now sat in a Dundee kitchen with three cups of untouched cold tea at his elbow and the telegram still in his hand, had done his last day's work well. He had fitted the type 47 pistol that morning and the celluloid was of one of the thinnest types used. As the bomb had left Lambert's bomb-bay a linen cord, still attached to the plane, had dragged the safety device from the pistol and rotated a pulley which screwed down a bolt upon a tiny bottle of acid. Now the acid had eaten through the celluloid until the spring-loaded striking pin had nothing left to restrain it. The pin struck the detonator and six hundred pounds of explosive destroyed the cellar and was heard across the whole town of Altgarten.

Two houses were totally destoyed and four severely damaged. Five people were injured, since by the time it exploded they had heard the 'all clear' and come back to their houses. Other delay bombs had been roped off but no one knew of this one. Seven TENO men, three policemen and Storp the old Blockwart from number 29, who was still digging down towards his wife, were blown to pieces, and a wristwatch belonging to one of the TENOs was found four streets away. No recognizable part or possession or garment of Gerd Böll, Anna-Luisa or Hansl was ever found, although even today splinters of Meissen and shapeless blobs of silver turn up in the gardens there.

One of the difficulties that the rescue workers faced was in the removal of dead and injured. Many bodies were glued to the road surface by the heat and were impossible to move without special equipment. The body of the Burgomaster's wife, for instance, held up traffic on Nehringstrasse for two hours.

Near the cinema a rescue team of TENO men were burrowing deep into a pile of debris. A whistle blew. 'Quiet, everyone.' There was still a lot of noise but every head cocked towards the rubble, listening for a call or groan.

'Stretcher party,' shouted an NCO.

'Wonderful,' said a policeman. 'There are thirty-eight people buried under that lot.'

'Morphia,' shouted the NCO, 'quickly.' The first light of dawn revealed deep craters in the streets and pavements littered with furniture salvaged from nearby houses.

On a piece of brickwork among the remains of Nehringstrasse 39 there was a chalked message: 'Kurt I am with Frau Weber love Kate'. Soon there were hundreds of such messages as the people of the town tried to reform themselves into groups: 'News of Herr Stroop please', 'Otto is dead', 'Peter is on leave', 'Mother stay here' were written alongside the bolder notes for rescuemen: 'Nine dead in rear part of cellar', 'Two dead first floor back room', 'Danger gas sump', 'Quicklime Danger'.

CHAPTER THIRTY-FOUR

The radar plotting-room was quiet enough to hear the electric clock jump each second.

'This fellow's a dud,' said Willi Reinecke.

'Keep the other aircraft up close and if this one makes a mess of this interception we'll not give him a second chance.'

On the Seeburg table the two men watched the dots crawling towards the coast. Both August Bach and his NCO had removed their jackets, but in the heat of the plotting-room their shirts showed patches of perspiration as the night wore on. It wasn't pleasant to see the destruction of a town happen before your very eyes, even if it was only represented by electronic dots. Willi picked up the glass of tea that had gone tepid. He drank without noticing that he did so. All the time the wax pencil in his left hand traced the moving dots across the table.

'He'll mess it up,' said Willi Reinecke.

It was all right for the others, thought Leutnant Beer, they all regarded flying as a mystical experience. For some of them there was nothing in life more important than becoming expert at controlling these uncertain flying machines. Beer, a motor-racing driver, had gone to his medical examination hoping to become a transport official or an administrative officer. The doctors had classed him fit for aircrew. The aptitude and intelligence tests showed suitable ratings and so he had found himself posted to the A/B School for pilot training. It was typical of the arrogance he'd met in the Luftwaffe that they all assumed he'd be grateful for the chance to fly.

Carefuly he followed every instruction given by the Controller at Ermine but he could tell the man was irritable.

Prussian arrogance! Beer was from Regensburg. His father and his family as far back as the Holy Roman Empire were Bavarian. To them all the so-called Germans outside the frontiers were Prussian. Bavarians were political animals, like the Austrians, and like the Austrians the world had labelled them *gemütliche* peasants and simple-minded clowns. Beer resented that.

Over his earphones came the voice of August Bach. 'Order: hold it.'

'Announcement: impossible,' said Beer.

'Give it some flap, man,' said August, abandoning procedure. 'You won't stall.'

Nor will you, thought Beer, in your cosy control hut, but he throttled back and put down more flap, although now he felt he must watch the air-speed needle very carefully.

Beer's radar man made contact. 'He's ahead of us and slightly below.' Beer eased the antlers forward a fraction.

'Kettle drums, kettle drums,' said Beer.

'The man's a genius,' said Willi. He put down his pencil.

'No, sir,' called Beer's radar man desperately. 'Much too much. I'll lose him off the top of the screen in a moment.'

The observer had his binoculars to his eyes. 'There he is.'

Beer cupped his hand against the Perspex to block off the reflections of the instrument panel lights, but his movement tilted the control column and they banked. He sat well back in his seat and brought the controls to normal. 'Still too far to port,' said the radar man. 'He's very close, you should see him.'

'I can still see him,' said the observer.

'Port and high?' asked the radar man.

'Yes.'

Beer still couldn't see it, but he cocked the guns anyway. The compressed air gave a hiss of anticipation.

'Too fast again,' said the observer.

'Yes,' agreed the radar operator from the back seat.

Damn them, they showed no respect for his rank. They spoke together as if he were superfluous. He put the nose up a trifle and watched the air-speed needle dip, but now the variometer was edging up to show that they were climbing. This business of matching speed with the target was not only the most difficult but also the most dangerous.

'He's turning left.'

'He must have seen us.'

'No, just correcting course.'

'Stop talking so much,' snapped Beer. 'I'm in command.'

The observer looked at Beer with cold disdain. The NCOs called him the cyclist because in the physical manner of a cyclist he trod upon his subordinates while nodding deferentially to his superiors. He wondered if Beer knew of his nickname and glanced at him again, but Beer didn't notice, he was staring ahead trying to see the *Tommi*.

Beer stared into the windscreen but could see only a pink sweaty face staring back at him. He could smell stale smoke in his nostrils. Damn that fire-fighting bastard too.

At first he could see only the reflections of the instruments. Then two flickers of light detached themselves and he knew that he was looking at the exhausts of an RAF Lancaster.

'We're right on top of him,' said Beer, staring down at the airspeed needle that was so close to stalling-point. Perhaps he should increase speed. Christ, the slipstream threw the Junkers aside and almost wrenched the controls away from him. Quickly Beer recovered control.

'We must get closer than this,' said the observer with a calm insolence. Beer reached for the throttles but changed his mind. He did not increase speed. He knew what a mid-air collision would mean. A giant like that would chop them into fragments and not even feel the bump. 'Much closer,' said the observer. There was a note of admonition in his voice.

Damned Prussian! Beer was the captain of this aircraft. Even if the target did not reach the edges of his gunsight, it was plumb in the centre. This was close enough, the Lancaster seemed gigantic and very near. 'Horrido,' he called and pressed the gun-button. He was yawing slightly, so the target slid to one side of the gunsight. He corrected with a touch of rudder. Not too much, he warned himself. Watch your air-speed.

The Ju88 was a fine aeroplane – a gentleman's machine – one that would fly hands off and respond gently and positively to the pilot. Yet it would not turn without plenty of rudder. Beer did not give enough and, as he tried to follow the Lancaster's turn, the Junkers slid sideways and Beer only recovered by means of a sudden burst of power that put his nose up.

Flash Gordon saw him because he was coming in high enough to be on the skyline. He saw the whole shape of Beer's Junkers pass across a piece of moonlit cloud. He had told Lambert and now the whole crew waited while these two pilots matched skills – and luck.

'He's a real expert,' said Flash. 'You can tell by the way he's waiting out there.'

'Scared shitless,' said Binty who was also watching him, but his voice lacked conviction.

'Keep off the air,' said Lambert. 'Flash, give me his ranges.'

'One thousand five hundred yards. Beginning to close now.' His voice changed to a more urgent note. 'Twelve hundred.' For an instant both gunners saw the Junkers as the moonlight struck the propellers and made them shine like a pair of spectacles in candlelight.

'Closing fast now.' Then, from between the glassy discs, there came white blobs that stretched and ran like spilt mercury. 'He's firing,' said Flash. 'Corkscrew port,' said Binty. Their voices muddled together on the intercom.

Lambert didn't corkscrew. He kicked the rudder bar and pulled both starboard throttles fully back. The Lancaster twisted abruptly to the right and jerked almost to a stop. Lambert prayed but also fearfully waited for the impact. Beer's Junkers came over them still firing, with only twenty feet between the tips of its propeller blades and the top of the Lancaster's rudders. The roar of it made the Lancaster's metal body sing with the vibration. Afterwards there was a kick of prop-wash.

'See him go, Skip,' said Binty gleefully from the top turret. Lambert was too busy to answer.

Battersby was not looking out of the window. He had watched Lambert's hands. It was the epitome of all he had been taught never to do. In theory Creaking Door should now have its tail ripped off. Battersby's hand reached out to the throttles as soon as Lambert's left them. Lambert nodded and with relief Battersby put the starboard engines back to cruising power. The Lancaster was sliding sideways like a sycamore seed. The compass went spinning as the nose moved right round the horizon and passed their original heading. The nose was inching upwards. The air-speed needle dropped towards stalling-speed and Battersby could see that the controls were mushy. Battersby watched the needle as Lambert pushed the stick well forward to put the nose down. The needle hovered at 160 mph, the aeroplane pulsating as it lost its airworthiness. Grudgingly the nose dropped and the needle started a return journey.

Lambert spared a hand for his microphone. 'Rear gunner, is the tail assembly OK?'

'It didn't half bend, Skip.'

'OK now?'

'Looks OK.'

'Happy, engineer?'

'Yes, Skipper, but at the HCU they told us never to do that or the tail would come off.'

'Not unless you give her too much rudder. Remember that.'

'I will, Skipper,' said Battersby.

'Any signs of the night fighter, anyone?'

'We've lost him, I think,' said Digby. 'Nice work, Skipper.'

'Bloody marvellous,' said Binty, 'you should have seen the bastard go. He was a thousand yards off to port and still firing.'

Beer was still firing long after the target had almost magically stopped in mid-air and sped off under his starboard wing. Now there was just the sound of the motors and the airstream. Beer's clothes squelched with sweat. They had only missed a mid-air collision by a few feet.

'I think we hit him,' said Beer.

'No, Herr Leutnant.'

'I saw the cannon shells hitting him.' There was no reply. Beer wanted a victory. He said, 'There were flashes, you saw them.'

'Your ammunition destroying itself at eight hundred metres. I saw them.'

Son of a stand-up, sawdust-on-the-floor *Wurstlerei* owner in a sleazy part of Nuremberg. How could you shoot down a real flyer? The observer had been washed out of A/B School with flying better than Beer's best attempts. He found it difficult to hide his contempt for this Bavarian peasant in officer's uniform.

So did Willi Reinecke. 'Messed it up,' he said, 'the stupid schlimiel.' The two blips had merged and when they separated again it was hard to know which was which.

'The *Tommi* is still going north-west,' said August. 'He's thirty kilometres from the main stream now.'

'He's making sure that the night fighter doesn't get a visual. Shall I call him?'

'Leave him,' said August. 'Call the other fellow in.'

'The *Tommi*'s coming a long way north of the stream, sir.'

'Shaken up a bit.'

'Faulty compass?'

'Could be.'

'He must be here, almost overhead.'

'He'll turn.'

'Yes, there he goes.'

'Bring in Katze One, Willi.'

Victor von Löwenherz looked at his wristwatch. He didn't trust the cockpit clock; the ground crews were not careful enough with them. He switched over to his main fuel tank and set the mixture to weak. He might need every last drop of fuel, for the *Tommis* entering his sector now would take another hour to return through it on the return journey. The last few bombers would be the most vulnerable ones. It was a simple matter of natural selection: the best pilots got promotion and the best aircraft. The best pilots would get the best navigators and would lead the attack. The least skilled pilots lagged behind, missed landfalls, lost their way, muddled their radio signals and had equipment faults that their careless pre-flight checks had not revealed. Sometimes such planes never found the target. Long after the Main Force had gone home they would be wandering alone over some remote heavily defended area presenting a keen Würzburg operator and controller with their only target of the night. If they did get to the target they arrived last when the defences were fully alert and the night fighters airborne with night vision adjusted. These crews got the planes that were slowest and the ones that could not climb. They were vulnerable targets and Löwenherz wanted to be quite sure that he was in the air when they arrived in this sector.

For Löwenherz was still in his assigned sector right over the beacon. Other pilots, like Himmel and even Redenbacher, had disobeyed the standing orders and followed the bomber stream along its route to the target. Löwenherz had not done that. He had patrolled his sector and obeyed implicitly the orders of his Controller, August Bach. Now Bach called him and told him that he had a four-motor *Tommi*.

'Announcement: a big car. Order: steer 300 degrees.'

'That's clear,' said Löwenherz. He increased his speed to overtake the *Tommi* before he was out of the radar range of his sector.

On the anti-aircraft cruiser *Held* 'Admiral' Pawlak and his K3 had had an eventful night of the sort that Pawlak had predicted. Now he reminded his friend of his prediction for the eighth time that evening. From the moon-rimmed cumulus to the south-east came the sound of a plane. Then other planes.

'From the south-east,' said Pawlak. 'Why from the south?'

'Night fighter.'

'Looks like it.'

'He's firing. He's got him.'

'Got him?' scorned Pawlak. 'Lost him, you mean.' He danced a little mime in which he threw a shell upon the loading tray, swung the rammer, spun the elevation wheel and the traverse and fired the gun. Klaus watched him dolefully.

The alarm buzzer made them rush back into their turret. Pawlak banged his elbow on the balancing-spring cover. Klaus smiled to himself.

In the fifty-five minutes that it had taken Lambert to fly from the German convoy one hundred miles to the target and back again the convoy had sailed only nine nautical miles along the coast – although the *Held* had done a little more than that, for it was now a mile ahead of the convoy instead of at its very rear.

Lambert's evasive movements had brought him well north of the Flight Plan. Not even the edge of the bomber stream passed over Scheveningen. So the only blip on the *Held*'s Würzburg was Creaking Door, until Löwenherz came creeping up behind them.

'Fire!' It was radar-controlled firing and twelve of the guns were 10.5s like the one that Pawlak manned. The explosions made a straight-line pattern of stars in the air.

The radar computer purred smoothly as it corrected the sighting so that the next salvo would compensate for the speed of the aircraft. The pointer moved and the gunners followed it. The guns fired in salvoes, so it was no advantage that Pawlak loaded at almost twice the speed of all the others. He waited. Pawlak only did it to demonstrate to his friend Klaus Munte the way he wanted the loading done in future.

That no better rate of fire was achieved by Pawlak's haste made the accident especially tragic. There was little for the naval surgeon to do. 'That damned breech has made as neat a job of amputation as I ever saw.' He clipped the veins and sewed up the wrist as best he could and let Pawlak sink into a deep, morphia-induced sleep.

Klaus Munte would not open the breech. The Leutnant in charge was about to insist that Munte did it but finally relented and did it himself. When they did open it the unused shell was difficult to remove. It was glued into the mechanism by an unrecognizable substance like raspberry jam.

Radar-controlled flak always bursts in patterns, one burst for each gun in the battery. Some RAF crews remained calm enough to make notes of the flashes for the Intelligence Officer. This salvo was well spaced on a south-easterly axis. The next one was even better and the third was the most accurate of all.

Whether using radar or visual sighting the aiming of an anti-aircraft gun is a complex skill. Both Lambert and Löwenherz were travelling at 240 mph, which required the shells to be aimed at a spot nearly one and a half miles ahead of them. Before each shot the fuse had to be set accurately and even if the target's course remained constant the range kept changing with the angle of the gun.

The rearmost shell of this salvo exploded seventy-one feet from Löwenherz's port motor. The theoretical lethal radius of an exploding 10.5-cm shell was fifty feet. This one fragmented into 4,573 pieces of which twelve weighed over one ounce, 1,525 weighed between one ounce and a fiftieth of an ounce and 3,036 were fragments of less than a fiftieth of an ounce.

Twenty-eight fragments hit Löwenherz's Junkers. Four pieces penetrated the port motor and others went into the wing and fuselage. The antlers were wrenched out of his hands as the ailerons were torn and buffeted by the shock-wave. The port motor's oil pressure and boost dropped, then the oil temperature shot out of its marked place and swept clockwise. The motor was losing oil rapidly. Mrosek could see it escaping into the air looking, not dark and turbid, but white and sugary.

Löwenherz put the nose down and closed the fuelcock. Then he gave the port motor a burst of throttle to use up the last of the fuel and thus lessen the fire risk. Feather the prop, ignition off, extinguisher on. He'd done the whole thing while subconsciously remembering the positions of neighbouring airfields. None was very near. Valkenburg, the nearest, was right under the stream; he didn't fancy that. In the moonlight ahead he saw the complex pattern of the islands and estuaries of Zeeland where outfalls of the great rivers of Europe fought a meandering battle with the low flat lands of Holland.

He recognized this coast. He'd done many forced landings here – in nightmares just before he awoke. Dump the fuel. He pulled the top off the emergency box beside his seat. The fuel came out of his tail like a fine silvery feather fifty feet long, glistening in the cold moonlight. He closed the cooling gills on the failed motor and gave the good motor a trifle more power. Then he changed the trim to keep her nose high. It was exactly like the emergency instructions in the instruction manual, except that the author of that manual had never flown on one motor in a plane with radar aerials stuck into the nose like a toasting-fork. He watched the 'turn and bank' indicator and saw that the Junkers was flying lopsided. It was sinking at five metres a second according to the variometer and he couldn't lessen the rate of descent. The altimeter crawled backwards.

'Strap tight,' said Löwenherz to his white-faced crew. The Ju88 was not an easy aircraft to force-land on one motor. They had all watched one burst into flame at the end of Kroondijk's main runway only seven weeks ago.

Löwenherz looked at the man beside him. Not a word was exchanged, but Löwenherz was convinced by the look.

'Bale out.' Mrosek wrestled with the floor hatch but it had been damaged and would not open. He looked up at Löwenherz in desperation.

Löwenherz detached the rear part of the cockpit cover and it flew off with a terrible roar that left them in an icy gale that whined and hissed across the edges of the windscreen. It spoiled the trim, so he touched the wheel to bring the nose down. Mrosek went first. Carefully he tucked his Zeiss binoculars inside his tunic. 'Lost in action' – he would not be asked to account for them. Agile as ever, he climbed out through the top like an acrobat. One of his boots swung dangerously near to Löwenherz's head, then he had wriggled clear. At first it seemed a perfect job, but a nasty thump told them that the slipstream had batted him back against the plane's tail. The slipstream threw him forward so that the binoculars crushed his rib-cage and broke four ribs. Tumbling head over heels his wrist struck the leading edge of the port tailplane and the fin gave his head a glancing blow before he was sucked away in a slipstream of fuel spraying from the jettison pipe. Overcome by the fuel and the blow on his head Mrosek fell 3,000 feet. Then night air blowing across his soaked clothing refrigerated him. Without fully regaining consciousness he pulled the ripcord and floated down under his canopy safely into a potato field.

Sachs had always been a bit timid. Löwenherz had seen his papers and knew that the pilot's section and officer candidate board had both failed him because of this. Löwenherz decided that he would need more than just an order. Especially to use the top escape exit.

'If you don't go immediately, I'm going to jump and leave the aeroplane to you.' Sachs climbed out then. Armed with the sort of luck that life had always provided for this rich young radar man, he was carried well clear and made a perfect descent.

The first sharp pang that Löwenherz had felt at the moment of the explosion had by now become a dull wet ache. It was as though an uncomfortably hot barber's towel had been pressed against his belly and wrapped around his middle. Its cause was a broken fragment of a knurled brass pin from the flak shell's nose-cone fuse. The pin had punched a tiny hole in the stressed metal skin of the aircraft's nose and split into three parts after hitting the gyro compass. This piece, weighing only one-sixtieth of an ounce, entered Löwenherz's belly. It passed through the abdominal wall and the peritoneal cavity, puncturing his ascending colon. It began to tumble as it lost speed, chewing its way through small arteries and a kidney before cracking open one of his lumbar vertebrae. There it nestled against his spinal cord, compressing it slowly.

It was not easy to hold the starboard wing down now that the motor had failed on that side and it was buffeting fiercely under his hands because of the damage to the metal wings and the tattered frabric of the ailerons themselves.

Löwenherz smiled grimly to himself. It was the very devil of a predicament. When he throttled back he began to lose height immediately. Yet with the good motor on full throttle to maintain height it carried him round in huge circles. No matter how much he tried to correct the turn with the ailerons it made little or no difference. The Ju88s were all like this, they needed a lot of rudder to turn them, and Löwenherz couldn't even feel his feet, let alone use them upon the rudder bar. He pressed a hand upon his left knee to use his lower leg as one might use a stick to prod at the rudder, but the pain on his spine was terrible. He continued to do it until the moment when he almost blacked out.

He called up the Controller and told him briefly that he'd been hit and wounded and was heading due west over one of the great islands south of Rotterdam.

'Get out, Katze One,' called August Bach urgently.

'Announcement: impossible,' said Löwenherz. 'I've damaged my back.'

'Order: turn back.'

'Losing height too fast. These damned aerials.'

'Order: keep the radio on,' said August. 'We've switched the emergency service into the circuit. They'll take a fix on you for the rescue boats. The Würzburg will hold you too.'

'Thank you,' said Löwenherz.

The life had drained from Löwenherz's lower limbs so that only the upper part of him was truly alive. His vision was affected too: the red and green lights on his panel and the bright blue moonlight became a neutral grey. The noise of the one good engine seemed quieter and he wondered if that was why it could not hold the heavy Junkers in the air. The grey aeroplane descended down to the grey ocean and the flash it made as it hit the waves was grey like the water into which it sank.

Sadly the Würzburg at Ermine followed the Junkers out over the ocean until the blip became a phosphorescent glow that died away. The tube was blank except for a rain of interference.

When the great red flash appeared far out across the dark water a sentry phoned the Control Room to tell them.

'He's gone,' said Willi. 'The sentry saw the explosion.'

'It's always the best ones we lose.'

'It was the Staffelkapitän,' said Willi. 'I know his voice.'

'One of the best pilots we worked with.'

'He was a count or a baron.'

'Damned bad luck.'

'That bloody flak ship.'

'There was no way they could know, Willi.'

'They're probably painting a ring round one of the guns.'

'Probably.'

Each of Creaking Door's encounters with night fighters had lasted only a few seconds, but between those encounters had come the tension and tiring concentration of one hundred miles of cross-country instrument-flying. After he had evaded Beer by the sudden turn to starboard Lambert continued on, nervously examining every quarter of the sky, but soon it was clear that they had escaped from that attack.

Binty Jones said, 'Skip, can Jimmy give me a break? I've got a touch of cramp.'

'OK with you, Jimmy?' Lambert said.

'OK, Skip.'

'Quickly, then.'

Lambert felt the trim change as first the wireless operator went back to the upper turret and then Binty climbed down from his seat in the roof and moved farther back to the Elsan just ahead of the tail. Jimmy Grimm, like most of the wireless operators, was a trained air gunner and he enjoyed the view that the turret afforded him. He touched the grips and the turret turned obediently, the machine guns tilting at the merest finger-touch. One of the worst aspects of the wireless operator's job was the heated-air outlet that emerged near his seat. Even wearing the minimum of flying kit, Jimmy had become uncomfortably hot. He slipped one side of his helmet off and pressed his face against the ice-cold Perspex of the turret. It was like a long draught of cold beer.

'OK, Jimmy?'

'OK, Skip.'

Lambert saw the flicker of the navigator's light as his curtain was pushed aside and guessed that Binty had come forward to the cockpit for a moment. Binty cherished a conviction that flying a bomber was little different from driving a motorcycle and he liked to watch Lambert's activities and tried to commit them to memory. He noticed that the altimeter was steadily turning as they lost height. It was the usual procedure to exchange height for speed from the time the enemy coast was crossed on the return journey.

'What about that photoflash, Binty? See if you can push it out, will you?'

'Can someone give me a hand, Skipper?'

'No,' said Lambert.

'I'll give a hand, Skipper,' offered Cohen.

'OK,' said Lambert. 'See what you can do.'

The moonlight that revealed the bombers to the night fighters was also reassuring to an alert bomber crew. Löwenherz was still dancing through the puffy cumulus far behind them over Rotterdam and no one in Creaking Door was aware of his existence. Leutnant Beer had been assigned to a southern part of the Ermine sector. In short, there was not an enemy in sight. Over the ocean one would not expect an 8.8-cm flak gun, but even if by some magic one was there, Creaking Door was nearly three thousand feet higher than the effective range of an 8.8-cm flak gun.

Lambert was relating these facts to himself when a 10.5-cm shell – with its superior range – burst near Creaking Door's tailplane. It came from the tail; a strangled thump. A giant's belch that rumbled along the metal throat of stringers and formers. Then came the bad breath of cordite and burning, speeding on the wave of displaced air that pushed Lambert forward against the controls, shook the extinguishers loose and sent Kosher's charts to fill the cockpit with fluttering paper. There was a flash of light too. That came from inside the fuselage. It made the screen turn white and blinded Lambert, whose eyes were adjusted to the dark night.

The control column came to meet Lambert's belly and even with all his strength he could not prevent it coming. Door's nose reared up like a frightened horse and the sound of the motors changed to a new note of anxiety.

'Micky,' said Lambert, 'Micky,' and Battersby rushed to his assistance, for he knew that he was the one that was needed. Binty Jones had been thrown to the floor by the explosion. As he picked himself up he knew that Door had been mortally hit. Then there was another great flash – bigger than any flak shell – a great white soundless explosion right under Door's belly.

'Take a look, Binty,' said Lambert. 'Back there.'

Binty got to his feet while Battersby put his foot on the pilot's seat supports and pressed against the column as hard as he could. His face was beetroot red and the veins on his forehead shiny with exertion.

The controls remained unyielding, although, with little Battersby there to push, Lambert was able to hold them still. Lambert checked the other controls: the rudder bar was slopping from side to side and the trimmer wheels did not respond. The elevators were unmovable and all the time the aircraft's nose was trying to come up. Both of them were using a lot of energy and Lambert doubted whether they could fight the column forward for the whole trip across the North Sea.

Binty pushed the navigator's curtain aside and was met by a blinding green light. It was so unnatural that he crossed himself and wondered if they had entered Hell as a crew. The green light flickered and died. Suddenly it was pitch-dark and there was a stench of burning cordite and rags. Binty Jones edged aft through the darkness. He groped towards Kosher's seat but he was not there. He continued climbing up over the main spar and past the bunk. The interior of the plane was billowing with smoke. Cautiously he stepped into it and walked as far as his turret before he saw the hole in the fuselage. He knew that the metal skin was thin and that a blow with a pencil's end could drive a hole right through it, but that did not lessen the shock of seeing a gap big enough to drive a small car through.

Because the explosion had broken a section of metal skin

away from its rivets and bent it back upon itself the hole was rectangular. The metal rattled angrily in the airstream like a monstrous letterbox flap. For a moment there was less smoke and Binty saw through the hole. There were tripods of grey searchlight beams somewhere near Rotterdam to the east of them, but the Lancaster was turning and the searchlights passed and the smoke closed in again.

'Jesus!' said Binty. He expected a reply from Jimmy Grimm in the turret but when he looked up he found that only the upper half of Jimmy remained. The leather-jacketed torso and masked head was staring over the gunsights as though ready to open fire, but the lower part of him was not there. There was just a boggy puddle of bone splinters, blood and liquidized viscera dumped on the floor and dripping from the flare stowage. Into it was pumping oil from the fractured pipes that led to the rear turret. Binty flashed his torch away from the obscene sight and steadied himself against the ice-cold metal skin of the fuselage.

Lambert had no rudder to steer with. Experimentally he held the control column and gently turned it sideways to operate the ailerons without letting it back an inch. For what seemed a long time Door didn't respond. The fabric covering on the starboard aileron was so tattered that most of the slip-stream was whistling through the holes. The port aileron was spoiling the lift on that wing but the starboard one was not giving extra lift to starboard. Door settled down like a fitfully sleeping dog and dropped fifty feet with a cranium-pressing lurch that pinned everyone to the floor. When she staggered across the sky Lambert feared the tail had broken but slowly the starboard wing came up. Inch by inch it came until it cut into the moonlit clouds. Then the nose began to slide sideways and ran gently along the horizon and the compass moved slowly until it pointed the way to England. Lambert knew that they had suffered severe structural damage at the rear. He wondered how much warning they would get if the airstream got busy and tried to rip the back end off. Already the drag was such that he could feel the rear part of the aircraft sagging and bucketing. He reduced speed, throttling back to minimize the strain upon the airframe.

Binty plugged into the intercom. 'Are you there, Flash?'

There was no reply. 'It's Binty, boy. Are you there, kiddo?'

Binty moved gingerly nearer to the gaping holes. Through them he could even see a ragged moon glinting on the black ocean. The floor creaked and tilted under him and nervously he stepped back. There were only a dozen stringers, an ammunition runway and that piece of metal floor-plate holding Creaking Door's tail on. Binty's weight might be the last straw.

'Binty, what's happening there?'

'Jimmy's had it, Skip, and I can't get no answer from Flash.'

'Can't you open his turret doors?'

'Can't get as far as that, Skip. She's full of smoke. There's half the bloody fuselage side gone. Her tail's hanging on by its teeth.'

'Kosher?'

For the first time Binty thought of Kosher. He seemed to have disappeared. 'Kosher, you all right?' said Lambert over the intercom. There was an answering noise.

'Where are you?' said Lambert. The intercom gave only a monosyllabic grunt. 'You hurt?' Again a bubbling sound came over the wires. Mother, perhaps. They never said Father. *Mutti*? Yes, it could be *Mutti*.

Lambert had carried dead and injured before. In 1941 he'd brought a Whitley two hundred and fifty miles with everyone, except himself, dead or semi-conscious. By now he knew the signs. The silent ones were either dead or unharmed. The screamers were slightly injured and scared, for no one who was mortally torn could spare the stamina for a long loud scream. It was the soft groans that needed tourniquets and morphine. Voices like Cohen's.

'Find Kosher, Bint.'

'I've found him, Skip.'

'Is he OK?'

'No.' A silence. 'You'll have to lose altitude, Skip. He needs oxygen.'

'Connect his tube.'

'Tube's OK. He's got no oxygen mask on.'

'Put it on.'

'Can't, Skip. It's gone.'

'What do you mean gone?'

'Burned away, Skipper. I'm going to have to get the morphine from the box.'

Binty went to the rear. This time he stepped lightly and leaned well towards the least damaged side. He tried not to look down into the clouds and sea below and tried to lose weight by willpower.

'How much of this tube of morphine do I put into him?'

'Give him half a tube into the arm. That's still a double dose.'

'It's difficult, Skip. I can't tell which is arm. Will the leg be OK?'

'OK, Binty. Digby, go back and give Binty a hand, will you?'

To say that Binty was not a close friend of Kosher Cohen would be an understatement. The two men had so little in common that the overtures of friendship that Kosher had made to the Welshman merely underlined the differences of class, education and interests. Binty had spent his childhood in a children's home and his youth at an RAF school for apprentices. He had always been shouted at and punished frequently and his life had run according to timetables and rule books. Little that was worth having came Binty's way and when it did he grabbed for it without worrying who got the elbow.

Cohen had been educated at public school and university. Also formalistic, male-dominated societies, but their rituals had ill-prepared him for conversation with men like Binty, who was truly knowledgeable only about crumpet and motorcycles. Cohen spoke like an officer, a fact that prevented Binty – and others – from being able to confide to him their inadequacies.

'Here, Cohen. Want a lift to London? Grrr!' Binty jangled a bunch of door keys. 'Last time I dropped in on my London piece by surprise she was in the bath. Took me the whole weekend to get my uniform dry.'

'Thanks, Binty, but some of the fellows from school are climbing this weekend. I said I'd go along.'

Binty flashed the torch around the bare metal interior: racks of signal flares, a first-aid box and the curve of the ammunition runways that sloped gently all the way to the rear turret. Ten feet ahead of him were the remains of his mid-upper turret, bent and bloody. There were no flames, but now and again there was the crackle of a bullet exploding with the heat.

'I say, what good luck running into you, Binty. Would you like to come down to my parents' place this weekend?'

'Not unless there'll be spare crumpet there.'

Binty tried to pull Cohen forward to the crew bunk built over the main spare, but Cohen was glued to the flare chute by cooked flesh. Binty was frightened that he might pull Cohen apart, for now with the morphia in him he would feel no pain until it was too late.

When the flak shell exploded Kosher had been trying to dislodge the photoflash from the bent chute. He had recovered his balance quickly, grabbed a fire extinguisher and hurried back towards the fire. A parachute was smouldering. It filled the fuselage with the black fumes of burning cloth. Some .303 bullets overheated and popped, making clinks and whines as they ricocheted around the metal structure. Very pistol signals, cartridges and other pyrotechnics caught fire, filling the narrow corridor with blinding light. Bright greens and reds lit up inside the smoke of a winddrift flare. Some of them burned through the metal skin and fell gently to the sea. Jimmy Grimm was past aid. Oh God! His torch was stabbing at the smoke and the lights exploding as Cohen looked back to the great multimillion candlepower photo-flash that he had been trying to dislodge from the damaged chute. It was smouldering. There was no one to help him and no one to appeal to. There was only one way to eject it from the aircraft and that was down the flare chute. He pushed at it with the new energy of desperation and dislodged it just a fraction of a second before it exploded. That was the soundless white explosion that had puzzled Lambert.

Perhaps if Kosher had been wearing his heavy leather aircrew gauntlets he would have been less burned but, like most navigators, he wore only his silk linings, having found it impossible to draw pencil lines and turn the circular slide rule while wearing thick gloves. And if only he had not looked down the flare chute to see what he was doing . . .

Binty cuddled the boy closely. After he had put the quarter of a grain of morphia into him Kosher began to shake like a man in a fit, but then he became still again. Kosher's eyes remained open but went glassy like a toy teddy bear.

Throughout years of skilled womanizing Binty had never needed words of tenderness, but now he began searching his memory for them. He found none. His childhood had been without kindness or love, but never before had he realized his loss.

'It's just a flesh wound, kidoo,' he said finally, but by then Kosher was sinking into unconsciousness. Binty had got an oxygen mask on him now. The burnt place in Kosher's chest bubbled with froth and the silk glove that held it disappeared under pink foam.

In the cockpit Battersby rephrased a question in his mind a dozen times before asking it. Finally he said, 'Shall I follow the elevator controls back to the tail?'

'Good idea,' said Lambert.

'I'm the lightest weight,' said Battersby. 'I might be able to get to the rear turret.'

'See what you can do, Batters. Take your chute with you.'

'Can you hold her alone?'

'Ease off your weight and we'll see.'

Lambert found he could hold the control column forward, but only by jamming his leg against it and twisting his body in the seat.

'OK.'

Binty shone his torch up at Battersby, who stepped over the two men huddled together on the floor. In spite of an icy wind the smoke still hung inside the plane. Battersby looked down dispassionately when he got to the hole in the fuselage. He had never been afraid of heights and he studied the edges of the damage with a technical eye. Battersby found the rudder control rod badly bent and kicked at it, but his strength was not sufficient to change the bend or even to make another. He reached along the rod to where it entered the tailplane spar but it was undamaged as far as he could reach. He flashed his torch but could still not see the damage. He plugged in his intercom to the connection near the Elsan. 'The rods are not too bad. Probably the elevators themselves, Skip.'

'Well, there's nothing you can do about that, Batters. See if you can get as far as the rear turret to see if Flash's OK.'

Suddenly they all heard Flash Gordon's voice. 'Rear gunner to captain. I'm all right.'

'Where the hell have you been?' asked Lambert.

'Sorry, Skip. My plug came adrift. I've been calling you and wondering what was happening.'

Battersby said, 'Skipper, would you let Flash come forward. His weight so far aft . . .' He left the rest of it to Lambert to imagine.

'Can you come up here, Flash?' Lambert said. 'We're in a bit of a mess amidships, so watch your step and bring your chute with you. Battersby is somewhere back there; do as he tells you, OK?'

'OK, Skip,' said Flash. 'I could tell there was something

wrong. My turret would only work on manual and there was a terrible smell.'

Flash came forward. He was stiffened by the coldness of his open-panel turret and impeded by his parachute. When he got as far as Binty and Cohen he sat down on the floor with them. It seemed warm there where the metal structure had smouldered.

The only true tiredness stems from the ball of the foot. First it makes the calves ache and the thigh muscles throb and moves along the spine to produce a pressure upon the cranium that almost forces the eyelids closed. That was the sort of tiredness Lambert knew now. He felt as if he had marched fifty miles in full equipment.

Yet with no navigator to help him and no wireless operator to obtain radio fixes he was trying to draw a triangle of velocities in his head. It was no use him remembering courses they had drawn up at the briefing, for those winds had proved to be hopelessly incorrect and were probably still changing. In any case he had brought the Lancaster down to 4,000 feet so that Kosher wouldn't lack oxygen and here the winds might be different again.

'Shall I see if I can work the wireless set for a QDM?' Digby offered.

'Stay up front. Help me get a pinpoint when we cross the coast.'

He had wandered far off the track of the bomber stream during Beer's attack. The moon was bright now, but all it showed him was the sea beneath and irregular formations of cloud ahead. He knew that if he was to make a landfall he must stay below the cloud and when the first particles wetted and darkened the Perspex he put the nose down until he could see again. The ocean was close below them. Those cold spiteful waves looked so gentle from here. Parallel and unmoving, they were patches of white cross-hatching drawn by moonbeams through the clouds.

Lambert had resolved that in this situation he would ask

the crew whether they wanted him to turn back over the enemy coast and bale out. But he did not ask them. So many times he had brought back dead and dying. Now once again he was doing it, while he himself was unscathed. Ruth said that he couldn't hold himself responsible for that, but she didn't understand. He steered the kite: a touch of the foot, a movement of the hand changed their position by half a mile. Anything that happened was his fault; there was no escaping it. No authority without responsibility. They did as he told them without a murmur of protest. Cohen had gone back to the flare chute. No one had asked to bale out, nor had they mentioned that had he reacted more quickly to the flak ship's guns they would not have been hit.

'Battersby, take an extinguisher and have a careful look round amidships. If you can find the Aldis lamp take a look at the engines through the wireless window.'

'The dials are fine, Skipper. All of them are running beautifully by the look of it.'

'Stay here, lad, I'm just being neurotic.'

'OK, Skipper,' said Battersby.

Racked by the guilt of not being disabled, Binty held tight to Kosher and tried to make amends. In a low voice, stumbling sometimes over the polysyllables and coughing because of the smoke, he recited nut for nut and bolt for bolt every component of the four motorcycles he'd owned. Flash sat on the floor listening to the litany and trying not to look up at the upper turret. At the controls Lambert and Battersby were struggling with the cantankerous unpredictable crippled Door. In the front Digby was staring down at the sea trying to make it into land. Finally he succeeded.

'It's the English coast all right: Aldeburgh.'

'Southwold, I can see the river.'

'Yes, well, I'm just a visitor here myself, sport.' Two searchlights lit and searched the sky, passing close to their wingtip.

'Skipper to crew. I can put down at the emergency field at Manston or try to find Warley.'

There was no answer for nearly two minutes. Then Binty said, 'Let's get Cohen back home.'

'Home it is,' said Lambert.

Masked by the effects of the morphine Cohen was slipping into a coma. Binty rocked him in his arms. 'Nearly home, Kosher, old son.' Then he began to cut his burned flesh away from the flare chute.

Tommy Carter's ground crew and aircrew were celebrating the pilot's twenty-first birthday by bumping him on the hard tarmac. His flying gear deadened the shock of the buffeting. After twenty-one bumps he got to his feet surprised and a little angry, although when he saw Roland advancing on him with a tray of glasses and beer he was suitably placated. Every one of the ground crew was holding a glass of beer before Tommy would take one. The Sergeant electrician held up his glass and said, 'Many happy returns, Tommy lad. And here's to you and your next posting, Tapper, old son.' They all drank happily. They'd hardly begun the second drink when one of them started up the song that had become Tommy's anthem. It was a well-known RAF ditty, sung to the tune of *In and Out the Windows*.

> 'The captain's name was Carter,
> He was a champion farter,
> He could play everything
> From God Save the King
> To Beethoven's Fourth Sonata.'

They all joined in the chorus of:

> 'Orbiting the beacon,
> Orbiting the beacon,
> Orbiting the beacon,
> As we have done before.'

They were so pleased with the harmony at the end of it that they repeated it all through again and there was more clinking of glasses.

'Here you are, Tom,' said Ben Gallacher, toasting his captain. 'You're the best bloody driver in the Air Force.'

By the light of the vertical searchlight and the flashing beacon Tommy could see that they were happy and the dangers and difficulties of the night were temporarily forgotten.

Lambert and Digby both saw the vertical searchlight and told each other. For a moment their tiredness disappeared. Using only his ailerons Lambert had brought Door around all the way from the coast. Degree by degree he had prepared the heading so that from fifty miles away he was approaching the main runway. Nine and a half miles from Warley he began his landing.

Flash and Binty held Cohen tight. The funnel lights were coming up too fast but old Door was trying. She really was doing her best. Lambert controlled his height by means of the throttles, letting the aeroplane drop gently through the air as it lost forward speed. The elevators were still useless.

'I'll need all your weight, Micky,' Lambert told Battersby.

The flare path was floating gently up towards them. Battersby put the undercarriage down and to their mutual relief it slid into position and locked with no trouble.

'Give me 20 degrees of flap.'

'Flaps down,' said Battersby.

The approach was good. 'Flash and Binty – OK?'

'OK, Skipper.'

'Hold on tight to the structure. If the tail breaks off it will only be the end bit. Don't slide out. Digby, come back here. Battersby, 60 degrees of flap, please.'

He was more than four hundred feet above the trees and still dropping nicely. Warley spire came up and pierced the skyline as Lambert struggled with the control column. Now he needed those elevators. Just this last time, Door, my love! Battersby and Lambert strained upon the controls until they both feared that they might bend the metal.

Neither of the men spoke. They were overshooting. Still the wheels hadn't touched. They were flying across the airfield at 100 mph with an altitude that could be measured in inches.

'I can't hold her,' muttered Lambert. They were sinking almost imperceptibly. Continuing on this shallow slope would bring them into violent and final contact with the ground in the middle of Witch Fen or, even worse, the copse just beyond it. Desperate, Lambert decided to slam all the throttles forward into emergency boost. He even started to reach for them; then paused. He doubted if the fragile machine could stand it and he knew that his subsequent circuit would have to be halfway across East Anglia since he couldn't use the tail to steer.

The air-speed needle quivered and dropped to 90 mph. Still there was no bump of wheels touching.

'This is it,' said Lambert. He cut the throttles right back. At speeds above its stalling-speed any aeroplane is a fairy princess caring nothing for the law of gravity. But, like Cinderella at midnight, a plane going even a fraction below its stalling-speed changes suddenly into a collection of metal components that, exactly as a brick, bomb or pumpkin, will drop earthwards as gravity demands.

Door did that. It fell upon the runway like a fist upon a counter, shaking every rivet. The tyres screeched like half-slaughtered dogs and repeated the scream as the bouncing plane reapplied their hot rubber to the hard ground. Lambert had every last inch of flap down now, but they were still racing at sixty miles an hour towards the line of trees that marked the far end of the runway.

'She's swinging,' said Battersby, but already Lambert was trying to correct it.

Two trees came up through the pale skyline, stabbing their

fingers into the air in a rude gesture at having been singled out for doom at the hands of a runaway bombing plane.

Then the world went mad. Battersby knew that it wasn't possible that they could sink into the runway, and yet he knew beyond doubt that it was happening. Lower and lower. There was a very loud bang that shook the whole aeroplane. There were flashes on every side and a shower of yellow sparks filled the cabin windows. The skyline detached itself from the air-field and danced first round to the port windows and then more determinedly to starboard. This time it kept going and there were hangers in front of them. Then the lighted windows of the Control Tower, and then those damned trees came round again. The noise was tremendous. Metal was ripping itself to pieces in a frantic rhythm that matched the dance of the trees until, as the horizon lost its energy, the tumult slowed and stilled and there was a silence such as they had never known before. Digby for a moment thought he was dead. Then he heard the gurgling sounds of petrol flowing from broken tanks and the creaks and cracks of the bent metal settling down. There was a smell of scorching and of one-hundred-octane fuel and with it the similar sweet perfumes of human juices and fresh blood.

They were all speechless and still. Even had the wreckage been on fire it is doubtful that they would have moved. Nowadays aeroplane accident investigators call it 'negative panic'; then they called it being stunned.

'Sorry, lads,' said Lambert. 'Had to bring the undercart up. Out as quickly as you can, there's a fire hazard. Got Kosher there, Binty?'

'Yes, Skip. We'll see to him.'

'Flash?'

''Kay, Skip. Have you got Flanagan?'

Lambert reached for the cross-eyed rag doll. 'Yes, Flanagan's OK,' he said. Lately he'd begun to hate that doll but never more than now. He stuffed it into his tunic.

'Dig?'

'Ready to go.'

'Unplug, get clear. Side door's best. Take it easy.'

Only then did the crew recover their senses enough to unplug their microphone leads, release their parachute harnesses and make for the exits. Lambert gave Battersby a blow on the arm to tell him to hurry and he patted the aeroplane an affectionate farewell. For a moment he sat looking at his aeroplane. He felt an irrational sadness at saying goodbye to the wreck.

There was a lot of noise now: bells and shouts and ambulances and fire engines. Flash and Binty carried Cohen about a hundred yards before they sank down with him on to the cold ground and looked back towards Door, bent and broken and well off the runway. One wingtip had snapped and was silhouetted. Pieces of tail were scattered everywhere. Digby came racing past soon after they had stopped. He saw them and dropped down beside them puffing and panting with exertion. 'Lord bless you, Mother Earth,' he said. The smell of the dew-wet grass almost overcame the smell of Cohen.

There was still no sign of Battersby. He was in the shadow of the wrecked bomber, standing by the exit waiting for Lambert to emerge. He could hear him moving around. Soon Lambert appeared in the doorway carrying something. Battersby moved to assist him, but then found he couldn't.

'You'll be all right, Jimmy,' Lambert was saying to the wet bundle.

One after another the Lancasters came in on the main runway that took them over the village roofs. Old Sam Thatcher gave up the attempt to sleep and switched on the light by his bed and looked at the clock. 'That damned wind. I knew she'd move round. I said so to young Cynthia.'

'Go to sleep,' mumbled Mrs Thatcher.

He switched out the light but did not go back to sleep. Finally he got up and made himself tea.

In the Briefing Room there was a shot of rum for every

returning crewman and a short dark WAAF with carefully applied make-up handed out cups of sweet milky tea. Two airmen were removing the shutters from the windows. There was a trace of watery pink colouring the eastern sky. The debriefing officers were sitting behind folding tables writing furiously as the crews grouped round them trying to recreate the raid. It was not possible; their descriptions relapsed into jargon and cliché. Their voices were shrill, and their grimy faces bore the red 'scars' of oxygen masks; like painted smiles on dirty clowns. The sudden realization that they had survived was far more intoxicating than one measure of Air Ministry rum.

'I got a real good burst in at him; definitely a Messerschmitt, wasn't it, Cliff?'

'I didn't see him, Dave.'

'You stupid sod.'

'And this is your twentieth trip, Captain?'

'Right on the target, but I couldn't tell what colour the smoke was.'

'Krefeld as a city no longer exists.'

'If you don't believe me, look at my photo.'

'It sounds like a good show.'

'A piece of bloody cake.'

For the bombs that missed Altgarten fell upon open land and did not burn, and so from the air the destruction of the little town appeared to be a highly concentrated and remarkably accurate attack upon the sprawling city of Krefeld.

Longfellow was pleased. 'It will be something to tell your children about,' he told Lambert, but Lambert had already resolved never to tell anyone.

The crew drifted away to their breakfast, still talking noisily. Lambert did not leave the room when the debriefing had finished; he waited. He always waited, but this time he waited in vain. He saw no sign of Murphy or any of Sweet's crew.

Out on the cold airfield half a dozen ground crew stood around on S for Sugar's tarmac pan. They'd heard distant singing from Carter's crew, but that had made them even quieter. They were wrapped in woollen helmets and long scarves. Their hands were thrust deep into their overcoat pockets and were only removed to light and relight cigarettes. The ground beneath their feet was dotted with white trampled butts. The men did not speak to each other except to ask the time. The Sergeant fitter had done his basic training with Murphy. Finally he said, 'Go and get some breakfast, lads.' The distant screech of the London train came clearly across the dark fenland. They walked slowly back across the airfield, staring at the ground and hoping they wouldn't see anyone they knew.

At Kroonsdijk Christian Himmel was the last of the Staffel to land. The dud engine gave trouble during taxiing but Himmel expected that. He came past the old wreck quite fast and then Kugel brought him into position with hand signals. He hit the port toe brake so hard that his plane swung round abruptly on its pan. He brought the motors up to maximum revs. The motor banged as he tested the faulty magneto. He switched both engines off. The gyros ran down with a sweet musical hum and the cooling motors chimed prettily. Beyond Kugel there was a group of men. The Medical Officer was there and Christian could see Redenbacher too. A nervous Flying-Control officer hurriedly switched off the runway lights.

'What's happening?' he asked Kugel as his feet touched the ground at the bottom of the ladder. Now that he had taken off his mask he was aware of the stink of the Junkers. Burnt oil, exhaust fumes, stale cordite and carbonized guns combined with the smell of his sweaty clothes. Kugel was looking at him in a curious way, perhaps because of this. Himmel stretched his limbs. It was a welcome relief after his cramped, closely fitting bucket seat.

On the far side of the airfield near the dijk there were flashing torches and motor-car headlights. He could tell from the movements of the torches that there was confusion and haste.

Kugel was bursting with news. 'A fellow from Twente came in to refuel and left pieces of his undercarriage scattered along the runway. His flaps and brakes had failed. It caught fire. Two officers were trapped in it. Horst Knoll rescued them but he's badly burned on the hands. Funny, eh? him hating officers the way he does.'

'Give me a cigarette, Kugel.' The old man selected one and pushed it into Himmel's mouth. They walked away from the aeroplane before Kugel produced his matches. Although it was still quite dark the birds were singing noisily.

'It's been a bad night, Christian. The Staffelkapitän has been snatched and now they think that Leutnant Kokke has also gone. The other Staffeln have lost four.'

'You'll have to change that engine, Kugel. She cut on me tonight in the middle of an interception.'

'It may not have been oiled plugs.'

'It was oiled plugs,' insisted Himmel, 'and the valves are dud too. You heard it. Anyway, the Kommodore said it should be changed if it gave any more trouble.' Kugel lit a match and Christian bent his head down to it.

'We'll put a new motor into her, Christian. By the way, Löwenherz's Knight's Cross came through on the tele-printer.'

'It will be best. Löwenherz dead, are you sure?'

'The radar people at Ermine saw the explosion out at sea. A shell from a flak ship they think. He would have got his Knight's Cross from Reichsmarschall Göring in person.'

'And Kokke?'

'At first they thought it was his radio but he's not landed anywhere.'

'Perhaps they'll turn up,' said Christian. 'Take good care of the dog or Löwenherz will be furious.'

'The Kommodore's waiting for you,' Kugel warned. 'And that old civilian fellow.'

'I was expecting them,' said Christian. 'In my locker there's a bottle of brandy and an American parachute canopy. You can have them.'

'And the Medical Officer is there too,' said Kugel.

'Yes, he would want to watch,' said Christian. 'He's a student of human nature.'

Kugel looked over his shoulder to be sure the crew were out of earshot. 'Hit me,' said Kugel.

'What?'

'Hit me and run. Hit hard so it's convincing.'

'You are a good friend, Kugel,' said Christian. 'Take good care of the dog.' He walked towards the group of men waiting for him.

At Warley Fen Munro brought his Lancaster down as lightly as a feather. He kept the wind under his port wing and held off his damaged tyre, tilting the controls gently so that it met the runway as gently as possible. So lightly did it touch that a gust of crosswind plucked the aeroplane back into the air and replaced it on a parallel run ten feet to starboard.

The lower a tyre's pressure the lower is the speed at which it will come off its rim. In spite of Munro's skill the soft tyre was punched flat by the hard tarmac rushing past at eighty miles an hour and then ripped into long rubber strips that scattered on to the runway, wriggling like hot black snakes as they curled into strange contortions and went hard and brittle. Devoid of its tyre the wheel hub struck a long gash of white sparks across the darkness before digging into the tarmac, bending and tearing itself into eight pieces that bowled along pealing like a set of bells. But when the oleo leg touched the ground it was as if the port wingtip had been grabbed by a giant and the Lancaster twisted neatly off the runway before settling lopsided on to the dew-wet grass almost undamaged. It was only two hundred yards from the wreck of the Door.

'Ground flight to ground,' said Munro, with formal precision. An aeroplane died each time that order ended its flight. The lights flickered off, the instruments ceased to glow, the intercom ceased to talk and the generators and gyros whined to a standstill.

'Ground flight to ground it is, sir,' said the engineer, turning the switch without any hurry. Munro released his mask, unplugged, unstrapped, turned and thumped his parachute harness release and reached for his peaked cap and walking-stick.

'Damn me, look at that, Jock.' He waved the broken end of his walking-stick. A tiny fragment of shrapnel had cut it in two. Munro shivered and decided he'd never carry a lucky charm again. If before trying that dodgy landing he had known it was broken he'd have been convinced he was for the chop.

'Congratulations, Skipper,' said Jock. 'Good landing and the end of a tour.'

'Thanks, Jock.'

The Briefing Room was littered with cigarette ends and the air was heavy with stale smoke and the odour of Air Ministry rum. When Munro's crew had been interrogated the room was almost empty. A large notice on the wall said, 'Crews: don't wait around to see your photos. Go to bed'. Before they used that sign the place used to be packed with noisy aircrew until the morning. The Intelligence Officer pulled his greatcoat tighter about him and looked at the clock. Munro saw him looking at it and shook his head sadly. The three missing planes did not have enough fuel still to be airborne. Longfellow gathered the sortie reports together and went out. The three men who had been waiting for friends near the entrance also left without a word to each other.

In the Sergeants' Mess they played the gramophone and

the Mess waiter went around complaining about sergeants who put their wet beer glasses on the billiard table. One Sergeant gunner punched a friend who had refused to corroborate his claim for a Ju88 shot down. A bomb aimer was sick in the bar after drinking whisky mixed with rum. One of the Sergeant cooks who was due on breakfast duty next morning came down to the lounge in his pyjamas and asked them to make less noise. He was greeted with foul abuse. Sergeant Binty Jones allowed his friend Flash Gordon to push his motorcycle out of the boiler house where he kept it. It started at a touch of the kick starter and Binty stuffed a toothbrush into his pocket and was off to his rendezvous with Rose in Peterborough. He bumped his bike across the unofficial footpath behind the Mess to get to the main road by the shortest route. He hurried along it, straddling the bike and letting his toes tap the ground just to keep his balance and giving the powerful engine little twists of throttle. He was almost level with a man coming the other way before he recognized who it was.

'Some of you fellows . . .' protested the Squadron commander in amazement. 'Were are you going?'

Binty was too surprised to lie. 'Peterborough, sir.'

'To see some woman. Is that it?'

'Yes, sir,' said Binty, unable to keep the nervousness he felt out of his voice.

Impulsively Munro said, 'Well, how about giving me a lift to Peterborough station? I might just be able to catch the mainline train home.' He touched his pocket and heard the crackle of his wife's letter.

'Certainly, sir,' said Binty in obsequious relief at not being charged with breaking out of camp. He turned the motorbike round. 'Jump on the back, I'll take you up to the Officers' Mess and wait for you.'

'That's the spirit, Gordon.'

'Jones, sir. Gordon's my oppo. I'm the mid-upper on Creaking Door, O Orange that is.'

'That's the spirit, Sergeant Jones. Peterborough, and don't spare the horses!'

'No, sir. I won't, sir.'

When Lambert left the Briefing Room he could hear the gramophone in the Sergeants' Mess and smell the fried bacon of the aircrew breakfasts. Tommy Carter, Tapper Collins, and Jock Hamilton from Munro's crew almost dragged him to the Mess to join them for a drink but he wouldn't go. He heard Digby say, 'Fair's fair, Sam's got to see his missus.' Tommy had a bottle of whisky that he had put in his locker. It was already half gone. They wished him goodnight and wandered away singing.

'Happy birthday, Tommy,' Lambert shouted after them. They were singing the famous soldier's song:

> 'That's my brother Sylvestre,
> He's got a row of forty medals on his chest.
> It takes all the Army and the Navy
> To put the wind up Sylvestre.'

The chorus was a tuneless chant sung as speedily as possible.

> Don't push, just shove, plenty of room for you and me,
> He's got an arm that's like a leg and his punch will sink
>   a battleship.

Digby ended long after the others and clinging to Tommy's waist he swung round to shout goodbye again to Lambert. Lambert waved again. Digby shared a room with Grimm and Cohen. Tonight he'd have the room to himself, that's why he'd not be going to bed.

By the time Lambert reached the changing-room it was empty. He was opening his locker when Battersby emerged from the crew toilets even paler than usual. He wiped his mouth and said to Lambert, 'Was I all right, Skipper?'

Lambert winked at him. 'Like a bloody veteran, Batters.'

511

The boy smiled.

'I phoned the sick bay.'

'I did too, Batters.'

'I was going along there but they said it was no use; they're doing all they can.'

'Get some sleep, Batters, the worst is over.'

The boy was full of unasked questions but he smiled and turned towards the door. Lambert reached for his shoes on the shelf and in them found the group photo. They were all there, grinning like immortals. He tossed it into the back of his locker and after it threw Flanagan. He pulled off his boots and flying suit and went to have a wash but changed his mind. Someone had been sick in the WC, there was a bulb missing and the only towel had been stolen.

He unlocked his bicycle and pumped up the rear tyre. He had to push the bike through the gap in the wire because the constant battle between the breakers and the repairers was going a little in the latter's favour. After that it was only ten minutes' cycle ride to the village.

The sky was dribbling with the first streaks of a new day and the air was cold enough to condense his breath. Lambert liked these rides. The countryside was still and aromatic and there were rustles of animal life in the hedgerows. For Lambert it was the moment to congratulate himself upon surviving another trip. He propped his bicycle against the hedge and opened the front door as quietly as possible.

Ruth was awake when he opened the bedroom door. She was always awake when he returned. He imagined she never slept while he flew, although he never asked her about it. He undressed slowly without the light. The moonlight that had shone so brightly over the Dutch coast was diffused by the thin cloud and dusted the bedroom with just a trace of blue gloom.

'All right, darling?'

Lambert didn't answer, and that she knew was bad. The only other times that he'd been silent was when they'd been shot up and lost crew. When he got into bed he lay full-length with his feet together like a block of wood. Or like a corpse, thought Ruth, and erased that thought. His skin was hard and his breathing was almost inaudible. She put her head against his shoulder. He didn't either respond or move away. He'd come back, there was that for which to be thankful. It wasn't only cowards who died a thousand times, it was wives and mothers and sweethearts. Fathers too, perhaps.

'Cohen and Grimm,' said Lambert, he didn't mention Micky.

She said nothing.

'I promised his father,' said Lambert.

'He made you promise,' said Ruth.

'I promised.'

She wanted to tell him about the Group Captain but she couldn't add another worry.

'It's Tommy Carter's twenty-first birthday. They wanted me to go for a drink.'

'You should have gone.'

'No.' A motorcycle came through the village at high speed, changed down at the crossroads and then opened the throttle with a roar as it turned on to the main road. Lambert bent over his wife and kissed her. 'I didn't wash,' he apologized. She could smell the awful night.

'I sent Dad a fiver.'

'You are a fool, Sam. He won't use it to pay his bills. He'll never be any different.'

'I know.'

'You can't be responsible for all the world, Sam. You mustn't try.'

'I'll not go again. They can do what they like, Ruth. I'm flown out, finished, kaputt.'

She reached to her bedside table and found a sleeping tablet for him. He took it like a small child, not caring what it was or where it had come from.

'Perhaps you should play cricket on Saturday. We can go to London the following week.'

'You're a good girl, Ruth.' He put his arm round her and closed his eyes but he did not sleep.

That was about the time when they found the Burgomaster. They all said it was the most obvious place to look, but no one said that until after he'd been found. A Hitler Jugend messenger almost ran over him on the wrecked site of his own house. He had collected as many undamaged bricks as he could find and he was building them into walls. He had no cement, of course, which is why they fell over when the boy's bicycle hit them. The Burgomaster was very upset and so the fourteen-year-old messenger helped him build his little hut again. It was almost an hour before the boy realized that the Burgomaster was trying to build the tiny hut around himself.

In Liebefrauplatz a team of TENO engineers led by Bodo Reuter were heaving at a block and tackle. The sound of the chains rattled around the ruins of the still-warm church. With each pull the tail assembly of Sweet's Lancaster rose higher until it was strung up in the town centre suspended from a buttress. It swayed a little in the winds that had so aided the great fires of the night, looking like a piece of some prehistoric animal, displayed thus to assuage the anger of the gods. Smoke drifted across the scene. On the rudders there were the red, white and blue markings of Britain and the white stencilled letters that were its identity. Some of the TENO men wanted to leave the body of Sweet's rear gunner in the smashed rear turret, but Bodo Reuter forbade it. Even before the cables were secured citizens had begun to gather to exorcize the species that had plagued them.

'Sieg Heil,' shouted one of them and the others also shouted. Sweet's wrecked aeroplane would stay there a week and then be melted down and within seven weeks fly again as a German aeroplane.

Luftwaffe Himmelbett Station Ermine was lucky with the mail. They were the first Luftwaffe unit along the coast on the mail route from Rotterdam. There were two letters for August Bach. One was from the jeweller in Altgarten. It was a receipt for the deposit and a bill for the engagement ring. As the jeweller said, an engagement ring is the riskiest item that a man can offer on credit. The other letter was from August's son. With characteristic confidence it was detalined 'near Leningrad'.

Pappi,
    Haven't got more than a moment. We were in the line until only four hours ago. Last night I was on patrol trying to get prisoners for questioning. Both died of wounds and tonight the company that relieved us will have to have another try. We are pretty sure that Ivan is all ready to attack us. When he does I shall get my promotion or a wooden overcoat. Either way it doesn't matter much, as long as I don't get wounded.
    Answers to questions: no. What we get to eat is entirely adequate. Eat your own rations. Yes, we shall be getting leave some time during the next two months. Yes, I am coming home. Do you think I'd miss another roll in bed with that juicy little housekeeper you've tucked away. I was telling the boys about her. As one of them said, 'Trust the Luftwaffe to get itself some civilian rations and then pretend they are going hungry.' He meant you, of course. And don't go all sanctimonious on me. See you some time in August and knock before coming into the bedroom.
Yours cheerfully,

PETER

PS. Answer to unasked question: I haven't forgotten and will pay you back very soon now.

*   *   *

August folded both letters and put them into his pocket. 'Reinecke,' he said, 'after breakfast I'll sentence the men who lost the bicycles. We'll see to the cash afterwards. Anyone sick?'

'Only me, sir,' said Reinecke and grinned.

'No,' said August, 'there are two of us.'

'You'll feel better after some coffee, real coffee.'

'The herons?'

'They've gone.'

At the guardroom at Warley Fen, Flight Sergeant Bishop was looking at his galleon in full sail. He couldn't decide whether to call it 'Cadiz ahoy' or 'Gold from the New World'. The phone rang. The operator spoke to Bishop who was for tonight the Sergeant of the guard.

'It's some police station with a message,' she said. 'I can't get any answer in Orderly Room or Operations.'

'OK,' said Flight Sergeant Bishop. 'Let's have them.'

'Warley Fen RAF?'

'That's it.'

'Cambridgeshire Constabulary here. Sergeant Ford speaking. We've got two of your people here. There's been an accident between a Norton motorcycle and a lorry. They were speeding, by the sound of it. Their names are . . .' There was a pause as he shuffled the document on his desk. 'Munro, John: Wing Commander. And Jones, William Gareth: Sergeant. Know them?'

'I know the Wing Commander but almost everyone is a sergeant on this station.'

'Very well. I take it your military police people will phone us in the morning to make your own arrangements and there's the damaged motorcycle to be moved too.'

'Wait a moment,' said Bishop, grinning to himself as he thought of it, 'you can't hold the Wing Commander in the cells until morning. Not for a traffic offence.'

'Ah, I'm sorry. I should have explained. Dead. Killed instantly. They hit the lorry at ninety.'

'OK,' said the Sergeant. 'I'll leave a note about it.' He replaced the phone. 'Cadiz ahoy' he decided would be better.

In the three kitchens at Warley the cooks were still heavy with sleep as they sat drinking their first mugs of sweet hot milky tea before they began to prepare the earliest of the early breakfasts. Maisie Holroyd the Catering Officer had a cup of tea and a joke in all three Messes in spite of having been on duty – supervising the aircrew's flying rations – until the middle of the previous night. The sun was clinging precariously to the horizon and killing the stars with its stare. Lambert turned in his sleep, groaned, laughed and went silent without waking his wife. For she had not yet gone to sleep and now she watched him like a mother with a sick child.

In the Medical Section two doctors stood upright for the first time in two and a half hours and let Sergeant Cohen die.

In Altgarten they had long since run out of death certificates and were using pages from children's exercise books with the rubber stamp of the Rathaus imprinted at the top. They had also run out of bandages, blood, splints, burn dressings, iodine and morphine.

There were explosions as the TENOs demolished houses and shops on Dorfstrasse. Voss' shop was one of many that had become a dangerous ruin. The metallic voice from a loudspeaker van moved slowly along the same road telling the homeless to report to Party HQ for information and assistance. It ordered next-of-kin to report missing persons to the new temporary police station – a house on Zieglerstrasse. The only way to get there was via Koller Meadow, for like many of Altgarten's streets it was partly roped off because of unexploded bombs.

Not far from Altgarten, Billy Pace was the only survivor from Sweet's aircraft. His landing, however, had not been a lucky one. He had seen the dark shapes of the fir trees only a moment or so before hitting them. A branch struck his leg and then he was assailed by the sharp edges of more branches before he was jerked to a sudden stop by his canopy catching the treetop. There was a tearing sound and he sank a few feet but then swung without descending more. It was pitch-dark in the forest and he tried to get a grip on a branch, but they were all flimsy and springy and would not bear his weight. He tried to peer into the gloom but could see nothing. He found matches in his pocket and struck one, but that only illuminated the branches close to him and seemed to make his surroundings even darker. He dropped a burning match but it went out before he could see beyond his dangling stockinged toes, for he had lost both flying boots. Suspended in the tight harness he was so uncomfortable that he was tempted to hit the quick release and chance it, but caution prevailed. Especially when he heard the cry of wolves nearby. He dangled there for three hours with his imagination working overtime until the sun came over the horizon and inch by inch lit up the dark forest. It was then that he saw that the earth was only eighteen inches below his toes. He let himself drop to the ground but was still nervous of the wolves until a forester came past and explained that they were caged dogs. Pace had dropped into the small wood behind the Wald Hotel and had heard the noise of guard dogs being rounded up by dog-handlers. He walked along with the forester to his hut and managed to exchange a few words of German.

Behind the forestry hut Billy Pace saw a stiff brown doll-like figure. Its little arms were drawn tight across its front like a boxer's high defence and its burnt mouth was stretched back in a demoniacal grin that exposed large even white teeth. Pace recognized the charred stubble of a moustache. It was young Speke, who had left S Sweet without permission. He had landed in a patch of blazing forest.

The forester let Pace look at it for a moment or two.

'Kamerad?'

'Ja, Kamerad,' said Billy Pace and he went into the hut feeling hot and faint and slightly sick.

The old man gave him a cup of bitter brown liquid that he claimed was coffee and then he used the fire-warning phone to send for an escort. Billy still had a chocolate bar left from his flying ration. The old man ate it with relish. As the old forester explained, he would be safer with soldiers than walking through the bombed town without protection. He showed the forester a photo of his mother. Pace wondered how long it would take for his mother to hear that he was a prisoner and not killed in action.

For Fleming and his crew no comrades grieved. Their only friends had been each other, and none came back. Their stay at Warley had not lasted long enough to form friendships with the experienced crews and who could blame the men who came back for preferring that their friends survived rather than seven strangers.

In the Officers' Mess at Warley the Education Officer was collecting together the personal effects of PO Fleming. He'd been made Effects Officer only a week before. He made certain that there were no pornographic photos and read the letters carefully to be sure that they could cause no distress to parents or wives. It was a solemn job. He looked at his list; the next one was Flight Lieutenant Sweet.

When the last of the bombers landed the work of Warley Fen's Photographic Section began. Each of the bomber's F24 cameras was unloaded and the five-inch-wide lengths of extra-high-speed film were threaded on to spools and processed. It was all done at high speed. The developer was at seventy-five degrees fahrenheit and they had only a three-minute fix and wash before going into a meth-and-water bath for rapid drying. The Flight Sergeant then took the wet film and ran it across the front of a light-box to check the exposure and development. He noticed nothing unusual, nor did anyone else until the films were being hung in the hot air of the drying cabinet by a WAAF corporal.

She went into the trimming-room and for a moment looked across the airfield. Several of the buildings were lit up, their windows making bright yellow patches, disembodied in the blue morning light. The paths and grass were shiny-wet with dew and the beacon still flashed a morse identity that lit everything like a lightning-stroke. The girl found a shiny photograph that had been taken during a previous attack upon Krefeld and studied it carefully before looking at the negatives again. She told an LAG before telling the Flight Sergeant. She didn't want to make a fool of herself.

'Flight Sergeant Booth here, sir, Photo Section. The attack hasn't hit Krefeld, sir, I've just been studying the negs. Street patterns are nothing like it. I don't know sir. It doesn't look like anywhere. It doesn't look like anywhere.'

Gericht der Wehrmachtkommandantur
Berlin   *Berlin* NW 40, den 23.8.43
L/W KS/78 ui   *Lehrterstr* 58.

To the Supervisory Board of the Penitentiary in Brandenburg-Görden

On Monday, September 13th, 1943, at 1 PM, the death sentence against former Unteroffizier Christian Himmel, born September 12th, 1922, in Ottobeuren, Bayern, Religion Catholic, will be executed with the guillotine in your prison.

Executioner Rötger is charged with carrying out the sentence. The sentence is to be notified there on the same day at 11.00.

Charged with the supervision of the execution is Oberleutnant Dr Henze who will be attended by Feldjustizinspektor Keyser.

The sentenced is in the remand prison of the Wehrmacht in Berlin-Tegel, Seidelstrasse 39.

The Polizeipräsidium Berlin as conveying authority is

requested to send the sentenced to Brandenburg on the morning of September 13th, 1943. Acceptance is requested.

The local prison doctor is requested to be made available for the execution.

by direction
(signed)

JOST
Oberkriegsgerichtsrat

Administration Officer
August 23rd, 1943   *RAF Station Warley Fen*

ACH/GD LAMBERT, Samuel Charles

The above-named has been found unsuitable for any further duties in aircrew capacity and his reduction from NCO rank has therefore been ratified by Air Ministry. With effect from this date he will report to the Station Warrant Officer for work assignments with cleaning, sanitation and refuse-disposal working parties.

While these duties are not intended as a punishment no privileges will be granted to AC Lambert until further notice. This to include passes or permission to sleep off the station.

To Station Warrant Officer
RAF Warley Fen

EPILOGUE

Some forgot the events of that night in 1943. Others could never forget and many did not live to remember. Löwenherz, Fleming and Sweet and the crews that flew with them were not the only ones to die. The Luftwaffe lost eight night fighters: three Ju88s, four Me11os and a Dornier 217 as well as three others that landed so heavily as to be written off strength. Ten Luftwaffe aircrew died and two more were hurt so badly that they never again flew in combat.

The RAF's losses were forty-four bombers, of which thirty-one fell to German night fighters. Three hundred and one crewmen were lost: of these sixty-eight survived to become POWs. Nine of this latter group were seriously injured. Of the RAF aircraft destroyed thirty had already bombed. Five aircraft jettisoned their bombs in the sea or in open country. One bomb-load accidentally fell upon a Dutch village and caused eight deaths and three injured. Of the RAF aircraft destroyed, nine were lost to flak and one was lost when an RAF night fighter mis-identified it and shot it down as it crossed the English coast forty miles south of the Flight Plan.

Three bombers made fatal navigation errors. One descended through cloud and crashed into a mountain near Stavanger in Norway. Another ran out of fuel one hundred and sixty miles east of the Orkney Islands. One crashed in the South of France after being shot up. All of the crews perished.

PO Munro (John Munro's brother), a Stirling pilot, survived the raid and completed his tour of operations. He now runs his brother's estates, having married Sarah, his sister-in-law, and brought up the child and sent him to university where he studied Law. Tommy Carter and his crew were killed four operations after this one.

Lambert never flew again. Ruth was posted away, became pregnant, left the WAAF and stayed near her husband for the rest of the war. After the war Lambert went to work as a draughtsman in an aircraft factory. In 1954 he patented a supercharger modification and went into business manufacturing it. He is happy and moderately wealthy, although like many bomber pilots he has a history of spinal pains and disorders. They have a daughter and two sons.

Battersby, Flash Gordon and Digby were reassigned to a new pilot. They completed their tour, were posted to Training Command and then returned to do four trips of a second tour before the war ended. On the last operation they were badly shot up and Flash Gordon lost his left arm. Many Lancaster turrets were modified to have a clear-view panel. The Group Captain persuaded Air Ministry to officially name this the Sweet Panel.

Battersby married the WAAF driver that he met that night. After the war he went to London University just as his father had planned and, somewhat to his father's surprise, chose to study English Medieval History. He has written a book on medieval fortification and is at present a visiting professor at a large American university.

Digby returned to Australia. He has the Australian agency for a British light plane manufacturer and travels round the country selling them to farmers on the assurance that if he could learn to fly them anyone could. Sometimes the customers ask him if he was in the Air Force during the war but Digby stoutly maintains that he was too young to be in the war. Now completely bald, he wears a toupee.

Jammy Giles left the RAF in 1949. He was drinking a lot

by then and couldn't get used to the fact that post-war Officers' Mess parties had become rather more staid than he liked. His mother died and left him a little cash with which he started to buy a pub near Stratford-upon-Avon. In the first year it made money but that led Jammy into a false confidence, for really he is not a good businessman. Careless book-keeping and generosity with credit made him bankrupt in 1954. However, after working as a waiter for two years he had another go at running his own place. While at his lowest point economically and psychologically he had met and married a beautiful girl named Bessie. Together they started a lorry-driver's café on the A1 only about thirty miles from Warley. Jammy admits that it owes its success to Bessie, who works twice as hard as he does. She handles all the buying and hiring and firing and, as Jammy says, 'more drivers eat here to see her than to see me'. However, sometimes Squadron people visit them to recall old times. There are dark fly-blown pictures on the wall of Jammy standing under Lancaster bombers and one of him receiving his DFC from the King. Only two years ago Peterson called in and they were laughing about the time he did a bombing run seated on the Elsan. Peterson lives in Montreal and is a vice-president of a small company that makes camping equipment.

In 1948 Cohen's parents both died within three months of each other. Nora Ashton still lives with her mother in the house down the lane. It puzzles some people that she never married, for they guess, rightly, that she had many proposals.

The Group Captain died in 1946 in a car accident in Germany while he was still in the RAF. Willi Reinecke also got a job with the RAF in Germany after the war, although he had to falsify his age to do it. He worked in Air Traffic Control for nearly five years before retiring to live in the Ruhr. His son now works for Lufthansa, also in Air Traffic.

Fischer got another medal soon after D-Day. He was awarded the Oak-leaves after rounding up a group of stragglers including cooks and clerks and, using Panzerfäuste, repulsing an attack by British tanks outside Caen. He was killed after being cut off from his division in the fighting near Essen. He established a strongpoint with one hundred and fifty men and refused all demands to surrender. Artillery fire destroyed them. He still had the three-hundred-year-old Kuba carpet with him. It was found in the ruins by an RASC driver and ended its days as a floor covering in his lorry.

Frau Voss survived the war. Using the few works of art that her husband had – with typical foresight – stored in his son-in-law's house, she was able to live comfortably in Portugal until she died in 1959.

Bodo Reuter also survived the war. He worked on a freight boat for a year and then met a man in Athens who gave him a job crewing a luxury yacht for a Greek millionaire. For the first time in his life he began to drink to the point where it interfered with his work. He was dismissed and went to work on various ships but it was on a Panamanian oil tanker that he continued for the longest period, working as a cook. On Christmas Day, 1952, two policemen found a derelict old man on a park bench in Le Havre. He'd sold his seaman's papers to buy wine so they were unable to identify him. They filled in his death certificate by guesswork. Shrewdly they guessed he was German, but, as one of the flics said, he looked more like a poet than a beggar. They compromised and wrote schoolteacher.

August Bach's SS son Peter, within nine days of writing his letter, won one of the Army's most coveted awards, a badge for the single-handed destruction of a tank. Three days after that he was promoted and four days later – on rest behind the lines – he died of shotgun wounds inflicted by a partisan.

August Bach is now a very old man with pure white hair and wrinkled skin. He went to Brazil after the war, married a local girl and had two sons and a daughter. The first job he got was with a small company that builds power boats for fishing enthusiasts, mostly from the USA. After four years the owner gave Bach a small share of the business and a few months after that made him a full partner and retired. Bach was an old man already but by bringing his son and son-in-law into the business he has expanded its trade every year. Bach's younger son Hans returned to Germany. Having already flown light planes in Brazil he got a job with Lufthansa and was trained as a pilot. He now has done nearly three thousand hours on jets. August Bach and his wife spend most of their days in their small cottage on the beach. In some ways it is not unlike the hut he had at Ermine and he still photographs birds and sometimes dissects them.

At Ermine itself there is virtually no trace of the radar station, although the concrete gun emplacements are still there. Dutch bird-watchers go there on Sundays in the summer but there are no herons there now. The nearby drainage workings have disturbed them.

The surviving Mausi twin served a six months' prison sentence for shooting the dogs but did not see combat until the closing weeks of the war. He was captured by the Red Army and served eleven years in a labour camp in the extreme north. He was a sick man when he was released and was permitted to go to West Germany where he had relatives. He is unmarried and works as a storekeeper in a plastics factory near Hamburg. He only got that job because the manager was also in the Waffen SS and felt sorry for him.

Hans Furth was taken prisoner by the British in 1945 and continued to work as a doctor in the camp and later for Allied Military Government. He ran as a candidate in the local elections but did not win. However, one of the people who worked for him on the election campaign was the Munich manager of an American public relations company. Furth was offered a job in the Chicago office. He worked for them for eight years and then left to start his own PR company in New York. Nowadays he works there only two days a week and is able to afford long holidays in Florida and a trip to Europe once a year. Originally, most of his clients were German manufacturers moving into the US market but now those are in the minority. Furth has become so American in his clothes and speech that very few of his clients guess that he is not a native. For this reason he only employs American-born staff with the exception of an English secretary, an English receptionist and an English telephone operator, 'for the image'.

Dr Starkhof, the Abwehr man, was arrested after the attempt to assassinate Hitler on July 20th, 1944. He conclusively proved his innocence and so escaped the death sentence. He was, however, sent to a concentration camp and although he was still alive when the American troops reached it he died only three months afterwards.

The Burgomaster went into a mental home and died before the war ended. The young Meyers who got married with Andi Niels' aid immigrated to Israel and now works on a fruit farm near Jerusalem. Redenbacher became an Oberst at OKL and was killed flying as a passenger in a Ju52 in January 1945. Old Krugelheim was killed when a low-flying USAAF Mustang shot up the Kroonsdijk airfield in late 1944. The airfield itself still exists, although it is only half its former area. There are only light planes flying from it today, although there is a two-motor aeroplane that for only fifteen guilders takes sightseers for a quick circuit of the IJsselmeer workings. Those same workings drained a vast area of sea and found the remains of Kokke's Ju88 last year. Although it was intended for a museum it broke up when being moved.

Warley Fen's runways are still in position although they cannot be seen for growing crops. If you go there today you will also find some of the other buildings. The Sick Quarters where Cohen died have become sheep pens and the remains of the Sergeants' Mess where the gramophone was once so loud now echo to the grunt of many pigs. Only the Control

Tower is in anything like its original condition, although if you ascend the iron staircase be careful. You might end up writing a book about it.

ACKNOWLEDGEMENTS

When finishing a book it is tempting to look back and try to remember the moment of its birth. Certainly this one goes back to an afternoon in 1944 when my boyhood friend Colin Smith – a flight engineer freshly returned from his first bombing raid – told me that during his briefing the crews had cheered when they heard that the more vulnerable Stirling bombers would be accompanying them.

Since then many people have generously given their time to help me make this story as accurate as possible. However, it remains a story and wherever research and story-telling have clashed I have favoured the story.

Flight Lieutenant Alfred Price started my research off on a sound basis and his fine book about radar – *Instruments of Darkness* – has been of enormous help. That remarkable path-finder veteran Hamish Mahaddie, DSO, DFC, AFC and bar, Czech MC, C Eng, AFRAeS, was an endless source of information about every aspect of the RAF. Vivian Bellamy while flying me to Cologne in a Heinkel III was able to make me at last understand the relationship between boost, throttle, and pitch.

I am grateful to Mr John Shewring for details of his experiences as a bomb aimer and the loan of maps, *Tee Ems* and personal photographs. Another bomb aimer – Miles Tripp – author of *The Eighth Passenger* and *Faith is a Windsock* completed what is perhaps the unequalled total of forty trips on one tour. He gave me access to his own collection of technical clippings, maps, and official publications as well as giving up his time to answering my questions.

My old friend Derek Coyte, publicity chief for the film *The Battle of Britain*, not only arranged my trip in the Heinkel but also arranged a meeting with Gunter 'Fips' Radusch. Herr Radusch, a Knight's Cross winner with sixty-three night-fighter victories, was the earliest pioneer of German night-fighting experiments. On this same trip Derek Coyte also arranged meetings with Hans Brustellin and Adolf Galland, to both of whom I record my thanks.

Herr von Lossberg, Knight's Cross holder and Luftwaffe staff officer, invented 'Wilde Sau' tactics for night fighters and was an operational pilot as well as a technical expert who flew almost every type of German aircraft used during the Second World War. Herr von Lossberg not only talked with me at great length but also went to the trouble of drawing a map of the radar scheme for 1943.

Karl Otto Hoffman, serving officer and author of a three-volume history of German radar from 1933 to 1945, gave me a great deal of his time and his book has been an important reference. Hajo Herrman, another Knight's Cross winner, also described for me his experiences as a night-fighter pilot.

For permission to visit Deelen airfield and see the buildings that had been constructed for the Luftwaffe I must thank Jonkheer de Ranitz. The commanding officer, Colonel H. J. Doorenbos of the Netherlands Air Force, was most hospitable, as were his staff: Majoor M. C. Breemans, Luitenant Lamers and Sergeant Majoor Bolderman. For access to technical information, photos and maps I must thank the engineer at Deelen, Mijnheer Tieleman.

Dr H. ten Kate of the Koninklijk Nederlands Meteorologisch Instituut provided me with details of winds and seas for the period of June 1943 and Mr Van Dee who was at the

Noordwijk lighthouse answered various questions about the district at that time.

Many residents in the small towns to the north-west of Krefeld helped me put together my fictional one: in particular, Johannes Hoeren of Gefrath, who also let me have personal contemporary documents. Also Frau Overröder who, together with her husband, ran the Park Hotel – now, alas, gone – not only sorted out for me the complexities of the wartime nursing services but was able to find her wartime uniform, now doing service as a kitchen overall.

My friend Fritz Sommer of Essen allowed me to go through his collection of documents and made available to me letters he had written while he was a serving Abwehr officer.

Don Elms and Mike Wooller helped me to find Anglo-American and German popular songs respectively. The latter also arranged a screening of his superb *Cities under Siege* documentary films. I must also thank Dr V. G. Radclyffe and A. Flowers for their kindness in helping me with some of the medical details.

The Imperial War Museum were wonderful – as always – and in particular Mr J. E. Sutters, the Film Librarian, found me German instruction films ranging from civil defence to Ju88 servicing.

In researching this story I have read more than two hundred books and I am much obliged to Pat Quorn of Hersants Bookshop for his remarkable memory and energetic help. For locating reference books that were no longer in print or of a special kind I am greatly indebted to the IWM Library, the Westminster Reference Library and *The Daily Telegraph* Reference Department, as well as to the kindness of Miss Howlett at William Kimber Ltd. A very special thanks must also go to Mr Jackets at the Air Ministry Historical Department and to *Flight* and the *Aeroplane*.

Advice about German shares and commerce came from Anton Felton. Other advice came from Ray Hawkey.

I am grateful to everyone at Jonathan Cape Ltd for their help and encouragement. Particularly to Tom Maschler who read the first rough draft. For their efforts in connection with this book I am also obliged to Tony Colwell and Jean Mossop, and for their careful work on the typescript thanks to Robina Masters and James Atkins.

When I drew a plan of the fictional town of Altgarten Mr F. N. B. Patterson, BSc, AMICE, MIMunE, MIHE, Borough Surveyor, Engineer and Planning Officer of Brighton, gave generously of his time to point out the basic working of town gas, sewage, water and electricity. As well as this he was most kind about explaining things to me by letter, often including the most lucid drawings.

Mr Jacques Maisonrouge of IBM must be thanked for his authoritative aid. This is perhaps the first book to be entirely recorded on magnetic tape for the IBM 72 IV. This has enabled me to redraft many chapters over twenty times, and by means of memory-coding to select certain technical passages at only a moment's notice. Ellenor Handley has operated this machine and given her expert and detailed attention to the MS at all stages as well as providing a cross-reference system that, together with colour-coding and reference cards, has enabled me to find my way around this very long book.

Last, and by no means least, Ysabele de Ranitz has patiently translated endless conversations, technical reports and books from both German and Dutch. Working from ancient recordings she has also provided the translations of German wartime popular songs.